Sharon ʒ Plight

JOAN HEPHZIBAH

DEDICATION

To everyone amid a plight

To all my readers, you made my dream come true.

To the sweet Sharon, can't wait to hug you once more.

To big J and little J, for calling me mum.

To the O'Loans, you opened your home to a strange

ACKNOWLEDGEMENTS

I would like to thank all those involved in sharing my vision.

All my editing team, for a successful job of editing.

To all friends and family, my gratitude.

ONE

Sharon jumped out of her deep sleep with the blaring of the alarm. *Oh, no!* Though she appeared calm, she was actually screaming in her mind. *My flight departs at 6.00 am. Oh no, I am so tired!* She lifted her hands to hold her weary head. The time was already 4:05 am, and it was the dawn of a new sunny day.

The sun was shining through the sides of her black summer curtains, installed with intent to sleep for longer during the brief summer months in Scotland. Sharon tried to remember what to do next as she pressed her hands solidly on the alarm.

Her memory of the night before was so faint that she could barely recollect anything.

I'm confused, what happened? She asked herself.

Oh! My MBA graduation party. I had a blast - I'm so glad I made Mum happy.

Mrs O'Loan, as she liked to address her mum, was one of seven siblings in her family. However, she could not have more than her only precious - Sharon. Despite their best efforts, they could not achieve the desired result. It was an ongoing joke in the family that the fault was from Mr O'Loan's side, who was himself a lone child in his family.

Growing up had been fun. She got all the attention wanted with no rival to consider, except sometimes from Mrs O'Loan's side of the family.

Early in the marriage, before Sharon came along, the large extended family was a bit tough to handle for Mr O'Loan, but he soon got used to it. Marrying his sweetheart made him realise that; Mrs O'Loan was a Nigerian graduate who had come to England for her postgraduate studies in the 1980s. Born into a very conservative, religious family, she aimed to settle down with someone having similar convictions.

Then along came the selfless, over-considerate Mr O'Loan. He was bi-racial child of a British man who had met and married the love of his life in Nigeria where he worked as an expatriate. The O'Loans soon moved back to the UK to give the family a British experience.

Later, Mr O'Loan's friend introduced her parents to each other during one of her young mum's one-off nights out with her friends. Their only mission was to get her mum a groom. Sharon interpreted her mum as one of the girls in her circle of friends in those days.

Sharon loved the tales of her parents' love-affair. She often dreamt hers would be as miraculous and God-ordained. Her parents raised her with a disciplined, loving, and firm hand, according to her parents' much-loved faith, the same faith she had embraced.

It was easy for her to focus on her studies. Sharon, at 21 years of age, had earned a first-class honours degree from the Scotland's oldest University, St Andrews.

Her degree in International Business Management was the step that launched her into her Master's in Business Management, where she also graduated with distinction.

Mother O'Loan had always drummed into her ears that the sky is the limit. That Sharon herself would be the only hinderance to achieving any success she aimed for in life. Mum was so right!

Although her higher education took a lot of sacrifice from her parents. Especially when the family had to struggle in the wake of Dad's job losses, they thought it worthwhile.

Her family's struggles had strengthened Sharon's faith. The love that bound her parents together weathered them through many storms of life.

Mrs O'Loan's beaming smile on her face as she danced with Mr O'Loan showed their joy at celebrating their daughter's success. They were looking forward to a bright future for Sharon in the United States.

Mrs O'Loan happily invited all her siblings to the graduation party. Four of them made it to the party with some more extended family members Sharon had never met before.

In an epic Nigerian party, the food, music, and dancing was a perfect reflection of Mrs O'Loan's culture. She never failed to exhibit anytime the opportunity arose. The party mood continued until about 1:00 am. Her parents dropped her home on the way to their hotel. Sharon, who ended up being exhausted, knowing early in the morning she would soon start a new era in her life.

She aimed to sail through the last stage of the five steps intense interview stages. It would be a dream come true.

Suddenly, Sharon jolted back to reality. A loud noise emanating from her streets shook the windows. Outside, it was already busy. She could hear the noise of buses and sounds of oncoming trains.

Don't I just hate living in the city centre? I have survived these living conditions for two years now. I pray for a change soon. Sharon recounted silently all sorts of peeves she had to endure the last two years.

Her one-bedroom flat (at the time) had seemed adequate for a student. She was looking forward to her dream job like a bat out of hell.

Or perhaps she could move back to her parents', which was just three hours from her current location. The latter she didn't want to do, because it was time to give back to them for all the years, they had supported her.

In a sudden panic, Sharon moved over to the edge of the bed and dragged herself into the bathroom.

I need to hurry! She brushed her teeth at the same time as picking out her clothes.

I have a job interview in 24 hours. I need to be at the airport in the next hour; she reminded herself as she jumped into the bath. I haven't even said my prayers.

What a way to show gratitude to my Heavenly Father!

She hurried out of the bathroom to utter a few words of prayer to thank the Saviour. Praying aloud, Sharon whispered.

"Lord, you know I'm grateful, and I'm normally not like this. But this morning, I am tired. I am grateful, and I'm thankful, and I want to say I love you. I want to say thank you for all my friends, the party, and most especially my parents. They have stood by me all my life. When times were tough and when I was naughty. When I good and when I was losing it. They had a bundle of patience, especially Mum. Thank you for a wonderful mum. Lord, I am heading for my first interview. Please, could you just give me the courage to say the right thing at the right time? Just as an icing on a cake, and a lovely flight. In Your name, Amen!"

At her last words, Sharon rose from the kneeling position, walking into the bathroom.

20 minutes later, an Uber driver parked outside her apartment to pick up her for the airport. Sharon bid her apartment goodbye as she stepped into the Uber.

It's the beginning of a new life,

Sharon thought, looking back at the old building. Her prayer was for a quieter environment, for her next apartment, wherever that would be! Sharon planned to board her first flight from Scotland to Heathrow Airport, London. From

London, she would take the connecting flight to New York, then on to Houston.

Once at the departure section, Sharon headed to locate her flight from the notice board. Her phone rang as she walked in amongst the busy crowd. In her haste to find her phone, coupled with the distraction from the cutest baby her eyes had ever seen Sharon accidentally brushed her shoulder against the gentleman holding a cup of coffee.

"I'm so sorry," Sharon exclaimed. "Oh, gosh, my clumsiness." She avoided looking straight up to his face.

The gentleman staring at her intensely, mumbled.

"Don't worry!" He muttered the next few words, "It's fine," still ogling her while his feet stuck to the ground.

Sharon, at a snail-slow pace, looked up to gaze at the 6 feet, 5-inch beautiful man towering over her. Like a thunderbolt, she realised.

"Oh my God, this man is breathtaking!" she thought.

Staring with her mouth opened, saliva almost dripped from her mouth. Sharon seemed to forget exactly what had happened a moment ago, until the stranger leaned down to tap her shoulder, bringing her back to the present.

"Hi! I'm still here. You accidentally poured my not-so-hot coffee on me!"

"Oh! So sorry again," replied Sharon, repeating her apology. Tightening her lips together in embarrassment, she managed to pull her gaze away from him to ask meekly,

"Can I buy you another cup of coffee? What about your shirt? How can I make things right? I have to check-in for my flight in 30 minutes. What can I do?"

Sharon's face showed a series of panicked expressions until the patient gentleman interrupted.

"I understand. We are all in a hurry to catch our flights. Don't worry about the shirt. I will get myself something to wear from the nearest clothing store. It was nice meeting you and have a great day."

The stranger walked away briskly to avoid any further conversation with her.

Wow! He was handsome and not offended. Quite a gentleman, the way he handled the situation. Besides that, he seemed shy!

Sharon glanced back as he walked away.

It's been a lengthy time since someone has made such an impression on me. Oh gosh! Yes, my second year at the University of St Andrews. I had an encounter with Tom. Unknowingly, he opened his car door directly into me as I walked past his car! I can recall that very well.

Sighing to herself, Sharon picked up her belongings, walking towards the check-in counter.

Her mind went to that first meeting with Tom - the apologies he gave, how after smacking her with the car door, he had insisted on taking her to the clinic for a check-up.

He later confessed a year into their friendship, he wanted to use 'the clinic' as an excuse to get to know her better. Her friends had distracted her from the encounter with Tom, which saved the day, as they knew Tom was already in a committed relationship. But she loved the friendship they kept, even after he got married two years ago.

Two weeks after her first encounter with Tom, she met him in the hospital again. He was sick. Although he had been diagnosed and being discharged for rest, Tom opted to stay with her.

The diagnosis of her condition was a fibroid condition needing surgery. Sharon wondered how she came about that situation. With corrective surgery planned immediately, the doctors informed her to contact her family members. Unfortunately, her parents were on their holidays, on the lifelong cruise Mrs O'Loan had dreamed of since she was a child.

Sharon could not break such a piece of ugly news to her Mum while she was away. Tom watched as her dilemma was discussed until he interrupted the discussion.

"I will be here with her throughout the procedure. I will stand in as her guardian."

"Sorry, Sir! Please, what exactly is your relationship with Sharon?" the doctor asked, looking at Sharon for answers.

"My name is Tom, and I am a family friend. Knowing her parents are unavailable, I would like to support her."

"I am sorry I didn't introduce myself. I am Dr. Alex, the physician on duty today. You look familiar."

Tom replied, "I know you treated my mother a few months ago. She is well. Thank you for your kindness to her."

"No. I mean, I have seen you around the hospital recently." Dr Alex insisted.

"Yes, I got discharged from the ward this morning when Sharon got admitted. I could not bear to let her stay on by herself."

"Interesting! A friend like you is rare! Sharon, you have a keeper here." Sharon smiled through her pain, muttered, "Thank you, Dr Alex."

The surgery to went on as planned, and the doctors successfully removed the fibroids. Tom remained in the hospital's vicinity as though he had nothing else to do. At least, she was glad his fiancée was on a business trip. She examined her feelings for her newfound friend.

After a week of recuperation, Sharon left the hospital with Tom. At home, they surprised her with a welcome-home get-together. Her friends had prepared meals for the next two weeks waiting in Sharon's freezer, and all she needed to do was rest. What friends!

After their one-off encounter, Tom invited her to church, but discovered they attended the same one.

Isn't it funny how you don't know you are sitting right by a pot of gold until you meet that pot of gold?

Tom's caring profile was beyond that of her immediate friends. He often volunteered to serve in various charities. One close to her heart was the homeless charity. Sharon, like Tom, had a heart to help others. She had signed up to support the homeless after the testimony of an ex-homeless drug addict and his encounter with a young lady about her age. He was not only endorsed unbiasedly by the lady, but he also met the Saviour through her.

After several months of unrelenting interaction by Tom, the ex-homeless agreed to enter a rehabilitation programme where he recovered completely from addiction. Life changed, and he returned to school. He ended up marrying the same lady that stood by him in his days of adversity. His recovery propelled her to reach out to others in need, like Tom.

Both Sharon and Tom had other common interests like movies, paintings and travelling. Tom,

Sharon, and other friends formed a circle of travelling enthusiasts, often traversing around to enjoy the country's scenery and beyond.

Both Sharon and Tom shared a love for fine food. Although they were superb cooks, Tom was better with his desserts and its associated artistic features. Sharon enjoyed cooking, but she was not a successful eater. She was very particular with her meals; a weakness Sharon had been dealing with since childhood.

After several visits to the hospital and nutritionists, she gave up the need to change for others. It turned out that Tom's girlfriend also did not enjoy eating. Sharon guessed their similar characteristic drew them closer. He did do all he could to make them enjoy food more. Poor Tom! Sadly, the two women he loved in his life did not share his joy of eating.

Sharon thought to herself, *Tom is a witty guy with smiles that often sends ripples into my heart. He is considerate and is always ready to go the extra mile for his friends.*

Sharon knew from his circle of friends that Tom was the 'go-to' guy whenever you were in need. *He does not, of necessity, have all the answers you want, but he knows how to get you from one point to another. He never leaves you worse off than before. You sought him for help.* To Sharon, Tom definitely was more than a pot of gold, both to his wife and his friends.

"She is lucky to have him," everyone commented at his wedding. Strangely, no one could be heard saying, "He is lucky to have her as a wife."

Don't get the wrong message, thought Sharon. *His wife is an excellent woman, but in all honesty, could not compare to Tom.* Sometimes, its broke Sharon's heart that Tom was not available but was already taken by someone else. She respected that fact and loved both as friends.

Back to reality now.

Waiting for her flight, Sharon longed for another encounter with the stranger as she thought about Tom. His memories fresh in her mind, Sharon whispered a prayer that she would meet someone like Tom for a husband, if another like him existed!

TWO

About an hour after the incident with the stranger, she had already boarded and settled down. As the pilot's announcement aired, she looked at other passengers. Lo-and-behold, the stranger appeared on the same flight with her. This time, he was wearing a light blue polo T-shirt in an exchange for the coffee-stained navy-blue shirt he had on earlier.

And though I don't know his name, I do know he likes navy blue clothing.

Sharon quickly looked away from him, after a realisation he had been gazing back at her, too!

What kind of man is this? He must have a lot on his mind. Why was he not willing to even ask for her name? I would have loved to know him better and at least exchange numbers.

He might just turn out to be another Tom. I might have to get used to meeting charming men who are not available for someone like me. Hey! Where did I stop thinking of my best friend? Holy Spirit, what do you think? Help me keep my heart on you so I will not wander away.

She furtively glanced over at the stranger. This time, he seemed to be reading a book.

How I wish it were a Bible, a man after His own heart. Right, young lady! You are overthinking this, criticised Sharon to herself. Remember, you have worked on this road several times. The Saviour promised you in Jeremiah 29:11.

"For I know the plans I have for you, declares the LORD, plans to prosper you and not to harm you, plans to give you hope and a future."

And somewhere in Isaiah 55, GOD told me,

"My ways are not your ways, and my thoughts are not your thoughts."

"You have a lot of trusting to do!" Sharon recalled Tom, reminding her to wait for the Lord's plan for a relationship. Sharon knew that for a fact. After her academic achievements and following career leaps at 23 years old, trusting was a gigantic leap for her. *But this mystery man, how I wish I knew him!*

Sharon put her thoughts together, picking up her notepad to scribble down her thoughts with feeble attempts to plan for the next events ahead of her.

About an hour into the journey, another peek to gaze at her mystery man revealed him to be fast asleep, like a child in a mother's bosom. He was so peaceful with his glasses stuck on the opening of his T-shirt!

On impulse, Sharon reached out with her cell phone and took a picture of him. Thirty minutes later, she excused herself to go to the restroom so she could get a better glimpse of him. As she walked back to her seat, he stretched out his long legs to reposition himself for better rest. She wondered more about him until she fell asleep.

Mystery Man woke up as an air hostess offered refreshments to the travellers. He used the opportunity to appreciate Sharon's beauty as she slept. Similarly, he secretly took pictures of her in the same way she had. The Mystery Man was thinking.

If only I were in a better place to speak to her. I am already too emotionally bankrupt to take a chance on another beautiful woman. I need to trust Him to give me another chance with her. If this is part of His plan, there will always be an opportunity to meet her.

She looks so peaceful, like the daughter of the kingdom. He remembered her apology. *Where could she be coming from? What is she going to do in Houston? I don't aspire to be a distraction. Perhaps she has a special person in her life. Perhaps she is married, but she does not have a commitment ring on. She appears as a young adult, probably between 20-25 years old.*

An announcement from the pilot's cabin accompanied by sudden turbulence woke all those sleeping. They were to adhere to all safety precautions. Sharon woke up suddenly to see the mystery man gazing at her.

He immediately looked away when they made eye contact. Sharon's heart threatened to pop out of her chest as she gripped her seat. Holding her breath and eyes closed in fear, she prayed in silence.

Lord, I know I didn't spend my usual time with you this morning. Please! Please! Please, for the sake of those that are yet to know you in this plane, can you keep us safe? I am just starting my life, God! Keep me safe! Amen!

The turbulence went on for the next ten minutes, and while all the passengers were in a panic, the mystery man seemed calm.

Sharon thought *the last person calm amidst the storms I know is Jesus. Is He? But Sharon, would I attract you to Him this way?* She nudged herself back to reality amid the surrounding panic.

Another announcement from the cabin crew brought of calmness. The captain announced the flight had just passed through the turbulence. He added that the passengers could enjoy a safe trip, as promised.

Floods of peace swept into Sharon's heart. Thanking the Saviour for answering prayers, Sharon flashed back to the last discussion with her mother with tears of Joy.

"Mrs O'Loan, thank you so much!" Sharon remembered spilling orange juice into a glass while sitting across from Mum at the kitchen island table back home.

She had said, "I have something to tell you, Mum. I got an interview invitation two days before the graduation party."

Her mother exclaimed, "Blessed am I amongst women!" Clapping her hands in joyful excitement.

"Mum! Mum, I have not finished." Sharon's eye sparkled as she shared her news with her mum.

"The position is for a business development manager. There's a possibility of a promotion in six months. It's a family-run oil production company, the CEO wants to chat with me. It's the last stage of the interview," she continued.

"I am so happy for you, my child," she said with a sudden sigh.

"I would be more eager if it was a piece of breaking news about your fiancé."

"Mrs O'Loan!" Sharon protested.

"It's true. I know it will come at the right time. But I can't help it!" she looked desperately into Sharon's eyes for answers to her concern.

"Sharon, you are my only child. For twenty-five years, I have been waiting to hear baby noises in this house. Your dad and I are not getting younger. We love to spend time with our grandkids."

Sharon looked away from her mother, distractedly picking fluff off her clothing. She was too embarrassed to discuss her love life with her mum.

"There is nothing to tell."

Her mother continued, "If there is any problem, would you kindly let me know? Your father and I can pray. We always pray for you, but this time, with a focus on marriage."

"Mum, I'm fine," Sharon tried to brush over the topic.

"When I meet someone, you will be the first to know. But till then... Is there anything I can eat before rushing off to complete the party preparation?"

"Uhh!" sighed Sharon, looking down at her shivering feet.

If anything had happened on this turbulent plane, not only will Mother lose me, but she would also lose the hope of grandkids her heart so longed for. Saviour, thank you once again. Her heart raced at what might be a frightening future.

Looking up now, she observed the mystery man staring at her. This time, he seemed to send a friendly smile her way. *A sense of reassurance to me?* She asked herself. *What a warm, flirtatious smile!*

Sharon smiled back to acknowledge her admirer. Heavy breathing accompanied by a racing pulse engulfed her. *What is wrong with you?* She cautioned herself, as the hair on her body sprung up in response to his flirtatious gestures. *Pull yourself together, Sharon, you don't know him.*

The cabin crew cut the fleeting moment of the encounter short as they went up the aisle collecting the rubbish from the passengers. He looked away, adjusting his broad shoulders before bending over to pick up his litter.

I need to exchange numbers with him. I need to explore why I feel this way with a stranger. In Tom's case, I did not need to explore. We both knew he was already engaged.

The pilot announcing, "The aircraft will prepare for descent, disrupted her thoughts."

She returned to her thoughts, *But I know nothing about this amusing and mysterious young man. What if he is engaged like Tom?* He has a calm disposition like him.

Her mind raced back to Tom. Tom's calm disposition endeared people to him.

As someone said, "People carry their madness about and only manifest it in unexpected situations."

For Tom, there seems to be no episode with him. Driving had provided considerable time to observe his temperament.

One evening about six months ago, she was sitting in the back seat behind his wife, while he drove them from an engagement. As the traffic light changed, the red car in front of him seemed reluctant to move.

Tom's wife, Shelia, and Sharon became impatient at the attitude of the vehicle. A few yards later, the car braked without prior notice. Tom, although sharp and calm, decelerated immediately to avoid a collision with the car uttering not a word.

The lady driving the red car jumped out of her car with her mobile phone. She headed to check the back of her car for damage. Tom's wife, already upset, got out of the vehicle to check if the lady had involved her husband in an accident. Tom remained calm.

Sharon inquired, "Tom! Are you not going to do anything?"

He replied, "By all means, I want the lady to calm down before making my move." Smiling generously, Tom got out of the car after his wife, alongside Sharon.

"Thank GOD! No damage!" Tom exclaimed, gesturing to his wife to return to the car so he could handle the situation.

To their amazement, the lady looked at us.

"Today is your lucky day!" she haughtily said.

Rolled her eyes, hissed, and walked away, apparently too busy to make a fuss over this annoyance.

Tom, though calm, looked over at us and said: "What just happened? Did she mean to brake heavily so we could collide with her and make an insurance claim?" He shook his head and headed for the car door.

Sharon knew something would have agitated her about the apparent drama and the arrogance of the driver. She wondered if Tom ever got angry.

Back in the car, Tom's wife did not hide her displeasure about the incident and how she thought the lady must have tried to stage her driving to cause an accident. Tom's simple reply reflected his internal, calm nature.

"My Love, let us thank the Saviour that we are safe from all harm, intended or not."

"You can now unbuckle your seatbelts," came the pilot's announcement, intruding on her thoughts again.

The announcer's heavy accent left all the passengers amused, causing them all to chuckled or laughed nervously at the same time.

Shortly after, the aircraft ground to a stop on the Houston runway, and the passengers stood to drag their luggage from the overhead compartments. The stranger remained on Sharon's mind. He was now several feet away from her, making his way to the aircraft exit door.

I must be calculating here and catch him before he disappears.

Upon reaching the entrance of the plane, she looked ahead of the passengers walking through the arrival doors. *We might meet at the baggage area,* she thought to herself.

Sharon rushed forward through the arrival doors. Excused herself as she barged into other passengers. Five minutes later, she was scanning the baggage area.

Mr Stranger was nowhere and had vanished. *Perhaps he had no luggage to pick up. I will have to rush to the airport exit.*

Sharon followed the signs to the entrance, panting along, dragging her heavy items of luggage behind her. Feeling exhausted and panting, she dropped her bags and all but yelled out.

"What is wrong with you, Sharon? The stranger had vanished for good! Get over it. If it's the father's will, you will meet him again.

She sighed at her foolishness, and the scene almost created by her outburst. Looking stressed, Sharon tried to find the address of the hotel she had booked from the United Kingdom.

A call-out jolted her into responding to the sound of her name.

"Sharon O'Loan! Miss Sharon O'Loan!" A middle-aged man stood yards away from her. "Is there any Sharon O'Loan around here?"

Sharon's eye lit up at her name. "Yes! Yes, I am Sharon."

"Miss O'Loan, I am a representative of Graceoak Incorporation, here to pick you up to your lodging," informed the uniformed chauffeur politely. Sharon declined the offer.

"That wouldn't be necessary. I can find my way to the hotel," she replied, still searching her bag for the hotel's address. Noticing he did not move, she gazed at him, puzzled.

The driver looked into her eyes and responded, "Miss, I apologise for the discomfort. However, I am mandated by the CEO to see to your comfort before you meet with him tomorrow. I would hate to not carry out my responsibility."
Smiling with gratitude, Sharon handed over the sheet containing her travel itinerary to him.

The driver picked up her luggage, proceeding towards the car.

"How long do you intend to stay in the hotel accommodation?" he inquired of Sharon, wanting to begin a conversation with her.

Sharon, looking puzzled at his direct question, "Not sure at the moment. I'm taking one step at a time. I guess the starting point is crossing the final hurdle with my meeting tomorrow. Once I get the job, I can decide what to do."

The driver chuckled at her remarks. "You packed as if you already got the job. You have planned well," he complimented.
Sharon smiled at the chauffeur and said: "You have a point, will have to trust my Father for answers."

The chauffeur opened the door to a Lexus UX Hybrid, while Sharon stepped in graciously and seated herself. As the car drove off from the George Bush Intercontinental Airport, Sharon straightened her clothes, then made herself comfortable for the journey ahead of her.

"Miss Sharon, you mentioned your Father's will. How do you mean? Is your dad making some alternative plans for you?" probed the chauffeur.

Sharon laughed.

"No, not at all. My daddy is good. My Father is the One in heaven. He is GOD and I have a relationship with Him. That reminds me, I need to call home to let my parents know I've arrived in Houston."

The chauffeur was about to ask the next leading question when Sharon interrupted him.

"The itinerary I gave you showed the hotel I booked; it is about 3 miles from the airport. I think you must have driven past it."

Clearing his throat, the chauffeur explained.

"The CEO arranged for an apartment a distance away from the company office. That will make it easy for your stay here."

This caused Sharon to become uncomfortable, so she said a quick prayer, placing her life into the Saviour's hands, trusting Him.

Sharon's mind raced back to the Stranger. *What on earth happened to him? Maybe he was now on a connecting flight to another destination? Why am I feeling attracted to him? I know nothing about the gentleman!? Oh; I see! I know a gentleman just like him.* She smiled to herself, remembering Tom.

Tom always wanted to act like a big brother soon as he realised, she was an only child. He seemed to take her under his wings. Sharon could do no wrong with him. On one occasion, Tom hosted a dinner party for his friends. Sharon strode in briskly through the doors, unaware of the new vase his fiancé got for Tom. Her legs hit the jar by accident, and it tumbled and broke.

"I am so sorry, Tom!" she exclaimed. "I was not expecting anything on the floor!" Sharon knelt to pick up the broken pieces. Tom reached over to pull her up.

"Please don't apologise. It's a vase. Any excuse will suffice for my babe. But the blood you will shed if the vessel cuts you might not be helpful to any of us."

Tom had greater concern for her than for the precious gift. Tom's smiling face was all she saw as she dozed off.

"Miss Sharon! Sharon, we have arrived at the arranged accommodation."

The chauffeur opened his door, hurrying to the boot to bring out the luggage. Sharon stepped out of the car as the chauffeur opened her door.

"Thank you, I appreciate your kindness," smiled Sharon.

"Don't mention it. I will pick you up for the meeting tomorrow morning."

Handing over a card, the Chauffeur continued, "This is my number. Kindly call me once you are ready. I will be on standby and don't lose the card!" grinned the Chauffeur.

"No, I won't!", smiled Sharon.

"Don't you think I should find my way to the office?"

Smiling, the chauffeur replied,

"Miss Sharon, kindly be ready in the morning."

Handing over the keys to the apartment, he bid her goodbye and drove off.

Perplexed, Sharon stood pondering. *Why on earth am I treated so especially well? I thought I only came in for the last stage of the interview. Does the CEO have any hidden intentions?*

Sharon knew she would not get any answer yet, plus Mrs O'Loan awaited her phone call.

She turned around, picked up her luggage, heading for the door. Using her key fob, Sharon entered the building and headed to Flat Number 2, as instructed by the chauffeur. Sharon was astounded at the sight of the well-furnished flat. The combined of colours of curtains and sofa were fantastic! The blend of maroon and light blue had a pleasant cooling effect on the ambience of the room.

Sharon dropped her bags by the door, walking meticulously around the flat until she heard her phone ring.

"Oh, it's Mum!" she exclaimed, picking up her phone and pressing redial.

She laid on the succulent bed, waiting for Mrs O'Loan to pick up her call. Sharon mulled over all that had gone on throughout her journey until she was in dreamland.

"Sharon! Sharon. Are you still there?" Mrs O'Loan shouted over the phone line. Poor Sharon, she was already in seventh heaven.

THREE

After a few hours, the alarm clock broke the silence with its sound, "Brring... brring!".

"Oh, I so hate jetlag!" Sharon exclaimed.

"I am so tired; I'd just rather stay in bed!!" Holding her forehead in pain, Sharon moaned, "I am still suffering from lack of sleep from the graduation party."

"What!" She quickly jumped out of bed. Sharon stretched out for the cell phone, turning off the alarm.

"I am running late again. Forty-five minutes to the interview or meeting! What am doing!?"

Sharon rushed into the bathroom and got ready in fifteen minutes flat! She made a cup of coffee while looking for the chauffeur's card.

"Where on earth did I drop this card? I need to call him." She searched through her scattered belongings around the room but did not find the card.

Filled with frustration, Sharon reached for her phone thinking, *Lord, I don't know what is happening! Is this a sign that everything will go wrong? Please guide my steps and lead me on this path of your righteousness.*

" Hello, can I get an Uber taxi?" called Sharon, ordering a taxi.

"Where would you like to be driven to?" came the accented voice from the other end of the line.

"I would like a taxi to Graceoak Oil and Gas, please."

"Where do I pick you up?" said the voice.

"Honestly, I do not know, let me check," replied Sharon, as she rushed outside to check for anything that showed the address.

The voice on the line said, "Is there an address posted outside the apartment building?"

"Let me check around, okay... 7 Palgrave Road," offered Sharon.

"I will pick you up in five minutes," said the driver.

"Thank you," she muttered.

Picking up her bags, Sharon proceeded to the apartment door, locking it behind her, wondering what the driver or even the CEO will think of her.

The taxi showed up precisely in five minutes. She quickly leapt into the cab. Three minutes early for the scheduled appointment, she walked through the revolving doors of Graceoak.

Once inside, Sharon found the building was not as attractive from the outside, but the inside was mind-blowing. The design was consistent with every current sustainability factor she had ever read from books.

Picking up a pamphlet from a table nearby, Sharon learned that recycled materials were incorporated into every part of the building. Sharon saw ventilation fans and vents used in the building for its ventilation; many water fountains helping to provide hydration, which served to increase the productivity of employees within the offices.

Sharon felt gobsmacked by the variety of eco-friendly materials used in the overall construction of the office building.

Wandering further in a daze, she observed PVC-free linoleum and water-based paints were well used throughout the building.

There were carpets in the building made from wool from the Trust's flocks of Herdwick sheep; ventilation snouts on the roof, which had come from recycled beer cans; a combined heat and power plant provided the building with its main source of heat; and the pamphlet stated the building laid claim to having the most extensive grass roof in Houston.

The densely planted roof with alpine sedum mosses trapped most of the rainwater falling onto it to reduce the risk of flooding; the solar panels installed in the building supplied 80 percent of the power used for heating; furthermore, rainwater collected in an underground tank provided flushing toilets and any other water function.

Upon her approach to the reception, the chauffeur hurried towards her.

"Miss O'Loan, good morning! Thank goodness! We were all anxious about you. I expected your call for a pickup. The Managing Director had, some minutes ago, instructed me to drive over to your apartment."

"Sorry," apologised Sharon. "I woke up jet-lagged and discovered I could not find the card you gave me yesterday."

"It's all right, Ms O'Loan. I am glad you are OK," assured the driver.

"I was so exhausted," explained Sharon, "And was not sure where I dropped the card. I called a taxi. Now, I am safe and ready for my interview."

"You are here now," said the chauffeur.

"Can I ask a question? Do you usually give the same courtesy to every potential employee of this organisation?" inquired Sharon.

"I wouldn't say that's true exactly, but I can say it would depend on the post. Let me walk you to the receptionist. She will take it from there."
He abruptly changed the subject, directing her to the nearby reception desk.

"Morning, Miss O'Loan," called out the receptionist. "You will meet the MD. He is waiting for you in his office with the Human Resource Manager."

Walking up to the desk, Sharon greeted the receptionist cheerfully, saying, "Morning, Ms ..."

"Oakland," the receptionist replied. "Please don't confuse it with Graceoak, as often happens." She smiled pleasantly, adding, "Although my first name is Grace."

"Miss Grace," Sharon replied with a twinkle in her eye. "I am supposed to have a meeting with the CEO, Mr. Finland."

"Miss O'Loan, I understand why you might be puzzled." said the receptionist looking apologetic.

"The CEO had a minor accident at the golf course yesterday morning and is unavailable for the interview."

"Oh, I am so sorry. Hope he was not hurt. We could reschedule the meeting for another day," sympathised Sharon.

"Not at all. The MD will duly handle the meeting. He awaits your presence."
The receptionist directed Sharon through the double door leading to the first-floor office.

They designed the workspaces to encourage collaboration and teamwork, with a unique pod desk set up for each employee. They organised the desks to promote personalisation, privacy, or collaborative working.

Graceoak continued to make a successful impression on her. *I should work here; I like it already.*

In front of the door of the office was a plaque for 'Mr Finland Jr.'

Alarm bells rang in her head. *I never read about this person online! The MD on the website is Mr William. I am in for more surprises.*

She knocked on the door, awaiting a response from the other side.

"Come in, whoever you are." *The response sounds like someone is upset and rude*, she thought to herself.

Sharon opened the door, instantly shocked. Frozen on the spot, she shook her head before recovering from her regular state of mind. It was the same stranger she had an encounter with at the airport!

The office was extensive, well decorated and furnished in the corner with an elegant sofa. There was a refrigerator and a coffee table to the right of the desk, beside which sat the handsome young man. She approached him in the familiarity of her last encounter with him.

"So, you are Mr Finland, Jr? It's a small world truly. I am glad I got to meet you again. Morning!"

He received the familiar greeting with an indifferent response. "Mr Finland, Jr?"

He is more smartly dressed in his grey suit and a matching tie and his lovely golden eyeglasses frames.

As she expected, he ignored the moment shared; instead, he arrogantly rolled his seat around as he expressed disappointment at the sight of her.

The young man stared into her face, answering unexpectedly with, "Excuse me, I don't think you have met me."

In an irritated tone, he continued, "Yes, I am Mr Finland Jr. I would have expected a level of professionalism from you. Even if we have met before today."

"I apologise for my over-familiarity and starting my conversation on a wrong note, Sir. My name is Miss O'Loan. I should meet with Mr Finland Sr for my final stage interview as the Business Development Manager. The receptionist told me that Mr Finland is not available. I would appreciate if I could be rescheduled for another appointment with him soon."

"Ha, ha, ha! Why am I surprised? I knew it! The young lady would be full of herself. I glanced at your profile. I wondered why Dad had any interest in hiring someone straight from the university with no professional ethics." said the young man sarcastically.

"I would be glad to hit the ground and work on my ethics, Mr Finland. If that is the only criteria I am lacking. I believe Graceoak will provide the environment needed to cultivate the values needed."

"She is so audacious!" He turned away from her, picked up the phone, and called someone to come into his office.

He is so rude. Was he never trained on how to talk to people? Imagine, I am still standing. He couldn't even ask me to take a seat. I hope I will not be reporting to him directly!! Lord, I need to change the direction of my prayers. Only let your will be done! Amen!

A few moments later, while Sharon still stood uncomfortably gazing at him, an elderly lady walked in.

"I understand you called me to your office, Sir."

"Yes! Yes, Mrs Resource, I called. Out of the blue last night, my dad informed me he had an interview scheduled for a new BD Manager position."

"Obviously," he continued, rolling his eyes from Sharon to Mrs Resource, "Because of the minor accident, he forgot to keep me in the loop!?"

Mr Finland, rather upset, had just blurted out his frustration in front of her! Startled, Sharon stepped back, confused. *Have I met this guy before? The stranger at the airport was calm and collected. Did God create in duplicate? So, there might be someone like me in another part of the world displaying the same level of insanity.... Lord, please see me through this. I feel so invisible here. There must be something wrong with this young man. The elderly lady seemed unable to stand up to him. In your name, I implore you, Amen!*

"George, I am sorry if her presence here disappoints you. There was a meeting planned by your father for this morning. He must have forgotten to inform you earlier. I am still awaiting word from the receptionist: the candidate has arrived." Mrs Resource added.

"Surely, she has. This misguided lady walked in as if I knew her from another planet." Sharon moved swiftly to deal with the rude nincompoop at the desk when Mrs Resource spoke up.

"George, a change of language or attitude might help! I know it upset you, but the young lady should not be the target. Wait! I left someone in my office. I will have to finish up with him, and I will be back." stated Mrs Resource.

"Please, take your time, Mrs Resource. Ms O'Loan is not in a hurry to head out of these premises," George stated in a sarcastic tone as the HR manager walked out.

Now I know Mr Finland's first name is George. Sharon felt trouble overwhelming her as he stood up.

He cast his miserable countenance on her as he walked over to pour a drink for himself.

"Rum in the afternoon!?" Sharon's aching heart said muted prayers to the Saviour.

Sipping the drink, he finally gestured to Sharon. "Take a seat. Let's have a chat. The CEO had already planned it. I am not informed, so tell me about yourself." Sharon remained bewildered by his sudden mood change.

Although still perplexed, recomposing herself, she sat in front of his office desk. Sharon summarised her academic experience. The few months of work experiences she had gathered before applying for this international role.

George uttered no word in reply as both stared around the room in grave silent. George's haughtiness blazed to scorch her as he took the seat opposite her, still sipping his rum.

A moment later, the door opened.

"George, don't you think it would be a better idea if we all sit on the comfortable sofa? The chat will be as informal as your dad would have wanted it,"

Mrs Resource suggested as she walked into the office. She took the lead towards the exquisite brown leather sofa.

"Sharon, would you like a drink? George has not been excellent company this morning. He has his moments. Deep inside, Mr Finland, Jr. is as gentle as can be. He has a beautiful soul. All you need is time to know him better."

Mrs Resource sounded as if she had a grip on the festering dissatisfaction expressing itself through George.

Sharon grinned at the uncharacteristic compliments showered on George. *A bully or an angel!? He must be a tormented soul,* she concluded.

Mrs Resource sat back on the sofa, offering her a glass of water from the bar.

"Thank you, water will be fine. I am thirsty," whispered Sharon gratefully.

At this, a George rudely interrupted, "Mrs Resource, I appreciate the kind words about me, but let's make this chat as official as possible."

He joined the two women on the sofa, crossing his legs with a disinterested look.

"Mrs Resource," Sharon called out.

"Yes, Sharon," she said, handing over the glass of water to her, smiling.

Sharon questioned. "How many more candidates are up for the same position?"

"I can see," replied Mrs Resource. Turning her gaze on George, she continued, "George has succeeded at scaring you off."

Shifting back to the interviewee, she added, "Graceoak is a family-run oil and gas business. We are looking to increase our business portfolio."

After a pause, she answered in a lowered voice.

"We advertised for someone keen to raise the profile of the company. Mr Finland Sr. spoke to some other candidates before your Skype interview. I guess you ticked all the boxes of his requirements. He was keen to complete discussions with you before his accident yesterday."

"Yes, he noted in our last conversation that this meeting would be the last discussion."

Taking a sip of water to gather her thoughts together, Sharon continued.

"But I was not aware that I was the last candidate. I got some directions from him about what plans he would like to develop once I start the job,"

Sharon added, avoiding any eye contact with George.

"I know the courtesy drive and fine lodgings surprised you, Miss O'Loan. Mr Finland will spare nothing to make his staff comfortable."

Sharon nodded her head in approval, remembering her first encounter with an unexpected chauffeur at the airport.

"George," said Mrs Resource.

"Sharon would be interested in knowing her employment package. I have enclosed all the details of engagement in this file. I would appreciate if you took the discussions from here."

Straightening his shoulders, George replied, "I think the discussion should go on without me. Miss O'Loan seemed not to be interested in an audience with me."

Sharon gazed at him, said a word of prayer before saying, "I was waiting for things to calm down. I appreciate the compliments made about you. I am waiting for the right moment to speak to you, Mr Finland."

Turning her gaze back to the assertive elderly lady, Sharon politely stated.

"Mrs Resource, this meeting has been more difficult than expected. I am still ready to take on the challenge of working with the Finlands', hopefully making the company profitable beyond the set targets."

Sharon expressed her words with all the courage she had left before returning her eyes to George.

"Mr Finland Jr., I once again apologise for the tiny identity crisis malfunction, I had the moment I met you. I..." She stumbled over her words "Don't worry, it's in the past now."

George interrupted them discourteously, saying to Sharon, "Let's get back to the reason we are here. I have a meeting in an hour. You stated you wanted to hit the ground running. I am hoping you will come along for the meeting to show off your new graduate skills," He jokingly laughed at her.

"That will be fine. I am free all day," Sharon responded courageously, countering all the fears roaring within her.

George handed Sharon the file after flipping through the details of her employment. "Interesting!" he sighed.

After accepting the file, Sharon said, "Do you mind if I take some time to go through the document?"

"No, not at all. Take all the time you need in the world," George replied grudgingly.

Sharon gazed at Mrs Resource, who gave her an encouraging look. "Sharon, I look forward to your response as soon as possible."

"I will get back to you shortly," Sharon replied with a grateful handshake.

Sharon took a taxi to the prime shopping area, entering the nearest coffee shop to ponder on the events of the last hour. Opening the folder once more, she quickly reviewed it.

The salary is fantastic, $105,000 as a starting salary to increase after her six-month probation. I am a fresh graduate. This is so unusual, she thought.

Sharon remained perplexed about George's attitude and how it might affect her acceptance of the job offer, leaving her puzzled. He was the boss's son!!

After three cups of coffee, she dared to call Tom and then her mum. The counsel they gave was the same, "Follow your heart. He will lead you in the path of righteousness."

If she followed the trembling fear gripping her heart and rejected the job, she might lose out on the Saviour's purpose for bringing her to Houston.

If she accepted the responsibility, she would describe it as facing death in the lion's den like Daniel. Taking a clue from the words of the HR Manager, the welcome she had received from the chauffeur and receptionist at Graceoak Limited might be the best thing to have happened to her in a long while.

Hmm... wonderful gifts come in inadequate covers sometimes, Sharon thought to herself.

The most unrealistic turn of event was the gentle, stunning looking stranger suddenly turning into a monster in broad daylight! The recent unpleasant climax, his level of insensitivity and display of memory loss towards her.

What happened to him? From the airport encounter to the nasty boss in the office! Do people switch with their environment? Perhaps he has a medical condition, bipolar or something. It will be an exciting challenge to take up, to unfold George's personality like the layers of an onion. One layer at a time. It will be helpful to know what makes him.

Staring out on the streets from the café window, her unsettling thoughts continued.

It would interest me to meet Mr Finland Sr. in person. They might be the opposite of each other. The way the rest of the staff spoke about him, he seemed like a lovely person!

Sharon smiled to herself and, leaving the uncomfortable thoughts behind, she walked out of

the coffee shop for a wander around the sky-blue
city.

FOUR

An Uber driver dropped Sharon off in front of the apartment about 3.30 pm. She still had enough time to call Mrs Resource to discuss her start date.

Unlocking the door, she saw a letter addressed to her.

"This is strange. Who knows me around here?" she spoke aloud with a well of insecurity rising within her.

The letter read: "Welcome to Houston, Miss O'Loan. hope you will join our family business! I look forward to meeting with you in the morning.

The doctor says I am all right to go back to work." Mr S. Finland informed her.

Later at home, Sharon dropped dispiritedly onto the sofa. "Is this a dream or what? If it is, Lord, wake me up."

The big question is, *why am I so out of sorts? Is there something wrong with this organisation? I researched and read all I could online. Everything seemed fine. Their profitability rose by 400% in the last year.*

Sharon dragged her handbag out from under the coffee table where she had dropped it, searching frantically for her phone to dial.

This time Sharon called her dad. He might be a better judge in a professional situation.

Twenty minutes after pouring her concerns and excitement to her father, he said. "Child, take the offer. You will know if it's not for you soon. But I would like you to clarify the situation around the accommodation you are staying in. What's the plan? Will you be staying there until you get to your apartment?"

Boosted by Dad's assurance, Sharon walked over to the fridge to store a few provisions she had gotten on her way home.

Afterwards, she picked up the phone to dial the office. "Afternoon, I would like to speak to Mrs Resource."

"Can I know who is speaking, please?" queried the receptionist.

"I'm Sharon O'Loan. I came in this morning." Sharon told her she had a final interview with Mr Finland Jr. and herself.

"Uhh... Okay," was all the response she got from the other end of the line.

"Could you kindly transfer my call to her?"

"Sorry!" apologised the receptionist. "She stepped out of the office earlier in the day. Let me check if she'd returned."

"Thank you," replied Sharon, tapping her fingers on the sofa in apprehension. The receptionist's muffled voice occupied the phone line until lovely sounds of classical Mozart followed for the next few seconds.

The receptionist came back online.

"Miss Sharon, I will transfer the call to her line. Have a lovely evening."

"Thank you and see you soon," Sharon smiled, waiting for the phone line transfer.

A few seconds later, "Good afternoon, Sharon, how are you?" Mrs Resource greeted.

Sharon responded. "I am well. Thank you for asking."

"What have you been up to all day? I hope our city is not boring?" asked the HR.

"Not at all. Been around some places and had a lot of time to think," Sharon answered.

"After thinking, what is your response to our offer to you?" questioned the HR.

Sharon laughed, "I must acknowledge it's quite a package. My response is, I accept. I am looking forward to meeting Mr Finland. Sr."

Relieved, the HR said, "I understand. As I stated earlier, he will be in the office tomorrow hopefully."

"Yes, I will. I saw a note from Mr Finland in my apartment. I am grateful he is taking the time to welcome me. But how long will the apartment be available to me?" inquired Sharon.

"Miss Sharon, I am not entirely sure how long Mr Finland has in mind. It would be a discussion you would need to have with him. The apartment plan came up after the accident," informed the HR.

"That's fine. I will take that up with him. How is Mr Finland Jr.?"

"He is fine. Hope you had got over your first encounter with George," commented Mrs Resource.

"Glad you mentioned the first encounter. Although the first impression says a lot, I will be better prepared next time." Inferred Sharon.

"That's the spirit!" cheered Mrs Resource.

"Thank you. What time should I come in tomorrow?" asked Sharon.

"10.00 am, should be fine. I will let Mr Finland's secretary know so she can put you down in the diary," replied the HR.

"10.00 am it is! Thank you!" Sharon replied, ending the call on a peaceful note.

Later at home, Sharon prayed, *Lord, please order my steps. If I am still making a mistake with the job confirmation, kindly redirect my steps.*

Sharon searching for the TV remote and after switching from one channel to another, she drifted eventually drifted off to sleep.

"Brring, Brring!" Her phone rang, interrupting her sleep. Checking out her phone, it proved to be Tom. In deep excitement, she jumped up to pick up her call.

"Hi Tom, how are you? How is your SH (Sweetheart)? I miss you guys!"

"We are good, Sharon. Miss you, too! What's the weather like now?"

"It's hot, Tom, but think I will love living here."

"Good for you," Tom sounded downcast.

"Are you OK, Tom?" Sharon tried to draw out answers from his reaction.

"I am Sharon and wishing you could be here with us. Anyway, what have you decided? Will you take the offer?" Tom chuckled.

"I have accepted; though, I am petrified with fears about the whole thing, Tom."

"Are you fearing your fears because of your feelings for George?" concerned Tom.

"Talking about George, how are we sure it's the same person? The stranger at the airport was different. Although I will not deny they share a complete facial resemblance. I'm quite confused, I am walking on the path of trust in the Lord!" shared a distraught Sharon.

"I believe you. I remember how you dealt with the situation with your friends. You have the courage to take on any challenge," counselled Tom.

"Huh!! That test shocked me to the core of my existence. I was almost running out of the office. I think the right word to describe it was 'terrified'!" she answered.

"You! Terrified?" Tom exclaimed. "It's not in your nature. Girl, you can fight a lion!"

"Then are you saying I am the present-day David?" Sharon replied, teasing him as she chuckled over the phone.

They went on talking until she heard over the TV the start of the 9:00 pm news.

"Oh dear, I have to go, Tom. I have not eaten, and I have to get prepared for work tomorrow." Sharon exclaimed, leaping off the sofa and walked into the kitchen, whilst saying goodbye to Tom.

The open plan kitchen joined to the one double bedroom, a typically designed bachelor suite for a single occupant, and a front porch facing the road for relaxation. Sharon got a readymade meal from a nearby shop. As tasty as it was, she missed a home-cooked meal. She was always too tired to cook a meal.

After a hot bath, she laid in bed, thinking about her discussion with Tom. Her mind flashed back to the dilemma she and her friends had to deal with. Rumours had it that a lecturer – Professor Walker was a hard nut to crack.

He was strict, crafty, and difficult to relate with, but he appeared very approachable at the same time. Unfortunately, by the third year, the same professor lectured one of their compulsory courses – International Business Relations.

By the first week, they knew it would be difficult to get by. They had no extra measure to deal with his impossible expectations towards their work.

Sharon and her friends met together with witty Tom to discuss a solution to their problem. Although initially he humorously counselled them to buy their way into his heart with their assets as females.

Tom knew they will have to handle the professor's stern attitude through hard work. He suggested with extra discipline and commitment, they would impress him.

The girls had several discussions with other past students and studied the professor's students' performance statistics and expectations.

The ladies gave him exactly what he wanted, dogmatically. They focused narrowly on his notes and deliberately set a target for the highest score in his exams.

Apart from studying, the girls talked to the Saviour about their next steps. They decided that on the final assessment, they would omit their names or student numbers on the exam's papers.

The results were eccentric! Professor Walker walked into his class and stood before them for a while.

Grave silence covered the lecture hall. They could hear the drop of a needle. He cleared his throat and said, "Something strange happened in his class set. Hmm, hmm, it has never happened to me in my thirty-odd years of lecturing."

There was an uproar in the hall, as the students discussed among each other and feared the class had cheated.

"Okay, guys, let's get on." He read out the students' names. As he called out, it was apparent the girls' names would remain anonymous.

The last name called walked forward to receive his paper. The lecturer noticed he didn't call out everybody's names. Clearing his throat again, he continued.

"Some of you think you can do what you like and get away with it, right!?"

The class watched as he threatened to take action against some 'unknown' female students.

After the class, he announced the students who omitted their names and ID numbers report to the Head of Department (HOD) office.

The five girls met together, spoke to the Saviour, and approached the office confidently.

The HOD – Professor McWilliams was the most respected person in the university. They knew the HOD had a relationship with the Saviour and hoped for a favourable outcome from her. Fortunately, Professor Walker was not in attendance at the meeting.

The HOD welcomed them into her office with a warm smile. "How has been this semester?" She questioned them with a sense of honesty as the ladies took seats on the sofa. The professor drew an extra seat beside them, waiting for an explanation.

Sharon took the lead, she replied to the session had great, although she was exhausted by the load of work. They were looking forward to a restful break. The HOD then asked if they knew why they were in to see her.

The students looked at each other, and Maya, one of them, replied.

"We understand we are here because of the anonymity on our exams papers."

"You are right," she replied with a stern countenance like Professor Walker. "Can you explain why you all took this action?"

Sharon was about to speak when the HOD signalled to Tamara, sitting across from her to talk. Although Tamara was one of the smartest of the girls, she was the timidest.

They all knew Tamara would have preferred to remain silent during the meeting. Blinking her eyes to show her discomfort, she shifted herself on the seat.

"Umm... we thought we should do something differently. We thought if we could disassociate Professor Walker from the student information, it might help to produce a more independent and fair marking."

Staring directly into her eyes intensely, Professor McWilliams asked, "Are you accusing Professor Walker of deliberate mismanagement of marks? Do you understand there is a term called peer marking?" Sharon interrupted the HOD in defence of Tamara.

"We wouldn't such a thing! Professor, we understand there is peer marking, but we felt like doing something different."

"Different! That would put you in trouble?" The HOD snapped back.

"No! No," they all voiced out in unison!

Maya continued, "We apologise and hope not to repeat this incidence. Once our papers are available, we will identify our papers through our writing. This action will hopefully sort out the misgiving."

"The only reason we will not be taking this case up is that Professor Walker had agreed not to do so." admonished the HOD sternly.

This statement brought a sense of respite to the tense atmosphere in the room.

"Answers to prayers," Sharon thought to herself.

Still waiting for further communication, the HOD stood up and walked off to her table.

"I am of the opinion that the five of you were not copying each other."

"Not at all!" they all echoed.

Sitting upright, Sharon continued, "We sat according to our last name, and none of have similar surname."

"That is the most astonishing thing we discovered. The words are original in some ways, but the same tone of discussion. Remarkably. that's the reason you were all called in today" observed the HOD wryly.

"There is only one explanation for this," Maya replied. "We are friends, and we study together."

"I see. Tell me, what led all of you to respond to the questions in the same manner?" inquired the HOD.

Timid Tamara responded to everyone's surprise!

"I learnt about his teaching pattern and how he liked his answers from past students. We did the same and produced the reports with no identification."

"What did you aim to achieve?" the HOD asked, returning to sit with the girls.

"His independent marking, Professor McWillams." answered the girls simultaneously.

"That still led to my earlier question," the HOD asked, sitting down with a folder.

"No!" they all responded. "We are not sure why we did, but we did," added one of the silent girls.

"Alright, these are the exam papers. Kindly identify yours and put the required information on it." Immediately, the HOD switched the discussion to ask the students what their plans were after studies. Sharon seemed to be the only one without a defined strategy.

The others had family businesses to run or a job waiting for them. She knew she had to work extra hard to make something out of the slight disadvantage observed. To Sharon, it was only the Saviour that got them out of that little mess.

As the HOD had nothing on them apart from the lack of identification, no action would be taken against them.

The girls' results were the best Professor Walker had examined since he started lecturing on the course. Sharon concluded he was quite astonished, which was why he made the HOD become involved in the verification process.

Similarly, Sharon had learned about dealing with relationships from Tom's way of dealing with obstacles, the best learning experience possible!

He had unusual ways of dealing with his relationships. He would always say, "Learn to tame a wild horse, and he will do as instructed. If you have a hard person to deal, learn about the personality, and you have nailed it. The tough point is the application to what you have learnt about the person."

In personal relationships, Tom knew all she needed to do was to take the route of understanding George. The combined help of the Saviour, her parents; and Tom would be a tremendous support to her. She repeated the last few words she remembered saying to herself in the meeting. "Work extra hard," a few times before she drifted off to sleep.

At 6:00 am the alarm blared, awaking Sharon from her deep sleep. She turned over, stretching out her hand to turn off the alarm in desperate need of more sleep time.

An hour later, she rose from her bed, entering the toilet to freshen up.
The next hour was spent with the Saviour, studying his Word, and praying. She got stuck with the passage in: Psalm 46:10

Be still and know that I am God. I will
be exalted among the nations; I will be
exalted in the earth!
It assured Sharon that the Saviour was with her.

She needed to take a step of faith. She remembered one precious Word that made so much meaning to her in this new season.

Isaiah 30:15 - In quietness and in confidence shall be your strength.

But was her season, winter, summer, spring, or autumn? She knows this present season is where the requirement of her stillness is needed. Sharon committed her ways, family, friends, Graceoak, and the nations to Jesus... Rising with praise, she fetched the cup of coffee she had craved all morning.

"Thank goodness!" she exclaimed, sipping the freshly made coffee. She picked up her phone to catch up with her social media.

Her friends were already in touch to find out how she was getting along. She messaged Maya and the rest of the girls, assured they were all good, and she would resume work in a few hours.

FIVE

The Uber driver arrived to take her to Graceoak Limited. Sharon wore the best of her wardrobe, which was her beautiful lilac dress with a silver lining shimmering in Houston's morning sun.

As she stepped into the taxi, the driver greeted with a "Good morning, Ms! You are looking dazzling this morning."

"Thank you for the compliments," replied Sharon confidently, with a smile beaming from ear to ear!

"Correct me if I am assuming I think you are the chauffeur that picked me up yesterday."

"Correctly assumed Ms ..." he intimated adding,

Sharon echoed, "Thank you for yesterday!"

"You are welcome. I assume your meeting went well as you are returning to the same office today." The driver replied.

"O, yes! It was a successful meeting!" replied Sharon excitedly. "I am resuming work today!" Unconsciously she whispered, "Praise God!"

Laughing graciously, the driver responded, "Amen!"

"Do... do you know the Saviour?" queried Sharon in surprise.

"Yes, going on the last two decades, I have attended the Grace Family Church not too far from Graceoak Limited." he informed her.

"Talk about the Saviour's leading," she thought to herself.

The chauffeur continued, "I am a leader in my church. I am Peter Hugh. We welcome you to join us for Bible study this evening. I can come over to pick you. You could meet my family. I have two smart girls, my mother, and my wife."

"Thank you. Can I think about it?" asked Sharon.

"Apologies if I bombarded you with too much information." Handing over his card, he added, "Here is my business card."

"Thank you, you are such a successful help in an unfamiliar environment." Sharon stretched out her hand to receive the card.

"You bet the Saviour knows how to place the right people in our way if we trust him wholeheartedly," he assured.

Agreeing, Sharon said, "Yes! He does, you are so right. I can see the Saviour directing my steps already."

"Ms Sharon..." he said hesitantly.

"Sharon, please," she interrupted.

"I don't want you to bother about space in the car. This is my business car. We will use the family car to church. There is always extra space for one person."

"Thank you so much," Sharon replied with a sense of relief.

"Can I make another small request?" he asked.

"Go ahead..." Sharon prodded him to continue.

"Can I ask my wife to invite you to church on Sunday to meet my family at home?"

"Oh... Oh!! That would be lovely! I will be glad to honour the invitation. It's like I have a new family already in Houston." said a misty-eyed Sharon.

Fifteen minutes later, they arrived at Graceoak Limited.

She thanked the chauffeur for the brilliant company he had been. "I will think about the invite and look forward to meeting your family."

She approached the doors of the vast complex, smiling broadly.

"Yes!! The Saviour got this! She told herself. Sharon walked through the doors, remembering her mother's word ... "You are never alone."

The receptionist's eyes lit up, and she broke out in an enormous smile, "Good morning, Ms Sharon."

"Good morning, Ms Grace. How are you today?" said a delighted Sharon.

"I am well. Thank you for asking."

"I love your dress, its suits you so well," said Sharon, complimenting Grace's flowery dress.

"Thank you, Ms Sharon. It means a lot to me coming from you."

"You're welcome," Sharon said politely.

"I am here to see Mr Finland Sr. Is he around today?"

"Yes, Ms Sharon," replied Grace. "I will let him know you are here. Do you want Mrs Resource to know you are around?"

"That will great, thank you," replied Sharon gratefully.

"Kindly take a seat. I will inform Mr Finland and Mrs Resource accordingly."

As Sharon took a seat, the chauffeur walked in towards the receptionist with some deliveries.

"For you, Ms Grace," the soft-spoken man handed her the packages.

Ms Grace put down the phone. "Thank you, Mr T. I will send this off to Mr Finland's office ASAP."

Mr T, as Sharon now identifies him, said, "Thank you Grace" before walking out of the lobby.

About 10 minutes later, smartly dressed, Mrs Resource walked toward Sharon.

"Morning, Ms O'Loan," she greeted her with a contagious smile.

"Good morning," Sharon replied.

"I will take you to Mr Finland. He has been expecting you." Informed the HR manager.

"As am I, Mrs Resource!" Sharon walked alongside the HR Manager towards the CEO's office.

Mrs Resource reached out to open the glass doors when the voice on the other side called out,

"Come in, Mrs Resource. I understand Sharon is already here."

"Yes, I have her here," she replied as they walked into his glamorous office.

The office layout was like George's office, but about twice the size. This office was a glassed-in oval-shaped expanse facing over the rest of the city.

The view was so breathtaking. Sharon, lost in the moment, walked towards the windows to admire the view.

Mr Finland Sr smiled appreciatively at the sudden expression on Sharon's face of wonder for his office and spoke, "Sharon, I could see you could not hold back your admiration for this view of nature!"

"Not at all. Forgive my impropriety. Morning, Mr Finland, I hope you are feeling better." Sharon said, turning back to him.

"I am well informed about the accident you had on the golf course and am grateful you recovered with no serious injury. Thank you for the warm welcome providing the chauffeur from the airport and the accommodation. I feel already indebted to your organisation from the first day."

Mr Finland stared at her with a surprised glance. "Miss Finland, I am not aware of any welfare gesture handed over to you. However, if anyone did such a thing, it would be my adorable Cynthia."

Mr Finland pointed at the portrait of his wife. "She has the magic ability to fix things behind me to make me look good. I must admire your courage to move to another country a day after your graduation to explore a new opportunity. Young lady, there is more to you that I need to discover. Take a seat."

Sharon accepted the invitation and sat on the sofa across from him.

Turning to Mrs Resource, he said, "Could you kindly tell my secretary to get us something to drink?"

"Sure!" She replied, walking toward Mr Finland's table to make a call to the secretary.

Moments later, she joined Sharon on the sofa, and Mr Finland continued.

"We will wait a few moments. 'My' Cynthia will join us. I think the meeting she's chairing with one of our clients is running late. Hopefully, you will step into the position of chairing these meetings in future so I can have my darling back by my side."

If anything emotional could affect Sharon, it was the affectionate way he had addressed his wife! She wished there could be someone somewhere in the world who would similarly adore her in decades to come. Her mind went to George.

"Should I consider him?"

The next person who walked into the office interrupted her thoughts.

"Talk about the devil." Mr Finland said, turning towards the open doorway, "You read my mind. I was about to mention your name in our conversation."

"Yes, Father, I bet you wanted to," retorted George, addressing his father.

"Morning, and how are you feeling? You know I can always handle things around here. You need to slow down."

Brushing away George's comment. Mr Finland said, "I believe you've met Sharon. I will leave her in your hands once we've settled her into the family."

"I have, and we had a lovely time getting to know each other yesterday," George muttered.

"Really?" Mr Finland turned his gaze on him.

"I believe Ms O'Loan will prove her worth in this organisation," George said. He took a seat opposite her, with his eyes focused brightly on her. Sharon felt her stomach tightened up. The feeling of tension between father and son was overwhelming.

Sharon stretched out her hand to pour herself a drink when George touched hers. "Let me help."

Looking away, Sharon whispered, "Thank you."

"A refill for me too, Son." Mr Finland added, reading his newspaper.

"I suppose your mother should be on her way."

Just as he finished his statement, Mrs Finland walked in, a wide smile beaming all over her glowing face and her husband turn to her, saying lovingly,

"Darling, I missed you all morning!"

Approaching her husband with a kiss, Cynthia replied. "What can I say? Missed you too. I have been busy!"

"Morning, Mrs Finland," Sharon said, rising to her feet with hands stretched out for a polite handshake.

"Morning Sharon, I have heard so much about you from Mr F.," Cynthia said, hugging her.

"Welcome, Sharon. I hope you are not too jetlagged. I always am whenever I return to the UK. Was Franklin helpful? Did you like the accommodation we provided?"

Sharon felt overwhelming joy as she watched the rest of the people in the office smile approvingly as Mrs Finland bombarded her with questions.

"Darling, she must have had a successful time so far. Let her speak." Mr Finland Sr. pulled his wife to sit on his lap with an affectionate cuddle.

"Embarrassed by this display, George protested, "Daddy! Mummy! Could you go home before? ..."

"Before what?" inquired his father. "I am still waiting for you to stop jumping from one bed to another with girls and settle down!

Really!" protested George.

His father added. "You keep saying I need to slow down. We need to see a sign of responsibility from you."

"How does marriage or being in a stable relationship define my responsibility?"

George voiced out angrily, "I will not go down this lane with you folks this morning!"

George stood up, obviously tense, put his hands in his pockets and demanded, "Can I request to take my leave now?"

His mum smiled at her son understandingly, "George, that's the first. You were pretty polite in your request. I guess it's because a certain Ms O'Loan is here. Should we assume you are already sweet on her?"

George, looking bewildered, ignored his mother and walked towards the door.

"I will be back for the 4.00 pm meeting with TB Ltd." He walked out without responding to his parents' request for his sudden politeness.

Meanwhile, Sharon sat reflecting uncomfortably, adjusting her dress at Mrs Finland's insightful observation of the slight aggression from George. *"Lord, teach me to work with this family."*

As though nothing out of the ordinary occurred, Mrs Finland kept smiling, holding onto the hands of her soulmate – Mrs Finland, reassuring Sharon, saying.

"Right! Ms O'Loan, please ignore George's attitude. He gets ahead of himself. He is not the lion he thinks he is. I am his mother. So relax..."

Her husband nodded in agreement, stating supportively, "If he does anything to make your stay here uncomfortable, our doors are always open to you. Remember, we are a family business and keep our workers as a family."

"Isn't that true?" said Mr Finland, waiting for a sign of affirmation from Mrs Resource.

"You're a right, Mr Finland. I can attest to that. Meanwhile, I will need to get Sharon familiar with TB Ltd files for 4.00 pm."

"And Sharon, we will see you in the conference room. I need to attend to my man," said Cynthia, caressing her husband's shoulder.

Mrs Resource rose to stand along with an unsure Sharon who thanked and acknowledged her new bosses.

"I am happy to be a part of the family and I hope to put in my commitments."

"We believe in you." said the Finlands in unison.

Those were the last words Sharon heard, feeling a log on her chest.

"But how, Lord? Not sure what I am getting myself into. I really hope that means we will remain within my job description."

Sharon was deep in her thoughts until Mrs Resource interrupted with, "Did you hear me, Sharon?"

She had followed Mrs Resource into her office while the HR discussed the relevant information of TB Ltd.

Sharon had heard nothing Mrs Resource had said. "Yes! No!" she replied simultaneously.

"Ms O'Loan. I know it's a lot to take in. I am sure you will be all right. We are all here to support you."

"You don't suppose I can sit down?" Sharon interjected, to fend off more sympathy.

"For sure, it's your office, remember? I am easing you in, as Mr George is in a state at the moment," intimated the HR, giving a reason for Boss Jr's outburst.

"What do you mean, in a state? Anything I should know?" questioned Sharon.

"Nothing much," shared Mrs Resource. "It relates to matters of the heart. You will appreciate it better when he opens up to you himself."

"Thank you, I appreciate it," Sharon responded as though her words did not bother her.

"So, you must take nothing to heart. George was not always like this. Constantly observing the two lovebirds makes nothing easy for his heart."

Ignoring her comments, Sharon responded. "I will look through these files, will be at the meeting at 4."

Sharon echoed as Mrs Resource walked out of her office.

Falling back in her seat, Sharon exclaimed. *"Oh, whoa, Lord! I did not know you would take me into the lion's den once I worked. George seemed like a challenge, but I believe your grace is more than enough. Your wisdom is all I need."*

Sharon settled down to familiarise herself with the files for the few hours, but she still felt troubled.

SIX

Sharon walked into the conference room at 4.01 pm. Her eyes glowered at George, Mr Grumpy.

The representatives from TB Ltd sat opposite George, who seemed to be having a chat with the two gentlemen, oblivious to Sharon's attitude.

George politely introduced Sharon as the recently appointed Business Development Manager.

His expression remained blank for the first time in almost 40 hours. Sharon felt supported by George's acknowledgement of her role within the organisation.

With an exchange of handshakes, she took a seat opposite George. She wanted to have an observation of George's body language to manage through her first meeting. Mrs O'Loan is so good at studying people. I have to put the skills she's taught me into practice.

Sharon watched, panicking, as the meeting started without the presence of Mr Finland Sr. He promised to be available for the meeting, she reminded herself, developing cold feet. A few moments later, Mr and Mrs Finland walked in. They exchanged greetings with the representatives of TB limited.

"Good day, Mr and Mrs Finland," both men greeted simultaneously, stretching out their hands for firm handshakes.

"Please take your seat," Mr Finland Sr. requested after the pleasantries, sitting beside his son with his Cynthia by his side.

George did a recap of the introduction, welcoming his parents into the meeting. He provided a reversed version to the business deal takeover, between TB Limited and Graceoak Oil and Gas.

The gentlemen from the selling organisation nodded in agreement with his reversed overview. They asked if Mr Finland Sr. had any other additional comments to make before signing the agreement documents.

Mr Finland Sr. stated he agreed to the terms and conditions of the agreement. Turning towards

Sharon, he asked if she had any comments before the deal takeover from TB Limited.

Sharon felt thrown into the spotlight without notice; but spoke up with eloquent poise.

"Thank you, Mr Finland Sr, for the opportunity to be present in the meeting and also, an opportunity to give my opinion."

Peeking at George, Sharon sensed a rising tension with his face posed with disapproval.

But she ignored him and pressed on. "In my candid opinion," clearing her throat with sweaty palms.

"From my perspective, I am concerned about the details of the terms and profitability of the business model. The clarification, as addressed in the copy I scanned through this afternoon, does not guarantee the turnover it as expressed in the documentation."

With every utterance from Sharon's lips, the representatives from TB Limited appeared increasingly uncomfortable. The first refilled his cup of coffee, while the second readjusted himself in his seat.

To support the gentlemen, George interrupted with, "Sharon, I have gone through the document, and I am quite satisfied with the outcome of the business proposal for the next couple of years."

"George!" said Mrs Finland, shifting in her seat, trying to interrupt him.

"Mummy, please, can I speak?" George snapped back at her.

"George!" His father echoed his wife's voice but directed his reply to Sharon.

"My family is quite interested, gentlemen! Can I request a break from the meeting for a private discussion with Sharon and George? Please excuse us."

"Dad, please, can I handle this? It's part of my portfolio." Ignoring George's plea and to shield their family's differences, Mr Finland Sr continued.

"As I was saying," directing his gaze to the gentlemen.

"We the family members need talk privately before we make the final decision," Words he spoke in explanation as he stepped out of the conference room.

George and Sharon followed him out of the meeting room. Sharon dragged herself behind George, expecting to lose her job on only her second day. She tried to compose herself as professionally as possible.

Mr Finland Sr. was standing, supported by his walking stick, despite the pressure on his sore legs. He turned around to meet George's angry face.

Attempting to placate his son, he told him, "I called both of you into the office to have a brief discussion, so we can have a common front for the takeover."

Turning to Sharon, he requested a detailed description of what she meant.

Sharon, with shaky lips, explained that based on the analysis and approach used in the proposal, along with the projected scores provided.

Graceoak could not make the projected profit margin. She further expressed that because of the level of debt to be acquired from TB Limited and the amount that the Graceoak is going to pay for the takeover of the establishment, it was a poor deal.

Sharon's analysis of the deal upset George so much he blew up angrily, retorting.

"Dad, this is exactly why I did not want anybody interfering in my business. I have already gone through it. I went through the numbers and am sure this deal is going to work. You shouldn't listen to this young lady with a limited background in business. That she got an MBA yesterday does not mean she has the experience and knows the business."

George's level of disdain couldn't be more evident. "Believe me, Dad, Sharon does not have a clue what the Finland family business is all about."

George went on expressing his distrust while Mr Finland Sr. waited for his son to let out all the steam.

After a brief moment of anger, George calmed down, after which Finland Sr. said, "George, you will agree that I enjoy taking business risks. I think I will take Sharon's suggestions. I am going to turn down this business deal."

Sharon stepped in and disapproving his comment, "Mr Finland, I wouldn't say you should step down from the business deal. I would recommend you allow me to speak to the company representatives."

George exclaimed, "Sharon, or whatever your name is. You don't even speak numbers. Now you want to speak on our behalf?"

"George!" his father tried to stop him, but it was useless.

George added, "You came in today causing chaos and confusion in my family..."

"Mr Finland looked down at his wristwatch, looked over at Sharon and George stating, "This is one of the biggest risks I have had to make for my business, but Sharon, I trust your gut!"

He walked toward the door, looking back, smiling at her. "Sharon, go ahead, take the lead."

Fifteen minutes later, they stepped back into the conference room. Everyone sat quietly, waiting for

Sharon to speak. George was expecting her to trip up, so he could pounce on her. Sharon spoke a few words to the Saviour for the wisdom to deal with her first business negotiation.

Sharon stood confidently by the edge of the table with everyone's eyes on her. She made refills of teas and coffee for the team representing TB Limited, while she got herself a cup of water.

Sharon sat back, facing the two gentlemen, and cleared her throat after a sip of water.

"I appreciate you want us to take over your organisation. And I also appreciate that Graceoak Oil and Gas is interested in buying you over. But, with the numbers you presented to us so far, I don't think that we can go ahead with this deal as is."

The gentlemen from TB Limited looked at each other, disappointed. They had not expected to meet an obstacle so close to the finalising of this deal!

Continuing, Sharon re-emphasised, "If you are really interested in negotiating the deal further, you will have to agree to reorganise your organisation and make it profitable for us. Your numbers will have to be reversed. At least, I would say that you have to cut down your numbers by 25% of the deal margin."

Thunderstruck, the two men bolted up in their seats. "I know it is coming to you as a surprise, but..." she slid the folder towards them.

"We cannot go on any further. If you cannot take 25% away from it, we won't take the deal."

The two men looked at each other and the leader said, "I am sorry Miss Sharon, but we've already decided. This is the amount we want to sell. We had an arrangement with Mr George Jr."

He looked at George for a confirmation, but George refused to make eye contact with him.

Sharon glared at them with a fierce emphasis and said, "I'm sorry, we cannot go less than what we have set. 25% off, then we take the deal."

The two men took their turn and excused themselves for a coffee break chat.

Once the gentlemen had gone out, Mr and Mrs Finland excused themselves from the rest of the meeting. They confirmed confidence in both George and Sharon to negotiate the last deal, but Mr Finland Sr, needed rest as he was still in recovery from the accident.

There was a grave silence between the two remaining individuals. Sharon prayed she would survive this first test of her business management skills.

After 15 minutes of talking with each other, the two men came back in.

Still looking unsure of themselves and wary of the fierce new lady they have never dealt with before this, they said, "If we take 15% off of the margin, we have a deal."

Smiling inwardly, Sharon knew she was better off. Observing that Sharon might make sense, George cleared his throat to accommodate Sharon's next move.

She looked at George and then at the gentlemen. "I'm sorry, but Graceoak will have to stand our ground, 25% off or no deal. Remember, the numbers speak for themselves!"

The men looked at each other and one of them countered, "20% will be our cut off. We take 5% off and we have a deal."

Sharon looked at George to determine his confirmation with eye contact.

Avoiding eye contact, George was too proud to accept defeat in his first attempt to ruin everything Sharon stood for. But taking courage from a lesson in believing in her gut, Sharon stared at George, waiting for his eye contact.

To agree to a certain deal to take 20% off from the deal he had already made, she had thus undermined his authority. With no premeditated intention, she had where George was concerned, dug a deep hole for herself.

Sharon had never done this before. She couldn't understand where the confidence had come from. Sharon knew that if this deal didn't work out as suggested, she imagined ending up in a Houston prison, not to mention Mum and Dad so far away unable to rescue her!

Looking away from George, she looked at the men and confirmed: "We have a deal." Standing up, she continued, "Successful doing business with you."

Sharon passed the documents to George for his signature. He checked each page patiently, as though he was cross-examining the length and width before signing the document.

George, still furious at Sharon's audacity, signed the papers before passing it to the gentlemen. He stood, shook hands, and walked out of the conference room. The men from TB Ltd exchanged goodbyes. They agreed on the dates for signing the final documentation with Mr Finland Sr.

The men were on their way with Sharon escorting them out when George appeared at the entrance.

Out of the blue, the image of the stranger she met at the Heathrow Airport struck her again. She suddenly became flushed.

Why I'm I getting into a trap with him? Is he or a ghost of the one I met? It's obvious I'm attracted to this him. Why do I repel him so this very much?

She was about to step out of his way when George walked up to Sharon and whispered to her, snarling fiercely.

"You have bitten off more than you can chew! I don't know where you came from, but if you would remain in this organisation with me, you have to dance to my tune or you will face the consequences."

He brushed past her, rudely stepping on her toes, and walked back toward his office. George detested Sharon more each day afterwards.

SEVEN

Peter, the Uber driver, picked Sharon from the office about 5.30 pm. Sharon, with excitement, discussed all that happened to her on the first day on her job. Both thanked the Saviour for the wonderful day as they headed to her apartment.

"Peter, I will join you at church this evening, if you don't mind." First, she requested getting something from the nearest store.

10 minutes later, she rushed back with a sandwich and a bottle of blueberry drink. "Apologies, I am famished, I could not wait till..." Peter interrupted,

"You shouldn't have bothered getting anything so soon. We might have headed to my home first. You could have eaten something with us."

"Oh no, not to worry. It's the first time I will meet your family. I wouldn't aspire to be a bother." Sharon quickly reclined his offer.

"It's not a bother, Sharon," Peter added. "You are now a sister to us, and we'll treat you like one." He replied heartily.

Sharon's heart was comforted. All things were falling into place the way he promised. She gobbled down her food, satisfying the hungry giants in her stomach. Peter drove her straight home and waited for 20 minutes while she changed.

Returning in the cab, they headed out for another 20 minutes' drive away from her apartment to Peter's home.

Sharon enjoyed the passing scenery... busy streets, the skyscrapers, the warmer weather. She couldn't get enough of that. Approaching a drive with tall evergreen trees on both sides, she peeped through the window to see two kids. They were jumping up and down with excitement.

As the car stopped, she heard their charming voices, similar to Tom's lovely little girls. "Hey,

Daddy! hey Daddy!" welcomed the little boy and girl rushing down towards him. They pulled him down by the shoulders with enormous hugs.

Peter gasped, "How are my heart throbs doing today?"

Ignoring his question, the girl demanded, "Daddy, who is this?" pointing toward Sharon.

Joining the small group, the boy added, "Hey, pointing's not nice! They taught you to be polite to strangers."

"I don't know her. I was talking to my dad and asking him who the stranger was!" retorted the little girl.

Taking each by the hand to stop the surge of verbal exchange, Peter admonished, "Oh, you two, get on! Go into the house and give me a little peace."

Sharon smiled at the exchange witnessed between the two children now both jumping up and down, waiting for answers. She would have introduced herself, but guessed their dad knew them better than that. Sharon watched the twins play with their dad, and walking towards the house whilst the little girl eyed her suspiciously, each time she swung her head towards Sharon.

"Hey, Darling!" Peter called out to a heavily pregnant woman at the open doorway.

"My Beautiful, I came in earlier today because we have a visitor," said Peter lovingly.

"Really, Peter, that's nice." The woman replied, hugging her husband.

"Who is our visitor today? You always have a way of bringing someone new every time. Now I understand, I am married to an Angel in disguise," she observed, hugging him even more tightly.

"Don't you start, woman!" Peter tickled his wife. "That's why you fell in love with me. Isn't it?"

Amused, the wife replied, "Of course! That's why I fell in love with you. Who else would be my Angel, If not, you?"

Sharon, getting embarrassed by the romantic exchange, focused her gaze on the floor. She heard, "Oh! Apologies! I'm Lovett, his wife. You can see I'm pregnant again."

Sharon nodded with a smile, acknowledging Lovett's introduction. "Thank you for having me." She mumbled with a friendly grin.

Lovett gently informed her, "These are my twins. Hope they didn't bother you. They always speak out of turn." One cheeky faced twin stood silently peeking out from behind Lovett.

"Oh no! They were not any bother. Most pleasant, I say." commented Sharon politely.

Lovett, with a surprised face, replied, "Really? That's a start. I didn't know you guys are now pleasant. I'm so glad you have such an excellent report."

The twins glanced back and forth, grinning, revealing their childlike nature.

"They're not that bad. I think they are just good-natured," expressed Sharon, making a cheeky face in response to the twins. They all laughed as the children jumped into the house, continuing their play.

The house was simply furnished, but tidy and colourful in every way. Sharon sat down while the family got ready.

A few moments later, Lovett brought in a tray with tall, water-filled glasses and snacks.

"I never asked what you wanted, but here is some water for your thirst," she said.

"Thank you for the warm welcome into your home, Lovett. You remind me of my aunt."

"I am glad, mind you, I get that compliment often. My DNA for hospitality is finely distributed abroad!"

The two shared a laugh as Lovett went off to get dressed. 15 minutes later, they were out, ready to head to church.

The kids headed straight into the car, as they knew exactly where to sit.

Both entered and started buckling in until their dad said, "Wait! Wait, you know Sharon is coming with us? Are you not going to let her take a seat at the back?"

"Okay, Sharon, come this way." The little boy got out of the car.

To Sharon, the boy seemed to be more considerate than the little girl. But she's yet to know them, so must be careful about forming an impression yet.

Once he was out of his seat, Sharon pulled the seat forward to take a seat at the back of 7-seater SUV.

Once everyone's door was shut, Peter shouted: "Everybody ready?"

"Yes, Dada!" shouted the twins and their mum in unison.

"Let us pray." He said a few words to the Saviour before turning on the ignition.

They drove approximately 15 minutes away from their house before pulling into the church parking lot. Everyone they met on the way into church exchanged enthusiastic greetings with them.

The service went well. It was so different from back home. Back home, it was more conservative. This here was upbeat in every way. The choir was so beautiful, Sharon felt she made the right choice coming to Peter's church.

In America, everything seemed absurd from the way they pronounce words to the broad roads and the design of the traffic lights.

Sharon knew she needed a lot of adjusting. She was glad the Saviour had already sent angels ahead of her, knowing things would be easier than it seemed.

Memories flooded her mind. Tom, I remember the first time we met very well. He was the guiding angel the Saviour sent to support me through those difficult times in university.

Those days, I didn't understand what the university was all about. Tom became the brother I never had. Now, another door is waiting here for me. A new family away from home.

After the service, Peter drove Sharon back to her apartment. Although the twins wanted to spend more time with her, begging to go into her house to see her flat.

"You will come back to visit another day," consoled Peter.

Stepping out, Sharon continued, "I am very grateful. I enjoyed myself this evening. Peter, you have the best of families."

"Thank you, Sharon, don't you worry, you have an extension of your family with us. If you need anything, don't hesitate. We will be right here to support you," Lovett added.

"Thank you much appreciated," expressed Sharon gratefully at the open invitation.

"Meanwhile, we should invite you to dinner," said Peter.

"If you don't mind, I will arrange something with my wife. We welcome you to spend the evening with us whenever you're able to. I know you just met us, so take your time." "Hmm, that's so kind of you," murmured Sharon.

"If next Saturday at six pm is OK, you can join us then for a meal." Lovett, turning her gaze to Peter, who agreed on the invitation.

"Oh, that would be great. I'll think about it, and I will let you know. Thank you so much!" accepted Sharon as she waved goodbye.

As he drove off, she exclaimed, "Oh, Peter! Please, please, will you be kind enough to come over tomorrow morning to pick me up for work?"

"Of course!" Peter responded.

"I'll be very glad if this became a regular thing, so I know that I have a plan in place for the time being," Sharon pleaded, with her hands pressed together.

"Oh no! No, no bother!" said Peter kindly. "I'll make it a point to take you to work until you can get your own car!"

"Yes! Oh, I'd love that too. But I need more time to settle down before getting a car."
She waved bye to the family as she walked into the house.

Sharon was so tired, but not too tired to make another phone call home.

"Hello, Mum!" she voiced wearily.

"How are you, Sharon? How are you? How was your first day at work? I've been waiting on the phone, waiting for your call. I thought you'd never call!"

"Mum, of course! I would. You wouldn't believe how things are falling into place for me."

"Really!? tell me, child." Mrs O'Loan exclaimed.

"It's been the most brilliant two days I've had in my life."

"Really!? More brilliant than days you spend with us?"

"No, Mummy, I didn't mean it that way. You know, but I was not expecting. Mum, wait! Where's my dad? Is he there?"

" Am I not here talking to you? Must your dad be here before you talk?"

"Mum, please, can I hear my dad's voice? I've missed him so much."

"He's here," said Mrs O'Loan, deflated.

"Dad! Dad, I have missed you so much." Her voice echoing excitedly over the phone.

"Hello, Beautiful, having been listening to you chat with my wife." joked Dad.

"Is Mom taking care of you? Are you eating? Is everything okay?" inquired Sharon.

"Sharon! Sharon, your mum is fine with me, and I've eaten. She's taking care of me and herself. How about you tell us everything that's been happening to you? We've missed you so much!" interjected her dad.

Sharon went on, discussing everything that had happened from the time she left the house in the morning. The meeting in the office, the second meeting in the conference room. George's attitude, the wisdom she displayed. Peter the Uber driver, the church service, Peter's family winning her heart.

"I can't believe the way everything worked out. Sharon remembers the Saviour is always faithful," her mother echoed over the phone.

They continued to discuss other news from back home. After about forty-five minutes of talking, Sharon said. "Dad, Mum, if I don't sleep now, I won't wake up in time to get ready for work. I need some sleep!"

"We understand you need your beauty sleep," her parents understood.

"First, I need to take some time out to talk to the Saviour," pleaded Sharon.

"You are right. Child, you need to do that. Remember the Saviour's words we wrote for you. Remember to read your scriptures every day."
Sharon joined in to recite the family 'remember' litany.

"Remember to be pleasant and remember to commit your ways into His hands. He would always direct your path. That you have joy that everything worked out today doesn't mean that every day is going to work out like this."

"I know, Dad!" Sighed Sharon.

"So, prepare your heart for difficult days, too." Mr O'Loan added.

"True, I know I'm keeping an open mind. I learnt that from both of you, my best teachers. Hopefully, every day is going to be this nice. But if it doesn't, I'll be glad to give thanks in everything."

"True," her mum echoed.

Sharon continued, "whether good, bad, or ugly... Dad, Mum, I love you!! But night, am sending my hugs through."

After the phone call, Sharon took a warm bath, after which she lounged on her bed to read aloud the Saviour's words back to him. She sang a few hymns before deciding to check out what's on the TV. She flipped through the stations, but giving up, she slept.

EIGHT

6:30 in the morning, a beeping from her cell phone woke her up. Sharon couldn't bear to wake up. She loved a good sleep!

Sharon considered her job. *It's time to go into the office.* The major obstacle she had to deal with this morning is nasty old George!

It is too early to give George any chance to find loopholes in her day's work. Sharon needed to be more careful about how to handle George.

Though he's trying hard to frustrate her, Sharon needed to appreciate how George worked.

On reflection, she must understand and not judge him.

The next morning, Peter was in front of her apartment by 7:30 pm. She called out a "Good morning, Peter. I'm grateful you came."

"And, how!" laughed Peter.

"Much more grateful for the dollars you're going to be dropping into my pocket," he said, chuckled.

"No problem, Peter! We are both benefiting from each other. Thank you for inviting me to the service yesterday."

"Thank you for joining us. Hope you managed a night's sleep," said Peter, peeking at her through the rearview mirror.

"I did!" commented Sharon, reflecting on last night. "I had a night's sleep. Everything that had happened so far has good."

"Don't worry, you will have many better days ahead of you, Sharon. Just have trust in your heart."

"Thank you so much, Peter." Sharon gazed out of the window. The rest of the journey was muted. Sharon's thoughts enveloped her. How do I exercise a professional self before her new bosses?

By 8:00 am, she was already at her desk. Sharon used the first moment to catch up with the IT equipment, connections and looking through her emails.

She figured out what the order of her tasks would be, prioritising each folder based on the deadline set by George written at the top of each folder.

Moments later, she got a call from Mrs Resource.

"Morning Sharon, we expect you in Mr Finland's office in the next 30 minutes. There is an urgent staff meeting."

Feeling apprehensive, Sharon replied. "I left early yesterday. Did anything terrible go wrong with the takeover deal with TB limited? I need to be aware of?"

Mrs Resource giggled. "Nothing terrible happened. Everything went well. Is there something I need to be aware of before the meeting?"

"I don't think so," said Sharon apprehensively.

"You can get ready then," Mrs Resource added.

"Oh yes, I'll be there in 30," Sharon replied, with a sense of uncertainty about Mr Finland's reasons for the expected meeting.

She took a few minutes to talk to the Saviour about her fears resulting from that call from Mrs Resource.

Sharon also remembered Peter's last words in the car: *"Trust." That is what I need now, she echoed to herself.* Proceeding from her silent moment, Sharon looked around the office and prepared all the files she might need for the meeting.

Five minutes before time, she strode out of her office and headed to the CEO's office. Stepping into the corridor, she met Mrs Resource and the Office Administrator.

"Is everything OK? Miss O'Loan, you look flushed." The administrator asked with concern.

"Everything is fine," replied Sharon, gathering her sense of courage.

"Mr Finland Jr. wants a detailed update from yesterday and the next target, how we planned everything. He's been out of the loop, and we all have to give him feedback about all the projects and commitments when he was away shortly after the accident." Mrs Resource added, updating Sharon.

"I understand," were the last words Sharon uttered before they walked into the office.

Mr Finland, George, his mum, and the rest of the team already seated greeted the rest of the team for the meeting.

"Good morning, guys. How are you?" Mr Finland greeted casually.

Wow, he's so friendly. Is this boss for real? Thoughts flashed through Sharon's mind.

"Morning, Mr Finland," the three ladies echoed after each other.

"Oh! How are you, Sharon? Are you settling in well? I know it will be overwhelming in the next few days or weeks." Mrs Finland asked with a caring tone similar to Mrs O'Loan's.

"I understand, Mrs Finland, and with the support of everyone here, it would be a peaceful assimilation into your company for me."

"Have you got everything you need to settle in? If there's anything you need, do not hesitate to ask." Mr Finland added, looking to the other members of the team.

"We're going to start..." the CEO continued. Sharon avoided any eye contact with George. She walked over to the table to get a glass of water.

"Sharon, it seems you prefer the water. Don't you like coffee?" observed Mrs Finland.

"I am trying to avoid caffeine as much as I can. But I'm very good with water. It helps me to settle down well." Sharon shared.

"You're healthy. I hope I can follow in your footsteps," Mrs Finland hinted with a smile. Sharon avoided the compliment of her healthy lifestyle.

She was glad as Mrs Resource came to her rescue with, "Things don't always look like it. For healthy living, if you're healthy, you are healthy. If you're unhealthy, you're not. Water might not be magic."

"You are very right, Mrs Resource! If you are unhealthy, there is only so much you can do about it."

Mrs Finland gazed over at her son, sitting with a nonchalant attitude. Sharon tried not to look at him as he was already had a furious expression plastered on his face this early in the morning.

Mrs Finland continued, "George, you need to give a smile, it costs nothing."

"Mum, can we start the meeting? I have a long day ahead. I have my diary full of scheduled meetings with clients."

"That's fine George, your Mummy enjoys pulling your leg." cut in Mr Finland Sr who anticipated a storm brewing, and to the calm down a fuming George.

"Can we go ahead," he started, "Sharon, we're going to start with you. I think you have some papers for my signature."

"Yes, Mr Finland," Sharon echoed, shifting uncomfortably on her seat.

"I negotiated the business deal yesterday. We took 20% off the asking price. We're able to take the business over once they return all the documentation. Hopefully, before the end of the day."

With excitement, the CEO and his wife responded, "Wow! Brilliant!! This is exciting!! Congratulations on your first Graceoak deal!!"

"The congratulations is all yours, Mr Finland," she replied, avoiding the compliment. "For believing in me."

Out of the blue, George, in his irrational nature, yelled out. "Sharon, can we just stop this...!

After a long awkward moment, Sharon proceeded, "Mr Finland, it's okay, no it is not alright. Mr Finland, thank you for believing in me. I'll be expecting TB Limited to send us the papers this afternoon. I will drop them at your office for signing."

"Oh! That would great." To add to the excitement, his father continued, "George, have you dropped all the other folders for the business takeover and business development to Sharon?"

"Yes," George replied in a flash, avoiding a rising resentment.

"Sharon needs to take the load off you." The CEO added, smiling at Sharon.

"Dad, dad, I have never complained, that I can't handle my workload," burst out George in protest.

"George, I know you can. I know you can do everything. But you won't be able to free your diary for all the clients and networking. So many ideas need to be run by you." Mr Finland continued in a relaxed, fatherly disposition.

"I don't understand," George fighting like an angry puppy.

"That I need you to explore new ideas does not equate leaving my files with Sharon. If nothing is broken, dad, nothing needs to be mended!!"
Angered by the tone George had used in addressing his father, Mrs Finland intervened.

"Get off your high horse, Young Man. Listen to your dad, and hand over all the files by the end of the day!!"
It shocked Sharon, the newbie, that no one seemed disturbed by George's behaviour. They must be used to him by now. His Mummy knew how to handle him.
Feeling cornered, George succumbed, muttering under his breath.

"I have already asked Mrs Resource to do that."
In an irritated tone, Mrs Finland continued.

"So why did you have to take us through this as if you were mad? Why do you have to make a mountain out of a molehill?"

Unrepentant, George looked away, quietly sipping a cup of coffee, while Cynthia held her husband's hands to give him some much-needed comfort.

"George, may I remind you that this establishment still belongs to me? As long as I am still alive, I make all decisions here."

Mr Finland's tone remained firm, though with a friendly face.

"Okay, just for now," George whispered emphatically.

"With this growing unbearable attitude of yours, it might take longer than you expect."

The CEO resolutely turned his gaze towards the window, to fend off his angry thoughts towards George.

The rest of the team stayed to discuss their usual business updates, changing the atmosphere back to the regular Graceoak meeting.

Mrs Resource discussed all the information related to the human resource department. The administrator and accountant discussed all the files associated with their offices while the CEO had been away.

One thing was apparent, the meeting was relaxing except for an angry George, which no one seemed to feel bothered about. To any outside observer, the organisation appeared like a family. After the meeting, they all dispersed to do the rest of their day's work.

The next six months became the beginning of a peaceful, yet challenging, period in Sharon's life.

George did not make things easy for her. He constantly attempted to undermine her work. Sharon seemed to always be a step ahead of him.

Sometimes files or documents on her hard drive went missing. Sharon, aware of his hatred towards her, had the wisdom she needed from the Saviour. She often remembered to trust Him for each day.

Sharon always made sure she had a backup at her home for every file or documentation related to her work. She knew it to be against company policies to take company information home, but she was not ready to take any chances with George.

On occasions when angry George would play a prank on her, she would always have a backup to prove her integrity. Rather than discrediting her work, Sharon received more acknowledgement for the good-work, precision, and attention to details.

In the fifth month, George knew her probation period would end in a month. He tried everything possible to get Sharon laid off.

Mrs Resource refused the evidence he produced, leading to a major disagreement. Every devious plan of his kept bouncing back to smack him in the face. That became an established pattern.

The CEO would rather let George off his responsibilities within the organisation than lose Sharon.

George ultimately gave up. He realised Sharon was a woman of integrity. Her job remained impeccable. Everyone seems to love her. Everything she laid her hands on appeared to prosper.

There must be a God above protecting her, he thought to himself.

Sharon left George with no choice but to get under her skin with questions.

What made her so different from other ladies?

Although he'd tried upsetting her, Sharon didn't even look upset. Even when she should be upset, she did not express it.

The next moment not only was she not upset; she was rather patient and understanding, despite all George's misgivings toward her.

"There must be some dirt about her, I don't know. Everyone has a cockroach in their cupboard somewhere." George's suspicions persisted.

George hired a private investigator who was also his long-time friend. His assignment was to find out all about Sharon's life. Was there something about her that set her apart from all the other ladies?

Thinking back to all the ladies in his life, they all had selfish agendas and had been girls who had worked in the office. He had successfully frustrated them, so why was Sharon so different?

The private investigator came back with his report after two weeks when they met at their usual night club.

"George, there's nothing dirty about Sharon. Who is this lady and what do you want from her? She is one of those people from a religious sect."

"What do you mean by that?" George asked, after clearing his throat with a sip from his water glass.

"Do you want to hit on her? Do you want to have anything to do with her? Are you tired of all the ladies in the club and your one-night stands? I can arrange a few of them for you," teased his friend.

"No man, that's not what I want! I just wanted to know ... I need to know why she's different."

"George, if you want to know why she's different; then, I think you need to go find out the traditional way."

"What do you mean, the traditional way?" his eyes sparkled.

"Sharon is not the regular girl. You need to cultivate a genuine friendship with her. I hope you have not sent her your usual vibes."

"You can say that again. I have wronged her worse than any other lady, and yet she seemed not offended. She is strangely weird."

"She seems like a keeper then." affirmed his friend. "Do you like her?"

"I can't like or develop likeness toward her if I know nothing about her, she bothers me or frightens me of late," George answered, gulping down the rest of the rum in his glass.

The next few days, George did more digging. He started investigating the description of the people associated with Sharon's religious sect.

George concluded that he would attempt to learn their language, to speak their language. It might help him get into Sharon's books. To know if things upset her, but unfortunately, she's being very professional with him.

He got himself the strange book used by Sharon's sect – the Bible. Maybe it could tell him what kind of lady she is. He started reading the Bible secretly, but strangely; he observed he was becoming calmer.

NINE

It's the first Christmas Sharon would spend away from her family.

She couldn't imagine Christmas without her parents. Sharon planned, from the beginning of December, how she was going to return home days earlier.

She prioritised all her tasks to finish a week before Christmas. With all plans in place, Sharon walked into George's office the third day in December. After discussing business, Sharon made her request known.

"Can I request leave to travel home a few days before the Christmas holiday? I want to spend time with my family."

"Return home?" George seemed to have woken up on his wrong side. "You could as well ask to leave now. Why are you waiting until the Christmas holiday?"

"Unfortunately, I still have tons of work to do here." Sharon's reply caught him unawares. George continued aggressively to push her to the limits.

"You know you have tons of work to do. Why do you even bother asking? said George dismissively.

"George, would you prefer I make a direct request to Mr Finland Sr!?" demanded Sharon.

"You know, I could. Yet, I approached you because you are my direct boss. Every holiday request has to come through your office as the Operation Manager."

"It wouldn't be your first." George snapped, adjusting his tie.

"I wish I didn't have to go through you about holidays or anything that has to do with my personal life," Sharon muttered.

George, who was looking for a way to get to know her, changed his demeanour. Before he could speak again, Sharon continued.

"Let's just keep it as professional as possible, George. I am as professional as possible here. I was not asking for any time off now, and I've never asked for any time off before. All I want is more time to spend with my family."

In his arrogance, George replied. "It seems I don't have a choice. You can do whatever you like. Sign yourself out and travel. Make sure there are no lapses in your job."

"Thank you, George, for being so polite and for always been helpful." Words, she pronounced with a smile.

Sharon dropped her holiday file on his table and walked out. She was not ready for any further comments from him. George, in a daze, stared after her with wonder.

"Sharon!" Mrs Finland called, peeping into Sharon's office. "Can you come over to my office?"

"Be right there!!" called out Sharon, smiling back at Mrs Finland, whom she adored.

She picked up her notepad and headed out of George's office. Knocking on Mrs Finland's office door, she heard, "Come in, Sharon. Get yourself something to drink and sit on the sofa. I will be with you shortly," her pleasant voice announced.

"Thank you, Mrs Finland." She headed to the coffee table. A moment later, Sharon walked over and sat beside her.

"Sharon, you have a passionate approach to your work, so I called you to discuss the Christmas party plans."

Mrs Finland discussed her elaborate plans with her. Sharon wondered where she would fit into in the picture created in front of her.

"Would you mind planning the Christmas party this year?" Mrs Finland's voice echoed in her wandering thoughts.

"Sorry, I didn't get that!" apologised Sharon, looking lost and bewildered.

"I said you should plan for the Christmas party this year, "broke in Mrs Finland.

To avoid responsibility and remove any roadblock on her Christmas plans, Sharon responded, "This is only my first Christmas in the company!"

"I am aware of this." Mrs Finland acknowledged.

"I would love it too, but I'm a nervous wreck," continued Sharon.

"I might make a mess of it. Would you mind if I ask Mrs Resource to handle it while I shadow her? By next year, I could learn from her and do something more professional and more dignified."

"I can imagine, Sharon," muttered Mrs Finland.

Sharon felt she was off the hook until she continued.

"You know, Sharon, you have a way of getting around super difficult situations. I didn't even imagine how challenging it must be for you. It's your first time in everything, but you have done exceptionally well so far."

Sharon prayed Mrs Finland would find an alternative, but she continued.

"You have a way of accepting the enormous task and making it easier for me," grinning at her.

"Thank you, Mrs Finland. I appreciate your thoughtfulness to ask me to do this. Can I request Mrs Resource to support me?"

"Oh, yes! You could arrange a meeting between the three of us. We'll discuss the details on how we will take this forward. I would be free anytime in the next two days."

"I will inform Mrs Resource and invite her to the next meeting." Sharon echoed and hurried out with a "thank you."

Walking back to the office, Sharon feared the worse about her holiday plans.

George might be right this time. I can't just make plans anyhow, anymore. Saviour, I trust you would work this out too. Sharon pensively, standing by the window, staring at the birds singing in the trees.

Later that afternoon, Sharon arranged a meeting. The three met together and agreed on a date precisely a week before Christmas.

Mrs Finland planned their holiday getaway week before Christmas after the office Christmas party. A miracle was the only definition Sharon had for this opening.

Some time for Sharon to travel, as she had already booked a flight ticket for three days before the Christmas holiday! Thank you, Jesus!

The Christmas party was fun. Sharon, however, noticed an unexpected turn of events. There was something strange about George. He wasn't his usual aggressive self.

Everybody knew he was always sarcastic, but something was different. George is acting. uncharacteristically like the stranger she met at the airport!

Occasionally nice here and there, opening doors and using his pleases and thank you.

She later hinted to Peter about George's new attitude. He smiled and told her not to get herself worked up. George is like a lizard camouflaging under the green grass.

"You are never sure what kind of person he would be in the morning."

Her mind consumed with thoughts of a changing George until she heard the emcee announce it was time for the gift exchanges.

Immediately, she discovered the secret gift she got was from George. Sharon wasn't sure who she got her surprise gift for. Hopefully, the person would like the $10 gifts you bought. Mrs Finland had specified gifts should be between $10 and $15, something to show a little appreciation.

Sharon was glad that she bought something worthwhile for the grumpy fellow.

After the party, George walked up to her. "Sharon, do you need a drive home?"

"Thank you. My Uber driver will pick me up."

"You know, Sharon, you can cancel your taxi. Please, I can take you home tonight if you don't mind." implored George.

"I do mind, Mr George," replied Sharon.

"I want to do this. Sharon, do you know you're not a bother to me? Allow me to drive you home. It would give me time to get to know you, right?"

"You want to know me more?" Sharon laughed in bewilderment.

"This is not the George I know."

"It is me, George." He cleared his throat.

"Maybe it's just Christmas. It's making everything different. You know, Christmas is a different time of the year. So, maybe a little kindness might help." He looked down, adjusting his tie.

Why does he keep adjusting his shirt when he is with me? Sharon thought. "Oh, really!?" she responded to his kindness. Thanking him, she picked up her phone and informed Peter not to bother coming over to pick her.

Like winning a trophy, George grandly walked her to his sports car. Getting into his car, they drove into the night.

The drive flowed smoothly, like many streams of water. Sharon questioned herself.

I wonder what in the world is wrong with me. Why am I in this guy's car? I'm not sure but let me play along.

After about 10 minutes of driving, George spoke up. "Would you mind telling me about yourself?"

Sharon gave him a suspicious look. "What do you want to know about me? Aren't we on professional terms?"

"Sharon, kindly remember - professionalism - stays at the office."

She decided to make it hard for him. She had already blocked everything that could allow him to approach her in a non-professional way. Looking away into the street-lit light, George continued.

"Sharon, I know I made it hard for you from the beginning. But please, understand that we can be friends and be professional, too. This is my olive branch of reconciliation. Can we begin again?"

"This cannot be happening!" Sharon exclaimed, not believing her ears!

George continued. "My name is George Josiah Finland. You know I am the junior while my dad is the senior."

"Oh, really! I never knew. Everybody knows that. Even the stone on the walls." Sharon replies sarcastically.

George doggedly added, "As I was saying, I'm the only child and hopefully, I'll inherit the company or..."

Sharon interrupted. "We already know that, thank you!! You've said that a zillion times. George, you can't even wait to take over the company."

"Sharon, I accept your sarcasm, but please, can you try not to be so cold tonight?"

"Oh George, I am always cordial, or didn't you notice? Thank you, but I am not interested in getting to know you."

"I appreciate your responses. I deserve that." George said contritely.

"Oh well. You deserve that. You deserve even more. I am very polite, you understand. But I would not stand you taking me for granted because I'm in your car."

Sharon snapped at him, belatedly realising she was finally letting out her pent-up feelings about him.

"Please, hear me out, Sharon!" implored George. "I know I hurt you."

"You're using this to wind me up or wind your way into my heart, right?" accused Sharon.

"Sharon, I am not trying to wind myself into your personal life. To be honest, I've watched you over the last few months. I have observed how different you are. I know I've tried to make the office and the job difficult for you. You have not treated me back the same way I treat you. Little did I wonder, why are you so different? I don't know why, and I think I need to know you because you are interesting. Not that I need anything from you, but because you are kind of a challenge to me, a hard nut to crack. I've tried everything possible in the book."

Speechless, trying to avoid his potential self-pity, Sharon exclaimed, "Oh, you have a book! Well then, George, I never knew you had a book!!"

"No-o... not a book, a physical book. Let's be serious."

"Do I look unserious to you?"

"I've tried everything to frustrate you, and I think I'm losing my mind," declared George.

"I've reached the end of my rope! Can we just be friends?"

"Oh yeah, George, we can be friends, professional friends." Words she expressed just as George parked in front of her house.

Sharon stared into his eyes and said: "George, let's get this straight. We are only professional co-workers."

"What can I say? I want us to be friends. Sharon. Have I ever told you that your smile is beautiful?"

"Hey, here we go! We agreed we are professional friends and thank you, I've always known my smile is beautiful. There's nothing new about that, but I'm grateful for your compliments. Can I say goodnight now? I need to sleep."

"That was a lovely party you pulled off!" George tried to change the subject.

"No, I didn't pull up that party. Mrs Resource organised it. I just supported it," inferred Sharon, refusing recognition for the job well done.

"Sharon, you were not here last Christmas. I know exactly how it was. If I said you pulled it off, I do not miss my words. You did!"

"George, thank you for being so supportive. We did the job okay. I accept the compliment. Thank you so much. George, I'll see you in the office tomorrow," as Sharon eased her way out of the sports car.

"Oh, you mean Monday? Today is Friday."

"Yes, Monday, I'll see you in the office. Have a lovely weekend, George. See you on Monday." Sharon stepped out of his car.

TEN

The image of the encounter flashed through Sharon's mind as he drove off.

"Sure, sure," she echoed to herself, climbing the stairs into the apartment.

"What an evening!" Sharon exclaimed, turning the doorknob. Rather glad to be home, she got ready for bed. In an unsettled frame of mind, she laid in bed thinking.

"What on earth happened to George, Saviour? I don't understand where his new attitude is emerging from. Is he all right? Is he sick? Am I his next bait?

Thoroughly exhausted, she dozed off to Dreamland. Sharon's subconscious swung back to the spot when she met the stranger.

The airport this time was empty and dark, terrifyingly gloomy. It was the same incident with a stranger. She was petrified with fear.

This time around, the dark distorted the face. The coffee spilt on the stranger, as in the real occurrence.

In shock, she exclaimed, "good grief!" But rather than respond with pleasant words, the stranger kept mute and walked away.

Sharon turned her gaze to find the image of the man had vanished before her into thin air. In a panic, she murmured cold shivers running through her body.

"Whattt... isss... happening...!?"

She jolted suddenly out of her sleep, sweating desperately in fear as one who had seen a ghost.

What was that dream about? Sharon examined her disoriented state of confusion.

What am I doing? Will George or whoever the stranger fade away? She tried praying. The images of the nightmare plagued her mind. Sharon couldn't get back to sleep either. She laid in the dark as the wall clock ticked the hours until the alarm rang.

Sharon had to get ready for work with a lot on her mind. Lots of deadlines to meet before she travelled. Peter drove her to the office that morning. He sensed her unusual reservation.

"You seem preoccupied this morning. Sharon, is everything OK?"

"Oh yeah, Peter, everything is OK. I've got a lot on my mind."

Concerned, Peter asked, "Do you mind sharing?"

"No, it's fine. I'm fine, it will be fine. I know it's one of those things."

After a long pause, she continued, "There are lots on my mind, Christmas travels..."

"Yeah! That's true," Peter interrupted. "Have you booked your tickets?"

"Oh yes, I have." assured Sharon. "I'm so glad that we threw the Christmas party just in time for me to also book my ticket."

"You know what? We will miss you," said Peter.

"I will miss you too, and the twins. Oh, I'll miss the baby. I know the due date is the 24th. I wish I would be here," answered Sharon wistfully.

Peter reassured her, "I know, in the new year you'll see the baby."

"I can't wait!" She exclaimed with a cheery face.

"it's a baby, and he's not going anywhere, Sharon."

"Not to worry. Have I ever told you I'm so grateful, Peter? You've been such a blessing and I'm hoping that in the next year I should be able to get a car."

"We will sort out everything, Sharon. I look forward to that."

Her mind flashed to the dream, and she became muted again. Peter looked in the rearview mirror noticed that her mind seemed far, far away. As he couldn't get her to speak, he quietly prayed the Saviour would grant peace.

Sharon walked into her office after an attempt to greet others with extra warmth.

Trying to settle down by organising herself, there was a knock on the door. George opened the door before she responded to the knock.

"What are you doing in my office this morning?" Sharon inquired, tension rising in her chest.

"Morning, Miss Sharon." He replied, denying her signs of aggression.

"I just came to say morning, bring you a cup of coffee and a thank you from miss..."

"George! Mr George," interrupted Sharon.

"Please, can you call me George? It sounds more friendly and professional?" His expression was the calmest Sharon had ever seen on him.

"Ok, thank you," Sharon responded, avoiding any eye contact with him. She continued, "Mr George."

After a pause, she continued,

"George, please, alright, I'm not used to us being friendly professionals."

"Makes two," George piped up, twitching his brows like Groucho Marx hoping to get a smile.

"I'm serious. You are offering a free ticket to LaLa Land!"

"I understand, Sharon. Would you rather I take the coffee back?" said a deflated George.

"Please, no, thank you. You should have observed I take water nowadays."

"I know, but I think I'm trying to walk you into the world of coffee again. Here's coffee, then!" George responded cheerfully.

"I know, thank you so much for being thoughtful," Sharon struggled to keep a stern appearance.

"You're welcome. I hope you don't have a lot to do these days. You don't have to stress yourself to cover everything. Leave the files with me," offered George.

"I appreciate the offer. If I can't handle it, I would leave them with you, but so far as I'm concerned, I think I can handle it. Thank you, anyway, George."

"I feel disappointed," he responded in defeat. "You have a lovely day. If you need anything, do not hesitate to chat with me."

"Sure! You'll be my first go-to person if I have a problem," assured Sharon.

George looked at her in an unusually kind way. Now she was sure something is wrong. He walked out of the office, looking back to wave bye.

What on earth has come over him? Wow! It's getting weird now. This George is scarier than the other George. Anyway, let's get back to work.

Sharon mulled pensively over the cup of coffee before her.

Two days later, Sharon headed to the Houston International Airport to take a flight back to the United Kingdom.

Walking through the airport was scarier since the strange dream still lurked in the back of her mind. Sharon was painfully conscious of everybody walking past her.

After twelve exhausting hours, Sharon arrived in the United Kingdom. She was finally back home and falling into the loving arms of Mrs O'Loan.

She planned to spend every minute with her mum and dad, but Sharon couldn't miss an opportunity to spend some time with Tom first.

After an evening meal with Tom and his family and they had put the kids to bed, there was some time to chat.

Relating to the life she lived in America, Sharon immediately brought up the strange recurring dream. She raised concerns about George's denial of any past interaction with her. She felt George was lying. The reasons behind it remained a mystery to her.

Although Tom did not share the same sentiments as Sharon, he was aware of the confusion that Sharon was going through, but he would not add any more stress to her. He committed Sharon to the Saviour's hand and told her to take a day at a time.

Tom and his wife suggested she should not attempt to figure out everything by herself; and advised Sharon not to push George away.

At some points, things eventually work out on their own. Sharon expressed her concerns louder than both their voices combined.

"Why? Why did he vanish? The stranger in actual life did not walk away from me. He did not look mean. Why can't I have the stranger I met in actual life? George, though becoming calm is different, it is something distinct. The stranger seemed at peace with himself. He was on the flight. I miss him. I should have taken the opportunity to know him better, at least take his number."

Instantly, she let out a flood of tears. Tom's wife, Shelia, wrapped her arms around her as the couple prayed love over her.

On Christmas Day, her parents surprised Sharon with breakfast in bed.

"Guys, this is the first! What's happening? Somebody wants to tell me?"

"Tell you what? We missed you. The day you left; we sensed your independence. The loss was enormous, and we wanted your old self back badly." Her Mum expressed her feelings, looking intermittently into her father's eyes.

"I agree! So any opportunity we have with you now, we want to pamper you as we have never done before," her father added.

Covering her eyes, her face soaked in tears; Sharon let go, stretching out her hands in demand for a hug. Her parents on both sides put the tray of food on the bedside table and hugged her.

They held each other close for a warm embrace until her mum broke up, saying, "Tell us everything about George."

Pushing away, Sharon found herself suddenly defensive.

"Nothing, nothing."

"Sharon, we know you too well. Your nothing is so loaded with meaning. This is not your usual reaction when you or we mention his name in the past."

"What happened, child? We have noticed your moodiness, but we know better than to assume the worst."

"Did anything happen to your job or with the Finlands'?" Sharon's dad quizzed.

"It's nothing much. Dad, Mum, I can't seem to hide anything from you guys."

Smiling, both agreed, "sure you can't, baby," drawing her close to them again.

"Okay, the truth...." Sharon narrated the incidence at the airport, the facial similarity between George and the stranger.

George's brutal attitude toward her at work, and the sudden changes she witnessed toward Christmas.

She related the drive home after the Christmas party. Throughout her communication, her parents listened to every single word uttered. When she finished, her dad replied after a long pause.

"Princess, let's pray." Surprised by his reply, she held hands with her parents.

After prayers, they expressed the same sentiments as Tom and Sheila. Their words were comforting to Sharon, although she did not bother telling them Tom had suggested the same.

The rest of the day; they spent with friends and families, and the quality time she spent with her folks. Christmas holidays went by in a flash and before long, Sharon had to get back to work.

By the first week of January 2005, she was back in Houston. Graceoak Oil and Gas Limited welcomed Sharon like a celebrity and depicted like a lost part of their family.

The only reason she could figure out for the special welcome back was her return from Christmas break.

Sharon was glad to be back as she had missed Mrs Resource, the best woman to work who remained welcoming and accommodating, becoming a mother figure with each passing day.

Sharon always looked forward to her warm hugs every morning. Though she was glad to be back, her first day in the office was full of meetings already previously scheduled from the end of the last year.

George, so kind, stood in for her at meetings, suggesting she must still be jetlagged, and he didn't want her to be drowsy. *This is a first-of-its-kind for George. Does he want to attend my meetings for me? It's a start of the new year, what can I say?*

Sharon ruminated while going through her files. He invited her for lunch in his office to get on top of things.

She remembered Tom's words, "Leave everything in the Saviour's hands."

A few days later, Sharon left with a note that she would be off for the rest of the day and the next. George tried to quiz her about her plans, but Sharon was reluctant to tell him, knowing it would ruin the surprise.

The next day, Peter accompanied Sharon to a car dealership to select an affordable car. For her, it was a new dawn, the beginning of her driving independence.

They drove her new Toyota Corolla straight to Peter's house. The twins were the first to test drive with their new favourite person in the world. She drove them to get ice cream and spent the rest of the day in the company of her extended family.

ELEVEN

Three weeks into the new year, Sharon became immersed in the business of contracts, development, and delivery. Graceoak's Oil and Gas portfolio had become larger with the acquisitions of more companies.

She remembered when she had first started the company had been more or less struggling.

To her relief, her ideas had been well received, she reflected as she got ready for work. The morning sunshine warmed her despite the cold weather, placing her in high spirits as she got to work.

On her way to a client takeover meeting, Sharon's phone rang. The ID was her mum, Mrs O'Loan.

It's strange she doesn't normally call me at work. What's wrong!? she worried.

"Hello Mum, I'm just heading for a meeting. Is there a problem?? Can I call you back, Mum, please?"

"No! No, Sharon, listen. Something happened."

"What happened? Mum, tell me what happened?" Sharon's eyeballs bulged out in panic. Not waiting for a response, she continued.

"Is everything alright, please what happened?"

"Calm down! I didn't want to call you. He's alright, he collapsed. We have rushed him to the hospital."

"What! Who, Dad?"

"Yes, your dad. I'm right in the hospital with him."

"Oh, my! What happened to him?"

"I needed to tell you..." a pause followed by complete silence.

Sharon interrupted, "Can you tell me, Mum, I am going crazy here!"

"He is in a coma, he's in a coma," whispered Sharon's mum tearfully forcing the dreadful words out.

Sharon's eyes, already filled with tears, babbled.

"Mum, Mum, talk to me. Is he going to be okay?"

"Sharon, he is alive. I don't want to lose your dad. I don't want to lose your dad!!" Mrs O'Loan sobbed.

"Mum, you will not lose him," Sharon spoke bluntly to refute her mum's fears.

"You don't understand. He is my life."

"I know Mum, he will be OK. He is a fighter. What did the doctor say?"

"The consultant is not sure, but his vital signs are OK." After a brief silence, she carried on.

"But I fear the worse because he fell and hit his head. He might have suffered some brain injury or concussion..."

Interrupting her again, Sharon comforted her mum.

"No, Mum, it's going to be okay," she exclaimed.

"I'm going to... Mum, please listen, I'm going to talk to my boss George. I'll take the next flight home."

"No! No, no, don't get on the next flight back. We will be fine," insisted Mrs O'Loan.

"Mummy, no!! This is my dad we're talking about. I'll be on the next flight, mum, I'll see you soon!"

Hanging up the phone, Sharon turned around, walking back into George's office. He was nowhere near his desk. She remembered he must have gone into the meeting, the one she was heading for just before the call.

Sharon headed straight for Mr Finland Sr.'s office. After a knock on the door, Mr Finland beckoned her in.

"Morning, Mr Finland."

"Morning, Sharon! You ought to be in a meeting now if I recall." Looking up from his sitting position, he inquired.

"Is everything okay? You look distraught."

"Mr Finland, I am... No, I am not!"

"So, what can I do for you?" still peering into her anguished face.

"Mr Finland, I have something to say..." Sharon broke down in tears, unable to control her emotions.

"What is the matter?" he murmured in a fatherly tone as he stood up to comfort her, holding her shoulders.

Sharon responded, wiping her dripping nose.

"I received a phone call from my mum a few minutes ago. My dad collapsed. He is in the hospital, in a coma."

"Oh, my! Is he all right?" Mr Finland exclaimed.

"We are not sure but praying for the best."

"I don't think you should remain here. You need to be with your mum," he suggested kindly.

"Thank you, yes, I will book the next flight out for tomorrow morning," Sharon mumbled.

"No, you can get on a flight tonight. Let me speak to Mrs Resource to get a flight for you." Mr

Finland picked up the phone and spoke to the HR manager. "Please, can you book the next flight to Heathrow? Sharon needs to head for London tonight, OK?"

"Any emergency?" asked a concerned HR.

"Oh yeah, Sharon needs to go home. Her father is in the hospital."

"I'll get the flight as soon as possible." Mrs Resource replied immediately.

His kindness amazed once again Sharon. She was standing by the door ready to hurry off, when she heard Mr Finland continue, "Mrs Resource, kindly book the flight on my tab."

Dropping the phone, he said to Sharon, "Everything is arranged. Go take care of your family. The flight ticket is my gift for your hard work. From me and not the company." He smiled with a similar facial expression as the stranger she had met at the airport.

A chill of déjà vu ran up her spine as Sharon responded quickly. "Thank you so much! I'm so grateful, so... so grateful!!"

"I didn't know how else to help. You'll be fine. I'll inform Cynthia and George about the current circumstances. They are in the meeting. I know you're supposed to be there."

"Yes, they are meeting with the clients," confirmed Sharon.

"I will call now and let them know and please keep in touch and let us know how you are doing." Ordered her boss.

"I will as soon as I know the true state of things. I'm grateful to you, Sir," her last words before Sharon walked out of the office with her tear-filled eyes.

The evening of the next day, she was already at Heathrow Airport. She rushed into the first available taxi and headed to the hospital.

Later, standing in front of the receptionist. Sharon inquired, "Good evening. I am looking for Mr O'Loan. Could you direct me to his room, please?"

"Yes," the receptionist replied. "Are you related to Mr O'Loan?"

"I am his daughter. I was on the phone with my mum a few hours ago. She said he's in this hospital."

Looking through her computer screen, the receptionist responded. "Yes, he's in room 336. You can take the elevator to the second floor. Look out for the signs for the ICU, the intensive care unit."

"What! Intensive care?" Sharon trembled, holding her breath.

"He's fine. Everything is under control. Don't worry, we are taking care of him."

Not waiting to hear the reassuring words of the receptionist, Sharon took off her shoes and raced to the elevator and took it to the second floor as directed.

At a fast pace, she walked, then ran through the corridor, searching for the ICU sign and then the room number. Approaching the room, she peered through the window.

Sharon stared silently at her father's helpless body. What a drastic change! He looked so pale! Her Mum sat holding his hands close to her heart.

Sharon watched with memories flashing through her mind. *These two people are inseparable. What is she going to do if she loses him? We can't even handle this, Saviour. Can you please bring him back? Not for my sake, but Mum's. Can you please bring him back?*

Sharon barely thought the last words when her mum lifted her face to see Sharon at the window. She rushed towards the door, each throwing their arms around the other as they wept together.

A few moments later, her mum asked.

"How long have you been standing at the window, Love?"

"Not long, I've been watching you." Sharon pulled her mum's head on her chest, and they held each other in a warm embrace.

"Mum, let's go." Walking up to her dad's bedside, Sharon touched his face.

"Dad, I'm here now. Your baby is here. Please wake up Dad, please. I've spoken to the Saviour. He assured me you'll be fine." Sharon cried, uttering more words,

"Dad, for once, I want you more. I can't let you go now. Please wake up, wake up!" Sharon laid her head on his chest. Her mum dropped her face into his hands, and as she said those words, the consulting physician walked in.

He approached them and asked gently, "How are you this evening, Mrs O'Loan?"

Sharon's mum replied, "I am coming to terms with things."

"Who is this young woman?" he asked with a comforting smile.

"This is my daughter, Sharon. She's just arrived from the States."

"Welcome. Not to worry, your father will be well taken care of."

"Any idea when he's going to get out of the coma?" asked Sharon.

"We do not have an idea. All his vital signs are okay, as we are monitoring him. We are hoping he's going to fight this and wake up."

"Will he be okay once he wakes up? Will everything be, okay?"

"Everything seems fine for the moment." The consultant completed his checks and further assured them, "we will keep checking on him."

Walking away, he turned around and looked at the women who echoed "thank you" together.

"Sharon, I dropped in to check on your dad. I think you should both go home and rest. Your mum has been here all night, and she needs rest. She needs someone to keep a close eye on her."

"I thank you, doctor," Sharon responded as he walked out of the room.

"Mum, you heard what the doctor said. I need to take you home now. Let's go. You can come back to stay with your husband."

"Sharon, it's all right. I'll stay with him, and you go home to freshen up. You just flew in. It was a long flight, and you must be exhausted!"

Insisting, Sharon spoke in a firm voice, "Mum, you know what? We head home together, and we come back together. We will stick together."

"What if he wakes up?" asked her mum emphatically. "I want him to wake with me beside him!"

"Mum, I hear the doctors and nurses are here with him." Holding her, and resting her palm on her worried face, she carried on, "Please let's go home. You will eat something, and rest and I will come back."

Still hugging her mum, Sharon continued, "Mum, have you eaten anything since we spoke yesterday?"

"I'm not sure Sharon, how can I eat when my darling is not awake, but I'm OK."

"Mum, I know you're OK, but you need to eat."

Sharon led her mum out of the room and walked her to the car.

The drive was silent; she observed her mum was completely exhausted. Each day, they visited the hospital with the hope Mr O'Loan would wake up.

Fear crept into Sharon's terrified heart that her dad might not wake up. The fear became all-consuming. Friends and family raised a prayer chain for them.

The medical reports seemed to suggest everything was fine. There was no medical reason for him to remain in a coma. Unexpectedly, she received daily phone calls from George to check on her.

Sharon still couldn't explain the sudden displays of kindness. *What is wrong with him?* After a while, she started avoiding his calls. *Why is he calling me? My dad is not dead yet. What is this all about?*

During one of his calls, Sharon denied his compliment when he hinted, "We miss you."

Who are the 'we'? she deliberated.

What is wrong with this guy?

Three days after she arrived in the UK, a flower delivery man came to the hospital. He delivered a bunch of flowers for her dad and a gift for her.

When she enquired who sent the flowers, the gentleman directed her to read the accompanying card with the gift. Sharon dropped the flowers by father's bed and looked at the card. Lo-and-behold, the gifts were delivered on behalf of George.

Sharon was glad Mum was not in the room at the time of delivery, as she would have had some questions to answer. *George sending gifts all the way from Houston? This is crazy.* By the time she got home each day, someone had again delivered a similar series of gifts.

George is spending so much money. Why all this attention? She could not understand how a professional friendliness had become unwanted, personal friendliness. This is taking it to the next level. Sharon left all the gifts in the room, opening none of them.

Late one evening, George called. Sharon expressed her heart-warming gratitude. "Thank you so much for your gifts and flowers for my dad. I wasn't expecting that."

"Is everything OK? Are you OK?" he asked in a soft tone like the airport stranger.

"Oh yes, we are still hopeful he will wake up soon."

"Sharon, I understand you were not expecting any act of kindness from me. I'm really concerned you left without notice. Dad informed me and I need to hear directly from you that you're OK."

"George, thank you. I am very OK. I wasn't expecting so many gifts."

"Yeah, I know. I aspired to be there but couldn't, so I sent the gifts."
Trying not to express her upheaving emotions, Sharon replied as calm as possible.

"Are gifts the way of making sure I'm, okay? And thank you so much. I appreciate the thought."

"I don't understand," George sounded confused at the other end of the line.

"Didn't you like me giving you the gifts?"

"Don't you worry about me! Mum, family, and friends are here! And I've got Tom here." assured Sharon.

"Who is Tom?" interjected George.

"Why care? Tom is a friend with a wife and kids. Are you bothered?" raising her voice, annoyed.

"Oh, not really. It good to know your other acquaintances apart from your dad and mum!" he responded cheekily.

"Is this what all that friendly professional is all about?"

"Of course it is!! Thank you for letting me know. I appreciate it." Although she got upset, George kept laughing.

"I have to go now. Goodnight, Mr Finland!" said Sharon tersely. "I'm heading to stay with my dad for the night."

"Please let me know how he is doing." George switched to his caring nature at once.

"I thank you for your concern!" she dropped the phone and walked into the hospital. Her mum was already sitting by her dad.

"Mum, are you not tired? You go to bed. You go home, and I'll stay with Dad."

"No way, I'm not leaving my husband's side!" stated her mum.

"It's been three days in a row that you've been here!" Sharon protested.

"Sharon, you've been here with me. That's what family is all about. I aspire to be here when he wakes up," informed her mum stubbornly.

"I agree with you. Mum! We stick together, right?" Both women held hands and prayed for Sharon's dad.

Sharon pondered. I need a love like Mum and Dad. It's like forever.

About 2 a.m. Sharon was holding onto his feet while she leaned her head on the bed. Her mum held his hands. She felt his toes moved as a tickle.

A few more times, of noticing the slight movement, Sharon jumped up, startling her mum. She began screaming, "Nurse! Nurse, something is happening here. Something is happening."

TWELVE

The nurse in attendance rushed in to check on her dad. Sharon rushed to her mum's side.

"Are you OK, Sharon? What happened?" her mum matched her panic.

"Mum! I felt his leg tingling."

"O, God! Please let him come back to me," pleaded her mum in tears.

Before they could ask a question, the nurse rushed out. They held his hands close, only to realise he responded with a firm grip.

Mrs O'Loan responded with excitement, "My heart, you are back."

As the words left her mouth, the consultant, and his team rushed in, with the previous nurse.

"He squeezed my hands. Sharon felt his toes move," Mother exclaimed with joy.

The doctor nodded in agreement and requested, "Can we take it from here, Mrs O'Loan?"

The physician got around to checking him. In a flash, Mr O'Loan sneezed three times, then opened his eyes. He came back to life.

Sharon leapt for joy and her mum leapt to embrace her husband. The medical team, in amazement, requested that Sharon and her mum excuse them.

One nurse led them to the family room, where she offered the much-needed calmness. Another nurse brought in a tray of tea and coffee. Sharon's mum all this while cried in joyful excitement, thanking the Saviour. Sharon, instead, picked up her phone to call their friends and family.

About ten minutes later, as they waited with no communication from the medical team.

Sharon's mum started panicking again.

"What is happening? Did anything go wrong with him, Sharon? I want him back healthy."

"Mum, take it easy. We didn't wake him up; the Saviour did. We need to trust him for his health; either what we want or what the Saviour desires."

Sharon moved her mum's head close to provide the comfort needed to dissipate the doubts and within 10 minutes, Mum fell asleep.

Sharon was glad she got her to relax. *I feel so sorry for Mum. She had not slept well for four days. Once her husband woke up from his coma, her sleep came back.*

An hour later, the attending physician walked in. "Mrs O'Loan, Sharon, I am glad to let you know Mr O'Loan is fine, and I will take you in to see him."

Mrs O'Loan rushed to him whispering a "thank you," and was instantly out the door.

Sharon, however, walked up to the doctor, taking his hand in a handshake, and asked, "How is my dad doing?"

"I must express my utter surprise," related the amazed doctor. "I would rather think of this as a miracle. He is in perfect health. We had to run some quick tests on him to make sure everything was all right."

"Thank you for all you and your team have done! Yes! the Saviour promised, and He did it," she stated as she walked out to see her dad.

"The Saviour? Saviour!? What is she talking about?" the doctor responded to her statement with a puzzled expression.

Walking into the room to say hello to her father, Sharon's mum called out. "You gave us a scare. What happened?"

Sharon followed on with, "I'm so glad you're OK, Dad," hugging him. They held each other, crying and singing Praises to GOD together.

The physician followed in to provide some plausible explanation for the events.

"Mr O'Loan, can you now recollect the event that led to your slipping down?"

"Not sure. I know I was heading to the fridge to get a bottle of drink for my sweetheart. The next thing I remembered was the sneezing and sneezing when I woke up." He muttered, gazing at his wife.

While his wife lovingly kissed his palms, he continued, "I should rather ask how I ended on the hospital bed!?"

While his family explained, the physician carried on confirming they had carried out the checks and there seemed to be no sign of anything wrong with Mr O'Loan. It was recommended he remained a night or two for further observation before discharging.

Sharon picked up her vibrating phone. Their church minister reached out for an update. With gladness, she informed him.

For the next thirty minutes, their phone lines were busy with calls from friends and everyone. Two days after her dad's resurrection from the coma, they returned home from the hospital.

Sharon took the plane back to Houston and work. *It's been two weeks of my life back in the UK at the beginning of this year.*

Proverbs 3:5-6 Trust in the LORD with all your heart. In all your ways submit to him, and he will and lean not on your own understanding; He will make your paths straight.

Landing in Houston, she took the next available taxi to her apartment.

Sharon's return to work came with unusual surprises. *Something strange must be there happening,* she informed herself.

Sharon observed a different George every morning! It was coffee on the table, invitations for lunches, surprise cards, and gifts. Rather than getting exciting, she became underwhelmed by his outburst of affection.

Each night, she struggled with several unanswered questions. The most difficult one, if answered, would tie it all together! The knowledge of the stranger and the new George!

A few days later, after a church meeting, she opened up to Peter and his wife, asking them,

"What could be wrong with George? I'm afraid he might think I am one of his regular girls. Peter, I am different."

Peter's wife, smiling from side to side, quizzed her.

"Are you not enjoying his company, or rather getting to know him?"

"I don't think my feelings are important at this point." she smiled, nevertheless avoiding that question.

Sharon continued, "I am concerned about his sudden change and the nightmare I can't walk away from."

Peter, after a long pause, said, "He's coming around."

"How do you mean?" Sharon interrupted with anticipation of his incoming thoughts.

"I think... I should tell you; he's falling in love with you." Peter implied.

"He can't fall in love with me! We are from two different worlds." Sharon protested.

"How do you know you are from two different worlds?" demanded Peter. From what you have discussed with us, he seemed different. He talks differently, so different in fact, that it seems as though the Saviour had met with him."

Sharon nodded in affirmation to his statement. Her eyes stirring aimlessly into the sky.

"Why don't you believe something special is happening to him somehow?" Peter added.

"Wow! that's prophetic. I didn't know you're now a prophet," his wife joked heartily.

"Not exactly. I just thought you should see the positive side of him. People do change, so you know," stated Peter.

"I agree," Sharon replied, pondering on how much she resented George, though she always thought she didn't. Reality seems to kick in fast.

"I think you should try to love him the way the Saviour loves you. I assumed from your reaction you only tolerated him and did not love him."

"I know he has been so hard on you, but we don't want you to resent him," His wife added.

Sharon, in honest submission to their counsel, let out her thoughts. "It's true, I'll be honest. Each day I resent him. I wish he remained the angry, bullying, George. I am already used to him, now he is so good and kind and calm. The option of loving him more than the Saviour requires..."

"Have you tried seeking or figuring out the reasons for his fits of anger?" interjected Peter.

"I don't know where to place it," observed Sharon. "I avoid prying into his private life."

"A little prying will let you into the window of his world." Peter's wife suggested.

"I didn't want to pry in case he is pretending. I don't aspire to be one of his sexual conquests."

"You can give him a chance. Don't rush ahead of yourself. Be a friend to him." Peter counselled her as the twins ran over for attention, which led to the end of the discussion.

As they exchanged goodbye, Peter suggested, "Why don't you invite him to church?"

"I never thought about that. I will try," she promised, driving away.

It was Friday evening. After a more relaxing week at work, George walked into Sharon's office.

"Are you doing anything tonight?" He enquired, dropping a client's file on the table without making eye contact.

"Nothing planned now, but they scheduled me to help at the shelter," she answered.

"Shelter? What do you do there?" George's eye sparkled to discover something new about the sect member.

"You suppose I live there," she responded, teasing him while she packed her belongings to head out.

"I help at the local shelter to feed homeless some Fridays. I am usually on the schedule today, but things changed. Someone else had to swap places with me."

"That's noble and interesting. This is another part of Sharon I am discovering," George expressing delight at in the new revelation of her.

"There are many parts of Sharon you don't know," Sharon responded, standing up from her table to pick up a folder.

"Now Sharon, it is 5:30 p.m. you're not heading to the shelter." admonished George. "What else will you be doing this evening?"

"I will go home and rest," she replied in an instant, avoiding eye contact with him.

Taking steps closer to her, George whispered, "Why don't you come over to my place?"

"To your place?" She lifted her gaze in shock to meet his beautiful blue eyes. "What's happening at your place?" Sharon enquired with a sense of defence.

"I've got friends coming around. We would like your company," implied George earnestly.

"Is it we or I would love my company?" Sharon demanded. Remembering Peter's words, she followed up quickly with a "Yes. If you don't mind, tell me what time?"

"For real, are you accepting the invitation?" George, surprised, stepped closer to her.

"Yeah! What's wrong? It will be good to meet some other strange people called George's friends," impishly replied Sharon.

"Wow! Is that the way you perceive me? Strange!?" barked George, taking some steps back.

"It's the truth! You've always been weird. You have even become weirder being nice."

George blurted out, "I'll text you my address," turning to leave her office.

"I appreciate the invite. I'll see you at 7 p.m." Sharon called out after him.

He didn't get upset though I wind him up; she told herself as she drove home.

A few hours later, Sharon drove to his house and knocked on the door. The size of his living room alone was three times her whole apartment. Though space discreetly decorated, it reflected a sense of taste and perfectionism.

George led Sharon to the dining room, where he introduced her to the rest of his friends. *In fact, he had a few friends in. They were having dinner.*

Sharon finally believed him and was glad she visited with a bottle of wine. She was further impressed to know that George did the cooking. It was a trait she would have never thought a brat like him would acquire.

The three coupled friends talked over the three-course dinner. Lips-pressed tight to resist asking when he had time to cook, Sharon controlled her negative regard toward him for the night. Rather, she observed him. They played games after the meal until late at night. After all his friends left, George walked Sharon to her car.

"Thank you for the invite. I will be honest here, you surprised me,"

"I am glad I did. Thank you for coming around. You made my day, Sharon."

"I have to head out now," Sharon interrupted, avoiding the compliments from George.

As she drove home, the scenes of the night flashed back. *Back to life, back to my reality. It's nice being around other people apart from church folks. Some of their jokes were dry, but that's fine!*

Settling down for the night, thoughts of spending more time with George crossed her mind several times before she dozed off.

Saturday morning, upon returning from a jog, a beep sound got her attention, showing a call from George.

"Good morning," he sounded excited.

"Morning, Master George," Sharon said in a sarcastic tone towards him.

"How are you? Thank you for coming around for dinner. I appreciated your presence. My friends liked you."

"Are you advertising me as your friendly professional friend?" Quizzed Sharon to get a hint of the reasons behind his invitation.

"Yes! You're funny, Sharon, and that's what I like about you," he replied.

"Wow, hang on a minute, you like something about me. I'm glad," she replied with a smiley face.

"What do you like about me?" inquired George. Sharon stared at the brewing coffee in front of her.

"I'm still searching, George," she laughed.

"That's okay," responded George, sinking in disappointment.

"Besides, George, will you visit my church with me tomorrow?"

"Oh, yeah, I'd love to! What time?" Pretending it did not surprise her that he wanted to go, Sharon continued, "10 a.m. I'll text the address."

"OK, I'll see you at 10," exclaimed George.

"Take care and I'll catch you soon." Sharon replied.

"Sure!! OK!" a flush creeping up her face. *What are you doing?* She chided herself.

Sunday at 9:50 am, George came right on time. He called Sharon from his car.

"I'm about 10-minutes from you. Are you already at the church?" She asked.

"Yes, Sharon, see you in a bit!"

George walked into the building, where the usher offered him a seat at a front pew. Seeing George looking around for her, Sharon was relieved she was not sitting close to him. At least he's far away from me!

The service went well. Toward the end, she thought George was going to step forward and accept the Saviour. Sharon reminded herself that, *no, it doesn't always work as planned.*

After the service, Peter invited George over to his house for lunch in the company of Sharon. She grabbed Peter aside.

"What are you doing, Peter? I'm not comfortable with this arrangement."

"Not to worry!! He's with us. Remember, we invited you home the same way we are inviting him. Is there anything wrong with that?" Peter reasoned with her.

Reluctantly, she dropped her argument and lead the way to George's car, informing him, "Lunch is at Peter's."

They had lunch in the garden. It was beautiful.

Sharon thought, *for the first time, I am observing another calm; gentle George.*

They watched as he played with the twins like they had always known him. They played hide and seek, followed by all kinds of games.

Peter's wife commented, sipping a drink, "George is wonderful with the twins.

With a sense of agreement, Sharon responded. "I have never seen this side of him," unaware she had spoken aloud.

Peter looked intently at her, and leaning forward, said, "You see! You just need to draw closer to people. He's a pleasant person, gets to know why he was behaving the way he did."

"I always felt so sorry for his parents. I can imagine they will be glad they have a new George!"

"Thanks to you!" Peter's wife teased.

"Thanks to me? How?" Sharon looked puzzled.

"Yeah! Yeah! Thanks to you. You do not understand how you have influenced him," Peter agreed, taking his wife's side.

"No, I can't take credit for that," Sharon refuted their suggestions.

"I know you're trying to be humble. God works in mysterious ways." Peter chuckled at his own comments.

"He allowed His working in us for His purpose." Sharon nodded, observing George's every move as he played with the kids.

Peter continued, "You shouldn't run away from this until you've accomplished the purpose."

"I hope I can accomplish this purpose," Sharon muttered as they watched George walk towards them with the kids.

The kids were running back with George for more food from the table. They ate and drank until about 10 minutes later. His phone beeped.

"Oh, my word, I'm sorry! I'm supposed to have a meeting with Dad and Mum. I need to hurry off."

"That's OK, I'll see you on Monday," Sharon replied, focusing on her shoes.

Facing Peter, George replied, "Thank you so much for inviting me. I enjoyed the company."

The kids protested. "No! George doesn't go. We have not finished the game yet. Please, one more round!!" they yelled.

"... Kids, he needs to go. George has an appointment." Their mum led them into the house.

"George will come back and see us. We've enjoyed his company," she added, comforting the twins.

"Of course, I'm going to come back as soon as your dad and mum say it's OK," promised George.

"You can come anytime. I think you are a friend already." Peter appreciated him.

"Have a successful evening." George shook hands with Peter, while Sharon stood up and walked him to the car.

"I'm grateful to you for spending your time with us. I'm sorry we took more time than necessary."

"No need to apologise. I enjoyed the company."

"Thank you. I hope to see you on Monday." George reached out his hands, and she responded with a cordial handshake.

"Hope to see you too, thank you." George shouted, driving away, but Sharon spent the rest of the afternoon with the Peters.

After dinner at Peters' residence, she drove home to find a package in front of the door. *Not again,* George, she muttered to herself.

Picking up the parcel, she walked in. It's a box of chocolates from George.

Her phone rang as she sat on her sofa. It was George. But this time, she refused to pick up the phone.

When did he have time to do this? I thought he was heading to his parents for a meeting. Anyway, I will enjoy this by myself this evening.

She went into the fridge for a bottle of drink, sat in front of the TV and guzzled the chocolates.

Sharon slept off on the sofa until her phone rang. It was Tom. Her eyes cleared immediately. "Tom! Tom, you can't imagine what's happening?"

"What's happening, Sharon? We felt we have not heard from you in a while. Lotte suggested we should check on you. Is everything alright?"

"Everything is perfectly all right, Tom. Surprise!! George came to church today."

"Wow! George was in church?" exclaimed Tom in surprise.

"Yes, I invited him, and he showed up. It was amazing. Not only that, but Peter also invited George to his house. Peter thought it was wonderful that George is churched."

"This news," Tim exclaimed.

"He spent the afternoon with the Peters. He loves children so much. I just imagine him running around with his own children."

Tom interrupted, "with you in the image?"

"Don't you go there, Tom, you're starting up again." Sharon protested, laughing.

"Yeah, anything is possible."

"I don't want to get my heart out there," murmured Sharon in a low voice.

"Are you not old enough? Don't you think about settling down and starting a family yourself like my wife and I?"

"With all these nightmares I'm having about the stranger, I don't know what to do."

"We will leave things in the hands of the Saviour. He knows how to direct everything and don't lose yourself in it. Release your heart, remove all your defences. I think he's a nice guy. I'll be praying with you."

"I understand, Tom, you are speaking like the Peters' now."

"Remember, remove all your defences, and learn to love again Sharon.

"I tried it before, at the University, Tom."

"I know, I know the feeling. I remember everything like a ticking bomb. This is your second year in the US. For you to enter a relationship now, Sharon, I think is a time. You're secure in a job."

"Tom, have you forgotten? He's, my boss? It's against the company policy, I can't do this."

"You can't do what? You can't be in love or work in the same office? Which one!?" Tom pressured her further.

"I don't want to lose my job, don't want to break the company's policy, Tom."

"Sharon, are you in love with him?"

"No! No, I am not. Not by an inch will I allow him all the way into my heart, even if he tries! Let me be straight, Tom." Sharon snapped.

"I'll lay off you for now," Tom backed off to make sure he did not rattle her feathers further.

"Can we talk about other things apart from George, or are you not bored already?" inquired Sharon, changing the topic. How is your wife and kids? I do miss them so much. How is the baby?" she asked wistfully.

They continued their discussion until she started yawning again.

"Tom, I need to sleep, going to work tomorrow. Talk to you again soon."

They said their goodbyes, and she landed in bed and slept like a baby.

THIRTEEN

For the next two weeks, George was away from the country to meet some clients in Japan. Graceoak's office was unusually quiet.

It seemed George kept the office operating like a beehive. And Mr and Mrs Finland were out of the office most times. Sharon was kept busy attending meetings and closing business deals.

It's approaching her second year in the company. Sharon was grateful the Saviour had been faithful to her.

Graceoak Oil & Gas portfolio had increased exponentially under her leadership, and Sharon got promoted three times. Everything about work seemed top-notch, but she couldn't get the surprise of recent events off her mind.

How could George get on a plane without informing me? I thought we were on a page together. Am I imagining things?

It took her by surprised when she arrived at the office Monday, after their lunch in Peter's house. Mrs Resource informed her George was away since Sunday evening.

She recalled George informing her about an urgent meeting with Mr Finland Sr. Then the phone rang, and she paused to take the call.

I had imagined the friendly professional terms would work out differently.

Sharon let her mind wonder, sipping a cup of coffee by the window, observing the busy road ahead until she heard a knock on the door. The office administrator popped in.

"Sharon! Afternoon - we've got a delivery for you."

"Delivery? From whom! Is it from England? You could have called me to pick it up."

Seeing smiles all over Grace's face, she continued, "Instead of delivering the parcel or envelope."

Grace started laughing. "I never knew you were to be having an English romance!"

"Roman what? Where is that coming from?" Her face popped out in innocent surprise.

"I was pulling your leg." Grace burst out with a laugh.

"Girl, don't try that again!" Sharon joined her. "Seriously!!"

"Oh," Grace informed her, Mrs Resource needs you in her office. She had tried to contact you. We felt something was wrong. Guess we were right."

"Right? How?" Sharon was puzzled.

"You did not hear the phone ring?" Grace asked.

"No, I walked in a moment ago, was in the ladies," Sharon replied in defence.

"Here is the parcel I came to drop off for you." Grace brought out the hidden package from behind her back.

"I joked about this with Mrs Resource earlier," Grace confessed, laughing.

"So, there was a parcel and there was no call from Mrs Resource? You are such a joker, Grace. Give me my parcel, thank you, and get back to work," she continued, laughing.

"Good to see you laugh, Ms O'Loan. You've been moody for the past few days. Who stole your cheese!?" Grace mischievously responded, walking toward the door.

Sharon walked back to her seat, talking to herself. *Have I been moody? Am I getting affected by George's absence? The nightmares wouldn't go away, too. Will he disappear like the stranger? Let me get back to work before someone else meets me in another distracted mood.*

Reaching for the box on her desk, she opened it to find a note. A single card note! Sharon picked it and it read,

"I'm sorry, I miss us."

This must be a mistake! Better still, who is missing us?

She remained in the office, occupying herself with paperwork to avoid further embarrassing teasing from her two colleagues.

Two hours after closing hours, she walked absentmindedly to the car, suddenly noticing a note under her windshield blade.

This time it read, **"Do you miss me?"**

Sharon, petrified for the first time, looked to see if anyone was lurking around. She hurried into her car and drove home, forgetting to get her dinner on her way.

For a third time on the same day, Sharon found a note slipped under her door when she arrived home.

The third note read, **"I missed you. You're all I've got."**

Alarmed, she rushed in and locked the doors. Sharon spoke a few words with the Saviour and expressed the deep-felt insecurity she had ever experienced.

Sharon, over the years, had described herself as confident, secure, emotionally balanced, but in the past two years, the experiences of the look-alike men had cast doubts on her feelings of security.

Her usual tendency would be to pick the phone and reach out to her mum, Tom, or Peter. This time, hungry Sharon curled into her bed and slept off with her battle-weary heart. As usual, the alarm rang, and Sharon woke up with a sore tummy and a headache from the night before.

She recalled not having anything to eat since lunchtime the previous day.

Her morning prayer was *Saviour! Please, can you stop me from having this stranger's nightmare? I don't understand where George belongs in all this. I am sure, or I think, he has become different, but that has me more confused.* She got out of bed, weary, but she nevertheless dressed for work.

The morning sun blinded her eyes as she stepped out of her house, stepping on a baby toy.

"Whose is this again? One of my neighbours' kids must have dropped it here."

Picking up the toy, a note dropped. "Another one?" She screamed, stepping back in horror.

Picking up the note, which had the same handwriting as the previous ones, Sharon read, **"I will see you sooner than you think."**

She squeezed the note in annoyance and threw it away. "This is not funny anymore. Who is the stalker?" she exclaimed.

Sharon drove to work, with thoughts flashing through her mind.

What if the notes are from George? He sent gifts to me while I was visiting with my parents. It couldn't have been George. His dad informed me he would be on a tour of Asia. Japan, Singapore, and... It is George, no doubt. What if George is in love with me? What do I do? Do I feel the same way? George seemed to be a shrewd businessman, like his father. Yet, the misery of Mr Williams. Definitely, a puzzle she had to solve.

Grace and Mr T greeted her warmly as she walked into the building, interrupting her thoughts.

"Sharon, Mr Finland would like to meet with you."

Sharon responded, "Any problems?"

"Nothing we know of. He seemed to be in his usual mood. Are you also in a mood today?"

"Yes, thank you for asking. Do you have any information about Mr Williams?" she whispered in a low voice close to Grace's ear.

"He's a wild card! I would have to discuss that with you privately."

Pondering her words, as Sharon walked toward the elevator and Mr Finland's office, her feet drew heavier, expecting nothing good. Her heartbeat faster with every step.

"Come in," the voice called out as she knocked on the CEO's door.

Sharon opened the door, but Mr Finland's seat blocked her view, and he didn't turn around.

"Good morning, Mr Finland. Grace informed me you called for a meeting."

After a long pause, Sharon continued, "Do you want me to bring you anything? Is Cynthia all right? Have you heard from George? Is everything okay? Should I become worried?"
Her voice grew faint as she expressed her concerned with still no reply from the leather chair.

So Sharon turned and walked towards the door. "I will come back as you wish."

As Sharon grasped the doorknob, a voice called out from the chair asking, "Sharon, are you okay this morning?" it was familiar but not Mr Finland's voice.

She spun around and yelled, "George! You can't be serious. Why did you pretend to kill me with suspense?"

George got off his father's chair laughing.

"I am so sorry. I didn't mean to scare you. Wanted to show you another side of George you don't know yet. Still on the friendly professional mood."

Though everything within her wanted to race for a hug from him, nevertheless she stood, pressing her feet to the ground inside her shoes.

"George, how could you vanish without a word? I was wondering if you had gone the same way as Mr William!! No one told us what happened to him."

"I apologise. After the meeting with Dad that evening, I had to leave to get some deals rolling. I planned to stay for the entire month, but I missed home too much. I have to set things right, ASAP."

"Did you miss your folks that much that you rushed back?"
She intentionally pretended not to understand what he meant. George ignored her line of enquiry and responded to her earlier question.

"In passing, greetings from Mr Williams. He is handling the recent developments in the Asian region."

"I thought Mr Williams vanished with the company's money?" Sharon quizzed.

"I thought so, too. Dad made me believe that until the Sunday I left. I guess it was the only way he could get me back into the company."

"I don't understand," Sharon protested.

"You will, if you agree to go on a dinner date with me!"

"Is this your way of being romantic, or are you bribing me?" Sharon winked, indicating that she was joking.

George laughed, expressing his beautiful set of white teeth like the stranger at the airport.

Sharon snapped back to reality when he demanded, "Did you hear me?"

"Oh, sorry, pardon me!" apologised Sharon.

"I said, it's all the above. That aside, I ordered for breakfast. Would you mind having some with me? We can talk all about business, nothing personal," he smiled cheekily.

"I, I have a lot to do this morning." Sharon excusing herself from being cornered even though she was famished.

"The breakfast is ready in my office. The rest of the team will join us if that will make you come along." George continued to convince her to change her mind.

"You never answered my question?" Sharon repeated.

"Which one?" he asked, looking bewildered. Remembering in an instant, he mumbled, "Time will reveal every hidden thing one day. Hold that thought!"

George led her and the rest of his leadership team to his office as the day's routine began.

So, he had planned all the notes; I guess? I think that dinner date will answer all my questions.

Sharon thought as she sat for a breakfast meeting. The entire morning, she observed George. He also glanced at her with every opportunity he had.

Her phone beeped with a text from George it read. "You are professionally beautiful this morning, Ms O'Loan." She smiled at him, drawing no attention to herself.

This guy is flirting in a meeting.

"You are in a strictly professional meeting, Mr Finland," Sharon responded in a text as she addressed the next question posed to her.

"I can't wait for our dinner. Any confirmation?" The next beep came in.

Sharon cleared her throat and adjusted herself to refill her cup of herbal tea.

"Ms O'Loan," George called out her name.

"Sharon, a preference, if you don't mind, Mr Finland." a pretend frown briefly flashed across Sharon's face.

"I can see that in the last two weeks you have turned to herbal tea," said George, both to show Sharon that he knew her likes, and to distract himself from the boring meeting.

"Mr Finland, it's just a preference for this morning, as my taste buds called for it."
Sharon announced as the other team members grinned in amusement. She squirmed with unease.

"Apologies, if I put you on a spot. When do I get a reply from you?" George was indirectly referring to the date with her.

"I will send an official memo as soon as I get to the office." Sharon texted a reply to his message with a coded response.

They exchanged silent facial expressions until the meeting finished.
Sharon excused herself before anyone trying to escape George's attention. She had missed for over two weeks.

It's lunchtime. The only plan is to leave the office or risk George asking to spend some time with him.

Sharon left hurriedly, informing Grace to receive any calls or information directed to her. Stepping into the car park, George was lazily leaning on her car as she walked toward him.

"Are you in a hurry to get somewhere?" He asked with a sense of empathetic victory.

"Not sure!" She deflected, taking a defensive position. "You tell me you are my boss!"

"Yep, friendly professional boss, I suppose?" He ably readjusted his tie.

"Let's cut to the chase! George, what do you want? I need to get some lunch."

"That makes two of us. Can I tag along?" persistently, George pushed further.

"Sure, your choice," Sharon sighed in defeat.

"You know, I'm not that bad a companion," George commented with a sense of anticipation. "How have you kept up with me and my weird attitude?" George opened the door, stepping into the car.

"Do you have any special restaurant in mind?" asked Sharon, ignoring George's comments.

"Sharon, anywhere you please. If I am in your way, I can leave..." George offered.

She interrupted, "You are not a terrible companion to hang around with." She replied, smiling.
Her smiles radiated like the glow from the sun's rays.

"Sharon, you are a remarkable lady, and you look today. Have I told you that before?" George seemed to drop his affectionate lines out of the blue.

Looking bewildered, Sharon replied, "No! You haven't and thank you. Can we leave now?"

"Sure, the lunch hour is almost over."

"Only for me, the employee, not for you, my boss," she teased him.

Sharon drove off to the nearest food truck. They got some hot dogs and drinks and drove to a serene park to eat. The lunch went better than she expected.

George openly discussed all his experiences during his travel through Asia. Most especially how he enjoyed the variety of food.

Sharon seemed unmoved because after having dinner with his friends, she knew he was passionate about food.

A call from Grace disturbed the pleasurable time they spent together. Sharon tried to avoid the call. But on the third ring, George requested she picked up the phone.

"Hello Grace, thank you for calling. Any emergency?"

"Sharon, it's an hour and a half after your lunch. Your 3.30 pm appointment is waiting."

"Oh, my word! I lost count of time." George smiled affectionately, loving Sharon's dismayed expression of a lapse in her work for the first time.

"I will be there in 30 minutes. Please delay with any reasonable excuse, but no lies!"

"Affirmative!" Grace echoed in agreeing to arrange for her coverup plan.

"What?" Sharon questioned George's calmness amid her storms.

"Sharon, you're having lunch with your boss. You need not panic." For the first time, he held her hands differently, more comforting than before. Denying his affectionate tenderness, Sharon stood up.

"Please Boss, I need to get back to my workstation, my meetings, and my reality."

"Why can't I be your reality?" George slipped in another unexpected comment.

"I have 30 minutes to get back, Boss, if you don't mind."

"Not at all, Miss Sharon." George indicated he would follow her lead. Leaving his car behind to be picked up later, they would go to Finland's in Sharon's car.

The drive back to the office was silent, except for a few side glances at each other.

Sharon ruminated on how to deal with this developing situation, which she was trying to understand.

Meanwhile, George's mind fixed on how to win the heart of the most rigid, difficult, and wonderful lady he had ever met. One thing was sure, presenting herself as a hard-to-get lady was definitely making her attractive.

No matter how tough and independent a lady is, she always appreciates it when a man has the guts to make the first move. George was determined not to wait too long before someone else did.

Back in the office, Sharon walked in for her meeting. George stayed in the car park to avoid any suspicion from colleagues. He was not ready to let the cat out of the bag.

FOURTEEN

With the thoughts of George circling her mind, Sharon thought of how best to escape from his jaws.

At the close of the day's work, she stayed behind to make sure everyone else had left the office before leaving. By 7.00 pm, Sharon tiptoed out of her office.

At the exit door, the security officers questioned her presence in the building at night. Her excuse, getting some work done for a presentation for a client in the morning.

Her drive home seemed the longest she had driven in a long time. The waves of a tormented sea were bashing against the walls of her heart.

She wished there was a straightforward way out of this. Her next move is to bring up the past with George and the unforgettable encounter with the stranger. How she would bring it up, she needed to figure out.

The morning sun shone onto her face from the window as she rolled over. Sharon begged the Saviour.

I don't want to face him today. Can I call in sick? Can I? George will know I am creating an excuse. I left without an appreciation for the wonderful time we had together.

In the nick of time, her parent, Tom, and Peter's words flooded her heart. "Trust in the Saviour to direct you and stop raising walls of defence."

Sharon jumped out of bed, when an email from Mr Finland Sr. requesting her presence at 9.00 am meeting popped up on her phone.

She consciously dressed, paying special attention to her choice of clothing. A blend of her lemon fitted pants and cream blouse with a blended coloured scarf.

Spontaneously, Sharon seemed to have added to her fashion collection in recent times.

Who am I trying to... if I do not get out now, I will have to explain why I am late? She reminded herself before locking her front door.

Graceoak's building was extra busy. She felt like an intruder.

"What's happening?" Sharon walked up to Grace.

"Sharon, I am as surprised as you are, but Mrs Resource hinted to me that some of Mr Finland Sr.'s old colleagues were in town. He is using it as a business opportunity to gather them, and some potential clients for a meeting."

"Smart move, opportunities, and people equal business deals." Sharon nodded.

"True," Grace echoed her sentiments.

"And I love working with smart people."

"Besides, you should be heading for the welcome. Mr Finland will very much want to show you off."

"Show me off!?" Sharon exclaimed, "Ha! As what?" she raised her eyebrow walking away smartly.

"Whatever!" Grace whispered with a sense of envy. "Wish I could be smart like her."

Sharon headed to her office to put away her bag. Immediately she opened the door, she sensed someone had been in her office.

It wasn't long before she confirmed it. A stem of red rose on her table and a note stared at her.

"Can we do lunch again today? Mr Weird. P.S. I got lost in every moment with you yesterday, and you?"

She got her answers! Digging into her bag, Sharon drew out the mystery notes. She looked through the writings, analysing them like a private investigator.

Sharon cracked the code. George is the brains behind all the surprise notes! The question becomes, how did he do it? She will have to interrogate him at lunch to find out more besides the questions he avoided answering in his father's office.

Sharon smiled, looked ahead through the window. I wish there was a simple answer, but I have to go through all the phases.

I only hope that George is the same person as the stranger, and he doesn't disappear like her frequent nightmare.

A knock on the door unsettled her reverie. Mrs Resource popped in, asking.

"Are you ready? You look fine!"

"Always ready, I learnt from the best." Sharon giggled back.

"Thank you for the compliments, let not keep the meeting waiting."

The ladies walked into a well-attended meeting. For the next few hours, they discussed one business opportunity to another.

Sharon was apt in the business vocabulary spoken around the table. But the most captivating story was the one George was writing on the walls of her heart. Every glance at him has met her with a smile, as he constantly looked at her throughout the meeting.

A few moments before the meeting ended, her phone beeped. "Do you have an answer for me? Can't wait"

"Hold your horses!" She replied to his text immediately.

"It's a yes or no. I'm telling you; a no will break my..."

"I will look forward to the break..." she hastily replied, interrupting him.

"It's a yes! Where are we going?" the unexpected reply text travelled into George's phone.

"A surprise!" he texted quickly back.

"As usual, stop distracting me!" She responded, looking at him with a cheeky smile.

Sharon left the conference room when her phone beeped again.

"Same venue for pick up. We will use my car," said George.

"Ditto!" she replied, walking into yet another boardroom for a meeting.

"That is so British of you." George echoed behind Sharon. This time, she did not reply.

Sharon exchanged greetings with her clients before starting her meeting. The meeting ran overtime.

By the time she made a quick dash to the car park, George sat waiting in his car, looking disappointed. A beam of a smile broke out over his face at the sight of her.

Sharon knocked on the window as he beckoned her to come in with joyful delight.

"I apologise. The meeting ran over." She leapt into his red sports car to sit beside him.

"I hope we do not overload you with work. Remember, I can take some workload off you. I've done little since I returned."

"Returned. That's only since yesterday." Sharon glanced at him.

"Yesterday to you, three days ago for me, Sharon."

"You are such an enigma!" Sharon exclaimed in a state of shock as George drove off.

"OK, tell me, how did you do it?"

"Do what?" as he glanced over at her with sudden surprise.

"Send all the notes to different places," demanded Susan.

"About that, I had some helpers," explained the Enigma.

"Oh, really," Sharon exclaimed, "I hope the helpers did not observe you have a crush on me."

"Have I?" George questioned her with delight.

"Can't you be serious?"

"Well!!" he responded teasingly.

Who would have believed that aggressive man is the same gentle, funny, and loving gentleman? Saviour, we need to take this slowly. I am falling in love in slow motion. George parked his car a short walk from the beach.

"Really, George. Do we still plan to get back to work today?"

"Do you? To be honest, I don't." He opened his door, came out, and walked over to the passenger door.

"George, I'm still an employee, and I am expected to spend my hours working." Sharon expressed sincere concern.

"That's so unlike me." He teased again. "Sharon, relax. We are out for lunch. I'll cover for you. Remember, I am your boss, and I am the Boss!"

"The Boss's son, you mean?"

"Whatever!" he responded, deflecting Sharon's cynicism.

"Shall we?" he continued as he led her toward a small elevation. As they approached, he asked her to wait, requested to blindfold her. She agreed, enjoying the fun she had never had in her lifetime. George gently led her over around the bend, directing every step until he said: "here we are."

"Sharon, thank you for accepting to dine with me."

"You're welcome. Can you so much as remove the fold on me?"

"Yes, yes," he responded with a touch of anxiety.

Upon George releasing the fold, Sharon's eyes beheld something that caused her to leap up in joyful excitement.

"Oh, my word! Did you do this for just an ordinary lunch?" Before her eyes was a picnic table laid out with a feast for a king, astonishing Sharon.

"Wait until you see what I have in store for you," he chuckled with glee.

"Really, George, thank you already!!"

Holding her hands to sit down, he mentioned one attribute that drew his interest in her.

"You know, one thing I love about you is your British accent," George stated emphatically.

"Whoa, I couldn't have imagined," Sharon dreamily reminisced.

"The first time you walked into my office, not only your beauty captured me, but your confidence, your British accent..."

"Alright George," interrupted Sharon, "can we eat now? I am famished!"

Masterfully, George clapped his hands, and immediately a young man walked out from the other side of a large boulder, approaching with trays of hot food.

"George!" Sharon shouted.

"Just eat it and enjoy! Today I want to know more about you, but first, we eat."

Sharon enjoyed not only the meal, but she opened her heart to George discussing herself, family, past relationships. Though she tried to caution herself, her mouth ran faster than she could stop tap water from running.

Two hours later, she had forgotten to ask him all the questions she had planned to corner him with.

They took a walk on the beach after lunch, discussing all the characteristics they admired in each other.

Slowly, a brick at a time, her walls of defence crumbled. George had walked into the unoccupied space in her heart.

Finally, like the sunset, Sharon requested she takes her leave.

"I have a Bible study tonight in Peter's home. Would you care to join me?"

"Without objections!" he exclaimed. "It will be my delight to share the Saviour's words with you," words he spoke as though he knew the Saviour personally.

Sharon was about to question him regarding the statement he made. However, he spoke first.

"I wouldn't miss the chance of having the twins for company. They are such a delight to be around."

"I couldn't agree more," Sharon mumbled as they walked towards his car. Unconsciously, he took her soft palm into his hands, a sign of the unknown journey ahead of them.

Driving off from the beach, Sharon suggested they drive to the office so she could pick up her car.

"Don't you want us to drive together in my car to the Peters?" George looked over at her, puzzled.

"No, that's not what I mean." Sharon lowered her eyes, trying to explain herself. "What I meant was..."

"I don't think you should have to explain," interjected George quickly.

"George, are you able to listen to me on a friendly professional term?" Sharon pressed her lips together.

George responded by smiling and asking, "Are we back to the friendly professional? I am listening." He glanced at her and back to navigating the road.

"I will drive behind you to the Peter's house," muttered George.

"I am thinking about tomorrow morning. I will have to get to work. What do you think?" Sharon threw the ball back into his court.

After a long pause, George peeked over at her, smiled, and continued driving.

"Is that your definite answer?" she probed.

"You are so smart, Sharon. I can't figure you out."

"Why? And don't you avoid my questions?" Teasing him of his remarks.

"Well, I didn't think about your plans for tomorrow. I guess I am only thinking of how I could spend more time with you today."

"I appreciate your compliment, George,"

"Sharon, you know what?"

Sharon lifted her eyebrows and replied, "What?" He drove past the office complex.

"I will drive us anywhere and everywhere you want till you get back to the office tomorrow."

"For real? You sure know how to make a lady feel special, George!"

"Thank you. I will take that as a compliment." George said with a sense of accomplishment.

FIFTEEN

The next morning, George packed in front of Sharon's apartment as early as 7.30 am. She walked down gracefully from the staircase in a purple-pink dress.

"Morning, Sharon! I hope I am early enough?"

"Morning George, you are as early as you can be," she smiled, approaching him with a hug.

"Thank you for the opportunity," as George thoroughly enjoyed her hug.

"You are welcome," her words flew out of her mouth as George opened the door for her.

The drive to work was the most unusual for her in a long time. She had never driven to work with another person apart from Peter.

Sharon thought, *this is new*, as they drove into the car park. Unfortunately for her, Mrs Resource stepped out of her car. Sharon could see the surprise in her gaze. But she smiled after waving to say, 'Morning.'

"Mr George, Miss O'Loan, morning. How are the both of you?"

Sharon responded, "Good morning, Mrs Resource. We are fine."

"I know," replied the amused HR, pointedly looking at George who croaked out, "Good morning!"

Mrs Resource walked ahead of them, while Sharon's face flushed with embarrassment.

"It's okay," he comforted her, "everyone will find out at some point whether or not we like it."

"True, but not until I can control myself what they find out. Friendly professional, remember?" she reminded George.

"Affirmative," George responded with his generous smile.

"Good!" Sharon chirped back, sweeping grandly into the office.

By lunchtime, George requested another moment together. This time, she declined, with an excuse for a meeting with Mrs Resource at lunch.

George knew from the sound of her voice she had made up an excuse out of the blue. He knew he should not push her. He had observed, Sharon can only cope with a little dose of affection at a time.

She personalised the statement, "she is not sure yet." He would do nothing to start her running off.

Sharon just made up an excuse to avoid another emotional rollercoaster with him. Too much, too soon!! I prefer to take it a little at a time. *Good! Saviour, I'm enjoying it, but it is too much too soon.* Sharon quickly walked back into her office, picked up her phone and called the HR.

"Mrs Resource, can I have lunch with you today?"

"No problem! Sharon, are you OK?"

"Sure," Sharon paused and continued, "I am OK. I just need your company. You know I look up to you." She added, distracting Mrs Resource from any potential suspicion.

"Very well," replied Mrs Resource in a casual tone. "I'll be in the lunchroom at 1:30 pm."

"Oh, you're having lunch a little late today?" inquired Sharon.

"Yes, Sharon I need to finish some paperwork."

"That's great! I will see you at 1:30 pm," consented Sharon.

Sharon arrived at the lunchroom to find Mrs Resource already seated.

"Here you are," Sharon said, pulling out the chair beside her. She opened a sandwich prepared earlier at home. Sharon ate immediately to avoid any conversation, pretending she was starving.

"You often go out for lunch, Sharon. It is strange to see you around here. Is everything OK?"

"Oh yes, everything is OK. Just needed some female company."

"So, I saw you with George this morning. Did you have an early morning meeting?"
Indirect questioning to make sure she does not make the worst assumption of both of them. With Sharon still avoiding making eye contact, Mrs Resource continued.

"I know something is ongoing between the two of you."

"How do you mean?" Sharon's expressions gripped with guilt.

"Child, sorry if I call you child," gently apologised the HR.

"That's alright," Sharon muttered.

"I know you. I know when a man is all over a lady. George has been mooning over you for the past 3 to 4 months."

"That's not true." Sharon once again avoided her observation, looking down at her feet.

"Can't you acknowledge liking anything about him?"

"You mean I admit nothing to myself?" Sharon sipped her drink.

"Oh, so you think it's gone unnoticed that throughout this week you two have been having lunch together?"

"I know! I know," Sharon finally gave up her pretence. "It's alright, I just wanted to run away this afternoon for some breathing space."

"Why? Love is a thing. Do you have a problem with that?" demanded Mrs Resource.

"I don't know how to deal with it! I don't know, it scares me." Sharon acknowledged, "George changed out of the blue."

"Do you mind explaining what you mean by that?"

"He switches from hating to doting love. How can I be sure when he is pretending?"

"Sharon, I'll be honest with you. George never hated you. Remember, I told you other things were bothering him, things I can't explain to you."

"Yes, you did, but why?" Avoiding her question, Mrs Resource clasped Sharon's hands in hers.

"I informed you that if you want to know, ask him. Have you made any attempt to find out from him, Sharon?"

"I haven't had an opportunity. Every time we went out together, he talks about work or we're discussing me. To be honest, we discuss nothing about himself."

"I honestly think you're getting acquainted with him is an opportunity to find out more about him."

Wise, Mrs Resource, knew what was best to do. Before Sharon knew it, they started talking about Mrs Resource's family, her grandchildren and how she loves spending time with them.

After an hour, Sharon announced, "I have to head back to the office. Thank you for the company. I appreciate you."

"Same here, Sharon," winked the HR.

When she got to the office, Sharon was relieved she had not encountered George on her way there. But George wasn't letting her off that easily. He had already dropped a box of dark chocolate on her desk.

Thinking to herself, *Oh, my goodness!* Sharon smiled, opened the accompanying card.

It read, *"I missed you at lunch today. When do you want to choose a dinner date?"*

Hanging on every word written in the note by George, a well of excitement rose within her.

Sharon sighed blissfully, looked up at the ceiling and then out the window.

Saviour, what do I do about George? There is a need to know him. I need to find out about him, don't know how to proceed.

She ruminated with him, and then the Saviour's words entered her mind.

"He will put the right words in her mouth to speak."

Like a revelation, Sharon whispered.

Please help me say the right words to him. I don't want to push him away, neither do I want to fall hopelessly in love. I shouldn't be thinking with both my head and my mind.

Words she was still thinking as she walked back to her seat when her phone rang. *It's him!!*

"Hi, George! I saw your gift. Thank you, much appreciated."

"You're welcome! Have you chosen a day yet... Friday, 7 p.m., good?" George proposed a time.

"Are you deciding for me? Or you want me to give you an answer because you've chosen the date, the time, and even then, you've ready picked the venue?"

"I still need permission, but the offer has been on the table for a while now."

To avoid any heated argument. She agreed, "Friday is good. But on one condition."

"Mention it and I promise to do it," assured George.

Sharon fell into her rolling chair, paused, swinging around before stating.

"On the condition that on Friday you will do all the speaking and me, the listening."

"Wow!" exclaimed George in surprise. "That's a tall order. Where did that come from?"

"Nowhere," said Sharon matter-of-factly. "I feel it's time for me to know you, the same way you want to know me. It's only fair if we are moving from the realm of friendly professionalism, Isn't it?"

"Interesting! That is surprising coming from you. Are we moving from the realm of the friendly professional?"

"George! You just invited me on a date. Don't you know what it means to invite a lady to a dinner date?"

George denied any wrongdoing, while Sharon protested till they both laughed.

"I'll see you on Friday. Pick up is 7pm." laughed George.

"That's fine, but keep in mind 7 is 7," Sharon reminded him.

It was now Thursday afternoon, and tomorrow would be Friday! Sharon didn't want a run-in with

George before their date. Walking into the car park after work, it surprised her that George sat in his car.

He just stared ahead, patiently waiting for her. There was no way she could run back but had to face him.

"Hey George, are you missing something?"

"Not really but come to think of it. I forgot something. It is you." He turned to her, engagingly pouring on his charm.

"Oh, please stop it!" Sharon insisted in embarrassment. "You can't forget me, I'm not a thing you know!!"

"Oh really! I had to say goodnight before I leave. Is that OK?" pleaded George.

"All right, goodnight!" Sharon sighed, pursing her lips together in response.

"Goodnight Sharon, I'll see you tomorrow," he mumbled quietly as he drove off.

"Interesting," she thought.

He had to wait in the car park to say night. I wonder why he didn't just pop into the office. Anyway, I guess he didn't want people to... whatever.

Switching her mind back to the road, Sharon drove on home. For the rest of the evening, George played in her mind repeatedly like a broken record. Images flashed into her memory from the airport encounter to that first shocking encounter in the office.

From the frustrated first meeting to the sudden fortune of a second meeting, or so she thought.

I want to know his story. What happened to the bitter George?"

This tempted Sharon to pick up the phone to consult with Tom or Peter or Mum. She always felt motivated, but concluded it would be better to eat, sleep, and pray. She knew she is on the right path. Besides, although Sharon would very much love to speak to someone, she did not want to share too much.

It wasn't long before Friday evening came. Sharon had to leave the office early to do some shopping.

Her mind in turmoil, at about six pm, Sharon started getting ready for the dinner that would likely change everything. Torn about dressing appropriately, Sharon wore a light blue dress which accentuated her appearance. And a pair of good-luck shoes, she thought, slipping her slender feet into a similar colour of pumps.

Ten minutes before seven, George was idling out front in his sports car, expecting her arrival outside.

To play down her eagerness, she stayed in the apartment until seven pm sharp peeking now and then down at him.

Finally, Sharon had enough of watching him and headed to the door. The anticipation of the night and her over-active imagination tingled down her spine.

George knocked at the door at the same time she turned the doorknob. He stood awkwardly in the doorway, clutching a lovely bouquet of red roses.

"This is getting to be much more than a friendly professional." Sharon commented with a further, "Thank you for the roses."

George's voice reflected his sense of amazement. She invited him to come into the apartment.

"This is your first time in my apartment. I hope you are pleased with the Finland standard."

In his cheeky expression, "I'm not here to check your apartment, but to take my lady out for our dinner," George replied stiffly.

"Totally focused! I see!" she teased.

"All right, it's a nice little apartment, but remember, the property belongs to my company." The arrogant words rushed out of his mouth before George could stop himself.

"You're right, I always forget!" agreed a startled Sharon.

"I can't wait to get out of your property..." Sharon's terse reply aimed at deflating his ego.

"And waste more money?" he interrupted. "Sharon, just save it." He fixed his gaze on her.

After a pause, they both laughed and looked towards the door.

"How about I put these flowers in a vase first?" Once she accomplished her mission to save the flowers, they headed to the door.

Outside, George led her to the car. He opened the door whispering to her, "Sharon, you look ravishing."

"Thank you, I thought you would never compliment me!" she smiled, taking her seat.

The drive to yet another surprise venue went gravely silent, as both seemed to have a lot on their minds.

Driving into the restaurant car park, petrifying images pierced her mind repeatedly.

How was she going to ask him questions?

It was a delightful surprise, as George had arranged the dinner in an Afro-Caribbean restaurant, 'Afroimbibe'.

"You brought me home!" She exclaimed, holding his hands in excitement. "I've always wanted to dine here."

Pleased with her response, George smiled. "Well, I thought you'd like a little reminder of home." He got out of the car to get her out from the other side.

A few moments later, leading her towards the door. Afroimbibe was a pleasant and exclusive place to dine. The background music emanating towards them, a piece of well-known afrobeat song.

Her mind flashed back to her graduation party. The images of her mum's family dancing to the music-filled her mind as her body swung to the rhythm. Each family member had taken turns to teach me how to dance to the rhythm of the music.

At some point, my cousin exclaimed, "Where did you get this gift of dance from, Auntie? Your daughter, she can't even move her body at all."

My mother had laughed aloud. "Leave my child alone. She takes after her father."

Another replied, "where did we miss it? We need to train her!!" They all laughed together.

She came back to the present when George pulled out a chair in the reserved area of the restaurant.

"George!" she looked around. "We are the only ones in the restaurant. George, what's happening here?"

She had astonished but amused look on her face.

"We have the whole of the restaurant to ourselves, don't worry." He responded, enjoying the startled expression on Sharon's face.

"You what? Booked the entire restaurant for the night? Are you serious?" Sharon questioned, with an increasingly tense tone.

SIXTEEN

"Relax Sharon, I've got this!"

"What are you doing? I'm serious."

"It's exclusive for you and me for tonight. Sharon, you are so modest, a quality I admire. That is why I reserved the whole restaurant." George winked at her with glee.

Sharon took a deep breath as George called up the waiter, who brought in the drinks.

He reached out and held her hands. "Sharon, you said tonight I am speaking, and you are listening."

"Correct," she replied, composing herself adjusting her seat.

"How do I start? Do you want us to eat first before talking, or you want us to talk first?" inquired George.

"I'm famished. We eat first," decided Sharon.

"You do always love your food," George signalled to the waiter to begin the service.

"Yes, I do like my food," admitted Sharon.

"Interest enough, you still manage to maintain your body weight."

"I take care of my body and remember to eat healthily."

"Oh, I can see that," he echoed as the first course of the mouth-watering meal of pepper-soup and fried meat hurried down her starving throat.

Then came the second course of Jollof, fried rice and assorted meat. Gulping down the meal in silence, Sharon noticed George was always glancing over at her. Not long after she slipped the last piece of the second course into her mouth, she asked her first question.

"Tell me about yourself, your childhood." Picking up her glass of wine to take a sip, she slowly made her move.

"To be honest with you, I can only tell you what I was told because I cannot remember my childhood." admitted George.

"That's strange, who doesn't remember their childhood, George?"

"Okay, Sharon, let's say I was born 32 years ago."

"About, you say?" Sharon regurgitated his words back to him.

"I know, right? Okay, let's start 32 years ago," he continued, sipping his glass of red wine.

"I remember. I was born to my dad and mum as a twin."

"You mean Mr & Mrs Finland." Sharon pressed her feet to the ground as the image of the stranger flashed through her mind.

"Yes, but somehow, as a living nightmare, my childhood tragedy occurred."

"What do you mean by tragedy?" Sharon asked while popping an extra escargot, into her mouth.

"After Mum's delivery, we were told that my identical twin brother died. The doctors tried everything they could. Only I survived."

"They informed them. Didn't your mum and dad see your identical twin?"

"Yes, they went through the mourning process for him." Sharon lost any further interest in the food.

"It's not all a sad tale. Sharon, I will tell you everything on one condition."

"You used my words for me," she smiled. "What's the condition?"

"Miss Sharon O'Loan, kindly finish the wonderful meal before us, then I continue my story." He looked desperately into her eyes.

Adjusting herself, she responded, "I agree," picking up her fork.

The dessert came after the meal. Sharon ate in silence, avoiding eye contact with him.

She feared the worst is yet to come... *What a sad story!* She pondered.

Once the waiters cleared the plates replacing their bottle of wine, George continued.

"I grew up as the only child. It was hard for my parents, knowing that I am one twin and the other dead."

"I can only imagine," she responded with empathy.

"Father stood by my mum, but I grew up a pampered brat. Over the years, my parents sent me to all the best schools possible. Best university, and you know, like every other young man, I became a rebel."

Sharon reached out, placing her hands on his hand. He responded, gazing at her beautiful smile of empathy.

"Along the line, I joined a rock band wanting to kick off my music career."

"For real? I can't even imagine you playing in a rock band." she felt compelled to draw from her sarcasm pot.

"Wait until you see my band members." They both joked as George continued.

"I left home pretending to be going to the university and diverted from my studies with my band for 2-3 years."

"Didn't your mum and dad object?"

"They didn't know! I faked letters and results, hired parent representative for any communication. Until one day, my father discovered the deception through one of his potential clients. His daughter was in the same class I was also supposed to be in."

"Oh, no!" Sharon exclaimed.

"I disappointed him and the secret life I have been living. He threatened to cut me from his inheritance if I continued in the music career."
Sharon nodded in agreement whilst he continued his story.

"At which point, my Mum intervened and pleaded with him for me.

She begged me, "Why don't you finish a university education first? If you want to go into the music industry, you are free."

"Although my father didn't agree with my mum, because of the love he had for her, he succumbed. Besides, he didn't aspire to be the reason for her second breakdown after my brother's death."

"I feel so sorry. I would never have imagined the hurt she's been through. She is a powerful woman," admired Sharon.

"You can say that again. You know mums, Sharon, they have a way of getting to their boys."

"I don't know. I never had a brother." She tried a tease with a smile.

"That aside, I went ahead with my university education. I finished about six years ago. I barely finished my course when Dad requested, I join the family business. Once again, we had a fierce disagreement. The next morning, I disappeared."

George refilled his glass of wine and did the same for Sharon before he continued.

"I suppose my disappearance took a toll on my dad."

In sad reflection, he continued.

"The company wasn't doing well with several failed opportunities..."

Sharon stopped him in an exciting tone. "Yeah, yeah! Yeah, that reminds me, where does Mr Williams come in all of this?"

"Oh yes, Mr Williams!" George laughed at her keen expression of wanting to receive a piece of forbidden information.

"What about him?" He took a long pause and then said. "Mr Williams was the managing director at around the time I was at the university. He was good with the company business, reviving every damage caused by my leaving."

"I see," Sharon expressed at the sudden revelation of Mr Williams' identity in the company affairs.

"Still my dad needed to get me back into the company. He created a scenario that Mr Williams had failed in his business commitments with him. Dad invented a story that the business was in crisis. His health was failing at the same time. He claimed he had a lot to handle between himself and my mum. Interestingly, Mum supported him. You know how they work together. No one can get in between them."

Sharon bursts out laughing. She knew what George meant. Her own two old folks were inseparable. De facto, they often finished each other's sentences!

"Well, I moved back home temporarily until things could turn around. With no managing director, I stepped into the post resentful and angry."

"Why?" asked Sharon, totally engrossed in his story.

"Because I later discovered the truth, that Mr Williams had gone to start the Asia regional business."

"But that's good," she exclaimed.

"Not good. While I may not do what I want with my life, at the same time I'm allowed to affect the changes I want in the company. But I was constantly being watched, always feeling their eyes looking over my shoulder. I had no sense of trust, so I became so mentally angry. I wanted out, I wanted to stay away. You know, I never could get the right timing. Dad started developing health issues from one thing to another. His health up today and down tomorrow. Everything went from bad to worse between us until the miracle of Sharon happened."

Wondering what he meant by the miracle, Sharon splashed out a laugh and responded. "What do you mean by the miracle of Sharon?"

"I don't know where you came from, but you made such a tremendous difference in my father."

"Tell me more. How did I?" Her eyes sparkled.

"You tell me. How did you meet my dad, Sharon? How did the employment come about?"

Getting back on the original topic, Sharon interrupted with, "Have you forgotten tonight is about you? Nothing about me."

"Oh, sorry!" apologised George, "I forgot. Pardon me, now back to my story!"

Sharon took a drop of drink, looking around. "I can't still believe you did all this for me."

"You are worth every dollar spent and more," staring helplessly into her eyes.

Sharon excused herself to freshen up to avoid his unrelenting gaze on her.

Don't derail the discussion. It was going so well. Why did you make that comment? She quizzed herself in front of the mirror in the ladies' room. You need to get back there and listen to his story! Today is about knowing him, understand Sharon!?

A few minutes later, she returned to George. Standing up, he pulled out her seat for her to sit.

"George," clearing her throat, she continued, "I love your chivalry." though she avoided his eye contact.

"You are so welcomed." He reached out to touch her hand with affection.

"So, where were we?"

"Right. When you appeared in the office, your beauty carried me away. I needed to keep expressing my anger and aggressiveness. I was angry, but it had nothing to do with you. But you were a convenient way to get back at my parents because I had become agitated. So, I tried to force you out, threatening you to get back at my dad."

"Whoa!" commanded Sharon.

"Honestly, it wasn't you, but the best of you happened. When you started showing my dad how good you are at work, you invited envy, right?"

"How?" Sharon stared at him, amazement.

"You seemed to soak in all the praise, while I seemed to shrink into the shadows. I couldn't beat you, so I created more frustration for you. Sharon, something about you was weird. Rather than getting upset, you would be more empathetic towards me. You took everything I irritated you with. Sometimes it was just hopeless, Sharon."

Trying hard to hold back her tensed emotion, Sharon replied, "what instance?"

George smiled in pain, paused a while before responding. "The first deal you handled. It amazed me at how easily you dealt with the client. You single-handedly changed the business deal to our advantage."

A breath of relaxation swept through her heart.

"Sharon," George touched her hands, "You gave us a 20% increase on your first deal, on your first official workday!" George exclaimed. Sharon's face softened with a glowing smile.

He confided, "That deal-breaker blew my mind."

Sharon started laughing. "It surprised me, myself, but it just happened. I am glad I thank the Saviour for that."

"That is it, the Saviour." He focussed attention at the mention of the word Saviour.

"The Saviour, He is the most important person to me," stated Sharon. Her heartbeat drumming as the mention of her Redeemer.

"How do you mean? Can I let you into the secret?" George's eyes let out in sparkles.

"Let me in on the secret." Begged Sharon expressing an eagerness to know more.

"You know, I was so concerned about who you are, where you came from. I used a private investigator, a friend. He followed you around town for about two weeks."

"What!?" exploded Sharon.

"Apologies, I am letting you know now," offered George.

"No, no, that's ok, apology accepted. Tell me more," invited Sharon.

"After trailing you around town for about 2-3 weeks, he came back with a report. He said you were clean," assured George.

"What do you mean by clean?" came her question.

"He said the only significant thing about you was your religious affiliation. This created a curiosity to discover you. My friend had no keen interest. He suggested other opinions of women of interest, as we chatted in the pub one-night," related George.

"For real? Have I met him before, George?"

"I told my friend my next plan is knowing you better." Sharon was afraid to ask.

"His response?" she queried, pressing her feet to the floor in anxiety.

"He said in all the years of investigating people of your kind, that the best way to know you is to know your Saviour. I guess that's why he wasn't keen."

"So, how did you go about that? This is becoming exciting," she leaned closer to hear him more.

"I watched you for several days and I didn't know what to do. I guess, should I say, I thought that the best way was to get the Saviour's book." George looked down as though he was shy.

"Are you serious?" A joyful sound leapt out of Sharon's throat.

"Yes, I walked into a bookstore one day and I got a copy of the Saviour's word."

"You did what? You mean you bought a Bible?" She moved closer to him.

"Yes, I did." His lips trembled as he began his transformation into a confession.

"Whoa, when did that happen?" asked Sharon, holding her breath.

"Around October or November last year," he revealed.

"Now I get it now. I get it! Get it." she repeated with a sense of a truth dawning.

"You get what?" George gazed intently at her with his beautiful blue eyes.

"That's when I started noticing the changes in your weirdness."

Sharon threw her arms into the air as she gave out a loud shout. George joined her as they laughed together.

"Keep laughing," he said. "Anyway, it's your evening. I'm continuing my story."

"It all sounds as if I'm watching a movie. Hope you don't mind." Ignoring her words, he continued.

"So, as I was saying. I didn't know where to start my reading from. I asked the shop owner, and he suggested I read from the book of John."

"Wow! Fascinating," commented Sharon.

"I started reading the Bible each day. As I read the life of your Saviour, I wondered, how can a man live like him?"

"You are right concerning that." She nodded at his sweet revelations about the Saviour.

George continued, "I thought, with every word I read, every conviction showed that, this was the way I should go. I didn't know-how. A few weeks into this new adventure, I only remembered that each day, I fell on my knees talking to him. Before I knew it, I started losing interest in my rockstar and the entire rock band dream. The change in my lifestyle became dramatic. Even my friends became confused. Remember the dinner I invited you to?"

"Yes," nodded in affirmation.

"Yeah, they asked me what was changing me. I said I was going to invite them to meet someone."

"So, you used me that day?" gently admonished Sharon.

"I know it sounded like I used you. I wanted them to see you are different."

"So, what happened to them?"

"Yeah, they feel I'm weird now. I've joined the weird group. But I'm praying for them that they will come to understand what I understand."

"You know, in the church when you came to visit the church that day. I was looking forward to you surrendering your life in front of the church," confessed Sharon.

George laughed aloud. "I did that in my room a few weeks before I came to church."

"I see now," Sharon slumped into her seat.

"Is everything OK?" inquired George, checking if they were on the same page.

Sitting back up, Sharon responded in relief, "Yes, everything is perfectly OK! I can see clearly now: the rain is gone; the sun is rising."

"Were you doubting me before now, Sharon?"

"I couldn't understand why the difference! Now I know that's how the Saviour truly changes lives."

"He has changed mine," echoing his gratitude.

"I'm glad to know you as a friend, a brother, and a boss."

"You won't forget that; because you are here on a date with your boss and that's before..." Sharon interrupted him.

"I have another question. I'm a little confused! Were you on any flight to the US, on the same day I was on a flight to Houston via Heathrow, George?"

"Can't remember why?" he said, puzzled.

"I met someone that looks exactly like you, George!"

"I could be several things, but I'm not a double. All I know is that my twin died at birth.

That's a long time ago. Less you forget, I interviewed you, so I was definitely in town. I remember Dad was in the hospital. They needed his only son beside him."

"That's weird." Sharon pressed her lips together, a sign of her uncertainty.

George continued, "What do you mean?"

"Someone just like your description! At the airport! On the plane with me! That's why the first time I saw you, you probably noticed I was a tad perplexed."

"True, that reminds me. Why were you looking at me that way, Sharon? Was I that breathtakingly handsome?"

"No, not really," she denied, "I said I met somebody out there that was a double of you! Now you said you're a twin."

"True," confirmed George.

"Could it be...?" George quickly interrupted, "But I just told you my twin died at birth."

"Anyway, George, it has plagued my mind for the past two years. It burned in my heart to ask you and finally, I realise you are one of a kind."

"Yeah, maybe a change will good." trying to distract her George, change the conversation.

"Would you like to dance with me? The floor has been empty all night."

"Wow, that is one weakness I have, George. My family knows I can't move to the right rhythm."

"Don't worry, I've got you. Remember, I'm a rock star!!" George stood up, stretched out his hands for hers. Sharon responded by placing her hands in his as she stood up to join him.

They danced together for the next 20 to 30-minutes. Undeniably, George had dance moves even better than she could imagine. He was gracious in teaching her to dance, too.

After a while, she requested to sit down. They talked and talked for the next couple of hours. George later dropped her off back home at about 12:30 a.m.

As he walked her to the door, George expressed his heartfelt gratitude.

"Sharon, I am grateful you went out on a dinner with me. This is the best thing that has happened to me in a long time."

"What do you mean?" she responded to the soft touch from his caressing hands and eyes.

"You were someone I planned to frustrate. I've changed my view of you. I'm getting to know you better."

"Thank you," she said as she hugged him. "For the opportunity to know you better."

George parted with a goodnight and watch her get inside the door, before driving off.

Sharon exclaimed as she walked into her apartment. Wow, and taking a deep breath.

I thought for a moment that he was going in for a kiss!

Walking toward her room to change into something casual, she continued. *Saviour, thank you so much. But to be honest, you give me the words to speak. I'm grateful for the assurance. I'm grateful that I'm going to know him more. I'm grateful for everything.*

She went on her knees, worshipping the Saviour for the wonderful day. Before she knew it, Sharon fell into bed with her dinner clothes on and was instantly fast asleep.

SEVENTEEN

Back at the office on Monday, Sharon pretended nothing had happened over the weekend. To the rest of the team, it was just a normal day, but as for Sharon and George, **use your imagination!**

Now that she had officially moved away from the bounds of friendly professional, it was like walking on eggshells around the office. Walking up to her meeting of the day, like a cat, George snuck up behind her.

"Hello beautiful, how was your weekend?" Moving to her other side, he continued, "How was Friday or Saturday or Sunday? I hope you rested well." He chuckled with a sense of triumph.

"George, get off my back. We are in the office."

"Hey, lovely, can the office stop me from finding out about your weekend?" That statement was made just as Mrs Resource passed by.

"Good morning, Sharon. Good morning, Mr George. It's lovely to see you two are getting along just fine."

"Morning, Mrs Resource," George responded, while Sharon looked down at her feet in embarrassment.

"A moment ago, I asked Miss Sharon how her weekend went? How was your weekend?"

Smiling back in satisfaction at his response. Mrs Resource replied, "Brilliant, I had fun with my grandkids."

"That successful, Mrs Resource." Expressing delight at the mention of the word - grandkids.

"Oh, that's it!" George exclaimed with renewed excitement. "Sharon, that's what am talking about. She had fun with the grandkids. So, there's nothing wrong with finding out how your weekend was, is there?" he stared into her eyes with delight.

"I'll let you two get on with your discussion, I'm heading to a meeting."

"See you soon," they both responded simultaneously. Mrs Resource looked back, smiling with a shaky head, and walked off.

"Okay! Okay, Mr George," Sharon responded defensively.

Sarcastically, she continued "I learnt my weekend was great. I had a lovely time and I'm back to work on Monday. Can we leave it at that?" she said with a smile, walking off to her meeting.

The meeting lasted longer than she expected and ran over her lunchtime. She thought about rushing into the cafe for a sandwich or something. Sharon opened her office to find a packed lunch on the table. There was an accompanying note, which read.

"I know you're very busy, beautiful. I covered up for your lunch. If you need some company, I am a dial away."

Sharon smelled the package, opened the lunch to dive into it. She was exhausted after the meeting. Another person's company is the last thing on her mind.

Taking the first bite, she heard a knock at the door. She panicked. It could be George, but this time around, it was Mrs Resource.

Noticing Sharon was eating, she asked. "If it suits you, can I come in? Are you busy?"

"Please, come in," mumbled Sharon, with her mouth full. "I'm just trying to get some lunch in. You know my meeting ran overtime, and I was not too good without lunch.

"Yeah, I know, Grace told me. I asked about you during lunch." She responded with a smile.

"Mrs Resource, can I ask you something?"

"Have the staff started noticing anything?" Sharon stared ahead with a grim face.

"Is there anything happening I need to know?" Mrs Resource drew a seat, sitting in front of her, pretending she is unaware of anything.

Sharon dropped her bowl of salad. "I discussed with you on Friday. No, Thursday, yeah, I think it was a Thursday."

"Do you mean regarding yourself and George?" Sharon nodded in response to Mrs Resource's question.

"Yes, Sharon, everybody has been noticing what is happening."
Sharon looked out the window and back. Mrs Resource, after a pause, continued.

"Do you think we have not noticed how George has been sweet on you for the past few months?"

Sharon explained, "I think I am the only one blind. I didn't know. I am trying to trust my heart, but..."

"But what?" Mrs Resource interrupted her. "What is bothering you?

"Can I tell you something?"

Holding Sharon's hands, which provided the assurance Sharon needed.

"You can trust me," Mrs Resource promised.

"OK. George took me out; we went on a dinner on Friday."

"Whoa! Tell me more." Mrs Resource exclaimed.

Sharon went on, discussing everything about her date with George.

"For the first time, I asked him everything."

"How do you mean everything?" probed the HR.

"Yes!" Sharon responded with sparkles in her eyes. "All the questions bothering me, plus the personal questions you suggested I ask him."

Admiring the courage that action must have taken the girl, the HR waited for more from Sharon.

"There were reasons for his inappropriate behaviour towards me and other stuff."

Mrs Resource smiled and continued listening intently to her, only asking, "So, did George tell you?"

"Yes, but I imagined incorrectly his reasons were more terrifying than what he discussed with me."

Mrs Resource questioned, "What do you mean?"

"I created the worse imaginations of his past in my mind. It didn't help the way you were secretive about it." Sharon echoed in between the sip of water after eating the last piece of salad.

"Yes, I don't always enjoy talking about other people. I often make sure they open up themselves when the time is right."

"Why? Is it a life-long policy of yours?" she enquired out of curiosity.

"Sharon, there's one thing I teach my grandkids. Your character is more important than silver and gold. So, if I teach my grandkids a lesson like that, I should apply the same to my life. Respecting other people's information and allowing them to communicate directly to others is my policy."

Looking at the HR with profound admiration, Sharon responded. "Mrs Resource, I have learnt so much from you. Thank you."

"You're welcome, Sharon. Let's get back to you and George. How do you feel about George and the dinner?"

Sharon burst out in a joyful exclamation, "I am flabbergasted. I wasn't expecting the experience. He swept me off my feet. I can't even explain it in words."

"George must have taken you to heaven and back!" Mrs Resource smiled in acknowledgement of the flame of love burning between the two lovers.

"What!" affirmed Sharon.

"Are you falling in love with him?" questioned the HR.

"That's it, I don't know where I am in this…" Sharon spoke hesitantly.

"Why? Didn't you just inform me you enjoyed the evening with him?"

"I did, but I am worried about the bigger picture…" she trailed off.

"I'm sure that should be the least of your worries. Enjoy every moment you have on this new journey. Sharon, let me assure you, nobody is going to hear anything from me. I seal my lips."

Mrs Resource made a zipping motion by her lips. "Thank you, I appreciate your sincerity," Sharon appreciated.

"To be honest, I keep hearing all the voices, all the things' people have been saying. How can you assume the staff don't notice George is always dropping gifts in and out of your office?"

Sharon smiled; her mind scanned through all the pleasant surprises George had showered on her. Mrs Resource continued, "When you're not there…"

"Yeah, exactly. I just wish he would keep out of my office when I am not available."

"I'm so sorry. I think that's going to be a long haul. For now, I just advise you to enjoy every bit of the surprises. You never know how things are going to turn out."

"For real!" Sharon lifted her hands to cover her eyes.

"Sharon, you captivated George's heart. I can't believe you changed George so much. How did you do it? He's such a changed man," inquired Mrs Resource.

"I know. I can't take credit for that. Lots more than Sharon O'Loan has happened to him."

"I'm wondering if it is temporary or permanent. How long is it going to be before..."

Mrs Resource glanced at her wristwatch and exclaimed, "I need to run off!! I have a meeting with Mrs Finland." She stood up and headed to the door.

"I'll see you later." Mrs Resource dashed out of the office. She popped back in to say, "Sharon, you have a beautiful personality."

Sharon laughed and grinned, "Thank you!!" Left behind and plagued with doubts, she continued thinking.

Is George the stranger? Is the stranger a real person? Who is the man my heart yearns for? George is not the kind of stranger I met and fell in love with at first sight. They look alike. Should I forget the unforgettable experience and cling to what I have? Here goes the saying, a bird at hand is better than two in the bush. George has a relationship with the Saviour now, the icing on the cake.

She recalled the discussion she had with Mrs Resource.

A few hours later, Sharon stepped out of her office. Heading to the ladies, she met Mrs Finland in the corridor.

"Afternoon Sharon," she called out to her. "I will expect you in my office. I hope you remember we have a meeting."

"Yes, I do. My last meeting ran over. Finished my lunch a short while ago. I will be with you and head to another meeting afterwards," Mrs Finland interjected.

"Before you do that, my party is on Saturday. I have an assignment for you."

"I will check my diary and will pop into your office later."

"Sharon, be there." Mrs Finland said affirmatively. "Good day Sharon," she added and walked off.

Sharon wished the ground would open to swallow her up, to avoid the exposure to the whole of George's family. *I'm going to be faced with George's entire family,* she pondered in her heart.

Moments later, Sharon's phone rang. The caller was Mrs Finland. "I am heading over to your office now."

"I spoke to Mrs Resource after I met you. She will give you instruction on what you will be doing."

"I will touch base with her before the end of the day."

"Remember, Sharon, last year, the Christmas party you planned was amazing. I understand you have a lot on your plate, that's why I didn't call you on this occasion. An event planner will be charge of making sure we sort out everybody this year," assured Mrs Finland.

"Thank you, I will be there on Saturday," came back Sharon gratefully.

The rest of the week went like a flash. Love, they say, is sweet. In every sense, Sharon was enjoying her new journey with George.

Every afternoon, they spent time together, visiting places she's never been to in Houston. His doting over her became breath-taking. She missed every moment not spent with him. Like every damsel in denial, she avoided the soft spot in her heart.

The increasing drumbeat following the sound of the voice of the singer, George, was singing the music her heart desperately wanted to hear. Her heart constantly skipped to the music, beating the drums louder and louder.

Sharon longed to speak to her parents. She didn't want to get them eager until she was sure which way her heart was leaning. *I really need to be honest with myself now.* The image of the stranger seemed to have faded with every moment spent with George.

A night before Mrs Finland's party, Sharon had the strange dream again. In the nightmare, she ran after the stranger.

This time, the stranger seemed to plead. Yet he was fading away with every step she took. The surrounding darkness loomed as it drew him away farther and farther from her. She woke up panting for breath, shaken by what had happened in her dream.

Saviour, what has George got to do with this? Please, if George has anything to do with my future, please take this dream away once and for all.

Sharon tried to get back to sleep but could not, as she tossed back and forth on the bed.

<u>EIGHTEEN</u>

Why do I feel so confused? Am I a fraud? Sharon scolded herself. She hurried out of her favourite gift shop after a long morning of shopping.

Stepping into the car, her phone beeped. The caller ID was Mrs Finland.

"Morning, Mrs Finland, and happy birthday to you."

"Thank you, Sharon, for the wishes. Looking forward to seeing you soon."

"You bet," Sharon happily answered. "I am finishing up in town, will head home for a change of clothes and be at your as soon as possible."

"That's great. Come to think of it, have you been to my place before?" probed Mrs Finland.

Sharon paused, as though thinking, before replying.

"To tell the truth, no. I am so looking forward to it."

"Let me leave you to get on with your busy day, Sharon."

A dilemma, to be sure! Am I eager about this party, or George, or been in the company of their family before? What will George describe me as? Does Sharon fit their desired description?

A sudden gust of wind carried her thoughts out the window and out of her mind.

An hour later, Sharon was driving towards the exclusive gates of a large, red-bricked mansion. She pressed the entry button after identifying herself. The gates to the driveway opened on its own accord.

Driving towards the grand mansion, tension tied her intestines into a fierce knot.

George, he grew up here! Now I know why he acted like a spoilt brat.

She drove to the front of the flamboyant building, where stewards waited to park her car. She stepped out into the setting sun. The main door flung opened, and George rushed out.

"You are here, Beautiful? I thought you would have..." breathless George paused.

"I keep my word, remember?" Sharon laughed.

"Sure, but not if you want to avoid George." Stretching out his hands for hers.

Responding with a glowing smile, she slipped her hands into his. "You bet."

"Sharon, on a serious note, I thought you would find a reason not to attend. I was already looking out, thinking that you would not come."

"George, oh no! This is for your mother. I can't, not appear."

"You have a charming effect on Mum." He drew her close to him, but she nudged away, avoiding his affectionate gesture.

She ignored it and replied, "You can say that again."

"You can say that again," Mrs Finland echoed as they entered the house. She walked toward them in a beautiful creamy diamond stoned dress.

"It's always been like that, Sharon. I never hear the end of his envious comments. George has even accused me of loving you more than him."

"For real!?" She slightly removed his grip on her, showing an expression of her disapproval and embarrassment in front of George's mum.

"Thank you for inviting me. Here are my gifts for your birthday," offered Sharon.

"Thank you, Sharon. That's so thoughtful of you. Sharon, you shouldn't have bothered."

"Oh no, I would bother, and I appreciate the invite," Mrs Finland said.

As Sharon walked on, she exclaimed, "Mrs Finland, you have an exclusive home. I must commend your successful taste."

Mrs Finland apologetically interrupted, "Please excuse me, I'm on my way to get my husband."
She handed over the gift to a steward, hurrying off.

George led Sharon to the garden fully decorated for the party as the guests poured in pairs. Greeting his mother's friends and their families, George got her a drink. She got introduced to most of the people at the party.

Sharon longed for a quiet moment, but none was forthcoming. The party went on and on endlessly. At what seemed like the end of the party, Sharon made moves to sneak out.

Somehow Mrs Resource appeared blocking her, indicating, "You can't leave. It doesn't work like that."

"I don't understand," Sharon pretending to not understand what she meant.

"Sharon, you need to know the Finlands more. They sense things, you know. If their son is developing an interest in you, you need to be more supportive during family events."

"Mrs Resource, I don't want to send the wrong signals yet."

"Sharon, a piece of advice... Stay here!!" she ordered as she headed towards the event planner.

Sharon entered the mansion thinking to explore. She walked into one empty room. She viewed one picture frame after another. The door opened with George popping in.

"Here you are. Thought you left without a word."

"You looked very handsome as a small boy." She observed, ignoring his sentiment.

"Do you mean I am not as handsome as a grown man?" He sounded defensive.

George sat down, beckoning her to sit beside him.

"Let me figure this out... it must be the end of the party."

She hurriedly walked past him, but George pulled her back. The sudden pull landed Sharon on his laps.

They found themselves caught up in an embrace, staring into each other's eyes. Until George muttered in sudden realisation of his action.

"I apologise for the sudden intimacy."

"Apologies? I would rather state your actions were deliberate. Thank you for the affectionate embrace."

Sharon stood up, straightening herself, with her face flushed with pleasant guilt.

"I apologised," confessed George, "because I shocked the church girl with my affectionate sentiments. My moves were not planned. Although I loved it."

"Thank you for being honest, Mr George Finland." Sharon placed her hand on his and sat beside him. They talked more about the pictures and his childhood until her phone alarm rang.

"It's 9 p.m., George, I have a planned call with my parents in an hour."

"That means you will have to be on your way. Sharon."

"That's what it sounds like, George!"

"Sharon," George whispered, holding her hands. "I would rather spend the rest of the night talking with you, but I understand what you have to do."

Stricken by his soft-spoken words, she fell into his embrace again.

What are you doing? Sharon, a step at a time, remember you told yourself.

The doorknob turning, interrupting the couple's embrace. One steward walked in.

"Master George, Mr Finland has some visitors he wants to introduce you to."

"Tell him I will be on my way."

"Certainly," the steward acknowledged George's message on his way out.

"Duty calls," George stood up.

"But I will need to walk you to your car before I meet with Father and his visitors."

As George walked Sharon to the car, she was about to open the car door when George turned her around and gave her a peck on the cheek.

Gently expressing, "I want to say thank you."

Sharon didn't see that coming. Still in shock with her lips pressed together and eyes blinking, she replied, "Thank you too, thank your Mum for inviting me. It was a lovely party."

"We should say thank you!!" emphasised George.

Sharon quickly got into the car. Avoiding any further eye contact with him, she drove off. She stared at his gaze through the window.

What do I do with him?... Or should I say, with these romantic feelings for him?

Driving along the road, she noticed an envelope on the passenger seat. How on earth did this get here? she thought. Once outside the gates, she proceeded along the road. Opening the envelope thinking it must be another invitation, Sharon read...

"Would you mind coming to the movies with me tomorrow? I've got tickets for a rock band if you don't mind!"

She looked into the mirror, stared at herself, and thought about what to do. She decided her best bet would be to send him a text immediately.

"I saw your invite. I can do the movies tomorrow, but without the rock band. I can't do two events on the same weekend. Do you mind moving it to another weekend?"

Sharon waited a few moments for his reply, which he did.

"Thank you, beautiful. Next Sunday we will attend the rock band then."

On Sunday, they walked together into the movie theatre to watch the new romantic movie of the next day. It was kind of fun. Spending time with George aroused her emotions, yet she kept denying they even existed.

She ruminated, *I would have visited the rock band on the same night, to spend a longer time with him, expressing regret at her decision. I've seen the time I spend with George recharges me because I am getting to like him.*

George was talking continuously about how he enjoyed her company.

Sharon, on the other hand, remained closed mouth about her feelings. All her responses were one-worded answers. It didn't seem to bother him because her presence with him satisfied him.

Their dates went from one now and then, to every weekend. At the movies or concerts or visits to museums or the charity gala for orphan kids organised by George, the head of the Finland Foundation.

Mrs Finland had set up the foundation in honour of George's twin to support the various orphanages. George once joked that his mum had always wanted more children. Although she didn't want to adopt, her greatest priority is to make sure they care for many orphans.

The foundation made sure the children get into successful adopted homes. Sharon's heart had always longed for a special person to call brother or sister. She could understand why this foundation remained dear to the Finland's hearts.

The days went into weeks and weeks into months.
A few months after their first date, Sharon was in without a doubt. Obviously, she is in love with George. There was a major hurdle to climb.

Our relationship is against Graceoak company policy, she quizzed herself. The problem is written in black and white... professional and non-professional relationships are prohibited between staff.

Mrs Resource's opinion was not forthcoming. Though she encouraged Sharon's relationship with George, she had deliberately ignored her need for clarification on this weary aspect of company policy.

Sharon's integrity was at stake. She had to be objective with George at some point. If she continued to follow the path of her feelings, there had to be a better solution to the impeding tsunami coming her way.

George announced he was heading out to Asia for an update on Graceoak business. The Asia region again, Sharon figured out it was becoming a biannual trip. A welcome break for Sharon. Though she wanted him around more than he would ever imagine, it would be a time for her to plan her next move.

Two days before he left, they were on a date. Out of the blue, George requested her company on the journey.

"I don't know what to say." She rubbed her forehead dealing with mixed feelings. Another of her crazy plans to elude her reality just got busted!

"Say nothing! Okay, say yes! I will sort your flight in the morning." George held her hands.
Sharon paused in silence with her lips pressed together.

"Say something," he pleaded, as though his life depended on it. Sharon could not deny the plea.

"Can I think about it? I will give you an answer in the morning, George."

"Don't keep me waiting. I am not sure I will survive the trip without you," he revealed in desperation.

"For real, don't flatter me, sweet tongue." Sharon denied his compliment.

"It's a working trip, remember, and not a holiday."

"You don't seem to understand. Sharon, you have become my primary work assignment." He whispered, drooling over her like syrup on fresh pancakes.

To escape his gaze on her, she redirected the discussions to question the affairs of the foundation. Another area of his life he treasures. He opened his heart to discuss story upon story about each child whose life had changed.

Sharon's conclusion: *you can't separate a man's passion from him,* she thought to herself.
After dinner, George opened the door for Sharon when she whispered.

"My answer is a yes!" George stood stock still. He wasn't expecting her answers.

"What changed your mind?" his eyes gazed into hers, waiting for an answer.

"Your passion! Nothing seems to stop anything you are passionate about." came her unexpected answer.

"Oh, really?" he challenged.

"Whatever!" she responded, slipping her legs to seat herself in the passenger side of his car.

The drive home was quiet. She questioned her decisions, she hoped she had made none in a haste. On the flip side, she's glad she accepted. *It was an idea to travel to another region of the world. What a grand adventure it would be,* Sharon pondered to herself.

George noticed her silence and stretched out his hands to cover hers. "There is nothing to fear, Sharon. I promise to be a man of integrity with you."

"Good to know. I must have feared that aspect."

"The Saviour used you to make me a changed man. The last thing I want to do is..."

"Don't worry, I believe you," assured Sharon. "Different rooms will be fine."

"Or can we plan different hotels?" George turned over to her with a cheeky smile.

"Ye are right!" she exclaimed, responding to his mischievous facial expressions.

Sharon, *George is officially into you. No getting away from this.* She responded to his warm, loving embrace, relaxing against his masculine frame.

George sorted out everything by the end of the next day. All she needed was her travel case. The trip took them from Thailand to Singapore to Hong Kong to Japan and the last stop on the journey, China.

Sharon found the experience life changing. The different culture, food, language, different ways of fellowship, etc. She only wished the entire world could be in unity under the Saviour's love. A near impossible dream to come to pass, she admitted.

NINETEEN

A month went by like a flash. It was time to return to Houston. Their flight was exhausting. Sharon had enjoyed every minute she spent with George.

Even when they disagreed, they seemed to crack a joke that could end any cold war between them. He stood by his words; he was more honourable than she could have imagined apart from his stubborn attitude. However, it was a little old habit here and there he struggled with. One could only assume Sharon thought George was getting close to becoming a perfect being!

How on earth did I get so lucky in life? A successful upbringing, successful education, followed by an icing on the cake, a successful man like George.

Upon arrival in Houston, George led her to the waiting car sent by Mrs Finland. He walked to the vehicle gallantly struggling with all the luggage. "An act of sacrifice," he often stated throughout the month-long journey.

He wouldn't allow me to carry my luggage or move a finger. Would he pamper me like this for the rest of my life?

Sharon concluded it is time to express her feelings to the people close to her heart. The whole George experience had turned her world upside down.

The stranger, the nightmares, seemed to have faded away. Sharon felt at peace with George, but had she driven the stranger away?

On returning from her trip, she was on the phone with her parents.

"I thought it was love at first sight with the stranger at the airport," she said, sounding downcast to her parents.

"You know sometimes, we think or plan things. But the Saviour's plans or intentions are more important," advised her dad.

"I know, Dad. I can't even stop this feeling I have for him. It's driving me crazy."

Her mum burst into laughter. "Child, I remember someone was once like that."

"For real, someone never told me." Sharon's father teased Mum back.

"Mum, Dad, get a life! This is my life, you know."

"You are the centre of it all. Sharon, you are the fruit of the love we share."

She countered, "Yeah! Yeah, I heard that a million times." They all shared a moment of laughter.

"Seriously, I feel better already," Sharon exclaimed.

"We are glad," they echoed together. "We know you will make a brilliant choice. As we say, don't shut your heart to love."

"Dad, I will have to resign from the company." She announced suddenly.

"Why?" they both responded simultaneously.

"It's the company policy, secondly George is my boss. It is wrong in all its aspects."

"Hold on. Have you discussed this issue with him?" Mum questioned her intentions.

"No, and I don't intend to. He doesn't even know the extends of my feelings for him yet."

"Do the rest of the people in the office know about both of you?"

"I guess so, but no one had asked me except," Sharon paused, "Mrs Resource."

"Then you are in excellent hands!" her mother exclaimed with a real Nigeria accent.

"No Mum, I'm not sure. I have tried discussing it with her. She seemed to shy away from any mention of it. I guess everyone, except George, would want me to be the one to decide what I should do."

"Why would you conclude for them, Sharon?"

"Dad, I have a reputation for integrity. It would be expected that I don't hide away from this decision. I must face it with the same sense of integrity you guys taught me, except you expect me to do otherwise."

"No, Sharon, we understand your point. We only pray the Saviour will sort things out, as you trust him."

"Have you spoken to Tom and his wife and your girls' friends?" Mother asked.

"No, I called to wish you a happy birthday immediately I dropped my luggage. I would call them as soon as possible."

"Yes, please do. We know they would be glad to know there will be wedding bells soon." hinted her parents.

"Muummmm...!! I never should have said anything!" Sharon shouted in protest of her parent's teasing.

"Why, do you know how long I have prayed for this news?" asked Sharon's mum.

"George has not proposed yet. Anything can change." protested Sharon again.

"Not to whom who believes in the power of prayer, like you two!"

"Okay, that's it! I must go, or I won't hear the last of this."

"You won't. We expect George's visit to us to ask permission," her dad added in amusement.

"Dad, you too!? Bye Mum, bye Dad and enjoy your birthday, send my cake!"

"Sharon, you gave the best cake!" complimented by her parent.

"Bye!" Sharon replied before dropping the phone.

Exhausted after a wonderful trip and a blissful phone call, she burrowed into her bed and slept.

Sharon woke up with a musical beep from her cell phone. Struggling, tapping her hands around until her hand knocked her phone off the bed. With a banging headache, she leapt up to grab the phone.

Her weary eyes lit to count forty missed calls from George. The recent caller, to her surprise, was Tom. She had been about to call him when she fell asleep yesterday.

O dear, I should be in the office three hours ago. This is terrible. I have not overslept like this before. She panicked for a few seconds, before deciding to say a few good morning words to the Saviour.

Moments later, stepping out of her bath, she heard a knock. She already suspected who was at the door.

"I will be right there," she shouted on top of her voice.

But there was no response. She dashed in to get some clothes on, as the door opened, and as she had speculated, it was George.

"You got me worried, Sharon. Are you okay? Everyone in the office is rather worried. I knew I dropped you off hale and hearty yesterday. I have imagined the worse." Worried words he stated as he rushed into her apartment.

"I would prefer a morning next time. How was your night? Mine was good." scolded Sharon.

"This is not funny! Seriously!! Are you okay? I missed you all morning!" declared George.

"George! Boss, get a grip on yourself! I am okay! I overslept, didn't even hear my alarm. I woke up about thirty minutes ago." George settled into her sofa as he enjoyed the vision of beauty in front of him.

"Listen," George, "before you swallow me up with your eyes, I better get dressed in something more appropriate." insisted a flustered Sharon.

Speechless, George slumped into the sofa, dissipating the exhaustion caused by the self-imposed anxiety.

"You are rather silent," Sharon called out from the bedroom. "You can get yourself something to drink, coffee or a drink from the fridge."

"I am good. The driver left. Hope you don't mind my catching a ride back with you."

"Oh really, George, you got it planned out, as usual."

"How do you mean, my love!?"

"George!" Sharon exclaimed. "Don't you know you have a way of perfectly planning all the surprises you have given me so far?"

"That's what I call false allegation," said George indignantly.

Laughing out loud, she responded, "False allegation indeed, I loved every moment spent with you and the surprises!"

"Thank you for such a beautiful compliment," he stood, walked toward her, reaching to take her close to his heart, like a lost lamb now found.

"You smell successful!" he complimented her.

"Can we go now?" she muttered, trying to extricate herself from his warm embrace.

"Of course! Whenever you are ready." George expressed his words coolly, yet he tried not to show his disappointment at being pushed away.

Noticing a drop in his excitement, she reassured him, grabbing hold of his hands.

"George, thank you for such a warm embrace, but I am running late to work."

"Running late, or you are four hours late."

"You are my boss. I'm delighted to be the accused, then forgiven all at the same time!"

"Shall we?" she said, leading him by the hands to the door.

Stepping into the car, George hinted, "I wouldn't assume you've had something to eat."

"Should you? I haven't George and I'm starving, too."

Tom's call interrupted their discussion. "Can I take this?" Sharon excused herself to pick up her cell phone.

"Hey, Tom, I came in yesterday exhausted. I slept immediately. I should have returned your call when I woke up."

"Your mum called me this morning to..." Sharon interrupted him to avoid any discussions about George.

"Can I call you back, Tom? I'm in a discussion with my boss."

"All right, speak to you soon."

Sharon adjusted her hair to dispel the discomfort of the brief exchange with Tom.

"Is that the same Tom, your friend?" asked George.

"Yes, we could talk from now till the morning if I don't stop him."

"Right, are we heading straight to the office or what?"

"My key priority is to get your stomach filled." He raised his hand to sweep her hair off her face.

The rest of the day, Sharon spent loitering around the city with George, eating and shopping. She soon forgot about other plans for the day.

They got back to the office after the close of the workday, only for George to pick up his car. Walking towards his car, George looked back at her with a love-stricken expression.

"Next time, Sharon, please don't scare me like that. 40 missed calls!"

"Hopefully, I won't oversleep again, heart crossed," she replied with an encouraging smile.

"I will be the first in the office tomorrow, boss!" Sharon continued, grinning.

"That's not funny! But love you still, Sharon, you make my heartbeat."

"Really!? Thank you, George."

George walked back, held her head softly, and kissed her forehead, saying, "Sweet dreams with George in it."

"Sure! Boss." Sharon avoided expressing any affectionate word and drove off.

With her unresolved feelings about George, she expressed her concerns with Tom.

As usual, Tom, and his wife expressed joyful glee, like her mum and dad. Judging from the day she spent with George – referring to her as his heartbeat. How can I deny the same for him? I need to come clean to him at some point, and soon.

"Please, Sharon, follow your heart. The Saviour has allowed your paths to fall in pleasant places." her friends encouraged her.

"There is one thing I need to do." She pointed out.

"What could that be, Sharon?" they questioned her.

"Company policy!" Sharon stated emphatically.

"That is not a necessary step. Sharon, we are talking about him! He is your boss and the potential CEO of Graceoak. He can make or break the rules!" Tom exclaimed.

"I know, but as an employee, I still need to abide by the company policy."

"We suggest you discuss with George before you resign."

"I will think about it." She had already decided lopsided their advice could change her stand on her decision.

They talked about Peter and his knowledge of her affairs. She acknowledged they were unaware and promised to visit her extended family as soon as possible.

After her call, Sharon composed her resignation letter. She promised herself to discuss with Mr Finland Sr. first thing in the morning.

The next morning, George hinted he would be away on a three-day trip to England. He offered to visit her parents however, Sharon declined and stated it would be better and more appropriate to visit her family together.

George agreed to her objections, only when she promised that his next visit to England will be a visit to her family, possibly to spend the Christmas holiday.

The more reason I need to resign, she pondered to herself.

Two weeks after her unforgettable official friendly professional travel to Asia, she reluctantly dropped a resignation letter on George's table.

George cancelled all his meetings for the day in hopeless disappointment. He sought some explanation for her actions, but Sharon informed him she had no choice but to abide by the standard expectation of the company.

"I am the company, can't you see? Sharon, your action to resign is unnecessary."

George's pleads fell unto the deaf ears. Sharon's heart flooded with an unexpressed tug of war, her overwhelming love for him; versus what she knew she must do.

"George, please understand this with me. I have to resign. Don't you get it? I can't do this!? We want a relationship that is no more friendly than professional. George, I'll still be working with you."

"Okay, let me get this. What is wrong with having a relationship with you and still working in the same office?"

"Do you want me to work against the company policy?"

"Yes, Sharon, I know it is in the company policy, but I am the company," pleaded George, with tears in his eyes. "I want nothing ..."

"George, it doesn't matter. We need to be an example. If you want what is happening between us to work." George's face lit up, awaiting her next statement.

"If you think this will work, we need a commitment beyond what I am to you now, George..."

"Excuse me, what are you to me?" he teased her, ignoring his teary eyes.

"George, can you be serious?" begged Sharon.

"I am listening." His cute expression made Sharon smile.

"You pay me all this attention. You can lobby your way into my heart. All these gifts you shower on me. George, how can you want nothing?"

"I'm sorry, I'm sorry, I want nothing. No, that came out wrong. I don't just want us to be friends. I want to know you more. I want to, I want to love you. I am..."

"That's what I mean, you use the word - love everywhere in the office. This is a professional environment. All the staff know what's going on. It is getting embarrassing."

"I get it," he exclaimed with a sense of understanding.

"When I was walking in today, I could tell everything was different. Do you know what they said when we went to Asia together?"

"I do. I knew everybody was talking about Sharon, but I closed my eyes and saw just you, you're all that matters."

"Yes, George, I am all that matters, but I also want you to portray the right image of this company. I would be friends with you professionally if I remain here, but..."

"But what?" He sounded agitated.

"If I want to have a relationship with you; if we have to take this to the next level..." Expressing her frustration, she continued.

"George, I want to know you more, but I cannot compromise the integrity of this organisation."

"Sharon, how would you do that?"

Flapping her hands in the air, she exclaimed, "by going against the company policy!"

"Sharon, I understand every word and your reflection of us." He held her hands close to his heart.

"I'll take it up with the board. I will discuss your resignation letter with Dad."

"Could you just sign it and let me go?" Sharon replied, upset, looking away from him. "I can get another job with another oil company."

"Do you think I will let one of our best assets leave this company to another organisation because I'm in a relationship with you?" He pulled her hands around him.

"George, please! OK, OK! I understand." She agreed to his compliments to avoid a further emotional grip on her.

"I understand. I can't eat my cake and have it. I can't have you in the organisation and in a relationship with you. Who wrote the company policy? Who wrote it? I need to know who wrote the policy?" George protested jokingly, pacing up and down the office.

"You're asking me? Ask your dad," she bluntly stated, while robbing his palm over his smiling cheeks.

"I see! Instead of smiling, I should say thank you for listening to me. Thank you for your attention." George composed himself in front of the straight-faced Sharon.

"George, I'm starting to like you." Sharon's whispering voice dropped in a profound confession.

"That's what I'm talking about!" George threw a fist in the air. "I've been waiting to hear that for a long time."

"Really?" Sharon walked toward the closed door. She felt the pain of deciding to leave the best job anyone would ever dream of.

Exiting the door, walking back to her office, upheaving thoughts raged in her mind.

All because I think I'm falling in love with him, and I need to accept this. No going back now, no more denial.

Sharon needed to delete any memory of the stranger from her mind permanently.

Sharon's Plight

TWENTY

Back in her office, Sharon pondered. *I think I need a breather*, tapping her ball point pen on the desktop. *It's time to check my calendar and reschedule all my meetings.* She checked for a few minutes, still lost in her thoughts.

The image of George had become permanent plasterboard on the bricks of her heart. A knock on the door ripped her away from her fantasy.

"Yes, please come in!" she said distractedly.

Grace popped her head in. "Sharon, have been trying to reach your phones, is everything okay?"

"Yes, why do you ask?" answered Sharon back in reality.

"All your meetings for the rest of the week are cancelled. Mr Finland called the reception desk to find out what's happening."

"Sorry, George, I mean Grace! Where is George?"

"He's been out of the office all day, Sharon." Grace gazed puzzled at her.

"Any idea when he will be back? I didn't see any meeting on his calendar for today." Sharon stared at her screen.

"Exactly my point!" hitting her hand on the table to get Sharon's attention back to her. "How do you mean, Grace?"

"Sharon, did anything happen between you two this morning?" She gazed at Sharon in awkward curiosity.

"I don't understand your point. Kindly elaborate." denial written all over Sharon's face.

"Mr G. F walked out of the building as if the whole of the 9/11 Twin Tower was crushing on him today."

"Tell me more," Sharon trying to hide her smile from the delight of Grace's words.

"He asked me to cancel all his meetings for the next three days before walking out briskly."

"Did you ask him what happened?"

"Sharon, out of the blue, the old Mr G. F we knew sprung up. He looked destroyed. We all know you impacted his life's total outlook recently. You guys had been getting on so well, we all thought..."

"Thought what?" she sounded upbeat.

"Gossip circulating in the office is that George is getting sweet on you. Did you reject him this morning? You guys are so good together," Grace said, flapping her cheeks with her hands.

"Grace, I did not turn him down, as assumed. Neither did he ask me for anything."

"For real?" Grace's face lit up expectantly for more from Sharon.

"We were talking about meetings, cancellation, and phone calls," Sharon responded, deviating herself from the interesting topic of George.

"Yes, cancellations and phones. What happened?"

Grace waited for more info. "Coincidentally, I will take some time off in the next few days. Don't worry, I have all my meetings covered by my assistant. He is more than able to handle them."

"I can see clearly now. The rain is gone!" Grace exclaimed, babbling nonsense. Ignoring her, Sharon continued.

"As for my phones, I switched them off because I had to finish some important reports."

Walking away and holding the doorknob, Grace said, "The entire world knows what is happening except you. Hopefully, you would make Mr GF smile again."

"Thank you for your gracious thoughts," Sharon replied, concealing her inner turbulence.

Once Grace was out the door, Sharon turned her phone on.

Fighting off her tears, she pressed the button on the handle of her office phone to receive calls. The phone came reeling off text messages and missed calls, most of them from George.

She waited for some time and re-dialled his number.

"George, are you okay?" she reached out on his voicemail. "Grace was in my office a moment ago. I didn't mean to hurt you with my decisions. I thought it would make things easier. I accept I might have taken it too far."

Sharon continued, "I should have discussed with you first ..." George picked up his phone halfway through her sobering speech.

"Sharon, it's okay. I understand you meant well. I talked with my dad. He advised I take some days off."

"Did you tell him about us?" Sharon stated in panic, sitting upright.

He replied with his usual chuckle, "Do you want me to lose my job today?"

"Don't be funny, I am serious! Anyway, I am glad you still have your jokes," she said, relieved. "I have not hurt that aspect of you."

"Sharon, you didn't upset me. I couldn't bear the image of an office without you. It would be unbearable. The rest of the staff are so boring. You light up everywhere. You are..."

"George, what did you tell your dad?"

"I told him, I lied, we had a disagreement, that you wanted to resign."

"What! George, did he request for more details about the resignation?"

"I had to lie upon another lie. Sharon, I admit, I couldn't tell him about us without your consent."

"Thank you for thinking about me first. You are considerate."

"George, I will be away for a few days too. I need to cool off."

"I understand you, Sharon. I only wish I could hold your soft hands now and comfort you in my embrace."

"Well, it's a good thing you aren't standing in front of me right now, since we would be at the office!" Sharon retorted, refusing to melt under his tender words.

"Sharon, how many days are you taking? I need to let Dad know he will need to wait to have a meeting with you upon your return."

"Three days, I suppose, I might extend it. I have reassigned all my workload and made sure nothing is hanging."

"I trust your work ethics. It is impeccable," assented George.

"Remember, whatever you do Sharon, you have stolen my heart and there are no replacement parts for it."

"Meaning, George?"

"Sharon, you are the only one who can cure or replace what you have stolen."

Suddenly overwhelmed by emotion, she muttered, "I have to go now. I will speak to you soon, bye!!" dropping the phone before George could express more of his tenderness.

There was one thing she will not be lacking for the rest of her life. George's affectionate words were becoming springboard.

The next three days were the worst of her over two years in the United States. Sharon made sure she left her apartment without Informing George as to location. She didn't want him to connect with her, yet her heart longed for him.

Her calls to her parents honed things, their words providing the comfort she needed. Once the calls are over, the thoughts of George, his cracker jokes, the way he whispers into her ears filled her thoughts.

By the third day, George still had not left her mind as she took a walk along the beach. Her history with George followed her still. Sharon sat behind the rock where she had her surprise first date with him.

Watching as the waves crashed in and out like the pendulum of time. Her indecision swung before her very eyes. If only George knows how much he means to her.

She picked up her phone intermittently to glance through her pictures, each one telling a story. The picture of her and George, a piece of a puzzle, a puzzle she alone could solve. Sharon watched a passing young couple expressing the much-needed affection she craved for.

Not able to withstand the scene any longer, she walked back to her motel, shutting the door against the image.

Exhausted, she fell on the hard spring single bed. Sharon was helplessly deep in sleep when she discovered herself on the path of another nightmare, only this time, the stranger did not fade away, rather he smiled as George would.

Everything was the same as during her first encounter with the stranger, he was dressed in the same shirt and jeans as at the airport. Sharon approached him wearing her dazzling wedding gown.

Slowly, she drew close to him as a bride would to her groom, but oddly he was bidding her farewell, and mumbling: "We will meet again, soon."

Sharon stood smiling, although confused, but not perturbed like all her other dreams.

She woke up to the musical sound of her cell phone alarm. Speaking to the Saviour during her morning prayers, she felt comforted she would be safe in the hands of George.

But for how long? Sharon pondered, does the *"see you again soon"* mean anything?

The next day: Sharon drove straight to Graceoak Incorporation, expecting an answer to prayers. According to her plan, when Mr Finland accepts the resignation, she would go get another job in the city.

She hoped to open her heart about her feeling for George with no reservation. Walking into the much-adored building, she thought about how much she would miss working with the most favourite people in the entire world. Grace's face lit up with smiles against the sadness she felt.

"Morning Sharon, hope you had a restful time?" inquired Grace.

"Yes," affirmed Sharon. "I did. How has the office been? I have missed everyone."

"Does everyone include George?" teased Grace.

I will miss Grace's all-seeing eyes, Sharon thought.

"Talking about George," Sharon changed the subject. "Is he back from his break?" she asked in anticipation of a positive answer.

"Mrs Resource informed me he travelled to England a day after you were off, Sharon."

"Oh, really?" replied Sharon, pretending disinterest.

"Did he not tell you? There must be a serious crisis in paradise. We want you guys to sort out whatever is happening between you two." Grace flapped her hands dismissively.

"Why are all of you so interested?" Sharon questioning their unwanted nosiness.

"You want to know? We do not want the old George. Everyone wants to keep the new one. I bet that includes you!" Grace winked her eyes in presumption.

Instead of answering her, Sharon changed her line of discussion. "Is Mr Finland Sr. around?"

"Yes, I understand. I have a meeting with him this morning."

"I heard another rumour. Is it true you are resigning?"

"Where did you hear that rumour from, Grace?"

"Sharon, news travels fast around here. You are the only one ignorant. Even the wall speaks loudly."

Sharon was laughing at her facial expression but turned to leave, saying, "I don't have time for you this morning. I have a meeting and need to speak to the CEO."

Grace muttered under her breath, watching as Sharon walked towards the elevator, "You mean your soon-to-be father-in-law, dear girl?"

A few minutes later, Sharon was in front of the CEO's door. With a slight knock, she heard his deep masculine voice, much like George's, respond with a "Sharon, come in. We've been expecting you."

Sharon stepped in with an expectation of leaving his office without a job.

"Morning, Mr, and Mrs Finland, how are you?" The two seemed relaxed as they sat on the office couch hand in hand, acknowledging her.

"Take a seat," Cynthia responded. "We are good, as you can see, taking a day at a time."

"Thank you," Sharon sat with a sense of discomfort, trying to analyse their body language. *Nothing seems to be off,* she summarised.

Offering Sharon a drink to set her at ease, Mr Finland asked, "Do you want anything to drink? As you know, we have both hot and cold drinks."

"I would like a cup of coffee," standing up to make herself a cup.

"How did you spend your time off?" Mr Finland asked, sipping his drink.

"Restful, quieter than I planned, but it good," Sharon answered politely.

"I guess you had some time to think over things," Cynthia added.

Not sure how to reply to her question, Sharon walked back to her seat, agreeing, "I would assume so."

"We understand there was a breakdown in communication between George and yourself." Cynthia started and her husband continued, "We thought we should try to talk things through, rather than sweep everything under the carpet."

"All right," Sharon added, "Did George give you the details of what transpired between us?"

Cynthia, holding tight to her husband, replied. "Not at all. We decided not to dig further. He was unwilling to disclose his side of the story to us. Sharon, you must know that in all aspects, you have made a difference to our organisation. We all have seen the dramatic increase in the share price of this company before you joined and what it is today. We all have worked hard. However, your contribution to the company had been too enormous to overlook. Or throw away because of an undefined disagreement."

Sharon sat stunned and speechless; her mind focused on every word as Cynthia's husband took over the discussion.

"Sharon let's get things straight. We received your resignation, but putting on my CEO cap and recalling the very reason we offered you the job, we are refusing your resignation. I know you disagreed with your direct overseeing manager; however, we hired you into this organisation, not George. We are not ready to let go of your services for any reason."

All Sharon heard was "we..." then she heard, "refusing your resignation".

Sharon tried to comment, but Cynthia took over from her husband again.

"We sent George off to England to put things in place for our new business venture. We have been speaking with our clients, and we think it is time to expand our businesses. George will not be back until Christmas. With this arrangement, he will be nowhere near you or be a distraction to you. We felt the need to reduce any tension. Although initially, we felt you two were becoming friends. But five days ago, when he spoke to us, we knew the only option left was to take him out of the picture temporarily. Once he can get the business up and running, the cloud would have moved on. Don't you agree?"

"I agree," Sharon responded in disbelief at the way the Finlands had planned things.

Now that we all agree on this point, Mr Finland carried on, "We are offering you a new post in our organisation. You realise that George's position is vacant and needs a replacement.

Therefore, Sharon, we are offering you his position, which comes with a new pay grade and all other bonuses."

He picked up the letter in front of the coffee table and passed it over to her.

"Does, does George know anything about this?" gasped Sharon.

"George is not aware of our decision. Although he would have assumed we would not accept your resignation," the CEO firmly asserted.

"Considering the fact that you are offering me his position, how would he feel if he returns?" Sharon responded in dismay.

"Don't worry Sharon, there is always a position for George, even if it means cleaning."

"Cleaning!" Sharon exclaimed, at which the three burst into laughter at the impossibility.

"I thought I was the only one who heard wrong until you spoke too," Stroking her husband, Cynthia faced him for assent, "Be serious, my son will never be a cleaner!"

"If he continues to stress my staff, he might just end up as one," the CEO in Mr Finland replied, bending forward to kiss his wife.

Sharon watched as they expressed affection to each other. A flashback of George crossed her mind. *How could I even manage without George's stress? It has become a routine to work with that stress, though a break from him will be a test of what we think we have.*

Cynthia's voice brought her back to the present reality. "Did you hear us, Sharon?"

"I'm sorry! Would you repeat what you just said?" apologised Sharon.

"Do you still need to take some time off, Sharon?"

"No, I am back to work. Anymore holiday so soon will weary me."

They asked about her parents, how they planned to further expand the business and other roles she might take in her new position. The phone rang, ending the meeting.

Sharon returned to her office in a daze, clutching the envelope of documents describing her new position, and amazed at what had just happened to her.

What is happening? Is this directly related to my dream yesterday? George or the stranger said, "see you soon." A few hours later, I am informed of a promotion to a new post with an increased salary. George is out of the picture. How will George take this? Will his pride be hurt? What about our friendly, non-professional relationship? Sharon walked through her office door. She noticed with the new signage, Sharon O'Loan - **General Acquisitions Manager.**

TWENTY - ONE

That evening, Sharon got home exhausted, filled with mix feelings. On the one hand, she was glad about her promotion, on the other hand, how would she deal with George? Now that he had left without informing her, Sharon wasn't willing to make the first move to reconcile.

She stepped into her apartment building and found a delivery note saying that something had been left with her neighbour. Knocking on her neighbour's door, Sharon was handed a parcel and bundle of red flowers.

Back in her apartment, Sharon dropped the flowers on the kitchen counter and hurried to check the parcel with her heart beating fast, like a galloping horse.

The box contained a beautiful red dress, diamond accessories, and accompanying dazzling silver shoes. She searched through the box to find a small card which read...

"By the time you are reading this card. I guess you know it's me. Thank you for agreeing to stay. My heart's torn into two parts. Apologies, I couldn't tell you I am leaving. Can we do dinner tonight? On Zoom... in an hour. P/S: do you like your dinner clothes?"

Sharon giggled with glee at the memory of all the surprises George had carried out so far. This surprise was beyond her comprehension.

How did he know when I would arrive? Or when I will have dinner to make time on Zoom? I can't even believe I will have a romantic dinner over, Zoom!

Not wasting more time, she rushed to refresh herself, dressed up and set up her dinner table with her iPad ready for George's call.

She felt her heart pounding in a steady rhythm. *How I have missed him, Saviour, give me the strength for this phase of my journey.*

"Hello beautiful," his deep loving voice echoed the rhythmic skipping beat of her heart.

"Hi George, how are you?"

"Beautiful, you look ravishing! I wish I were with you right now, cuddling you!" gushed George.

"Oh, you sweet talker! Thank you for the gift. It's a lovely surprise. I could not expect any less of you, George! You are such a charmer."

"The same way you charmed my heart, dear girl," George on-screen revealed his amazing set of teeth grinning from ear to ear.

"So, Mr G. F, what are we having for dinner? I know you planned it already!"

"You know me too well," sighed George. "Before we start, can we talk?"

"Of course we can," relented Sharon. "What do you want to talk about?"

"How did you settle things with my parents? You know, they are not giving me any details."
Sharon laughed as his eyes shone out of the iPad screen, desperate for answers.

"George, I will give you all the details you want. Please, I need to eat. Do you mind?"

"Not at all. Your appetite is one thing I like about you," at the same time George took out his phone and sent a text.

"Sharon, do you mind waiting for five minutes?"

"Not at all," she agreed.

"Tell me, what were you up to during your days off? I imagine you reposting every moment we spent together in Asia."

Sharon smiled, making no comment, pressing her lips together.

After a brief pause, she replied. "I spent my time in reflection."

"I hope the reflection was about me?"

"Don't flatter yourself. George, what are you doing to me?" she spoke aloud blindly.

In a swift whisper, he replied, "I'm sorry I cannot hold your hands now, Sharon. I am trying all I can to make this work."

"Exactly my point. How will this relationship work?" words she uttered before her doorbell rang.

"Excuse me, someone's at the door." She stood up gracefully while from the screen George's eyes fixed on her every move. Still, she disappeared from his sight. She opened the door to see Peter.

"Hi Peter, it's been a while. I have not been to church in a few weeks now. Lots on my mind."

"I understand you are having dinner now, and I am on a mission to deliver your meal."

"Are you serious?" she screamed and ran back into her apartment.

"George! George! Did you organise this? Oh, my goodness! O, dear!!!"
Still enjoying the emotion he aroused in her, he replied.

"Do you love the surprise? Hey! You left Peter at the door, remember!?"

"Yes! Yes, yes," she replied, leaping back towards the door.

"Peter, how did you arrange this without my knowledge? I can't believe it!"

"I am glad you like it, Sharon. Remember, I told you, he could be the rare gem you waited for all your life."

"Thank you for your support," Sharon said as he handed over the basket to her.

"Do have a lovely dinner date with your Prince Charming," teased Peter.

"You can say that again, and I will tell you all about it, my friend!" assured Sharon.

"Can't wait!" he said, turning back to leave.

"Enjoy the ride, every day is different but beautiful."
She walked back into her apartment where the gallant George waited patiently for her.

"Hey, Beautiful! Do you like the surprise so far?"

"Like is an understatement." Sharon settled back on the seat and revealed the basket. They hard filled it with a pre-prepared three-course meal and a variety of drinks for her choice.

She gently set her table while George watched her. Breaking the silence, Sharon asked, "George, are you watching me eat alone?"

"That's the next part of the surprise," he hinted. Once Sharon was ready to eat, George stood up and set his table. It was time for Sharon to watch him patiently.

"You know this is crazy, a dinner date on zoom! George you are getting to be a real perfectionist..."

"Sharon, you are the impeccable one."
For the first time, Sharon seemed a sense of satisfaction with his compliments. Another brick had fallen from her wall of defences.

They enjoyed their meal together, exchanging jokes, and talked about the business and their parents. She informed him about her new position and, amazingly, George was not perturbed.

He seemed content with the arrangement. George confessed he preferred travelling and expanding the business rather than work within the building.

They agreed they could use their strengths to expand the business. Though he was not physically with her, it was the best evening in a while.

George made her feel so special. She prayed in her heart she could return the affections he had showered on her.

Sharon stepped into her car, heading for work, when her phone beeped musically.

It's George! I am yet to recover from yesterday, she thought, glowing with happiness.

"Rise and shine, beautiful!" His text read.

"Hi, cold and windy, handsome!" She replied. Seconds later, her phone rang.

"Beauty of my heart, I got an upgrade!" They shared a laugh until she asked.

"What upgrade?" she questioned. George called in reply.

"Did I hear you call me 'handsome'? Glad about that," he added.

"Don't flatter yourself. Did you sleep well?"

"I have yet to close my eyes. Couldn't get you off my mind."

"Really? That's good, George, I have hope!! Hope the weather is not too crazy for you?"

"If you lived here, I could have you as my source of strength."

"George, I am running late to my first official day at work in my new role."

"A question for you?" He was drawing her attention to every word he spoke.

"Listening, my handsome George."

"What plans do you have after work today?" inquired George.

"Thank goodness, you asked. I was thinking you had me all planned out."

"Remember, you are running late," he cautioned her.

"I plan to, to..." he interrupted her saying:

"I see. My friends will pick you up for dinner. They aspire to be in your company. Hope you don't mind?"

"Oh wow, George! Do you think that's an idea?"

"I can't help if my friends are urging, they want to spend time with you. If you are not feeling up to it, I will cancel it all."

After a long pause, she asked. "With their girlfriends? Or guys alone?"

"Don't worry, I will not plan to leave you alone with my male friends." With a chuckle, George laughed heartily.

Driving off, Sharon continued the conversation on her Bluetooth car phone.

"You are not comfortable about this?"

"Oh, I am comfortable. I just feel sorry for them," confessed George.

Both broke out laughing until Sharon stopped to ask, "Why?"

"You are too respectable for some of them. They are in awe of you. They are still trying to understand the Saviour like the old me."

"We will take it a day at a time with them."

"That's what I am saying! The same way you have shown the difference to me, the way you lived before meeting me. They have to see the difference in the way we live and relate to each other now."

"Whoa, George, this is coming from you? Thank you, I appreciate your sincerity.

"What's the plan?"

"My friends will pick you from the office at about 3.00 pm. I planned out the rest of the day. I am hoping you will enjoy every moment."

"I will miss you..." she said wistfully.

Can't you just tell him how you feel, rather than chicken out? You can't run away. Don't you think he knows you are in love with him already?

"Are you there? Is everything okay?" George's questions suddenly brought her back to reality.

"I'm okay, George. I was just distracted."

"I'll leave you to drive safely then and let me know how your day goes, Sharon. I'll check on you as often as possible."

"As support or distraction?" she teased playfully.

"Both, I know you love it," and George expressed longing, "I am missing you so much, beautiful."

"You need to tell me why you call me beautiful, Georgie."

"I will, by and by, meanwhile, speak to you soon, Love." He started blowing kissing sounds over the Bluetooth!

The evening went better than she could imagine. Sharon got home, narrating the events of the day with her parents and then Tom.

She later called Peter to thank him for delivering the surprise dinner. They all encouraged her to enjoy the journey and keep her eyes focused on the Saviour's promises.

Turning in for the night, her phone beeped with a text. She knew it was from George.

"Hey, beautiful!" George texted. "I met someone who knew you today in a client's office." Sharon dialled his number to talk in a never wink.

"Tell me more, George. Who, where, handsome?"

"You don't want to know."

"Did you do something terrible today, Georgie?" demanded Sharon impatiently.

"I was in a meeting with a client and his partner. In the course of our discussions, rather than call her name, I called your name and on three different occasions."

"What! How did you manage that?" she raised in a loud voice.

"Funny you say that. It shows how much you have turned my world upside-down, Sharon."

"I had to open about you and at the mention of your name, the client called out, "I know Sharon O'Loan, we were in university together! It's a small world."

They discussed Sharon's friend she knew during their undergraduate days and how he took the client out to dinner to find out more about Sharon. He was eager learning about the news of her consistency and forthrightness over the years. After about two hours of talking, Sharon slept after continual yawning.

A month went to another. It appeared as if George had never left. His constant dates and surprises were a glee Sharon looked forward to.

George would stop at nothing to show how much she meant to him and his longing to be with her at any cost.

In the first week of December, Sharon had a discussion with George about visiting her parents for the holiday. She only wished she would be around when he visited his parents for Christmas.

George remained silent and only replied, "We will figure it out."

After a day of pouring rain, she discussed her plans with Mrs Finland, and she agreed on a condition Sharon must leave after the company's Christmas party.

However, Sharon was disappointed, because it only meant that she would leave for the UK at the same time George might return to the US. Sharon didn't want to disappoint George's longing to see her, so she refused to discuss her concern with George's mum. The next day, she got a text from him scolding her.

"When are you going to tell me what my mum told you? Are you beginning to hide things from me?"

"George, I am waiting for the right time. I am trying to figure out how we manage our first holiday apart."

"I am sorry for being too forward. Sharon. Don't let my mum overwhelm you with an obligation to the company. You need to think of all the parties involved, of course!"

"George, remember there is a possibility she's going to be in my future. The earlier I learn to work with her, the better for our relationship."

"How did I get so lucky? You are so wise!" He exclaimed with a sigh. "You are a better person."

Several weeks went by, and in no time the Christmas party came. Sharon was busy with the event planners at the Finlands' house for the party.

She was making all the final arrangements for the evening when she felt a light tap on her shoulder. She turned around, and it was George. Sharon dropped all she had in her hands and fell into his embrace. Uncontrollable tears of joy streamed down her cheeks.

"Hey, Beautiful, why are you crying?"

"Nothing, nothing." Cleaning her face, pretending nothing happened. The ladies with her excused themselves so they could have some time together.

"How did you manage it? You still have client meetings planned till few days to Christmas? Did you cancel all your meetings?"

"Sharon, can you please leave work for a few moments? I need a drink."

"The party is in the next few hours. I will meet you in the lounge so we can talk. Kindly give me a few minutes."

"Few minutes it is" pulling her hands against his chest affectionately, he planted a kiss on her lips.

The party ended with Sharon and George talking over drinks with his parents. Mrs Finland was once more filled with admiration for Sharon's organisational skills.

Cynthia was glad to see her son, even though he had appeared unannounced. Sharon sensed Cynthia knew something was going on between George and herself.

She refused to show any form of affection for George in front of her. Throughout the evening, she deliberately spoke to him with sarcasm, and George graciously played along.

The Finlands' soon complain about their disagreements, encouraging them to remember the ethos of their business to treat every one of their employees as family.

George's mum made it mandatory that George drive Sharon home to improve their relationship.

To both, it was the best part of the evening. George drove with one hand on the steering with the other holding onto her as if she would vanish from the car.

Though they drove in silence, there was a lot of discussion going on in their minds. Sharon couldn't get the image of George's first kiss away from her mind.

It came unexpectedly. He is coming stronger at me each day, and at least ten bricks of my defences fell off the wall with a single kiss. He sure knows how to get a woman to lose her mind in an instant.

She ruminated and smiled with a flush of tension, beads of sweat forming on her forehead and palms.

Clearing his throat, he informed her, "You are a successful con-artist."

"Me! Con artist? Don't accuse me falsely, George. Do you want me to continue from where I stopped in your parents' house?"

"That's my point! Why do you do it? You created a front before them as though nothing is happening between us."

"Did you not play along as assistant con-artist?" Stroking her hands on his cheeks.

"How long are we going to do this, Sharon? Don't you think they would have heard all the rumours from the office?"

"I know, George, but would they have proven any of the suspicions tonight?"

"Not a chance," he replied. "You know your job is safe now and you have my heart. My question is, what are you waiting for?"

"What do you mean?" she asked him as he parked in front of her apartment.

"Sharon, stop playing games. You know what I mean. When will you give your heart to me?"

"I don't understand." she looked away, pretending not to get his point.

"It's been over a year and a half. You have never expressed your feeling nor mentioned or tell me you love me," gazing away, George continued.

"Don't you know you can tell me! let me know? I am in love with you, Sharon, and have loved with you from the first day I set my eyes on you."

Sharon's racing heartbeat shouted. *Same here! I am dealing with you and the stranger's shadows. I have to deal with this alone.*

Sharon looked away into the night and, after a long silence, muttered.

"George, I am honoured you love me. But I cannot talk about this tonight. My toes are hurting, and I need my bed." She answered abruptly, avoiding his questions.

"You need the rest, Sharon. I hope you are taking the day off tomorrow."

"It's Saturday, and I am leaving for the UK tomorrow evening, George. Have you forgotten?"
She secretly hoped George would head back to the UK with her. It could only be his choice and on his terms. George reached into his pocket and brought out a present.

"I waited all evening to do this. I got this for you." She opened the package to a set of diamond jewellery.

"You got this for me? Are you serious?" she shouted, throwing her hands around him. "You did this for me?"

"Do you remember before I moved to England? I suggested I would like to meet your folks. I figured out we might not..."

Interrupting him, she said, "So, you bought me more gifts instead."

"*What better way to get your mind off things, right*?" he told himself, pressing his lips together as though he were hiding something. "I only wish I could meet them during the Christmas holiday."

"Whoa, me too! But this is the best of all the surprises! George, you are adorable." She gave him a surprise peck on the cheek kiss.

"Thank you. It's my glee to make you happy all the days of my life. Hope there's an extra room in your dad's house..." Clearing his throat, he added... "when I will visit."

"Funny! You would find out in the morning. Night handsome!" she called out, stepping from his car.

George rushed out of his car to walk her to her door. "Can I come in for a drink, my love?"

"What, and watch me sleep, George?"

"You don't know how long I have longed for that. I would love to do it for the rest of my life."

Gazing into her eyes, he lifted her hands and placed an enduring kiss on Sharon. Instantly. he moved to kiss her forehead, and then her lips. Reluctantly, she moved to push away.

"George, have a restful night." She turned her yearning flesh further away from him and opened the door. Without looking back, Sharon quickly shut the door.

Taking a deep breath, a stunned George in love froze, waiting in vain for a more affectionate moment with her.

In her apartment, Sharon ran over to the window and felt a drag towards him. In a moment of unrestrained freedom, she rushed forward, opened the door, threw herself at him, and returned the kiss he had so longed for.

Embarrassed by her show of vulnerability, she whispered, "That's for the past one and a half years of goodnights."

George watched her with his lips pressed, fixed together, trying to recover from the surprise gesture of intimacy.

A few minutes later, Sharon watched through the window as he drove away, flinging his fist in the air, yelling, "Finally!"

TWENTY - TWO

The next day an Uber driver parked in front of her house at 3.00 pm in the heavy rain. George stepped out with a giant umbrella and ran up the porch to press the bell.

"Yes, give me a minute," she called out. Sharon zipped her luggage and walked to the door.

Sharon opened the door and, with a surprise, yelled, "What are you doing here, George? A surprise trip to the airport, I suppose."

"Beautiful, at least. Would you ask me in?"

"Of course! Pardon my rudeness, oh handsome one!!"

"Thank you," George walked in, folding up his umbrella, as he continued, "Are you ready for the airport?"

"Kind of! My flight is 6.30 am."

"I know, you told me." He looked away.

"George, come on, what's on your mind? You look absent or mischievous."

"Nothing!" he kept staring at her TV.

"George, I am sorry things are not working so well. You are back here and at the same time I am leaving for the UK on a holiday."

"I am sorry too, but yesterday, I hoped..." George interjected.

"We need to leave now, or I will be late. We will always have time to talk during the drive."

"Definitely," agreed George, as Sharon handed over her luggage to him. Avoiding eye contact, he headed to the door.

"It's still raining, Sharon. I will put your bags in the trunk and get back to get you. We have to share an umbrella."

With a puzzled glance, she replied, "Sure." *What in the world is wrong with him? For the first time, I gave him a glimpse of my affection yesterday, and today he is cold. Saviour, you need to help me out here.*

Sharon walked around the apartment to make sure she had left nothing behind.

A few moments later, he popped his head in. "Am back, shall we?"

"Sure," Sharon said pretending, his awkward attitude did not bother her.

Sharon followed him, feeling like a lamb being led to the slaughter. As usual, he opened the passenger door for her to get in before getting in the driver's side.

"George, why an Uber?" She questioned him pointy.

"We need to talk. Is everything okay?" She continued sharply.

"Hey, hey, take it easy, beautiful. Nothing is wrong. I didn't feel like driving today." He sighed.

"Can we go now?" George touched the front seat, informing the driver to start the journey.

The journey to the airport was weird and uncomfortable. However, as a reassurance, George held her hands in his. Every so often, he lifted her hands and planted kisses.

Although comforting, Sharon could imagine the next surprise he had for her.

Is this how I would be in an emotional shuttle with George all my life if I say yes to him?

She stared outside the window, avoiding looking at him, even though she loved the feel of his touch on her hands.

Once at the airport, George paid the driver and rushed to open Sharon's door. He opened the umbrella for her and suggested she walk ahead of him. He decided he would join her with the luggage.

Sharon was in the boarding queue when someone tapped her shoulder. It was George with additional luggage apart from the one she packed herself.

"Are you planning to send my luggage to the UK and use me as a courier for this bag? These days nothing would be a surprise to me," she quizzed frustratingly.

George pulled out his wallet, drew out a ticket, handing it over to her. Sharon looked and once again, she fell for his trap. Blindly, she threw herself on him.

"Seriously! Are you on the same flight with me!? You are so mean! You should have told me! You got me worried with a zillion thought."

George, taking in all her excitement, held her close and whispered.

"This is the part I am always looking forward to, beautiful."

"Which part, George? You..."

"Your perplexed face, for one."

"How and why? Now I understand why you asked if there was an extra room in my parent's house!" She hit his chest with her tender hands.

"Have you forgotten we are outside, and we need to check-in? We lost our spot already."

George held her close, planting a kiss on her forehead and leading her through the departure lounge towards the check-in counter with, "We do have the entire trip to talk."

"Now I understand, the Uber, George, you are such..."

"The best thing that ever happened to you, Sharon!"

"Sure! You are right," she agreed, dragging him into the line.

For this particular flight, Sharon couldn't dream of any better company. A stranger in the form of 'George'.

A renewed man, a different man who had become a friend. George made this journey memorable with his funny rib-cracking jokes. He is the best thing that had happened to me in Houston.

Now he is coming over to meet my family at last. How will my parents react to him? I hope there would be no extended family surprise visit this Christmas. He seemed not bothered as I am.

Sharon leaned on his chest as she dozed off in comfort of his presence.

Tom was already waiting at the Heathrow Airport to receive her as requested, became surprised at the sight of George.

First, Tom embraced his most favourite friend on earth with a fatherly observation, "You are all grown, Sharon."

"You can't be serious, Tom. I've grown since I left Mum and Dad."

"I know, honey, but today is with a difference,"

"Ha, Ha! Big brother." Tom, the big brother she never had.

"Sharon, who do we have here?" Tom asked, stretching his hands to greet George.

"My bad, Tom, this is George. George, this is Tom." Shaking each other by the hand, George greeted Tom.

"You must be Tom. I have heard so much about you."

"The same, I must confess. I hope it is all excellent reports?" Tom asked, still in a handshake with George.

"Can we go now!? You guys have a lot of time to catch up with each other." She pulled Tom's hands away from George, leading him to the car park.

"Hey, you changed your car, Tom, you never told me."

"Sharon, you have been so busy with work, and George nowadays, we rarely talk, remember?"

"Don't tell me you are jealous," she reached out and held George's hands.

George looked on as Sharon and Tom exchanged a beautiful interaction as friends, thinking, *Sharon is a rare gem. It seems like everyone that knows her gets a bit of the goodness that comes from her. I would give up the entire world to have her.*

They got into the car for another two hours' journey until they drove into Oxford suburbia. The traffic was horrendous. Sharon had forgotten how hard it was to drive back to Oxford through rush hours.

"Here we are." Tom parked his car in front of the home of the older O'Loans.

Sharon hurried out of the car and rushed toward her mum and dad, who were already walking forward to welcome her back.

"Mum, Dad, your only baby is back for Christmas!!"
They held each other in a warm embrace. Since after her dad's return from the hospital, she had not spent enough time with him. Sharon was looking forward to this special time with them. They were in the arms of each other until Tom cleared his throat.

"Mr and Mrs O'Loan, evening. I came to deliver your special package."

"Thank you, Tom, you can say that again. Special package well received," Mr O'loan replied, still hugging his princess.

"And who is this gentleman?" Mrs O'Loan asked, as though she had never seen George's picture before.

"Mum, Dad, this is George. George, this is Mr and Mrs O'Loan, my lovely parents."

"Evening, Mr, and Mrs O'Loan," George politely stretching out his hands to greet them.

"You are welcome to our home. Kindly come in, it's freezing out here." Mrs O'Loan stated.

"Of course," echoed everyone as they walked into the warm Christmas decorated home.

George stood quietly as he observed the sweet rapport between Sharon, Tom, and her parents.

I now believe it for myself. The apple does not fall far away from the tree. I see Sharon gets her beauty from her mother. George looked around the room decorated with amazing African art and pictures of her family.

"Tom, George, what would you each like a drink?" Sharon's mother asked if she could make some hot drinks for them.

"I have to leave now. My family awaits me for dinner. I can't be absent from it." explained Tom, excusing himself.

"We understand. We appreciate your picking up our princess," Mr O'Loan replied lovingly, stroking his daughter's cheeks as she sat on the sofa beside him.

"George, what would you like? Although dinner is almost ready, we have coffee and Sharon's special Christmas cookies."

"I would very much love that. Thank you, Mr O'Loan."

"It was nice meeting you, George," Tom shook him again. "We will plan a visit to our house if you have time."

"I am sure we could."

"Tom, thank you. I will bring George over some time and thank you again." She hugged Tom as she led him to the door.

"Mr and Mrs O'Loan, I will visit again."

"Thank you, Tom," they all echoed as Sharon and George walked Tom out to his car.

After taking refreshment, Sharon led George to his room for a change before they served dinner. Dinner was a combination of Nigerian and English cuisine.

George enjoyed the meal, expressing contentment with the taste of the food repeatedly. Sharon and her mum cleaned up the dishes and whispered about George and the surprise ticket at the airport.

The two ladies excused themselves to spend some time together chatting in Sharon's room.

Similarly, her dad and George headed to the sitting room, where they chatted about business, sports and ended up talking about the Saviour.

Mr O'Loan began yawning, showing him his need to rest. He excused himself, calling out to Sharon to spend some time with George; after providing her with a fatherly kiss of a night.

"Tell me George, wouldn't Mr and Mrs Finland miss their favourite son not spending Christmas with them?" Sharon asked, placing her tender hand on his cheek.

George removed her hand, planted a kiss on it and recited, "It is written, for a man shall leave his father and mother alone and..."

"Please, don't screw with the Saviour's words, Georgie!"

"Or rather, I'm about doing my father's business." Laughing aloud, Sharon quizzed him. "Which of your fathers, heavenly or earthly?"

"Both, my love, both. I am spending my days recklessly pursuing this beautiful gem until she is mine."

George looked upward as if praying. "And then what, my handsome George?" Sharon quizzed.

"Hmm..., I will treasure her for the rest of my days on earth! Sharon, you are so like your parents, lovely and soft-spoken and accommodating. Your Dad is so down to earth compared to Mr Finland."

"I take exception to that. Your dad is a successful man, George, and I respect him, especially his trust in me."

"I bet you do. They can throw me off the bus to replace me with you. I am glad I am in love with you, else I would have been jealous."

Both talked into the night about Sharon's childhood, family, and her past relationships before she started yawning herself.

She called it a night and walked George to his room.

Holding her hands and drawing her close, he whispered, "I want to watch you sleep. You will look so adorable."

"I know!" Sharon fell helplessly into his embrace, as he gave her a light kiss before whining that, "Sweet dreams, about only me."

"Only you!" George replied, closing the door behind him, and leaning against it, holding his breath to exert some self-control.

TWENTY - THREE

The next day was Christmas Eve. Sharon had a long list of things to do before Christmas, the biggest being how she would fit George into her plans.

At 5.30 am she stepped out of her room for a morning jog when she met George waiting for her, ready for a run.

"Oh, morning George, you are already awake?"

"I should ask you!! I know you need rest too, Lovely One!"

"Are you planning to go out, Mr Finland?"

"I made plans, Sharon. You know you are not the only one who makes plans."

"Tell me about them," she asked him curiously.

"You know this is my home, right?" Looking at him, she continued, "You either asked my parents, or you have been here before and know the layout of my house."

"I'll take the former," George replied, defeated.

"Oh, I see. You asked my Pops yesterday before he went to bed."

She walked towards the door. Pulling her back to lean against his chest, George whispered into her ear, "How did I get so lucky to have this smart girl to myself?"

"Who says I am yours? I can't see any ring on my finger." She extended her left hand with bare fingers, pointing towards him.

"My hearts tell me you are mine. I dreamt about you yesterday! Did you dream about me?" asked George, trying to deflect her line of questioning.

"Talking about dreams, I should start jogging or I will dream on the rest of the day."

Changing the topic, she released herself from his tender grip. Sharon turned around, opened the door, and stepped out, while George stood looking at her, puzzled.

"George, are you coming or not? I will like your company if you don't mind."

"I do mind, Sharon! I only jog with people that dream about me."

"For me, that would be a nightmare, then. Let's go. George, we have a lot to do today."

"Tell me, my assistant has planned my entire day for me!" He said, stepping out grumbling.

"It's not that bad. I am a brilliant assistant to George Finland, am I not?"

"Talking about assistant, I need to be in London in a few hours to see a client, so do you want to go with me, Sharon?"

"It's Christmas Eve, and it was not part of my holiday plans. I planned to visit the Toms and my girlfriends."

"Sharon, please! You are still here till after Christmas. You can still chase up with family and friends. Remember, I hinted at you on the plane, I would like to spend New Year with my parents and head back to the UK in the New Year."

Sharon stopped and stared at him confused, "George, are we boring you already? Why can't you spend the holiday with us?"

George, with sweat all over his brow, held her hands around him. "Sharon, every moment I spend with you is precious. I would love to spend each second with you, but..."

"But what, George?"

"Sharon, do you love me?" George gazed hopelessly into her eyes in the mist morning light.

Ignoring George's pleading, Sharon reminded him, "You know what? We should head back. It's about two hours to London and I don't think you aspire to be late for your meeting."

"Can we talk?" determined, George led her towards the bench ahead of them.

"Look, I can postpone till next year. I only wanted to spend time alone with you outside this village."

"Oh, really?" Sharon yelled, "So, you don't have a meeting?"

"I do have a meeting and I want you to go with me?" George pleaded.

"I need to know how you feel about me!" Sharon looked away from him, but George continued.

"For the past two years, I have loved you, cared for and pampered you. But I still don't know..."

Rather than saying a word to comfort his weary heart, Sharon drew him to herself and kissed him as she had always dreamt of kissing the stranger.

She thought, *I rather get this ghost off my chest. It's been too long. The stranger might never exist.*

To George, her kiss was the most passionate of any woman he had ever been with. Her tenderness broke down every wall of doubts in his mind.

He knew with no qualm; Sharon was his forever. She had finally found her way back to his heart.

Moments after the passionate kiss, Sharon felt a sudden mix of insecurity and vulnerability.

Sensing her sudden shame and the goose pimples on her skin, George swept her into his embrace once more. He wanted the moment to last forever.

"I have found my home," Sharon whispered under her breath.

"I have waited for this moment forever, Sharon," he whispered. "You had my heart, and you have it forever, my Angel, my Beloved, and my Beautiful. Even in my bouts of anger, you still loved me. I can't ask for more."

In the tranquil embrace, she soaked in every word until her dad approached them.

"Here you are, Sharon and George. We were wondering if you guys have missed your way." Suddenly detaching from George's warm embrace.

"Morning Dad, where is Mum? Guess she is still sleeping. I know she likes her beauty sleep."

"Don't you both love your beauty sleep? Besides, are you okay here?"

"Yes, Mr O'Loan, we took a rest to spend some quiet time together," answered George. "

Yes, course, I can see how the time together will mean to my princess. Take care of her."

"By all means, Mr O'Loan, she is in excellent hands. We should be on our way. We have a long day."

George took hold of Sharon's hands as he held her up to jog back home.

"Breakfast is ready," Mum announced as they opened the door, walking in hand in hand.

"Morning Mum," Sharon cheerfully greeted her mother, though still overwhelmed by the emotionally draining experience of George.

"Morning, Mrs O'Loan,"

"Morning, George. Hope you both enjoyed your time together?"

"We did," they both echoed, looking into each other eyes.

Offering them coffee, Mrs O'loan added, "Do you want to freshen up first, or eat first?"

"Mum, I am eating first. I need to fill my tummy." Sharon took the mugs from her mum to enjoy breakfast.

Mrs O'Loan continued pleasantly, "So, what plans do you guys have today? I bet Tom's kids can't wait to see you. Moreover..."

"Mum, I wanted to ask. I hope we are not having a large party tomorrow. I would prefer something quiet. The four of us will be perfect."

"Did you put her up to this?" Sharon's mum turned to question George.

"It wasn't me!" he protested. "She is on her own on this one."

"Really!!" Sharon replied, hitting him tenderly. "You couldn't bear the blame!"

"Miss O'Loan, not this time!!" he burst out laughing with Mrs O'Loan leading.
Sharon felt left out of the mirth-filled moment.

"Is this the way it's going to be, George? It good I know where I belong now." She looked really crestfallen.
He reached out to hold her hand and placed a kiss on it.

"Sharon, you always belong in my heart and nowhere else."

"You both will have to excuse me. I need to start my day." Mrs O'Loan excused herself to allow the lovers some space.

The two lovebirds took a trip from Oxford back to London on the coach. She held onto George's hands and every word he spoke as though her life depended on him.

George resolved not to take lightly Sharon's expressions of affection towards him.

After two years, George had realised Sharon's a lady of few words. Her actions often spoke louder than her words. He only wished she could be more expressive of her heart towards him.

She spoke softly after their unexpected encounter that morning. George's next goal was to protect her heart, which she had handed over to his safekeeping.

He realised he would have to secure his position in her heart. It had to be as soon as possible.

George's meeting with his client lasted about thirty minutes. Afterwards, they spent the rest of the day together, doing some Christmas shopping for the family.

They wrapped all the gifts they purchased in the shops to reduce time. On one occasion, George randomly excused himself to get something special for his mummy. He returned with a beaming smile, as though he had won a trophy.

"Where on earth did you disappear to?" she whispered as if to someone who was a missing treasure just found.

"I am sorry, Beautiful, I got..." George replied, holding up the bags of shopping.

"How are we going to manage all these? George, don't you think it would be an idea to drop by Tom's house first and drop off their gifts?"

"Yes, but what is the guarantee they will be at home?"

"A call to them should sort that out." Sharon retrieved the phone from her bag to call. After several attempts to call with no response, she gave up.

"I guessed as much, Beautiful. We can take a taxi home from the train. We will take all the gifts home to your mum and dad, then freshen up and visit them at night. What about that as a plan?"

"Aye, aye, Captain George!!" Sharon saluted his suggestion with a smiled.

"I will call for a taxi at once." George echoed, planting a kiss on her forehead.

"We have much to carry," she called back. They were having a coffee break in front of a nearby Starbucks, when 30 minutes later, a taxi arrived to take them home.

I wish he was not returning to the US immediately after Christmas. Now that I have opened the windows of my heart to him, the last thing I want is to be apart. I struggled with my defences for two years and finally gave up. I love George; I pray the stranger was an image of George to come. Giving my heart to him means no going back.

Sharon reflected, as she rested her head on George's strong shoulder. Meanwhile, George held her in a warm embrace from the winter cold.

TWENTY – FOUR

"Morning, Princess," Sharon turned her head to gaze at her mum.

"Merry Christmas, Mum!" Sharon sat up in the bed.

"Breakfast is ready, Love!"

"Thank you, Mum, you spoil me! Is George awake?"

Laughing aloud, her mother replied, "I think the question should be, has George finished his breakfast? I like that he has a successful appetite, like you."

"You can say that again." Sharon echoed her mother's sentiments. "I will finish freshen up and get dressed in 10 minutes."

"Sharon, take your time, self-preservation, remember what I taught you!"

"You are the best Mum," Sharon got out of bed to hug her mum.

With her warm embrace, Mrs O'Loan kissed Sharon's forehead and said, "Don't keep the young man waiting."

"Mr O'Loan is getting himself a new son," Sharon replied, teasing her mum.

"He's glad there is another man in the family, since he's waited patiently for this long." Mrs O'Loan whispered as she opened the door and left Sharon to get ready.

Thirty minutes later, Sharon sat on the kitchen island with more food, wondering where everyone was.

With every piece of blueberry pancake she ate, images of living with George scrolled through her mind, in which both were running around the house having fun. Yesterday, she couldn't believe it. *Saviour, thank you for leading me this far.*

"Hey, beautiful, you finally woke up," George exclaimed.

Her parents and George walked into the kitchen as doors. swung behind them. He immediately held her in a close embrace, stroking her cheeks and neck.

"Missed you, Love, but I've been spending quality time with your Mum and Dad."

"Morning, Mr GF. I couldn't stop dreaming about you, the reason for my late morning." She teased.

Turning to her dad, Sharon greeted.

"Morning, Mr O'Loan, I can see you're keeping our guest occupied in my absence."

"Morning, my princess, you can imagine! Hope you had a restful night."

"I did. I am trying to catch up with breakfast. Mum, Dad, when do we start cooking Christmas dinner?" Sharon asked with a show of innocence.

All laughing together, they teased, allowing her breakfast to digest before starting the next meal.

"We will go for a short walk to allow you guys sometime together," announced Mr O'Loan.

"But we love your company, Dad!!" Sharon protested.

Her dad held his wife's hands. "Mrs O'Loan, we need each other's company, right?" kissing her cheeks.

"Right." she sensed her husband wanted the lovers to have some privacy.

"You have lovely folks; I couldn't ask for more!" George announced as the O'Loans stepped out.

"Hmm... I see where you get all your..." observed George.

"George, are you going to leave tomorrow? Can't you spend a few days more?"

"Let's say we enjoy today together and see how things go tomorrow, Sharon."

"Okay," she reluctantly agreed, with no small amount of dissatisfaction.

"Sharon, The Saviour's words comforted me this morning."

"Tell me more, George. I am so happy to hear that." George related the comfort he got from the amazing story that the Saviour had come into the world. Then how George was saved through the help of a beautiful soul called Sharon.
She watched as he created a love story starting with the Saviour and leading to himself and Sharon.

It was the first time she experienced him speaking this way. She knew the business side of George. She had experienced the romantic part of him, but the spiritual was a pleasant surprise.

As he dropped his last words, she turned around and held him in a sweet embrace.

"Thank you for letting me see another reason for Christmas, to bring His sons and daughters closer to Him."

She briefly imagined George at a pulpit talking about the Saviour's love.

"Yes, to unite this son and this daughter." George kissed the top of her head, holding her close to his heart.

Suddenly, they heard the doorbell. "It's Christmas Day. Are my parents expecting any visitors?"

Staring blankly, George replied, "I don't know. I should be asking you." Sharon released herself from his embrace.

Walking off, she called out, "You know, George?"

"Yes," he replied.

"We forgot all about Toms' gifts here under the Christmas tree and we have opened none ourselves."

"We still have the entire day, my heart!"
Upon opening the door, it shocked Sharon to see the whole of Tom's family.

"Hello, family! I can't believe you would all come over today."
Tom's two girls rushed towards her.

"Sharon, Sharon, we missed you. We got Christmas presents for you and Grandma and Grandpa."

"You girls are so sweet. I couldn't ask for anything less." Holding them close, she continued, "I got you something, too. Come in."

"We couldn't imagine you not visiting since we arrived two days ago," quietly muttered Tom walking into the house.

"Dear, did I just hear a hint of jealousy in his tone?" Tom's wife asked, looking back at him.

"You can say that again," Tom replied, handing the baby over to Sharon.

"Hello, my cutest boy in the entire world," she kissed the baby,

"I have not met you. My name is Sharon. I have waited for so long to see you."

As the family entered the warm house, she shut the door and turned to settle everyone in.

The girls were shouting, running around, getting acquainted with George. Sharon was trying to get some refreshments out for the guests when her parents walked in.

"Mum! Look who we have here!!"
Tom and his wife walked over to exchange greetings with the O'Loans and everyone settled to talk.

The males formed the usual group to converse, while the women walked towards the kitchen.

"We have to start dinner," her mother announced.

"I have done a lot of preparation yesterday, so things should be fast."

"Mummy, I hope there are no more surprise visitor."

But as Sharon uttered the words, the doorbell rang.

Tom opened the door to greet her aunt and her family.

"Mummy!" Sharon exclaimed. "I was hoping for a special day with you."

Her mother reassured her. "Princess, it's Christmas. It is better celebrated with a large family."

She embraced her sister, who ushered in several dishes of food along with all her family.

"Sharon, wouldn't you introduce me to George?" announced Sharon's aunt in her strong Nigerian accent.

"The last time we met was at your MBA party, and two years after..." Sharon interrupted her.

"George, this is my aunt and her husband, Bola, and Niyi. They are two of my favourite people on earth."

"It's a great to meet you," George replied with warm handshakes and then hugs.

The rest of the aunt's family came over to greet him while they placed more gifts under the Christmas tree.

The entire house remained in an uproar for the rest of the day. Even though Sharon was enjoying the vast company, she longed for a restful time with her nuclear family.

George is leaving tomorrow, and my head has not dealt with that yet, she thought amid the noise.

More members of her extended family on both sides joined in the Christmas celebration, including her grandparents. But Sharon sensed something was up.

After dinner, the men cleaned up the dishes, while the women sat talking over coffee. The kids were getting tired when Mrs O'Loan announced it was Christmas present time.

Each member of the family took a turn to open their gifts from the kids to adults, everyone by age.

However, when it was George and Sharon, they excused them because they were the Christmas hosts and should be last.

At last, all that remained were gifts from all the family for Sharon and George to open interchangeably. Until suddenly, George handed over the last gigantic box to her.

"Whoa, you left the biggest till the end. When you bought this yesterday, I thought it was for Tom's kids."

"Beautiful, could you kindly unwrap your gift?" George replied patiently, while the extended family remained silent, looking in awe.

She unwrapped the first box. Inside was another small box. Sharon continued to unwrap into the eighth box to find the last smallest box. George was on his knees when Sharon lifted her eyes.

"Sharon, Beautiful, in the presence of your family, today I am requesting a joining of my life with yours. I have loved you from the first day I set my eyes on you. You stole my heart, and I don't want you to return it to me. I offer this ring as a promise to keep your heart forever in the love of our Saviour, if you would be my wife."

Sharon, completely surprised, looked all over the room filled with her loved ones. Each one nodded with excitement, awaiting her positive response.

During the long pause, the kids started shouting.

"Sharon, say yes! Say yes!!!

"My knees are killing me," George whispered as a plea.

It was yesterday I expressed my feelings for him, though I had hidden it away all this while. I love him. I can't doubt that again. By now, it is no doubt that George loves me. With the Saviour the centre of our love, I have to say yes.

Sharon began to tear up as she realised her dream was coming true.

"Sharon, what do you say?" George's voice awakened her from her thoughts.

"Yes! Yes! I say yes to be the keeper of your heart forever if you would keep mine," assented Sharon.

In a flash, George carried her into his embrace and gave her the longest kiss they have ever shared.

"Ehhhmmm!!" the kids shouted together, while the adult clapped, sharing laughter and rejoicing.

"We need to prepare for the wedding now," Aunt Bola announced.

"It's going to be the party of the year," someone added.

The rest of the family resumed their fun time, while George and Sharon excused themselves.

"Are we heading outside?" Sharon asked, clinging to him.

"Yes, I will get the coats," George rushed ahead to get some warm coats to cover his new fiancé.

Once outside, Sharon turned to him.

"George, you did not plan all this. Who helped you!? I need to know my allies, not those that will sell me out."

Smacking his chest joyfully, George shouted, "Yahoo!! My heart is ready to burst!!"

"Don't be silly, tell me how you did it, George!" ordered Sharon in her professional but playful voice.

"All right, Sharon, I visited your parents before I came over for the Christmas party to ask for your hand in marriage."

"You did what!? You never told me! George!!" Sharon had her hands on her hips by this time.

"I remember you informed me that in the Nigeria tradition, it is important I ask for consent first," George meekly informed her.

"You remembered? But that's my mum's family tradition."

"Both your mum's and your dads are your families."

"True," agreed Sharon.

"Apart from telling them what else happened?" shouted Sharon in her eagerness, which increased the production of adrenaline. The love for the precious soul she gave her whole heart to was bursting forth.

George staring into her thunderous flashing eyes with excitement, continued.

"Your parents and I decided that I would have to ask you, and we left the final decision to you. I informed them I was concerned you could not express your true feelings towards me. They advised I wait until you were comfortable in expressing how you feel before I asked your hand in marriage."

"Oh, really!? And all this went on behind my back, George?"

"The night I dropped you home after the Christmas party, I pleaded with the Saviour for a sign. That was when you kissed me, Sharon! I knew then His eyes had shone on me."

"Oh dear, George! I am so very sorry, I struggled so much to accept all the affection you showed me but could not reciprocate."

"Immediately, I got home that night. I called Tom for his advice. He suggested I ask you directly how you felt about me."

"Whoa, even Tom is in on it?"

"Yes, that's why during the jog on Christmas Eve, I had to ask you."

Sharon felt a sudden intense sweet affection toward George, reaching to hold him close, while he planted several kisses on her face.

"How about the surprise family guests? How did that happen?"

Clearing his throat, George continued, "Tom and your parents are all involved. They invited all the people close to you for the Christmas party. Most declined, but we still got the room filled."

"Do you mean they didn't know you wanted to propose to me?" wondered Sharon.

"Not really. I called Tom while we were shopping yesterday. We met in the jewellery store, where we chose the ring."

"Wait, don't tell me. You called him while we were in the store."

"Yes, that's because he was around the corner from where we were. I guess, he didn't want to mess up the plan. He didn't pick up my call."

"George, have always known you were full of surprises, but didn't know you would go this far."

"Sharon, your parents knew about the proposal, that why we tried to occupy you all day and distract you from the gifts.

"Talking about gifts, why nine boxes?"

"I fell hopelessly in love with you the ninth month after you started working in the company. Also, Beautiful is a nine-letter word. It's the name I have often called you these past two years."

"Thank you, Handsome," she uttered under her breath in contentment, holding on to him as if it meant her life.

They walked quietly, silently communicating with each other's heart, as the warmth they shared eradicated the cold winter breeze.

Suddenly, large flakes of snow began to drift down from the sky. A sign of heaven's favour?

George held her closer than ever, as they decided it was time to return to their awaiting family.

Now we need to take ourselves back, announced us to the Finlands' and the company. I hope George had figured everything out as he did with my family. I am not ready to face any questioning or... This is a precious moment with George, and I wouldn't ruin it.

Sharon's mind jumped from one thought to another as they walked back home.

TWENTY – FIVE

In the early haze of dawn, Mr, and Mrs O'Loan drove the newly engaged couple to the international airport for their flight back to the US.

Sharon could barely open her eyes at 4:30 a.m. on the 28th of December. One thing was sure, she persuaded George to stay a little longer for travelling back with him. Though she would have wanted more time with her parents, she knew it was time to take the last flight away from the nest and not return to be a 'Miss' again.

Still showing symptoms of persistent, sleepiness, George supported her as they waved goodbye to her parents. She promised to be back as soon as possible to start the arrangements for the wedding.

"Hey, Beautiful,"

"Yes, Handsome Heart?"

"I like that, H.H.", agreed a happy George. Sharon smiled with a sense of approval from him for the new pet name she made up on the spot.

"Do you want some coffee to help wake you up, my love?"

"Thank you, I would like some and do get a cup for yourself, Handsome Heart!" giggled Sharon.

"Sure," George responded, walking away from her, blowing kisses in the air. He returned not only with coffee but with some extra selection of snacks.

"I remembered we had eaten nothing, so I got something extra."

"Thank you, Love," she replied sweetly. Looking around, she commented, "I wonder when we will get through the checkpoints and airport security. It seems the entire world is travelling today."

"Ha, ha! You read my mind! It's the festive season and folks are catching flights for the New Year."

Their plan to spend the New Year with his parents was facing its first test. The airport was busy with travellers trying to catch the last flights of the year.

After a two-hour delay from the planned flight of 7.45 am, they finally boarded the aircraft at about 9.45 am.

They checked into their seats as soon as possible. After talking and laughing at all his jokes, Sharon soon laid her head on George's shoulder and fell fast asleep.

It wasn't long before her recurring nightmare began. This time, the stranger was in the same position as he was on the first flight, the flight to Houston to resume her employment.

Rather than looking back at her from his seat smiling, he looked back with tears rolling down his cheeks. Sharon, uncomfortable and simultaneously confused, tried to reach out to him.

In desperation, she leaned out her hands to reach him. She sought to find out why was he crying, but there seemed to be a deep chasm between the stranger and herself. Sharon pleaded and groaned in pain, but the stranger closed his eyes. His tears continued.

"Please tell me. Tell me! Tell me! What is wrong?"

With a loud cry of *Noooo*, she woke up from the nightmare.

George held her close, murmuring to her that it was only a dream. He tried to find out what type of dream she had had and what caused the fright.

Sharon, not ready to disclose the dream, responded, "George, it was not clear. I am not sure what happened. All I know is that it was a nightmare, a terrible dream. I don't know why, but I hope it never comes to reality," her hands and lips trembling in fear.

George held her hands close to his heart. Both said a few words to the Saviour, comforting her.

The remaining part of the twelve-hour trip was silent. George knew there was something terrible bothering Sharon, but he did not know how to reach her. This was his first test of getting to understand her.

On arrival back in Houston, George got an Uber. In the days following their trip, he tried making her happy and so forget the nightmare.

Although he planned a surprise welcome home party to get together with his friends, her fragile state of mind was more important to him.

George changed plans and dropped her off at her apartment. Sharon excused herself and headed to the shower. She returned to a sleeping George on her sofa. Knowing not only was he exhausted by the journey, but he must also be worried about her too, Sharon covered him with some blankets, took some painkillers before resting her head and going to bed. The sound of the alarm at 6.00 am woke both of them.

Upon waking and after a time of fellowship with the Saviour, George made and ate some breakfast before heading out to his parents' house for the annual Graceoak Strategic Business Meeting to start off the New Year.

"I hate to leave you alone, Sharon, but I have to give feedback on the state of affairs to the Finlands."

"I do understand, George. I know it is going to take the entire day or two. Remember, no one knows I am around."

"I do and I will spend every moment that I can with you," he said, affectionately kissing her forehead.

"I know, but you need to hurry along, or you will change your mind soon enough."

Sharon dragged him towards the door where the taxi driver was already waiting.

Calling out to him as he walked off, she shouted. "H. H., it would be a good idea if you headed to your house and picked up your car before going to your folks' place."

Turning back, he replied, "Good idea beautiful, why am I so lucky to have you?"

Smiling back, Sharon replied, "Love you! See you soon." Within her, she pondered on his word, 'lucky'.

You could be right, George. I need some of that, especially when I don't understand these dreams and why they happen.

    Throughout the rest of the day, they barely spoke on the phone. Sharon thought George must be busy with several meetings with his parents and the board. Sharon missed his voice and sense of humour.

    Sharon had not informed anyone she was back in town, she had to remain indoors. She longed for some interaction with her friends. Sharon constantly reminded herself of George's endless surprises and plans which had changed everything in her life now.

    Working within the agreed plan, according to George, they were to spend New Year's Day with his family. He would introduce her to his parents. But the day couldn't have become any worse.

    After George left, she took a nap. Not long into her nap, she had the same horrible nightmare.

    Sharon woke up in a panic because the stranger not only cried but disappeared from her sight! With dread ravishing her mind, she feared that these new threads of nightmare were a portent of something bad to come.

In contrast, the last dream about the stranger stating 'see you soon' was a sign everything would turn out well. The peace she had gotten from that dream made her say yes to George.

Was this present nightmare a sign that something terrible was going to happen to George and herself? How could she go through this?

Sharon called her mum and dad. They discussed her dreams and the effects on her relationship with George.

Mr and Mrs O'Loan encouraged Sharon to trust in the Saviour to lead her relationship with George. Though she did not have answers to the several questions bothering her, Sharon knew her heart only beat for George, as much as she had for the stranger at the airport.

Every time she heard his voice, her heartbeat thudded like unhampered horses racing over a mountain top.

Later in the evening, George, and Sharon would share what happened throughout the time they were apart.

However, Sharon did not open up to share about her nightmare. She didn't want to alarm or scare George because she was wary of repeatedly harping on the ghost of the stranger haunting her. It was all too weird!

Before he ended the call, she asked him, "H. H, tell me?"

"Tell you what, Beautiful?"

"George, do your parents' sense anything going on between us?"

"I think you are an expert in hiding your feeling, Sharon. I am sure my dad does not. But my mother is a woman like you. I wouldn't be able to tell."

"What does that even mean, H.H.?"

"It means you are a special creature, crafted to protect my heart, more than my mother had done. Sharon, I could imagine all our kids will look like you."

"Really? Thank you. I know you love being around kids. I pray we make babies as soon as possible."

"Why the rush?" George exclaimed, not so sure he agreed.

"For starters, our parents want more kids, and I don't mind. We are not getting any younger, George."

"I think I would prefer to spend more time with you, my darling, before we raise kids."

"Ditto," she concurred, laughing. "But George, there is a topic we have not discussed to a large extent."

"What could that be, Beautiful?"

"Can we video chat?"

"By all means, this sounds scary," he noted before redialling her on video chat.

"Hey, beautiful, you look tired," George commented after observing her weary face.

"Is everything okay? Do you want me to come over?"

"I am good. I think I still need more of my beauty sleep," she responded.

But changed the tone of the discussion. "But we've not discussed sex!"

"I thought you would never ask." George adjusted himself on his bed, humming a tune. "Let's talk about sex, babe, let's talk about you and me..."

"George, listen, listen!!" Sharon exclaimed, as she laughed about his keen interest in sex.

"I am listening. I will so much enjoy every step on the way to sex..."

"Save it until the wedding night, George!"

"For real, then why are we talking about it?"

"We have to. It's important we discuss where it stands in the marriage and our relationship with the Saviour."

"Interesting, educate me." Pushing his head back to his pillow, he waited for Sharon while she stepped away to pick up her scriptures. Sharon flipped pages of scriptures to several references related to the sexual relationship within marriage: its role in solidifying the relationship between a man and a woman.

George waited patiently, staring at her until he said: "You enjoy talking about sex, right?"

"Yes, why?" Sharon looked up from the pages of the book.

"I am hoping you will enjoy it the same way you love talking about it, beautiful!"

"How do you mean, H.H.?" staring with a puzzled gaze

"For starters, Darling, have you experienced sex before?" There was dead silence on the other end, a test to prove Sharon's openness to talk about the topic she had raised.

"Are we on the honest road to disclose all-out dirty linen?" asked George.

Continuing, "Is that not what all this is about, Sharon, or are we only to discuss it from the perspective of the Saviour?"

"Right, shall we? George! have you ever gone all the way before?"

"Could you expand on the 'all the way' part?" George quizzed waiting to launch into her naive worldview of sex.

Hesitating, but insisting on making good on this discussion, she continued,

"In secondary school, I experienced the oral part with my first boyfriend. I knew from the Saviour's words that sexual intercourse should be within the context of marriage. Peer pressure played a sound part in the broken walls of my virginity."

George, impressed by her brief speech, adjusted himself and exclaimed, "Is that all?"

"Naughty boy, were you expecting more? Don't forget, my parents raised me well."

"I don't doubt for a second, the outstanding job, and the fine daughter you have become."

"Thank you, George. It's your turn. Tell me about your dirty linen."

"Are you ready for this complete revelation?"

"Really, George! It isn't that you have HIV or some sexual diseases!?"

"Sharon! So typical of you!" George protested at her extreme imagination of his past sexual life.

"Truth be told," George admitted. "I had an incidence of sexual disease, but it's treated and its history."

"Whoa!" Sharon was looking very alarmed.

"Do you want me to continue? Sharon, you knew I lived a boy's life. You want to know. My first sexual experience was in primary school."

"Primary what!!?" shouted Sharon. "Who has sexual experiences in primary school?"

"Calm down, Sharon. It was just touching and peeking! However, I have had several sexual partners, but thankfully I have got no girl pregnant. So don't be afraid of any 'baby mama' issue. There is nothing."

George tried to make light out of the tension his past might cause Sharon.

After a long pause, he continued, "Sharon, do you want me to tell you more?"

Sharon blinked her eyes at him, a sign of her acceptance.

"Please do continue," she indicated mutely.

"If my past makes you uncomfortable, kindly let me know, my Love."

"George, we all have our past and remember the Saviour has cleaned all our sinful history away. What we make of our future with him is the most important."

"Thank you for your kind words, beautiful."

"Tell me, when was your last sexual experience, H.H.?"

350

"After the week I got my Bible from the bookshop. I couldn't do it anymore. Each time I read the Word; I had a strong restraint not to continue in my lifestyle. It confused my friends, Sharon. I was the playboy in the rock band. I knew three things: money, power, and women."

"Thank you for sharing your truth with me. I respect you for your honesty. Don't worry, wouldn't bother to ask you how many partners, H.H."

Laughing aloud, George responded, "To be honest, I cannot count. I am grateful I met you. The Saviour used you to change my worldview."

"George, one thing comes out of all our experiences."

"What's that?" George asked with a curious face.

"One of us has experience in the act, and I have a skilled teacher already!" said Sharon, determined to put a positive spin on things.

"I will be very gentle with you all the way. Baby steps together. I love you so much, Beautiful."

"I love you too, Handsome Heart." yawned Sharon, stretching out her arms.

"I better let you have your beauty sleep, Darling."

"Thank you for your kind consideration, H.H. Goodnight!"

"Sweet dream about me only!" George blew kisses through the screen door.

"I sure will," she responded, although she feared the nightmare will hamper her beauty sleep. Once off the phone, she thanked the Saviour for everything and dozed off.

TWENTY – SIX

It was the last day of the year and a knock on the door woke her up from sleep. Sharon rushed to the window to discover George's car in the front of the apartment.

What on earth is he doing here this early? It's only 6.30 am. Opening her door, George rushed in from the chilly breeze with two bags and cups of coffee.

He dropped the bags on the coffee table and walked back to a surprised Sharon, expecting some explanation for his actions.

"What happened? Are you okay, George?" queried Sharon as George held her close and kissed her lightly.

"Nothing is wrong. I tried sleeping, but I couldn't. After tossing all night, I felt the sensible thing to do is to get us breakfast and enjoy your company the whole day!"

"Handsome Heart," Sharon sighed.

"Thank you, but don't you have a meeting? Please don't cancel because of me. I can keep myself company..."

"Hush, Darling..." He held his finger over her mouth. "Listen, I rather spend the entire day with you than at any other meeting."

"For real?" she responded, unconvinced.

"I am not joking, Sharon. I told Dad I needed some time for myself today. It surprised me he didn't object to it."

"Don't be too hard on yourself, George. Your father knows you need some time."
Holding her hands, he kissed them and led her to the couch.

"Listen, sit, I will be back," he dashed away with the bags to get breakfast ready.

"What are we having?" She shouted as he waddled off.

"Surprise, as long as it's not poison. By the way, thank you for being so open about yesterday. I dreaded the day I would have to speak about it. You made it so easy, darling."

"You welcome, H.H.," Sharon giggled back.
The breakfast was an amazing collection of fruits, fresh warm pancakes, bakery toast, and fried eggs.

Sharon wagged so surprised she exclaimed, "Tell me, did you go to a cookery school?"

"Don't ask. Please enjoy the meal. I promise it won't stop after we are married!"

"I pray that, too," she smiled contentedly, taking a bite of a juicy strawberry.

George enjoyed the company of Sharon for the rest of the day.

Their day was spent wandering from one store to another. They shopped for gifts for George's family.

George guided her on the perfect choices of gifts she needed to get. They teased each other and even teased the delighted people around them.

George and Sharon enjoyed a delicious afternoon meal to celebrate the last day of the year and their engagement before heading to his mum and dad's house the next day.

To Sharon's amazement, Mr, and Mrs Finland seemed shocked to see their son wanting to spend time with them on New Year's Day.

"Hello George, it's late! Why are you here?" his father asked as he opened the door.

"Hi Dad, good to see you too, Dad." He replied, ignoring his father's statement.

His mother, hearing their voices, came out to stand beside her husband.

"Welcome George, I am glad you are here. I agree you didn't tell us you were coming, hmm?"

Seeing Sharon coming up beside George, she readjusted her tone.

"Come in here with me, Sharon," holding out her hands, leading Sharon with the men to sit in the living room.

"Good evening, Mr and Mrs Finland," Sharon greeted them with the embarrassment of sweaty palms, not looking forward to breaking the news of their engagement.

"I didn't know you were back. We were expecting you in the New Year. Is there anything wrong, Miss O'Loan? Come and talk to me."

Mrs Finland patted the seat beside her on the luxurious sofa.

"Hello Sharon, this is an unexpected surprise!" George's father interjected.

"Dad, Mum, please don't make a fuss. Do you want us to leave?"

His mum intervened, turning towards Sharon.

"George, we welcome you any time you show up at home, especially with Sharon, don't we? Mr Finland?"

"Yes, we do," her husband backed away from his confrontational attitude toward his son concerning his presence at home when he should be out with his friends wildly celebrating the New Year.

"Thank you, Mr and Mrs Finland, for welcoming me into your lovely home," Sharon covered as she tried to smooth over the awkward situation.

As the four sat in front of the fireplace in the huge private sitting room, a steward brought in drinks after a few minutes. Sharon became relaxed, temporarily forgetting about the stormy tension within her enjoyed the discussion they had about the business.

After lunch, Mr, and Mrs Finland led the couple to a relaxing walk in the garden, where George found the best opportunity to spill the beans.

Although he walked with the women between him and his dad, he gathered his courage and cleared his throat.

"Mum, Dad, you know you're being pressing me to be responsible and..."

Mr Finland interrupted, "Talking about responsibility, we must thank you for all the effort you had put into building the business in the UK."

Turning to George, his mum added, "Son, you have noticeably improved your game at Finland's UK office."

"Thanks, Mum, but that's not what I was getting at."

The statement halted everyone, and they turned to George at the same time. Like he had swallowed a stone, George seemed to shiver.

Sharon noticed this demeanour and reached out to hold his hands. Her touch gave him a boost of energy as George gushed out.

"Like I was saying, we are engaged!" he rushed out the words before his courage could fail him.

"That's splendid news!!" his parents exclaimed in unison.

"Why was that tough news to tell us?" Mr and Mrs Finland hugged Sharon with the excitement of the news that their two favourite people were in love.

Sharon, smiling, added, "I do not understand why it was so hard myself, George. We are home!" she exclaimed to lighten the air.

She placed a light kiss on George's lips, who responded positively in the presence of his parents with a kiss on her forehead and tight-fitting hug.

"I think we should drink to this," His father responded, turning back to the entrance of the bi-folded glass doors to pour drinks at the ornate cart carrying several bottles of fine liquor.

Sharon felt the Finland's were not surprised as much, especially his mum. She smiled in approval at Sharon and said as they walked to the cart.

"I saw this coming. Why am I not surprised?"

These words comforted Sharon because she dreaded how the parents were going to handle the news.

Mrs Finland and Sharon took time to talk about George, most especially his childhood. While the men went out to discuss business in the UK; Mrs Finland soon started talking about wedding plans with her soon-to-be daughter-in-law. The Finlands were so excited; they spent the rest of the night getting to know Sharon better personally.

How they got engaged... her family... This was by far the best New Year's Day ever in Sharon's life and it was spent with her new beloved family!

To Sharon's amazement, she's already thinking about the wedding with her mother-in-law to be, just a week after becoming engaged. To convince her otherwise would have been impossible.

At 10:30 pm the following night, George, and Sharon said their goodbyes to his parents and headed back to Sharon's house.

The next day, Sharon walked into the office building as usual, but the welcome was different. Everybody sang her praises for capturing George's heart. Grace led her to the cafeteria with a banner on the wall which read.

Congratulations George and
Sharon on Your Engagement!

She stood stock-still as George walked in behind her, wrapping his arms around her in a surprise hug.

The entire room cheered, each person telling her the first time they noticed something was amiss; noting that her walls of defence had collapsed after the strong pursuit by George. As though they planned it, the staff gave the couple hugs and celebrated with an engagement cake.

Sharon never expected it would be so acceptable or easy. Her greatest fear of going against the company policy had vanished into thin air.

After a day or two, the staff settled down to the routine, while for Sharon settling down into the new format of life together as a couple in the office was a bit too much.

George took her out for lunch in the afternoons, and every now and then they visited the beach where they spent their first romantic experiences together.

Holding hands as they walked one day, Sharon expressed concern regarding the amount of time they were spending together, neglecting work.

Holding her hands to his chest, George replied, gazing into her brown eyes.

"I am too, but I am ready to maximise my time with you. Getting to know you and enjoy each other's company is more important to me than Finlands right now."

Not satisfied with his response, Sharon felt a growing agitation within her that all the attention was stressing her out.

One week after their announcement, they organised another surprise engagement party in the presence of their friends and family in the Finlands' mansion.

Sharon and George walked into his parents' home filled with guests shouting, "Happy engagement!!" To top off the evening's surprise, Mr, and Mrs O'Loan appeared from one of the rooms to grace the occasion.

Tears of joy rolled down Sharon's cheeks as she held her parents in warm embraces.

"Mr and Mrs O'Loan, were you in on this?"

"Don't ask," her mum replied. "Just have fun. It is the Saviour's doing. We rejoice in it."

Holding on to Sharon, George whispered. "Sorry for the surprise. Dad and I thought it was an idea to bring a few family members together to share the joy."

"George, should I be expecting everything with you to be a perpetual surprise?"

"Not a load idea, is it?" he replied with his cheeky smile.

"Not so sure! I think you should allow me in on things from now on." She responded in a serious tone, kissing him on the cheek before walking out to the garden.

George set down his glass of wine and rushed quickly to follow her. Catching up with her in the garden, he pulled her back, but she shook him off, annoyed.

"George, I need some time alone. It has been so overwhelming for the past few weeks. It is still a dream." Rather than leave her alone, he gathered her into his arms and explained.

"I know you would prefer a conservative engagement and wedding, but it doesn't work like that for the Finlands."

"Yeah!" she pulled him away protesting.

"What about the way I feel? What about what I want for once? What about planning things together, like we did when we announced to your parents? First, the office and then a massive family engagement party. How big will the wedding be? I can't even get my head around it. You invited my parents without my knowledge!? George, I want to go home!"

"I apologise. I planned to surprise you, beautiful! Please don't go," George pleaded.

"Wait, am I supposed to be treated like a trophy and kept out of things, or will I end up being a guest at my wedding?"

"I agree, Sharon. I took things too far. But at least let us disagree somewhere else. Not at the party. Please, can you pretend everything is alright?"

"No, I can't, not now or ever, George! The fact that I don't express my feeling all the time should not make me a doormat for your heavenly surprises."

Their absence in the room caught the all-seeing eyes of Mrs O'Loan. She began a solo search party for the whereabouts of her daughter.

As she walked out of the kitchen, glass doors leading to the garden, she heard muffled exchanges of Sharon's and George's voices. When she approached them, Sharon ran into her mother's embrace, crying.

"George, is everything okay? Why is my princess upset?"

"Mrs O'Loan, it's my fault. I made all these surprise plans without letting her in on them. It had gotten too much for her to handle. Especially being left in the dark, that her dear Mr and Mrs O'Loan; would be guests for the party."

"It's okay, George. Would you mind if I spend some time with her? You need to attend to the guests before people ask questions. She will be fine, I promise."

A few moments after George stepped away, Sharon stopped crying. Her mother spoke about the strength of the girl she gave birth to.

She reminded her to learn to communicate her concerns at the right time and place. Likewise, it was important for George to know her boundaries before starting the marriage.

The disagreement with George was a sign that things were getting complicated or a good sign of getting to understand each other.

She prayed the Saviour would grant both of them the wisdom to work out their relationship.

Later that night, George, and Sharon talked about the importance of open communication. She requested that her opinions be taken seriously.

Sharon stated she would prefer surprises for personal stuff. However, things that have to do with the extended family and friends, she would like a united front.

George agreed that he had not learned to do things this way before. But, with the support and understanding of Sharon, their relationship would work out fine.

TWENTY - SEVEN

Five months after the surprise engagement party, Sharon knocked and entered Mr Finland Sr, office.

The images of three look-alike men she saw shattered her to the core. Sharon quickly shut the door behind her and headed back to her office to recover from the shock.

But she made a quick detour into the ladies' powder room. *George won't come after me in here! I need a breather. What in-the-world did I just see? Was that a dream or not!? I must be losing my mind. Now I am sure I am not.*

Sharon later picked her bag and dashed out of the door. George was already at the reception awaiting her.

"Sharon, here you are! I have been searching all over for you."

"What's happening? I was dashing out for a quick meeting with a client and wanted to brief Dad, but it seems he was busy."

"The exact reason I am searching for you, George. There is a surprise awaiting you in the CEO's office."

"For real?"

"I hope you're ready for this, beautiful!!"

"Ready for what, H.H.?"

"Another of your surprises," pretending she had no clue what this was all about.

She prayed and pleaded, *Saviour, please can you help me out here? I am confused, I fell in love with one and I am getting married to another in a few weeks!*

"Let me take you into my office first." George held her hand, but she resisted.

"I will be back soon. I will be late for the meeting."

"Sharon, please why don't we talk in my office, then you can head out." Sharon succumbed to his pleading, leading her away to his office.

Shutting his office door behind them, George held her hand and led her to his sofa.

He reminded her of the discussion they had during the dinner in the African restaurant about his brother, the twin who had died.

"Yes, I remember," Sharon responded with a sense of surprise.

With excitement, George continued. "I think he just came back from the grave."

With sparkles in her eyes, she replied, "What? What do you mean?"

Her behaviour and cover-up continued. At present, Sharon knew what he meant. The fact is, if his brother was back, there was a probability she had met him at the airport. That was why she couldn't shake off the creepy feeling the image created in her mind.

George led her joyfully to the CEO's office. Sharon became depressed as she walked with him like a sheep led to the slaughter. George knocked and led her into the office.

Mr Finland, in an exhilarating state, exclaimed, "Oh yeah! George, thank you for bringing Sharon. I remember I have an appointment with her today."

"How are you, Mr Finland? I can see you are having a delightful day."

She avoided looking at the man seated to the right, like George.

George held her hands securely as Mr Finland continued. "I would like to introduce someone to you."

The man stood up, turning to face her. "This is Luke!"

At the mention of his name and appearance, Sharon fell into a faint upon the sight of him!

George grabbed her in his arms before she landed on the ground; desperately shouting, "Dad! Please call the emergency!! Call emergency, I can't lose her!

Mr Finland picked up the phone in a panic, while Luke rushed to George to help.

"Can I?" He asked, attempting to conduct a CPR on Sharon.

After several efforts, Sharon coughed back to life, and simultaneously, the ambulance service arrived.

George followed the ambulance to the hospital to check on her. His parents and Luke came along with him to find out what had happened to her.

Mrs Finland suggested pregnancy could cause it and quizzed George about his sex life.

"Mother, that is a personal issue between Sharon and I."

Trying to reassure him, she continued, "There is nothing wrong with that. Everyone has sex now and then, except you guys think to hold off until your wedding night."

"Darling, can we drop this? He is going through a lot at the moment. He needs our support, not questioning," requested George's father.

"You are right, dear," Mrs Finland sat down beside the couple to offer support.

Soon, the doctor arrived. He confirmed Sharon's vitals good, and they had nothing to fear.

He suggested she needed rest, and she will be back on her feet in a day or two. Once discharged. Sharon gave an excuse that she still felt light-headed and requested to be home for a rest. She had a perfect excuse to be off work for the next two days.

She needed to stay away, to get her senses back. George became concerned because her parents had instructed him to make sure their baby was okay. He kept a tab on her to make sure she was all right.

The next two days, everything to Sharon became a nightmarish reality. It was three weeks before the wedding. How on earth was she going to sort this mess out?

Three days after the terrible messy episode in the CEO's office, Sharon returned to work. Luke, once more, was formally introduced to Sharon.

This time around, she had gone through the previous shock and could politely acknowledge Luke. She wanted to have nothing to do with him. Sharon remained cold toward him and avoided any conversation.

Often, she had problems distinguishing them apart. She remained certain that for now, Luke would not impersonate as George.

One evening, Sharon was rushing off from work to avoid any encounter with George or Luke when Luke caught up with Sharon in the elevator.

"Sharon, I think you recognise me. Don't you?" He spoke with such tenderness, exactly the way the stranger spoke to her on their first encounter.

"Hi Luke, I do," she replied, looking away from him.

"I am still in shock; I never knew you..."

"Yes, I know. It's a small world. So, let me formally introduce myself to you. I'm Luke, the guy you spilt coffee on at Heathrow Airport about two-and-a-half years ago."

Still trying to pretend the emotional connection between them never existed, she continued, "Yes!?"

"I'm sure you are the lady that was so distracted, staring at me like I were a ghost..."

Sharon interrupted him and added. "Until you got me back to my senses. So, I see you remember."

"I do, I do." Luke smiled passionately, melting Sharon's heart instantly.

Get yourself together, she screamed inside her mind.

"How are you?" He added.

"I'm good. I can remember you have asked me that before." She responded, avoiding any expression of the compliment on the subject of her adulation.

"Do you mind going to dinner with me, Sharon?"

"No! no, no!!" she protested.

"Please don't misunderstand me. I know you're getting married to my brother in three weeks."

"I'm glad you know. Thank you." She responded sarcastically to annoy him, but he continued,

"That's not the reason..." Sharon cut in again, but she was becoming increasingly tense.

Now sounding uncomfortable, Luke continued, "I want us to talk. I want to know if there is anything wrong with getting to know my brother's soon-to-be-wife?"

"No, definitely not!" Sharon pretended it's a fair bargain for him to get to know her.

"I accepted the invite on one condition, if you don't mind..."

Luke interrupted her. "Do you want me to do something?" he pleaded.

"I think I have a place in mind." Sharon wanted them to visit the same restaurant as she did with George. A chance to enjoy talking to him, to measure them together.

"We have ourselves a deal." he stretched out his hands to shake hers as a sign of peace between them.

Just then, the elevator doors opened. Sharon watched Luke walk away, but deep within her heart, she knew she had not gotten over her encounter with him.

One thing she was glad about was that George was out of town. She didn't need permission from him to dine with his twin... her supposed 'love' at first sight.

7:00 pm that evening, Sharon looked out her window to see Luke parked outside her apartment. She recognised the car as the same one used to pick her up from the airport the first time she arrived in Houston.

Another similarity to the twin, she pondered. *They are both punctual for a date, a little too early for comfort.*

Sharon dressed in her exclusive lemon green dress and a favourite lemon and green scarf.

She questioned herself about the extra care she was taking, as though she was going on a first date.

It is my first date with Luke, I suppose, justifying the need for the time she took to dress up. Two hours, Sharon, you have not dressed for two hours for a date with your soon-to-be husband. This is a conflict of interest and needs instant resolution.

Deep within her, Sharon knew something was exciting about going to dinner with Luke.

She shared on the phone with Tom, "I have never felt different from the first day I met him. Should I not go out with him? What if I become confused? I can't bear to break either of their hearts!"

"You will be fine," Tom's words of sage advice reassured her as she left work.

Besides, Luke promised he will not impede my relationship with his brother.

A knock on the door interjected her thoughts.

Luke at the door 10 minutes early. He must be tired of sitting in the car. Sharon opened the door to a well-groomed 6'5" handsome version of George.

Her heart melted. *You won't faint*, she cautioned herself.

"Wow, Sharon! You look gorgeous! I am honoured to dine with you tonight. I can't imagine any reason George would willingly pass you by unless he was blind."

"Evening, Luke, you are not bad yourself. Remember, tonight is not about George, but about you."

"You are so kind. I got flowers for you." He handed her over the same flowers George would often get her.

I hope I get through this evening, she whispered to herself.

"Did you say something?" Luke straining to hear her whispered comments.

"They are beautiful, thank you," she responded, looking away.

"I chose something not romantic, as we have a mutual understanding about this date."

"No problem!" she replied sharply, noting the Luke was trying not to hurt her. He is so thoughtful. What a beautiful soul. Hopefully, he has a woman in his life.

About 7.30 pm, Luke opened the door for her to step into the restaurant, commenting on how good she smelled.

He has a way with words too, like his brother. The only difference, Luke, is so much more soft-spoken than George. He might be a better listener, too.

Sharon had directed Luke to this African restaurant, repeating the same event with George and herself walking into that moment surrounded by the rhythmic sound of music.

Such a beautiful evening! The staff directed them to the exact table where she usually dined with George. What a coincidence! Sharon watched every of Luke's mannerism. No different from George.

The way he opened the door of the car for me. The same way George skip across to my side door with eagerness. They both place their hands on the table, move their legs the same way. Everything is exactly like George. How can two people be so similar? How do I describe to anyone that I am in love with two brothers? Oh, God! Save me. How can I sit with him? I'm so torn!!

Sharon cried to her Saviour for help.

Taking his first sip of a drink, Luke said, "I... I... I need to apologise to you."

"Luke! Why on earth are you apologising?"

"I'm sorry. Back then I should have introduced myself. I needed to tell you how I felt that day! Sharon, I was too... your beauty rendered me speechless!"

Staring at her, Luke continued. "I felt attracted to you on the spot. I... I didn't know what to do, so I ran off."

"Same here," Sharon sighed. Looking away from him, "But we were on the same flight to Heathrow. I looked for you. What happened?"

Luke gathered his breath before continuing. "Once I got out of the airport, I knew you were around somewhere. After I got into the arrival area, I popped into the first men's room toilet, and about three minutes later, I saw you disappear into the baggage collection area and lost you."

"That was mean! Why didn't you search for me?" Sharon tensed with dissatisfaction.
Luke looked like a puppy, forlorn and abandoned. He continued quickly, not wanting the distraction of more questions.

"I take responsibility for what didn't happen! I know, it's been two-and-a-half years. I have regretted every single day for not telling you how I felt. I look back again. I didn't know how you would take it."

"Hush, don't," Sharon placed her finger on his lips. Immediately, Luke's heartbeat started to race, his breathing grew heavier.

He gasped and held her hands the same way George would, breathing on them and whispering, "Thank you."

They sat in grave silence, with both hearts roaring like a December blizzard despite the beautiful music and people eating and having fun around them.

Sharon finally broke the wall of silent unspoken words and softly encouraged, "Luke, can you continue, please?"

"I didn't know who you were and had no way of finding out. I don't know why. I knew I should have taken the first step. By now, you have observed, I am more reserved than George. As you can see, I am more of fewer words than he."

"I can see that," she flashed her beautiful smile, revealing her even teeth.

Luke responded with a wide grin saying, "When I first met George, I realised he was so loud compared to me."

"Yeah, that seems to be the only difference I can see." Sharon teased back.

"But whatever, you're the one who should observe the difference, not me," Luke whispered to himself under his breath.

"I see, Luke, where this discussion is going," Sharon protested, drawing her seat backwards in discomfort.

Restraining her hands as she got up to leave, he said, "Please listen to me, to get my side of the story."

Gazing into her fierce eyes, he continued, "I release you to George. I am not sure what I was thinking." Luke uttered hopelessly romantic.

TWENTY - EIGHT

In defence, Sharon snapped, "That's it, we are done! There is no reason to order any meal. Can I leave now!?"

Rather than reacting like George would have to control the situation, Luke bows his head in defeat. He had lost the battle. She felt so horrible for thinking the two brothers will act similarly when confronted.

Sharon, longing to escape the whole evening, pretended she needed the toilet. Sharon slammed the door behind her. "What do I do!!" she screamed.

An elderly lady stepped out of one of the cubicles and replied, "Say yes to him."

Looking away from her, she replied, "It's complicated."

"It all boils down to one thing: your choice. Every lady, at one time or the other in life, reaches this junction. But one thing is sure, that is a choice. Make a wise choice." Patting her shoulder, the elderly lady walked out.

Sharon refreshed herself and got back to Luke. He spoke first, extending out her seat for her to sit.

"Do you feel better? I am sorry that I upset you, Sharon!"

"You can say that again," she muttered under her breath while he took his seat.

"What would you like to eat? Can we order something?"

"Of course," she replied. Luke called the waiter, and they ordered their meals.

"What do you think about him, Sharon?"

"Pardon, who are we talking about, Luke?"

"I mean my brother, George. I'm getting to know you. I have to get to know him, too."

"Speaking of getting to know each other, do you want to tell me what happened at your birth?" words she spoke before the waiter brought their meals.

"It's a long story, Sharon." She remembered George's replied with similar words.

"So! We have the entire night. I am here to listen. Can we eat first because I don't play with my food?" Sharon announced.

But Luke did something that surprised her. He held her hands and said, "Can we pray?" Sharon's heart melted and replied, "Sure."

His prayer was short and serene. She admitted it ushered in the much-needed peace her heart longed for.

She smiled at Luke and said, "Thank you, I needed that."

They ate as Luke explained how it all happened.

"I started searching for my birth family a few months before we met at the airport. I guess you could imagine I had a lot on my mind then. The connecting flight took me to Minnesota. I visited the hospital and other places to get more information about the events surrounding my birth. But that journey was not productive and couldn't help to reconcile what was happening."

Sharon interrupted him after taking a sip of her drink.

"Okay, do you want to start from the moment of your births, because I'm going to get confused?"

Her ears perked up like that of a rabbit, wanting to hear every sound. Something might differ from what George had narrated.

"Sure, Sharon. All I know is what I gathered from my mum now. My Dad has passed away some years ago."

"I'm so sorry to hear that," she replied with empathy.

"To be honest, his death led to my quest. My parents are Christians, and I grew up in the church. Sharon, I understand you are a Christian. My mum loves the Saviour, and I am a disciple."

"Oh! Thank goodness, that was why there was the attraction."

"I bet you could say that" Luke laughed the same way George would.

He is so handsome and peaceful. Sharon ruminated, pushing her fork of food in her mouth.

"Like I was saying, we moved to England when I was about 3 months old. From the story my parents told me, they adopted me as a desperate child who needed a loving home."

Sharon was stunned because this tale was a complete diversion from what George said. She was about to question him, but she refrained.

"My parents were blessed with 50 years of marriage, before my dear father died a few years ago at a good old age. They married late and unfortunately; they didn't have a child of their own. My dad finished his PhD program at the University of Minnesota. They were determined not to go back home to the UK without..."

"Why?" Sharon interrupted him. Luke paused and signalled to the waiter, requesting for another bottle of drink and continued his story.

"They didn't want the embarrassing questions from his family, asking about his wife not having a baby. Instead, Mum and Dad found a way to adopt a child and return to the UK to start a new life. It happened around that time there was a young 15-year-old girl pregnant with twins."

"Are you serious!" Sharon exclaimed.

"I think she was 15 and her partner 17. Mum told me her friend, who was a nurse, informed her of a young girl that wanted families to adopt her babies." Luke paused and took a sip of his drink.

"The young teenager was herself still a child and was in a real predicament with two babies! They started preparing for the adoption of the second child. Though, from what I was told, my mum wanted the two boys so she could raise them together. But the girl would not allow that to happen. They finally agreed to take one boy, the junior one. Well, George was the first of the twins. Immediately, I came out of my biological mum's womb. They transferred me to my adopted mum with no contact with my birth mum."

"Why would they do that?" She questioned his narrative.

"The given reason? To make sure there was no physical bonding between mother and son from birth. The adoption agency handed me over to my current mother. According to the story, mum told me, after two weeks in the US they signed the papers and we returned to the UK."

"I tried to find out the background of my parents from my mum," said Luke.

"She explained that my biological mum had been a pregnant teenager from a rich Jewish family. She had to choose between losing her inheritance, or getting married to the poor non-Jewish boy that got her pregnant. It was a taboo back then to have a baby out of wedlock because of her Jewish heritage. She and her boyfriend ran away from home in Houston to Minnesota, where they lived with her boyfriend's grandma.

"Oh whoa" nodded Sharon.

"The boy's family was from an economically unstable background. It would have been difficult for them to survive with one baby. How could they manage with two? At that point, keeping the two babies was not the ideal option for the two young people, so they gave up one twin, and left the second with her boyfriend's grandma."

Luke continued his narrative, "In the early days with the money they got from the adoption proceeding the couple survived, however, when things became unbearable in her boyfriend's grandma's home, the girl and her baby went back to live with her wealthy family, leaving the boyfriend behind."

"That's hard! Now, that would have been a terrible decision for the young lady to make," sympathised Sharon.

"You can say that again, Sharon! On top of my head, when I was told the story, I don't know how she came up with such an idea." After a long pause, Luke continued.

"According to my mum, she kept in touch with the nurse even after the adoption. The nurse in touch kept in touch with her in case she changed her mind to give up the other twin. The girl got home and somehow reconciled with her wealthy family, finished her education while losing contact with her boyfriend."

"Wait, how did your mum know all this information is true? How did she know the nurse was not making it up?" Sharon raised an eyebrow of doubt.

"Like I said, mum said, the nurse kept in touch with the young lady, but after her university education, she lost touch with her."

Sharon took a sip from her glass with her eyes fixed on Luke's lips.

"From my private investigation, I discovered she married the same man who got her pregnant as a teenager. I believe because there was a history between them, the reason they got married. Her concerned family passed all the inheritance to her as the only child. That was the foundation of Graceoak Oil & Gas Incorporation. The company is owned by my biological mum's family, the Finlands."

"Oh! Now I see the link. I see. I now understand." Sharon exclaimed.

"How do you mean?" asked Luke.

"The first day in the mansion, I entered a particular room with pictures alone. Luke, I was looking at all the pictures, which seemed like pictures of generations of one family."

"Did you ask George about them?"

"No, Luke. George does not talk much about the past, but until the Saviour changed him, he lived in a world of anger and rebellion. He might not be the best person to give an objective view of things."

"You seem to judge him rather harshly," Luke questioned her disapproving tone regarding George.

"You would understand if you had been there. I had a very difficult relationship with him when I started working in the company. I am glad you met a better version of George. The Saviour changes lives."

"He does," Luke agreed to the sentiments about the grace of the Saviour to change lives.

"Back to the pictures. Yes, they were totally generational. So that's where we Finlands are from. After my mum told me everything, I was disappointed at all they had kept from me for so many years."

"Really," empathised Sharon.

"Though I know they adopted me, they kept the whole family saga a secret. A secret kept between my mum and my dad. But after my dad passed away, she accepted responsibility and disclosed everything."

Adjusting himself on the seat he continued. "If she had known about what happened to them, she said, she would have told me. However, since dad was out of the picture, she didn't want to go to the grave with the information. After mum told me, for the past two-and-a-half years, Sharon, I've been on a quest to find my actual family."

"Whoa, it's like a real-life movie, Luke!"

"Every time I came over to find my real family, I faced a brick wall. I always returned disappointed. My biological mum had used fake names in the hospital, so it was difficult to trace. I guess because her parents were influential. She hid her actual identity and that of her boyfriend. It took a bit of work to get back home. I'm glad I am reconciled to them, but unfortunately, I'm not glad I'm losing you to my brother."

Sharon was disappointed because George had given her a different story about what had happened. However, she reminded herself, George might just have no clue as to the actual story himself.

"Up till now, I think George does not know the whole truth. I am not ready to disclose to George the truth as I know it, Luke!"

"Why, Sharon?"

"So many things are at stake, because sometimes it's just easier to let sleeping dogs lie, Luke. George is getting on well with his parents, and as you testified, he is getting married to the most beautiful woman. You and I are uniting a family of 32 years broken history. I would rather wait for him to find out from our parents himself."

"This is hard to accept, Sharon. It seems better if George knows everything and faces the consequences. If George is now a Christian, he needs to know everything."

To Sharon, with a deep feeling of discomfort thought, *Luke should not be the one to decide what method to ease him into the truth. It is wiser to let George know, or at least leave it to the Saviour.*

Later, after Luke dropped her off at home, Sharon fell into the comfort of her bed, exclaiming,

"What an eventful evening!" and promptly fell fast asleep. The whole night was still a dream, a dream she did not want to wake up from.

TWENTY - NINE

Monday morning, Sharon entered her office to find a bundle of flowers and a card on her desk. Picking up the card, she thought it was from George. She opened and it read.

"Thank you for Friday. You are the
best. George is lucky."

Closing the card, she closed her eyes, seeing the visions of the beautiful evening she had with Luke.

If only he knew I was the lucky one, in love with two brothers. Her mind flashed back to George, the one who her heart is betrothed to. She longed for him.

It had been a week since he's travelled to the UK to deal with some clients. Although they had been in touch constantly, Luke's presence every day chipped off the edge of the ice building up in her heart.

At lunchtime, she knocked on Luke's door; he was not around. Sharon turned around to meet Grace, staring pointedly at her.

"Miss O'Loan, are you looking for something? Sharon reacted like a guilty child caught with a hand in the candy jar!

"Hmm, Hmm, I... I was checking on Luke. Where is he?"

"He stepped out with Mr and Mrs Finland a few hours ago."

"Oh, I see," she responded, pitching her lips together in embarrassment.

"Are you okay, though? You look flushed." Grace probed like a mother who has caught her child in a wrong.

"Why would you say that?"

"I mean, it is easy to get confused and wrap yourself around Luke as though he is George."

"Am I that obvious?"

"What is obvious is that we all know George; you two meant a lot to each other. I mean, we know you are missing him. Thus, Luke is in the right place at the right time to hone you feel. Is it not?"

Looking as though she agreed with Grace's sentiments, she nodded, "Certainly, you are right, Grace."

Sharon prayed Grace did not suspect otherwise.

"Good. Glad we see things the same way. I am just about to drop these files on George's table. I think Mr Finland is thinking of expanding his portfolio. You know what? Luke is not only handsome, but he is also so smart."

Grace giggled and continued, "He can easily fit into Graceoak. I only wish he would look just once at me, and I will fall into his arms forever."

Laughing aloud, Sharon replied. "I bet you would. I am also glad you have a man in your life, except..."

"Miss O'Loan, you know, I am only thinking aloud. Can we call it a day, then?"

"Yes, day then, I will see you soon," Sharon clenched her fist as though she won.

Do you mean Grace observed nothing about my demeanour? Whoa, I should be more careful. Nobody observed my two-timing love of the two handsome brothers. She walked into her office, locked the door behind her, and fell on her knees beside her office sofa. *Saviour, will you not help me? I can't help the way I am feeling about Luke. It is so hard to let him go. I need your help. Do you want me to tell him the way I feel? He let me into the window of his heart during the dinner, but since then, he has been avoiding me. Did I do anything to encourage him? George will be back in a few days. My wedding is in two weeks. My heart is vacillating between two men. This is not right. Can you help? Speak to me.*

A knock on the door interrupted her fearful prayer. Sharon opened the door to see the wedding planner introduced to her by the Peters.

Seeing the troubled state Sharon was in, the planner was very concerned.

"Are you okay Sharon? Your eyes are red? Have you been crying?"

Trying to avoid eye contact, Sharon invited her in while she walked to her desk.

"Sharon, you know I will say nothing until we sort out your problem for you. I can't have an unhappy bride. That is not good for business."

Sharon looked away, took a deep breath, sipped a drink from her coffee cup, and spoke.

"You are right, but it is okay. I have been speaking to the Saviour about it. I know he heard me, and he has already sorted me out."

"That's my beautiful girl! You are so full of faith! And if you need me, I am just a dial away."

"The first dial on my phone," Sharon replied with a smile.

"Did I tell you you're more than a wedding planner for me? You are a friend, too. Thank you," Sharon said, holding her hands out for a hug.

"Thank you for trusting me, Sharon." She crooned retaining the embraced. "Okay, now that you feel better, let get right to business."

They discussed the wedding plans and what they needed to do. The wedding planner shared the progress they have made working with her parents' wedding planner in the UK, where the wedding will take place.

Once George and herself get back to the UK, she reminded them to go for the cake testing. She promised to keep everyone in the loop about the plans.

She requested that Sharon provide the final number of people going to the wedding from the US. She informed her she would confirm the total number once she discussed it with George's parents later in the evening.

The wedding planner left the office at the same moment Luke walked into her office.

"Sharon, a pleasant afternoon to you! Have you signed the documents for the..."
Sharon took the documents lying on her table and handed them over to Luke.

"Signed and ready, Luke. How was your meeting with the clients?"

"It went well! Learned from the best, Miss O'Loan. Your record at Graceoak is impeccable."

"I appreciate your compliment." Sharon's face went pink because of the commendation.

Luke noticed her countenance and laughed. "She is blushing. George is so perfect for you." Luke teased.

"It's a smart move, Luke. It is time for you to go to your office before Miss O'Loan boots out!"

"Thank you, Mrs George Finland." He teased her back, walking out of the door.

"You are sure right." Sharon smiled as she closed the door behind him.

Luke dragged his feet back to his office, his heart sick with desire at the sight of his unattainable love. He opened his office door and seated on the sofa was Cynthia.

"Afternoon, Cynthia," Luke greeted his biological mother.

"Afternoon, Luke," but before she continued, Luke spoke.

"How can I help you?" He asked, hoping she would not mention the complicated situation between the two brothers.

"Luke, you realise you have been avoiding me."

"Cynthia, I rather not discuss this now. You should talk to your number one son about his past and not me."

"I hear you, Luke, I hear you have forgiven me and your dad. I can't forgive myself, neither has your dad."

"Cynthia, I have a lot of paperwork to do now. Can we leave this till we get home?" insisted Luke.

"Luke, you've not been home to stay since you came, remember?"

"Cynthia, I think I am a full-grown man and can make a choice where I live. Besides, George's place is okay."

"Yes, till he gets married in a few days. Then what? Hear me out." suggested Cynthia.

"I am listening," Luke said, walking toward his desk.

"Luke, I need you to talk to George. We regret not telling him the truth. When we saw you for the first time, I sensed you were different. Thank you for coming back to us. I am looking forward to meeting your mum."

"We share the same sentiment, Cynthia. I am not sure I understand."

Luke puzzled but continued, "If I do, your point is that I should bridge the gap of communication between you and the pain you caused George since he was born?"

Cynthia paused and fell back into her seat, helpless. Luke walked up to the drink cart. He filled two glasses halfway with drinks and handed it over to Cynthia.

"Thank you, son," she acknowledged the courtesy.

"You are welcomed," he said, sitting close to her. After a few sips, he continued, "Can we speak honestly?"

Cynthia nodded. "Before we talk about honesty, Luke, George is hurt. He is pretending everything is fine because of the wedding. I don't want Sharon to get the brunt of his anger."

"How does this even matter to me?" Luke protested.

"Are you suggesting my coming back is going to destroy the pillars of lies you have built all these years? I see the marvellous foundation of orphans, yet you couldn't find your own son. Shouldn't I be the one hurt? You sold me to take care of him. Why only George, for 34 years? I cannot deal with this right now!!"

After a long pause, he showed his hopelessness by asking, "Do you think it's even an idea for me to stay?"

"I am sorry," apologised Cynthia, near tears. "I feel terrible for botching my responsibility as a mother for both of you..." but Luke interjected to continue.

"Look, I thank the Saviour for making our reunion possible. I am glad to reunite with my family. I am glad to know everything great and have allowed me to fit into the family business."
Luke's words came as comfort, placing his hands over hers.

Luke continued. "But Cynthia, I am not responsible for your actions, and I mean no disrespect. I think a discussion with George about his past is your responsibility. George needs to find out about his past and the earlier he finds out, the better for the entire family."

Luke's words were like a sword piercing Cynthia in the heart as he walked back to his seat. After a long pause, she sipped her drink, stood up and walked towards the door.

"Thank you for not letting the cat out of the bag. I will tell George at the right time, I will..." she assured Luke as she left his office.

A few seconds later, she popped her head back in and whispered, "Thank you, son, I am glad you are back. In the meantime, kindly check out your tuxedo before your brother's arrival."

"Thank you, Cynthia! Have it planned in my diary already." Luke's heart raced as the words left his mouth.

However, he bowed his head on his desk and wept quietly, praying from his heart to the Saviour. *How will I manage this, Saviour? How will I bear to see my Love walk down the aisle to marry my brother? Can I cope with this? It's getting more complicated than I prayed for when I started this adventure to find my family. Could you kindly help me deal with the raging war within me? Take this love for Sharon away from me. But why should George be the one to have her? I met her first and have loved her ever since the day I met her. She has never left my mind. I have dreamt, cried, and prayed for her for months, yet she will be with George. Should I tell her the way things are with me? I need your grace each day, dear Saviour! I want what's best for us all. Please, don't want to confuse her or my relationship with her. Help me, Saviour. Your word says you keep in perfect peace those whose heart is stayed on you.*

Luke avoided Sharon for the next two days as much as possible. He made sure they had no scheduled meeting that would bring them together.

His prayers that the Saviour would help him seemed to give him strength. Luke could not promise himself that he would not reveal his vulnerability in her presence.

On the third day, George called, he would arrive, which is earlier than his planned return. Sharon thought since Luke was staying at George's place, it would provide a bonding time for the brothers to be in each other's company.

She requested Luke drive her to the airport to pick up his brother, George. Sharon headed to Luke's office to talk, leaving George behind in her office.

When she knocked, she heard his sweet, calm voice calling out to enter. She adjusted herself before stepping into his office.

"Hey, Luke, how is work going?" She asked, as though she was genuinely interested in his work.

"Good," Luke replied, standing up for a formal handshake.

"Is there anything I can do for you, Miss O'Loan?" he asked in the sternest tone he could produce.

Clearing her voice, Sharon pretended she had not noticed the change in his body language and tone.

Responding, Sharon requested, "I was just off the phone with your brother, and I would like to ask that you drive me to the airport to pick him up."

"Sorry, is George back?" He asked, wiggling his eyebrows to elicit a reaction from her and to lighten the situation.

As expected, Sharon burst into laughter. "Be serious, Luke!" she exclaimed. "We don't have more time. He is waiting for me at the arrival terminal at this very moment."

"Miss O'Loan..." Luke echoed.

"Sharon," she cut in, "I prefer Sharon. In the next few days, I will change my name, but not yet! Also, why are you addressing me as Mrs Finland? You did that a few days ago."

The last thing Luke needed was a probe into his feelings. Why prolong his dying day? He changed his tone, turned to face Sharon from the drink cart where he stood facing her.

"I look forward with glee to you joining my family! I wouldn't miss the opportunity to spend time with my brother and his lovely wife."

"Thank you. I was almost sensing some reservation from your tone."

"Sharon, I am getting used to everything around here. I should be grateful to you because you made it a lot easier for me."

His comments made Sharon smile, and she gladly replied, "Thank you too."

Deep within her, she questioned the sincerity of his statement was as easy as he claimed in his statement. To her, every minute spent with Luke would last the eternity of not having him in her life.

On the way to the airport in George's sports car, Luke kept his eyes peeled on the steering wheel. Sharon searched for an avenue to start a conversation with him.

But Luke had already made up his mind not to talk until she said, "Luke, is your mum not attending the wedding?"
Sharon was desperately trying to break the ice wall between them.

"My mum?" He echoed her words as though the question was not directed to him.
Without turning his face to her, Sharon replied.

"Yes, your mum!" Smiling to him to encourage him to have a go at her line of questioning.

After a pause, he replied. "I told her George is getting married. I supposed she would prepare to attend."
Looking for a way to direct the discussion to her, Luke added,

"Do you want her to attend your wedding?" Peeking over at her before refocusing on the road.

"Obviously!" Sharon exclaimed, touching his hand on the gearbox. Luke subtly slipped his hand beneath her hand, lifting it onto the dashboard.

Ignoring the slight embarrassment she caused, Sharon continued, "Why not! I'm looking forward to a relationship with the woman that raised this wonderful man."
Sharon pointed at Luke and laughed that Luke adored.

"Sharon, you flatter me too much," he said with sparkles in his eyes, enjoying every word spoken by Sharon.

"No, seriously, Luke, you are a man. I see through your heart."

"Thank you for the compliment." Luke looked at her before facing the road again.

Sharon continued, "If you weren't a man, you wouldn't make peace with your family or try to sort out the hidden past between George and his parents."

"Sorry, it's quite the reverse. I'm not doing anything to reconcile their differences," Luke stated without looking at her.

After a long pause, she continued. "I know. It's one day at a time. Luke, you're making everybody know they have to take responsibility."

Luke replied, "Don't you think you should talk to George?"

"Me?" Sharon protested. "No, it's not my role to do so."

"Why? If I may ask, Sharon."

"Off the top of my head, I believe that the Finlands should have an honest conversation about George's past."

She turned to Luke and continued, "Also, I wonder why George keeps brushing the topic aside every time I talk about it."

Luke chuckled and replied, "I should ask you, since he's going to be your husband."

"Is that so?" demanded Sharon.

"Don't take so it seriously," Luke pleaded, "I was only joking!"

"Why are we all hiding things? If you think it never bothers him, you are wrong."

She sounded upset before continuing, "it bothers George... bothered about why a 'brother' suddenly shows up out of nowhere?... Why he'd be bothered about everything!"

Getting upset, Sharon continued. "You stay in his house. Why did you not say anything!?"

"Take it easy, Sharon." He tried to tone down the tension in her voice.

"I asked him. He refused to discuss the past. He'll only discuss the present."

"You guys should talk about the past."

"My point exactly. Initially, when I showed up, he was eager, but that was where it ended. George knows my mum is alive and my dad is dead. But he never asked me any question about my past. Even when I try to say something, he brushes it aside."

Sharon asked, "How come George is so weird?"

"Well, you are getting married to the weird one." Sharon smiled, looked out of the window. Her mind dashed between the features of the brothers before she replied to him.

"I know, but I love him. That's just the funniest thing. I know it is hard to get through to his heart, but once you do, he is very kind-hearted." She reflected on the brother she had betrothed her heart to.

"That I can imagine," Luke's voice sliced through her thoughts as he reflected on her words.

Luke became silent as he drove into the airport. Streams of unspoken words flowed between them.

Luke battled with his emotions, his heart tearing apart.

It's too late, Luke, he muttered under his breath.

THIRTY

Nearing the arrivals exit, Sharon immediately saw George waiting outside the building. She hopped out of George's sports car and raced towards him.

His arms wide opened, Sharon jumped on him. Sharon gave him a well-deserved embrace, a very strong hug.

"I missed you so much, darling," kissing him on his forehead.

"I missed you every second I was away from you, beautiful," George responded to her passionate kiss.

Meanwhile, Luke leaned on the car, waiting for the lovers to exhaust their welcome.

After a while, Luke exclaimed, "We thank the Saviour for journey mercies. Can we go now?"

As both walking towards Luke hand in hand, he saw a deep reflection of the love they shared, realising it would be evil to tell her the way he felt.

If I truly love her like I said I do, I need to let go and let God. Genuine love should be free to be!

George interrupted Luke's thought, pulling him in for a manly hug.

"How are you, man?"

"I'm good," Luke replied to his hug and ended with a firm handshake.

"Thanks for taking care of the love of my life. At least, this time, she would have missed me less because she saw me in you, every day."

"You bet!" Luke laughed in agreement, while Sharon gave George some light punches for embarrassing her. She blushed while George cuddled her.

"Can we go now?" Luke added to get everyone back to focus on the task at hand.

"Yes, shall we?" George added, his arms draped across Sharon possessively.

They all boarded the car. George and Sharon sat in the back, holding onto each other as if they might be ripped out of the other's arms.

"How was the trip, man?" Luke asked once they settled in and drove off.

"The journey was fine, apart from missing you all, especially my heart." He turned and gave Sharon a peck on her forehead.

"That's good. I can't wait to get you back so I will have less work." Luke teased.

"You will wait for a long time. I am getting married in a few days, remember!"

"Ha, ha!! You are right, if only I can escape the slavery."

As Sharon watched the brothers trade banter, she tensed a tone of defeat in Luke's voice.

A flash from the dream entered her mind, "Oh my!" she exclaimed.

The twins turned to face her, replying simultaneously, "Pardon!?"

"Oh! Nothing! I am enjoying both your company," she admitted.

"It's good to be back in England where you are both from," George turned his gaze to Luke and Sharon.

Luke replied, "I am glad you like it there, though I wouldn't have thought you would."

"Maybe not before I met Sharon, after Sharon I have fallen in love with Britain."

"And the royals?" Sharon added.

"You can say that again, with the royals." They all laughed because of the excessive sentiment placed on the royals by Americans.

"I am so looking forward to a British wedding with my beloved," George added, kissing her palm.

"For sure!" Luke confirmed George's undying love for the royal family and Sharon.

"Have you contacted my mum?" Luke added to move George to talk about something more personal.

Although the statement caught George off guard, he replied.

"Sure, I spoke to her on the phone. We went out together for coffee. She invited me for a meal."

"Thank you for reaching out to her." Luke appeared emotional at the thought of his mum and George together.

"You're welcome. She asked me to give you some things. It's in my luggage."

"Oh, thanks, George!"

"I look forward to eating more of her meals some time."

"Yeah, she's an excellent cook."

"Lucky me!" Luke teased him.

"You can say that again, lucky you!" agreed George. "I have all the stewards in the house, but there's nothing like having your mum cook the food and not stewards. You know you have a unique mother."

"Thank you," Luke reflected on the blessings of the Saviour despite all the odds against him.

"I guess the next few days, we need to focus on the wedding and get back on track. I will hopefully help in closing the gaps you suffered from the lack of your Mum's..." Sharon comforting word slid out.

"... Cooking! I couldn't agree more." Both echoed.

The three of them laughed at the way the twins ended each other's sentences.

"You guys are really twins!! Your brains process similar words at the same time!"

They are so similar. No surprise I couldn't tell the difference when my heart fell in love with both of them on different occasions.

Sharon's heart fluttered at the thought of the two brothers.

That evening, the twins, and Sharon had dinner in the Finlands' mansion.

They discussed the Nigerian traditional wedding, pre-wedding dinner, and church wedding in the UK. They would wait to hold the grand reception when the couple returned from their honeymoon.

Sharon explained how the two wedding planners had worked together to provide both the glamorous wedding for Mrs Finland and the modest wedding she dreamt of. Sharon noticed Luke seemed to be distracted throughout the dinner.

Luke avoided looking at her face and talking with her. The only time he replied to her comments was when she made it mandatory to have a conversation. Sharon knew where his attitude was coming from.

She was so ready to open the door, because once she opened that door; she was fearful of where it would lead her. *What if Luke's still in love with me? What if he's also feeling the same way I'm feeling every time I stare into his blue eyes? Sharon, you better let sleeping dogs lie.*

On the flip side, George talked away with a joyful expression, cracking jokes, and teasing his parents and sharing his experiences with the British people.

This revelation of George and his interaction with his parents was new to her. On one hand, she felt George was overly expressive at the expense of Luke. She was glad to see a new side of him. She felt the need to pull Luke out of his shell.

Sharon decided not to deal with the matter of his heart as she watched the new family dynamics on the table. Mr Finland Sr. was also unusually reserved at the table.

She could understand that he had a lot on his mind, and he might be thinking of ways to bring his family back together. As for Sharon and Luke, she announced to herself, *the dead should be left in the grave.*

After dessert, the boys went off to spend time together, a sweet relief for Sharon.

All the ladies continued to talk over their plans. By the ending of the evening, they agreed that George and Sharon would be on the flight to the UK in the next two days.

After the wedding clothes and the tuxedo were delivered as planned. Luke, their parents, and the rest of the close family would join them three days before the big day.

As envisaged, wedding preparations went into full gear. Sharon passed on most of her client portfolios to her assistants. She focused on making sure her wedding ran smoothly.

George and Luke went over for their suit fittings. Sharon, the wedding planner, and Mrs Finland headed to do the exclusive bridal gown fitting fully paid for by the Finlands'.

Sharon felt overwhelmed by her soon-to-be mother-in-law's decisions concerning the plans, especially her choice of a wedding dress.

Often, when she complained to Mrs O'Loan, she was reminded to maintain her boundaries the way they raised her. How would anyone do that when Mrs Finland must cross and dot every tee?

She was all too glad that her family had some independence about the Nigerian traditions and wedding arrangements without a constant checklist.

George and Sharon sat inseparable on the plane heading back to the UK to celebrate the love they shared. After a few hours of beauty sleep, Sharon lifted her head from George's shoulder, who seemed to be busy on his laptop.

"What is my heart doing?" she quizzed him with a yawn, stretching her hands to cover his ears, caressing his face.

"Patience, my lady! A few more days and I will eat you up! Tell me, considering the way you are rather expressive with your hands, what did you dream about?"

"Mr George Finland, keeper of lady Sharon's heart, of course!" Sharon playfully replied.

"Hope you will be ready to express how flirtatious your dream was," he teased her, placing a kiss on her forehead.

After a pause, he turned away from his iPad and continued, "I am writing my vows and to be honest, for the first time, I am finding it difficult to describe the way I feel about you."

Sharon took his hands in hers and said, "Do you want me to help?"

"No, I can handle it, it's just that since my brother showed up..."

Sharon interrupted him, "Glad you mentioned him. What has Luke got to do with this?" Sharon asked in defence because she was afraid George must have noticed the unspoken communication between Luke and herself.

"Sharon, please. I am unashamedly in love with you, but this is hard to say."

"Say what!?" Sharon was expecting the worst from him.

"Give me a moment to clear my head." Sharon waited for him to regain some composure before he continued.

"A few months ago, before you said 'yes' to me, Sharon, you told me about the stranger at the airport and the attraction with him. I looked like him yet differed from him."

"Yes, that is all true, but..." she shifted closer, still holding his hand.

"Luke was the guy you met at the airport. You fainted when you saw him in Dad's office." George expressed his words with his beautiful, tearful eyes. Sharon, speechless that George knew all along, waited anxiously for him to continue.

"I was afraid I would lose you when he showed up. My best option was to arrange a trip to the UK to give both of you some space."

"Oh, stop!" Sharon exclaimed. "You mean you set a trap for me? Why did you do that?" she questioned with tension in her voice.

"Sharon, wait, please! I learned something from you. You taught me love releases and gives. If I must give you up to Luke because of the attraction you had with him, I will!"

"So, let's fast forward. What changed?" she asked in eagerness.

"The day I arrived, I saw you guys, knowing there was no connection between you two. At the dinner, Luke seemed defeated. I knew I got my heart back. But sincerely, if I have to write an honest vow, I needed to let you know the truth from my heart."

Sharon embraced him in a fierce hug, speaking over his shoulder.

"Oh, George, when I said to you, I meant yes to you and no other. We laid our future before the Saviour to lead us, and I intend to follow through with you. Several times I tried to connect with Luke, he met me with resistance. My heart remains with you forever, and not Luke's."

Why have I not been able to get over Luke? He made a lifetime impression on my heart with only a single interaction. She was still hugging him tightly.

"Thank you, Beautiful,"

"Besides, I fell in love with you, the good and bad. I don't know Luke's good and bad yet." She smiled, placing her hands on his heart.

Laughing out, he replied, "You are the best!"

"Now that we have cleared the air, are you now able to write me the best vow any lady can ever imagine?"

"Beautiful, you are my vow. If the Saviour gave you to me, what else could I want in life?"

"Wait a minute!" something occurred to Sharon. George paused.

"Is that why you refused to talk with your parents about your past?"

"Sharon, I'd rather not allow any pain of the past to affect my future."

"George, sometimes the past is the doorway to the future. You need that healing, with the help of the Saviour for our future together."

Her words barely left her lips when the pilot announced the aircraft would descend. They advised all passengers to put on their seat belts.

"We will continue when we get home," George replied, holding his fingers gently under her chin.

Mr and Mrs O'Loan picked them from the airport at about noon. They drove George to his apartment in

London. Later in the evening, before they left him, George handed Sharon and her parents some bags of shopping.

"When and how did you get these?" Mrs O'Loan shouted in surprise.

"I'm sure we drive you from the airport without...

"Mum. Dad. You should be used to George's surprises by now. He must have done all these shopping months ago." She glanced at George with adoring eyes.

Smiling with the acceptance of the compliments for his benevolence, George added.

"Thought I should get my family something exclusive for the pre-wedding dinner."

"I understand Tom is arranging a bachelor's night for you."

"How kind of Tom! I am following all the instructions of my Beautiful Sharon and her wedding planners," said George, "obediently."

At which they all laughed at the solemn head bow he gave to Sharon, who added blissfully,

"You'd better!" she giggled.

Finally, they headed off to the village where Sharon's parents could spend the last precious

moments with their princess before they married her off.

The three of them spent the evening together chatting in the kitchen. Mr & Mrs O'Loan updated her on all the arrangements for the wedding.

According to her mum, once George's family arrived in the country, they would hold a close family dinner, followed by the Yoruba traditional wedding the next day. The third day will be the wedding celebration, invited-guest reception, and the late-night party before releasing the couple for their honeymoon.

"Mum, Dad, I am confused. Why was I told about these elaborate arrangements? I thought I was only coming to my wedding, and I will be off for my honeymoon."

Smiling, her father replied, "Same as you Sharon, I would have preferred the easier option, but your mum's family rarely takes the simple route. I guess you should know that by now."
Mr O'Loan stroked her lovely hands to reassure her.

"But, Mum, how do you plan to surprise the Finlands with all these arrangements?"

"Princess, calm down. Your aunts, uncles and I will not allow my child to get away with a simple wedding. We are Nigerians and you are, too."

Sharon's father chuckled and replied, "I told you, Sharon."

"Honey, don't make it harder for me, stop it!" her mum responded to his teasing with a flirtatious smile.

Facing Sharon, she continued, "Sharon, the two wedding planners had been working hard together to make the journey easy for us. I believe George's family is aware of all the arrangements and all requirements are already in place."

"That excludes me." Sharon brushed her comment about the wedding planners aside, standing up to refill her glass of drink.

"Anyway, Mum, George and I will be at the cake designer tomorrow to confirm our selection. We are running out of time."

"I understand you guys have made a choice already," her father observed.

"Yes Dad, we have, but we needed to make sure..." her mother interjected.

"Sharon, can we use the time more appropriately? I agree George will be here tomorrow. We will involve him in the finishing touches. If we've already sorted out the cake, I don't think we should spend more time on..."

Sensing the tension between his girls, her father stepped in.

"Okay, my ladies, let's take it easy. I think we should call it a night. I am tired. I bet my precious ladies need their beauty sleep, too."

"Thank you, Dad," Sharon said, standing up from the kitchen chair.

"Mom, Dad, I would like to head to bed." She gave her parents' hugs before heading to her bedroom.

"Darling, you should have allowed us to sort it out before she went off to bed."

"I know," he replied, embracing his wife.

"The girl is rather exhausted. It's been a long day. She might not be functioning well. I will get on the phone with George to be here first thing in the morning. Could you kindly get on the phone with the wedding planners? Shirley has flown in already, has she?"

"Yes, she has." With sparkles in her eyes, she continued, "I think what you said is brilliant. With the planner around, she will understand better. How did I get so lucky marrying you, my wise owl?"

"I love you. The best wedding organiser ever lived." Holding her closely, he kissed the wife of his youth.

Releasing her, he turned around to pick his phone so Mrs O'Loan could dial the two planners for a meeting at 9.00 am.

THIRTY – ONE

Before the Yoruba traditional engagement, there would be an informal introduction of the couple to create a cordial environment, a to get to know everyone.

In George and Sharon's case, both the formal and informal ceremony was scheduled to be a single event because of time constraints since George's family was to arrive from the US. The wedding planners explained the schedule for each participant at the wedding the next morning.

The invitation card included the date of the wedding and other information including the colour code, purple for the bride's family and ivory for the bridegroom's family.

The meals to be served for the engagement agreed upon by both wedding planners and Sharon's family, mostly Nigerian foods. Sharon's family covered the traditional wedding. George's family would cover the church wedding.

According to the explanation provided, the venue for the traditional dinner and wedding will be the Palace Hotel, a large hall able to hold up to 500 guests. Only 200 invites were sent out something unusual as for the average Nigeria wedding. The expectation was for twice as many invited guests.

Decorations would be an interpretation of the colours chosen to complement the joyful union, and requiring proper consideration of seating arrangements, cutlery, flower vases, floral arrangements, coloured balloons, tapestries of purple and ivory schemes.

White tablecloths, and chairs covered in the couple's ceremonial colours. The plan included the decoration of a prominent couch in front of the crowd for the bride and groom, and a top table for dignitaries.

The O'Loans contracted the catering to professional caterers to provide assorted Nigerian foods including jollof rice and moin-moin, which is beans pudding, pounded yam, amala (yam extract), fufu, and wheat meals, along with a variety of vegetable dishes.

Meat dishes were chicken, fried or roasted, fresh fish, and catfish and small chops like sausages and meat pies. Sweet snacks include small cakes, chin-chin, and other small traditional delicacies.

The drinks could be the responsibility of the hotel. The drinks include alcohol, juice, punch, fine wines, brandy, mineral water, and bottled water, based on the needs of the guests.

The lilac damask and lace outfit of the bride will match the purple female guests will wear.

Other items for the bride *aso-oke* include *gele*, which is the head tie, the *buba* top, and an *iro*, which is a large, ankle-length piece of material tied around her waist.

The bride's colours complimented the groom's outfit and a similar look. Sharon's accessories would be gold chains, beads, bangles, gold earrings, and shoes to match, already purchased by her special aunt Bola.

Mrs O'Loan said "This is her one and only daughter, and she deserved the best." George would dress in Agbada, which is a two-layered piece of material of heavy texture: ivory and lilac damask and lace aso oke.

After overseeing the thorough preparations, Sharon felt comforted that Mrs Loan had had her best interests all along. Meanwhile, George headed out to receive his parents.

Luke's mum had agreed to open up her large many-roomed home for most of the expected guests, but accordingly, the Finlands planned for all the three days' events of their son's wedding.

At 6:00 pm, all close family members from the two families gathered for the dinner, a formal introduction to get to know each family.

Sharon wore her new fitted cream dress decorate with diamond stones; an exclusive dress George chose on one visit to downtown London.

Her hair flowed over her shoulders in a wave of black to complement the exquisite gown. Sharon's parents dressed in purple and lilac coloured dress and shirt, the same gifts he got for them that time before they dropped him off in his flat.

Sharon walked into the dining room to the admiring awe of everybody. George recovered in an instant from his amazed gaze and walked up to Sharon.

"Sharon, my beautiful, you are impeccable."

"Thank you, Handsome Heart." as she released her body into his strong embrace, placing her sweet lips on his.

The bride and groom were lost in a world of their own, until George's mother walked up to them, pulling them reluctantly back to reality.

"Sharon, you looked breathtaking! My son is blessed to be marrying a wife of such beauty."

Taking Sharon by the hand, Mrs Finland led her to the rest of the family. Each family member introduced himself or herself to the others and then sat down to have dinner.

Everyone was enjoying the fine meal until suddenly, Luke quietly excused himself and walked out of the room. Sharon knew why Luke was finding it difficult to go through the dinner.

Sharon's marriage to his brother was proving too much for Luke to deal with! Her heartbeat raced faster with the knowledge that Luke loved her and was hurting. She quickly whispered a prayer.

Please, Saviour, could you help Luke? I don't know what to do. I love George and I love Luke, but I made a final choice for George.

Soon after her prayers, Luke returned to stay the rest of the evening. The dinner became bearable because his mum distracted him.

A constant puzzled gaze from Mrs O'Loan constantly peppered Sharon with silent questions of "What's going on with Luke?"

Sharon told herself. *No matter what happens, I am determined not to let Mum know the mess I am in, with my love for both brothers!*

Later that night, after the wedding banquet, Sharon spent some time with George, walking off the meal on the grounds of the hotel.

Tom, Luke, and his male friends approached them to whisk George away from her for the bachelor night.

Strolling back to her hotel room, she met Tom's wife and her friends, exchanging pleasantries before retiring to her hotel room to spend her last night as a spinster.

The wedding planners have managed their plans very well, with a perfect blend of UK and Nigerian customs. Though she was in the company of the girls, Sharon's mind travelled between Luke and George and the marriage vows she had to make to George.

I can't make Luke go away. He is part of the family, and we will occupy the same family mansion and see one another every day! Saviour, your words say you will keep me in perfect peace if I keep my heart stayed on you. I am trying to, but I am getting cold feet and I don't know if I should go through with marrying George.

Unable to open her insecurities to anyone, she trusted the Saviour to give her peace in her heart for each poignant moment of the coming days.

The long night stretched into late morning. Her wedding planner and chief bride's maid woke her up to eat and prepare for the traditional wedding.

"Sharon, wake up!! You can sleep as much as you want during your honeymoon! We don't have all day. Everything is ready except you. Stand up!"

They urged her to wake up. The wedding planner opened the curtains. A ray of sunshine shone in her eyes.

"Okay, I heard," she cried out and sitting upright on the bed, covering her eyes with the duvet.

"Can I at least have some time alone with the Saviour? Please let me start my wedding day, right?"

"We will give you some time," they said, walking out to give Sharon some privacy.

Forty-five minutes later, Sharon's mum knocked on her door.

"Please, come in," invited Sharon.

"Princess, I bless you among women," Mrs O'Loan swept into the hotel suite with a flourish.

"Mother, your entrance is grander, but I need to dress quickly."

"Princess, everybody is waiting for you. I came to announce we are about to start. I will send the ladies in to help you..."

"Thank you, Mum," Sharon replied, running into her arms. "Please, Mum, pray for me. I am scared to death."

"It's okay to have cold feet. Remember the Saviour has got this!" Holding Sharon in a firm embrace, her mother raised her voice and muttered sweet words to her Saviour about her daughter.
As she ended her prayers, the ladies flocked in.

"Sharon, Sharon, we need to hurry!" The ladies implored her. "Aunt Bola is keeping everyone on their toes."

"Thank you, ladies, I need help with dressing up," she pleaded with stress evident in her voice.

"Calm down, take a deep breath. Your dresser and makeup artist are here with us."

A Nigerian lady appeared from behind them announcing to everyone, "Madam Sharon, I am Tinu. I am here to..."

"Please, Tinu. I appreciate the introduction, but as you can see, we are behind schedule."

"Yes, Miss Sharon," agreed Tinu.
The ladies rally around with Sharon, helping her with the elaborate traditional dress, and putting finishing touches on their own dresses. Soon, they were all ready to step out of the room when Aunt Bola called for them.

The lengthy traditional engagement and marriage started in the banquet hall of the hotel.

The Alaga Ijoko (traditional master of ceremony) was the anchor, a contracted professional organised by Aunt Bola. *Alaga Ijoko* introduced herself. "My role is to officiate and coordinate the proceedings so that each provision of tradition is strictly adhered to."

Once she finished introducing herself, there was a collection of cash which the Alaga keeps, collecting cash every time she speaks through singing a traditional song and talking drums. She further questioned George's family as to their intentions and reasons for calling the gathering.

Later, the groom's family professional representative called the Alaga Iduro (Master of ceremony who follows the groom) introduced herself.

She provided the reasons for the gathering of the groom's family to beg for the hand of Sharon in marriage. The guests were allowed a question-and-answer session in the groom's absences and his friends.

Once the message was accepted by the bride's representative, she collects more cash and asks the groom and his friends to be formally introduced to the bride's family.

At this moment, George had a role as the groom which he didn't particularly enjoy since all attention would be focused on him!

Despite all the coaching he had with the Nigeria wedding planner, it never dawned on him how difficult it could be to get married the Nigerian way. He was glad to have familiar faces like Tom, Peter, and some Nigerian friends they had introduced him to since he met Sharon.

Above all, George had the support of his brother Luke and all the other friends selected from Sharon's family.

George danced into the hall gallantly, like a Yoruba warrior returning from a triumphant battle. The bride's master of ceremony put the friends of the groom through some battle moves until she was satisfied and accepted them.

Once George stood in front of Sharon's parents – Mr and Mrs O'Loan, they instructed him to bow to the parents and formally requesting their daughter's hand in marriage. This was carried out several times; until the bride's master of the ceremony had either gathered enough cash for herself or was satisfied that George had made his request known to the family well enough.

She was only ready to move to the next level of the ceremony when George showed signs of exhaustion from bowing down and prostrating in front of his in-laws.

All the guests cheered George for doing a job of conquering the hearts of his in-laws to allow the ceremony to move to the next stage.

The whole ceremony fascinated the groom's American family, though many had been coached about the process. The reality, they say, is better than they imagined.

George was finally allowed to take a well-deserved seat on the artfully decorated couch provided for the bride and groom in full view of the guests on the couch in the ceremonial colours chosen by the celebrants.

Seated on the couch swathed in fabrics showing the ceremonial colours, George waited to be joined by his bride, knowing full well he had earned his due in cash and kind.

Now, it was his favourite niece who read the formal letter from the groom's family. The guest cheered about her accuracy in delivering her lines, persuading Sharon's family of her uncle's undying love for her.

After she read the letter, the master of the ceremony from George's family hand delivers the letter to Sharon's parents on their knees, receiving cash delivery fees as prescribed by the bride's master of ceremony.

After Mr & Mrs O'Loan accepted the letter from Aunt Bola, their mouthpiece, her parents read a letter of response to either accept or reject the love or marriage request.

From Sharon's family, her niece, Kemi, read the letter of acceptance. Thus, finally, Sharon's family accepted George's family's request to marry her.

The next stage proceeds with the guests eating and drinking because both families are now at the engagement stage. George's family presented the list of the items for the engagement, under the strict arrangement by the wedding planners.

By now, unable to watch any more of the lengthy celebrations, Luke stepped out and took a walk in the garden.

He mournfully decided he would never love someone again for the rest of his life, the way he loved and lost his Sharon to his brother George.

George's parents presented general gifts for each traditional ceremony. These included a bag of sugar, a bag of rice, alligator pepper, many bitter kolas, a bag of salt, kola nut, a Christian Bible, a keg of honey, about forty large tubers of yam, non-edible items including expensive materials like lace, several pairs of shoes, a wristwatch, a gold engagement ring, and head ties.

Each of these items had different meanings and significance for the life of the new couple.

George and his family watched and were fascinated by the exchange going on. The only thing on George's mind was having Sharon sit next to him. He envisioned her beauty when dressed in African attire. This would be the first time he would see Sharon in her native attire.

If I like it, he thought, I will not mind encouraging us to wear them occasionally after our wedding. Seems I am converted to Nigeria's traditions. Aunt Bola suggested I would fall in love with it, and she is right, though the dancing is exhausting.

His wandering thoughts dissipated upon the announcement that they should usher the bride in. George searched for Luke. He was seen nowhere. He beckoned on Peter to get a group of friends to find him. George was afraid his brother might not handle the sight of Sharon and himself married. They found Luke in the garden.

He jumped up in shock when Peter touched his shoulder. "Luke, are you okay? Do you want to talk about it?" Peter asked in a supporting tone.

"Nothing, I am fine. I just needed some fresh air. It's exhausting to marry a Nigerian lady," Luke teased, trying to distract from the main issue.

Peter continued, despite his distractions. "Sharon once told me she had an encounter with a stranger while on her way to the US for the first time. She fell in love with that stranger."

Luke, still looking away, he continued. "I believe she was not wrong. We all encouraged her to trust the Saviour and heart to make her choices."

Luke stood up to leave, but Peter touched his shoulder. "She loves you still, please, you need to understand. It took her a long time, but she gave in. I believe the Saviour will work out His plans for you."

Turning back with teary eyes, Luke replied. "I understand."

But he refused to admit to anyone the extent of his genuine feeling for Sharon. Even his mother, his closest confidant since his dad died, did not know. One thing was sure, he was not wrong in thinking Sharon felt the same way about him. But should he let go?

The two men walked into the hall in time to meet the bride with her face covered. The guests heralded her in with dancing and singing. They led her in with her friends and bridesmaids.

All the ladies wore the traditional *buba* and *iro* matching the bridal colours. The ladies twirled in a boisterous dance down the hall. They ushered Sharon in, similar to what had happened with George.

The master of the ceremony followed the same etiquette. The only difference is, they will give the money collected this time to the bride for her keep. Sharon swung left and right to the sound of the music.

Even though this would be the only time she would have to dance this hard, she made all effort. George watched with pride as his bride danced before his parents and her parents, and the guests showered her with cash. George and his bride were becoming tired when the master of ceremony requested the singing band turn down their music.

The two masters of ceremony worked together to introduce Sharon into the groom's family. A formal welcome into Finland's family was made official by asking Sharon to sit in-between Mr and Mrs Finland.

George's parents prayed for their new daughter. Sharon was led to her parents, and seated sandwiched between them, and her parents prayed for her as well.

"What a rich culture!" George whispered to Luke, who was standing beside him.

"You are a blessed man, George." Luke patted George on his shoulder, forgoing his desire. Sharon assumed her place beside George, her groom.

Traditionally, Sharon and George were already married by this ceremony. After a brief pause, to encourage some alone time between the couple, the guests requested that Sharon picked her favourite gift. She stepped out elegantly to pick the Bible. Then everyone cheered at her choice.

"Why did you choose the Bible, the smallest of the gifts?" asked the bride's masters of ceremony.

"The Bible is the source of life. I find here all the wisdom I need to build my home." Everyone loved her response and cheered her on.

They requested George to join his bride in front of their family and they showered prayers of blessings on them. The new couple then danced over to the engagement cake stand, a beautiful two-tier velvet sponge cake with lovely ivory icing.

There were small figurines of the couple in traditional wear. The cake-maker explained the significance of the cake's contents to the guests before the cutting. The groom, master of ceremony, assisted by George and Sharon.

"Now to the latest couple in town, at the count of J-E-S-U-S, you cut the cake."

Everyone joined in the counts and as she echoed the last "S," thus the couple in unity cut their cake. At the joyful sound of the mixed English and traditional music, George fed Sharon some cake and wine. Sharon did the same for George, and they shared a kiss, to the amusement of the guests.

They had completed the contract marriage between the two families. The only item on the agenda is to dance, feast, and make merry. A live band performed.

The dancing time started with the couple on the dancing floor. The music was ethnic but combined contemporary popular songs blending with both English renditions, and Yoruba's native tongue with talking drums.

The band members sang traditional songs from juju music, afro juju music, highlife music, gospel music, hip hop, and current Nigerian sounds. The traditional engagement party ended with taking photographs of the two families, guests, and friends.

It was only about 10.00 pm when George and Sharon had the first chance to be alone all day. She collapsed on his lap with George wrapping his arms around his Bride passionately.

"You did well today, beautiful! You, your family, your traditions are so amazing! I know we talked and practised, but nothing is the same as reality."

"Thank you, my Handsome Heart!!" Sharon hugged her husband happily. "The Finland family did well, too. Thank you for everything."

"I should thank you for having me." acknowledged George.

They shared the memory of the entire day, the colours, decorations, music, foods. Suddenly, George echoed.

"Sharon, I pledged to you beautiful, your people shall be my people and your God my God."

"I know those words too well, and it will do me well as we begin this new life journey together." As they shared a romantic moment, her mind wandered to Luke. She whispered a few words of prayers for his wellbeing, until Sharon fell blissfully asleep on George's lap.

THIRTY - TWO

The next morning, Sharon woke up with the insistent beep from her phone. Finding she was still on George's lap, Sharon panicked.

"George, George!" Waking poor George up, she asked, "Where is my phone? Do you know we slept on the couch?" she said with her eyes wide opened.

"Take it easy, beautiful, you slept off and not me, and I could not disturb your beauty sleep," assured George.

"You sound just like my dad!"

"Don't be surprised. I'm part of the family now," George teased back.

"Seriously, George! Where is my phone?"

"The question should be, where is your bag?"

Both searching non-stop until she found it tucked between two sofa cushions.

"How on earth did this even get here?" Sharon exclaimed.

Opening her envelope clutch bag, she checks her phone to see the caller and the twenty-odd, missed calls and congratulatory messages from Mrs O'Loan and others.

George, staring flirtatiously at his Bride from the couch, replied.

"Is everything okay, should we become worried?"

"George, the look on your face isn't one of concern. Can't you be serious?"

Adjusting his position on the cushion, he continued, "Right, do I have a more serious face now, my beautiful Bride? I pray for all the kids to look just like you."

"Okay," ignoring his mention of kids, Sharon continued, "I have twenty-odd, missed calls. Where is your phone? Nobody called you! How did I sleep so soundly?"

"Talk about the snoring!" he teased back, leaning toward the sexy figure in front of him. "I want to eat you up right now."

Impatiently, Sharon pulled away from him and shouted, "George, what if something has happened? I need to call Mum back immediately!!"

George took hold of her hand and drew her close into his embrace. While Sharon dialled her mother's number, George whispered gently, caressing her neck.

"I switched off my phone. I didn't want anyone to bother us yesterday."

"Did you hide the bag, too?" Sharon sounded annoyed.

"No, I didn't," George drawing her to himself with ease.

"Beautiful, you slept like a baby. I couldn't even let go of you for fear of waking you. I needed to sleep, too. You were too beautiful to disturb while asleep. I am grateful that I will be sleeping and waking up to see you each morning for the..."

"Oh, hello Mum," interrupted George's words, as Sharon held the phone to George's ear while her head laid on his shoulder.

"George, I have been looking for you two all night. We thought something happened to you."

"Why, Mum? I thought you guys saw both of us sitting on the sofa yesterday."
Sharon said, releasing herself from George, standing as though annoyed with his romantic gestures.

Turning to see his sad expression. Sharon held his hand, sat back on his lap, and continued on the phone. George could not get his hands off her, melting every sense of resistance she had left from before her wedding night.

"Mum, I am married now," Sharon protested.

"I know, Princess, but it is unlike you not to respond to calls. You got us all worried."

"Mum, I am with George, and we slept in. Guess what, I am still in those heavy clothes from yesterday."

"You mean the lace or the...?" her mum teased.

"Mum don't be naughty. It was our wedding night. Why would you even call us?? I know what you are thinking! We did nothing as George and I were too exhausted, and we were out in public on the sofa. I slept on his laps until this morning."

"Princess, we worked you hard this time," continued Sharon's mother.

"Morning, Mrs O'Loan," George called out into the phone, rescuing his Bride from the teeth of the dragon.

"Morning George, how was your night? Did you hear...?"

"Mrs O'Loan, I heard every word. I have kept your daughter, my wife, safe in my lap all night!" reassuring her.

"Look at that, Mum! George is protecting his territory." They all laughed together as Sharon commented with satisfaction, "Your daughter, my wife, I like that, H.H., it sounds cool to me."

"Same here," her mum laughed back.

"Where is Dad?"

"You should know your dad by now, he is out already. He planned with Mr Finland and the rest of the men to go golfing this morning."

"Oh, gosh!" George exclaimed, "I am supposed to be the reason for them meeting to golf." The two women laughed at the sudden remembrance of his morning schedule.

"When you have this beauty in front of you," kissing Sharon, George the Bridegroom continued, "You forget the entire world still exists."

Leaving Sharon talking to her mum about the plan for the day, he hurried off the hotel suite to dress and to catch up on a few golf rounds if he could still meet the men at the hotel golf course.

Mum repeated Sharon's comments to the other ladies with her on the breakfast table. While the ladies echoed their joy, teased, and repeated how fond they were of the twins,

Aunty Bola shouted as George appeared fully dressed for golf.

"Is his brother Luke married or engaged? We can get him a beautiful Nigerian girl. We've got lots of them."

The thought of giving Luke up to someone else dawned on Sharon, but she did not give herself away.

George responded, "No, Madame Aunt, he is not engaged. I know Luke would love that. He is fond of my Nigeria Babe."

Hitting him pleasantly, Sharon replied, "don't mind him, Aunt, he is on his way out."

To George, she held her hand over the phone and whispered.

"You look sexy in those pants, my man. God help me!"

Hearing his Beautiful' s hinting comments about him, George walked back, planted a kiss on her forehead, working down to her lips, leaving his Bride breathless.

He then walked away with, "I will be back to eat you up."

"Eat you up!?" shouted the ladies at the other end of the phone line.

In dismay, Sharon admonished, "Mum, don't let them listen in. It's a private conversation!!"

"Young woman, you better head out to get yourself cleaned up and get ready for the last stage of your wedding celebration."

"Yes, Mum," Sharon obeyed.

"Can you join me in my room? I would like us to talk to the Saviour together for the last time before I am officially married off from the O'Loan family."

"Off course, daughter, I will see you in fifteen minutes."

"I am going back to the room, Mum. Please send food to my hotel room. Is the makeup artist about? I have not spoken to anyone in my bridal team. Everyone must be worried sick."

Mrs O'loan teased, "Everyone is ready except you, Princess. I sent a message to Faye, your chief bridesmaid. Immediately I located you. They should all be waiting for you in the room."

"Thanks for that, mum," she said, dropping her phone into her clutch and heading to the door.

The next three hours, every hand was on deck to celebrate Sharon's summer afternoon British wedding. The section of the hotel used faced the breath-taking sunset.

At the end of each seated aisle, Angel's trumpet -scented candles hung from naked tree branches. Ivory coloured leaves spread down the floor of the aisle, as far as the eyes could see. They were slightly moist so they would not crack as the guests stepped on them.

All the close family and friends were formally dressed in the colours for the occasion, varying shades of purple and ivory. On either side of the aisle, they sat in covered white chairs with lilac and ivory sachets hanging from the aisle chairs to complement the green summer grass.

As each guest arrived at this pre-wedding reception, they were served with drinks, and everyone exchanged pleasantries. A memory box displayed shared memories about the couple.

The decorations exclusively catered to the taste of the Finlands, who were covering the cost of the entire day. They left no stone unturned to reflect the best they wanted for their eldest son's wedding.

Back in Sharon's hotel room, she was a case of nerves. She was at least glad that the photographers had already taken the pre-wedding shots. Noticing her tense face cracking up her beautiful makeup, she heard a faint voice,

"All Right, okay, right Sharon, you need to breathe...

"Can you do that for me?" one bridesmaid asked.

Only five minutes remained before her wedding began. Sharon was as nervous as she was the first time George asked her on a date with him.

And the struggle she had to go through the past weeks to walk away from her love-at-first sight did not help at all. *Saviour, should I go through with him? There is no turning back from here, till death do us part.*

Her heart was torn apart, like a predator had reaped the heart of its prey.

"Sharon, calm down!" Toni, her chief-bridesmaid, and longest-serving friend, yelled, "Can I get Aunt Bola? She knows how to handle you better than anyone else?"

"I can, I can breathe," Sharon responded to her, "I need my Mrs O'Loan to calm down."

All the ladies-in-waiting stared at her wide-eyed. "Uh, Sharon... about that. Seconds lapsed...

"You mean, you can't get my mother!? I can't get married without seeing her!! My Mum is my lucky charm. No way!"

"Hey!!" Jenny, Maid of Honor, rushed in and yelled, "Everyone's here. Your mum is seated. The wedding is about to start. I see George and his handsome brother Luke waiting at the end of the aisle, and he's just as nervous as you."

Another bridesmaid asked, "Sharon, did Luke come to the wedding with a special someone?" All the ladies laughed at once, which seemed to ease the tension. Gazing into her eyes, Sharon replied.

"Not that I know of. You could walk up to him and ask him out." The bridesmaids giggled.

"Do you not want to marry the love of your life over the craving to speak with your mum for the last time before taking your vows?" interrupted another, taking hold of the situation.

Sharon shook her head. "Good, because if you don't marry him, I know plenty of women in this room are ready to change into your amazing dress and marry him."

Luke, George's best man and his friend, cracked jokes about his bride to keep the groom calm. They watched as the guests moved from the pre-wedding reception area to take their seats as silence grew to show respect for the soon-to-begin service.

The officiating minister stepped in front of the erected podium, preparing to bless the couple.

The minister of the day was Sharon's pastor from her parents' church. George had enjoyed every pre-marital counselling session they had together via zoom and a few times they met with him.

He is just as open, honest, and kind as the O'Loans, although he has a shy disposition until you speak to him. George understood that to be a common trait of British folks until they get to know you personally.

"Please lets us stand for the bride," the minister announced to the guests, as they stood smiling with excitement.

As the music began, the flower girls threw the petals on the floor. The little ring bearer walked confidently behind the two girls down the aisle. The guests whispered to each other, expecting the incoming bride.

It is my turn at last! All eyes will soon be on me.

Mr O'Loan greeted Sharon at the entrance to the sanctuary, taking her arm.

"I wouldn't miss the world for this chance," he whispered into her ears. "My princess, you look gorgeous," he escorted her down the seemingly endless aisle.

Her father became the strength she needed and without him, Sharon would have fainted. The guests looked at her, waving one after another, taking pictures, smiling, each other trying to get a view of the beautiful bride.

One thing was for sure, though... no one made a sound. Up ahead, Sharon beheld George, her future husband, the love of her life, her everything.

George stood taller than usual, his shoulders back, and his eyes on her. If Sharon wasn't mistaken, she could have sworn tears filled his eyes. Unlike George, her nervousness kicked in tenfold. The attention of all the guests felt too much to handle.

The thing was that she only had ten more steps to go when her eyes turned on the groom's men. Next to her groom was Luke, her all-time first choice. For the first time, they had the same haircut, the same tuxedo, the same broad shoulder.

I wanted to marry you, Luke. If only you spoke the day we met, we would have....

Her thoughts interrupted when her father led her to the end of the aisle. Mr O'Loan hugged his fairy princess, said, "Princess, I'm proud of you," handing Sharon over to her groom, placing Sharon's hands in George's smiling tearfully.

Before turning to walk away, Mr O'Loan patted George on his shoulder. He indicated George was part of the family.

Standing next to her 'Handsome Heart' she felt overwhelmed. He was the safest place on earth for Sharon at the moment. George and Sharon, hand in hand, approached the minister. From the corner of her eyes, she observed Luke. He seemed rather discreet.

Maybe he had finally gotten over me. *It's time I let go of this guilt and self-pity and begin this journey. Is this happening? Will I soon be Mrs George Finland? Luke called me by that name a few weeks ago. It's becoming a reality now.*

The minister said to the guests, "You may now be seated." The guest and families took their seats.

"Dearly beloved," he began, "we are gathered here this afternoon to witness this man and woman joined in holy matrimony."

The minister led them into exchanging vows. George read his vows, first a poem he wrote on the plane and then.

"I, George Josiah Finland, take you, Sharon Oluwatobiloba O'Loan, to be my lawfully wedded wife, my heartbeat, the very reason my life makes any meaning. The light that shone on the dark path of my life. The beauty that brings the best out of me. My constant friend, my faithful partner, and my love from this day forward. In the presence of our family and friends, I offer you my solemn vow to be your faithful partner in sickness and in health, in good times and in bad, and in joy as well as in sorrow. I promise to love you unconditionally, to support you in your goals, to honour and respect you, to laugh with you and cry with you, and to cherish you for as long as we both shall live."

Standing flushed by the words used to describe her, she expressed her heart in words to him.

"I, Sharon Oluwatobiloba O'Loan, take you, George Josiah Finland to be my lawfully wedded husband, my only handsome heart, the day I saw you I was smitten. A double vision, I call it. God knows you were hard to reach, but once I did, I am grateful to choose you above all. You have a teachable heart that makes me reach to know you more. My best friend, my partner in mischief and my heart belongs to you from this day forward. Each of your surprises brings my day to a graceful close. The way you look at me makes my heart melt for you. Praying never to solidify again. In the presence of our family and friends, I offer you my solemn vow to be your faithful partner in sickness and in health, in good times and in bad, and in joy and in sorrow. I promise to love you unconditionally, to support you in your goals, to honour and respect you, to laugh with you and cry with you, and to cherish you for as long as we both shall live."

After exchanging their vows with tears filling both their eyes. Sharon sensed some guests wiping their eye too. The ring bearer came forward and presented the rings. Sharon placed George's ring on first, then he placed on hers.

The minister nodded and asked, "If anyone objects to the marriage, speak now or forever hold your peace."
Sharon feared Luke might speak, as this was his only last chance to tell her how he felt. But no one said a word. She watched him, staring straight ahead, his mind many kilometres from them.

"With the power vested in me by the English Government, I now pronounce you, man, and wife. You may kiss the bride."

George leaned in and kissed Sharon softly, like he had never done it before. Everyone cheered for the couple, however, Sharon barely noticed as her full attention rested on George.

In the Christian tradition, the couple took individual candles (lit earlier by their mothers) and used those candles to light a larger candle (called the unity candle). That symbolised they are no longer "two" but now "one."

Soon after, they did the whole candle ceremony. The minister shared a few lines from the Scriptures. He then prayed for the couple, and then the immediate family, and blessed all the guests for a successful wedding service.

The newest couple in town gallantly walked out, hands in hand, heading to the reception, followed by their attendants. As they left the church, Sharon thought to herself, I am beyond hungry for food and my beloved.

A little while after the wedding evening dance at the night party; the recently married couple left their families for their room. Heading off to a well-deserved honeymoon.

George and Sharon knew the company was in the excellent hands. Luke and George's parents were more than able to cover up for them for the next month.

George's dream had come true. He had his heart secured in the hands of his lovely wife, Sharon. True to form, he planned their honeymoon trip before he proposed to his wife.

She had always wanted to visit one of the exotic countries in Africa. When she suggested Kenya during their discussion, George was more than excited that his longing to experience Africa and a safari would also include having his new wife at his side.

THIRTY - THREE

A month flew by, Mr and Mrs George Finland came back to reality. Their return completed with a reception for the new couple by George's parent, the last part of the package deal with the US wedding planner.

They hosted the reception in the Finlands' mansion. They littered the grounds with lights from the gates to the garden, the 10 acres of grounds filled with visitors from all walks of life.

George and Sharon drove in, the grounds buzzed with eager chatter. They could see children running around the meadow in a good-natured game of tag. As the newlywed couple entered the crowded hall, applause broke out across the room in welcome.

There were the scraping feet as friends and family got up for a standing ovation and the happy couple made their way through them, smiling and holding hands. They greeted folks with hugs.

George leaned in for a kiss time and time again. Amid the crowd, Sharon's eye went back and forth, looking out for Luke. Sharon pondered anxiously.

Has he stayed away because of me?

After a few moments, Mr Finland raised his glass clearing his throat introducing everyone to his home and the reception. He and his wife led everyone to the garden where lots of people were already eating and drinking.

The food corner showed a display of different dishes, snacks, both contemporary and local. Sharon sighted the two-tier lemon cake she chose with the wedding planner. The icing on the cake was the colour of the lemon green dress she wore on her first date with George.

The memories of that night would be present forever. She couldn't wait for her tastebuds to work through it. Stepping out suddenly, Luke approached them.

"Hey big brother," Luke said, coming over to give me a handshake.

"How's it going? Hope you had a relaxing honeymoon. Are you liking your party?"

Sharon held her husband's hands intimately as George nodded.

"Very much so. We're delighted to be welcomed home so joyously!"

Luke hugged and slapped him on the back.

"Stop with such nonsense!!" He muttered his words. Sharon sensed something was wrong with him.

"Luke, are you okay?" She reached out as though on a rescue mission. She had never heard him use the word "Nonsense" before.

"Sharon! Oh, Mrs O'Loan, you talk too formally. And loosen up, George, don't be so stiff." Luke shoved the drink in his hand in front of his brother's face.

"Hey, drink it. You need it more than anyone in this room."

Sharon stood motionless, staring at a Luke she did not recognise. *I think he is tipsy. Does he drink? One month away, and Luke's changed.*

George smiled and reluctantly took the drink.

"We don't plan on staying long, Luke. We wanted to see Mum and Dad."

Holding Luke's hands, George continued, "Luke, is everything okay? You rarely drink."

"Okay," George's brother confirmed, "Having a few bad days. I am okay."

Turning around, Luke put a hand to his ear as if listening to something far away.

"Hear that.... that's your song. Go ahead, the dancing floor is waiting for you guys."

George let go of his Sharon's hands and dropped the drink. "Did you do that, brought in my band?" George exclaimed, with delight grin over his face.

"Yep. But, unless you stay for a little longer, there is no way you will enjoy the whole evening. Leave if you guys want."

"Uh, no," he grinned, looking at his wife, "We'll stay."

"Are you sure?" Luke picked up the drink from the ground and handed it to George.

"You know, your wife played a major role in getting them here.

"Such thoughtfulness!" George said eagerly. Turning to Sharon, he pulled her off her feet and planted kisses on her lips.

"I could not get these guys around since they know I am changed. How did you do it?"

"I learned from the best teacher."

"You can say that again," he led his wife towards the room where the band was playing. Luke stood watching the happy couple like a lost sheep.

That evening, George, and Sharon danced and shared the memories of their first dance as a couple in the UK.

The dances were the sweetest moments, followed by kisses shared between them. Others joined them from time to time, but Luke was nowhere to be seen. Soon, Sharon's heels hurt terribly.

She whispered into George's ears, "If you don't let me stop now, we will head to the emergency soon."
Laughing at the expression on her agonised face, he led her into a bedroom for a rest.

A few months after the wedding reception, Sharon sensed her Handsome Heart withdrawing from her. She tried reaching him, but he was closed to sharing what bothered him.

George's relationship with her was loving, yet she knew all was not right. She noticed tension rising between George and his parents.

The reasons were not far-fetched. His refusal to speak to his parents about his past was gradually taking a toll on him. She, as a wife, spent time with the Saviour discussing her husband with Him.

Maybe she should have impressed on George to sort out his relationship with his parents before the wedding. Wisely, Luke suggested it.

However, she had learned from Mrs O'Loan some matters of the heart need time for healing and a rush will do no one well. She only prayed this situation would turn out well.

Without Sharon's knowledge, George requested a meeting with the family lawyer to find out about his inheritance. George wanted to know what to expect when the time came. He was desperate to know if his parents would treat his inheritance the same way they had hidden the information about his childhood.

The lawyer refused to discuss any information with him. An opportunity came up when his parents went on a well-deserved holiday. George went to his family home to visit Luke, who had moved in with their parent after George's marriage.

Luke welcomed him to lunch with no awareness of his intentions.

"Hello Brother," greeted Luke. "I wonder why you are here alone. Where is your heart?"

With unanswered queries, Luke continued,

"She is fine. I requested a visit alone with you, as you and I have not spent time together since we married."

Nodding his head, Luke replied, hugging him.

"You are right. Come in."

"They must have settled you in. Mum and Dad must be glad to have you all to themselves."

Talking toward the dining room, Luke turned around. "Talking about Mum and Dad, have you discussed with Dad?"

"Discussed what?" George feigned ignorance, with tension rising in his tone. Sensing George's discomfort, Luke ignored his line of questioning and replied, "Let's get lunch first! I am famished!"

"I know Sharon loves her nutritious food and would want you to eat that way as well," Luke replied with an endearing grin. He had to step carefully, never sure where he stood in George's mind.

They ate lunch as George discussed the direction, he would like Luke and himself to drive the company. It seemed to Luke that George spoke as though the company belonged to him.

Luke was not ready to take over the company, something he should tell George. His life belonged in the UK. His mother lives in the UK and ultimately, he could not wait to disappear from seeing his lost rib, Sharon.

The heartache he had suffered since the marriage had led him to consume alcohol, something he had not taken since he was a teenager.

Luke was glad Peter supported him, although he refused to open up to Peter about Sharon. He sought an opportunity to return home, away from the complications of his new family relationships.

Luke wondered if he would ever meet a woman who, with a glimpse, could capture his heart. If Sharon was meant for his brother and they were married, Luke could not understand why he could not say goodbye.

Though he staggered for a while, he thought he could begin again. Yet he was not sure about his place in his brother's heart.

After lunch, George excused himself and headed to his father's safe. It was not long before he got the combination.

He knew they would include Luke in their will. "Suddenly it seems the world rotates around Luke," he muttered with jealousy under his breath.
His search led him to an unwanted discovery. Mr and Mrs Finland had set two-third of the inheritance to be handed over to Luke.

"This is impossible!" he exclaimed in anger. "Why on earth would they do this to me? That means they never forgave me for my past mistakes. Does it mean Luke just shows up and gets everything?"
In anger, he took pictures of the documents, safely returned them. George headed to his brother to pick a fight with him.

But at that moment, Sharon called. Staring at his phone, he deliberately refused to pick, when a text popped up from her, "SOS!!"

"Are you okay, Beautiful Heart?"

"I am missing you since I woke up and I need my husband. I can't live." She pleaded like a small child.

"I will only return on one condition, beautiful."

"I know what you want. I am ready. The bath is also ready," she teased back.

"I will round up with Luke and head out." promised George.

"Talking about Luke, is he okay?"

"Yes! Why?" George chuckled.

"The Luke at the reception was a one-off. I believe he turned a new leaf. He has to be on his behaviour around his beloved sis-in-law."

"For real! Sis-in-law." Sharon inwardly felt the weight of pain she must have caused Luke by turning a blind eye to the unspoken feelings between them.

"And I chose you as my 'one and only' Handsome Heart." Sharon shifted herself on her bed as her eyes filled with tears of thankfulness and her undying love for her new husband. She fondly reached to rub over his pillow as she as she always does with his head.

"I caught you, my beautiful inseparable heart," George whispered, as the tension within him fizzed out at the sound of Sharon's voice over the phone.

Sharon has a positive effect on me, George believed. *Saviour, please send her my way when I feel the need for undesirable actions as I just intended.*

"Luke, I have to go. Duty calls," George echoed at the sight of his brother.

Clearing his throat, as though he could not decode the meaning of the words "duty calls," Luke said.

"I just made coffee for both of us. We were still discussing the new takeover plans for the UK."

"We can talk business later, for now..."

"You aspire to be with your new wife," he stretched out his hands for a goodbye handshake and turned towards the door.

George walked out, leaving Luke wondering what his visit was all about. *We barely spent time after lunch, though he spent a considerable amount of time doing what he came for.*

Luke felt a sense of deep-seated unease.

Something bad is going to happen, I just know it!! Luke stood shaking his head, puzzled.

Weeks afterward, George's changed behaviour was getting on Sharon's nerves. Sharon tried all she could to reach into the cave of her husband's heart.

One day, not long after, when visiting the mansion, a fierce George stormed past Sharon into his father's office to confront his parents.

What is going on with George this morning?

She hurried after George to find out what could be wrong. All apparently was not well. Sharon was terribly concerned about him.

"No, you are totally unfair, and I deserve to know why!!" George's angry voice echoed through the walls of the office.

"Keep your voice down," his mother pleaded.

"No, not this time! You kept everything hidden from me. Who am I? What am I to you?"

Sharon's feet were in front of the office door as she deliberated whether to enter.

"If your son did not show up, I would have had to wait until you guys were in the grave before..."

Sharon interrupted by stepping inside. She thought, maybe if I step in, I can calm my Handsome Heart down. The room fell silent as all eyes fixed on her.

"I can come back," she stepped back hesitantly, holding on the door ready to bolt, shrinking from the troubled faces.

"Sharon, you can stay." Cynthia whispered, "You are part of the family. Your presence here would calm the storm."

Walking to George, Sharon placed her hands over her husband's, comforting him, while Sharon's eyes searched the room.

The eyes of the four Finlands focused away from the others in the room. She stepped towards George's side, choosing to sit near George on the arm of the leather sofa. Luke sat face down, tears rolling down his cheeks.

Moments later, after a prolong silent, clearing his throat and cleaning his brow, Luke spoke up.

"Mr and Mrs Finland, George, Sharon. I came searching for my family to know my roots. I found my roots and I embrace my roots."

His eyes filled with tears, he continued, "The last thing I want is to be the centre of friction. I'd rather return to my old life and pretend all you my beautiful family never existed than to cause a breakdown in..."

George interrupted, "Luke, I do not imagine you are the reason for a Finland family breakdown. I rather think you came in and shed light on the darkness I have been living in."

George stood up, walking toward the ornate drinks cart. Sharon followed him, holding her hands around his waist to comfort him.

He responded to her tenderness gratefully.

"They lied to me all my life. They lied. Now they take all my inheritance and hand it over to a total stranger." he sobbed bitterly.

Their parents sat muted. *I guess it was the best they can do now. They must have their reasons. I only wish they were honest with George, so it would not end in such pain.* Sharon rubbed her hands over her husband's temples to help soothe his extreme emotional stress.

Luke continued, "I would like to request that you write all the inheritance over to George's name. He will be at liberty to do what he wants with it."

With a grin, looking at Sharon, then his parents and George, Luke said, "With Sharon by his side, I trust he will make the right choices. Saying that, I guess, I need to take my leave and start packing my things."

Luke stood, picked up his mobile phone off the coffee table, taking a few steps towards the door, when Mrs Finland pleaded with him,

"Luke, my son, I lost you once. I pray I do not lose you again," tears streamed down her cheeks. She turned toward her husband, begging him to say something.

Mr Finland was about to say something, but in the confusion, Sharon stepped in.

"I know things don't always turn out the way we planned out. We all have to learn to talk things over as a family, the family we are trying to build."

"I can't see that," Luke whispered in frustration.

"Can we all sit down and talk it through? It will be good for everyone to air out all their pain in the open."

Looking at Luke, she grinned her beautiful smile at him as usual. His heart melted at the sight. Luke turned around and took his seat.

Mr Finland broke the silence, clearing his throat. He slowly started expressing his thoughts.

"It all started when your mum and I were in primary school. We spent most of the time together, but they wanted to keep us apart because of our families. Cynthia's family is Jewish and strongly forbade her from making friends with me. We were from two separate worlds. Her parents were extremely rich, while I was the son of the housekeeper. Our differences never stopped our friendship."

Holding his wife's hands, he continued in a low voice.

"Cynthia and I swore an oath to stick to each other no matter what happened. Thus, we continued seeing each other into our teenage years until the inevitable happened. I made your mum pregnant at fourteen. When her parents heard, they promised to disown her unless she chose to keep her inheritance and give up the twin babies for adoption."

The silence in the room was thick until cut through by the ringing phone.

Sharon walked to the desk, picked up the phone and said, "Good day, Sharon Finland on the line. Can I help you?"

"Morning, Sharon," the familiar voice answered back.

"This is Mrs Resource. Can I speak to Mr Finland Sr?"

"I am sorry," apologised Sharon. "It's really not a good time. He is in the middle of something important. Could you cancel all the Finlands appointments for the rest of the day, Mrs Resource?"

"Which Finland do you mean, Sharon?"

"I mean, every one of us." Sharon raised her voice slightly.

"Sharon, is everything okay? Grace hinted me, she heard a disturbance coming from the office."

"I assure you everything is fine, and I really have to go now. Thank you for cancelling all our appointments." Sharon dropped the phone and walked back to sit with the rest of the family.

"Thank you for doing that, Sharon," said Cynthia with relief.

Sharon replied calmly, "You're welcome."

Cynthia continued to narrate their story. "My husband's dad lost his job with my family. We couldn't handle the pain we caused everyone, so my boyfriend and I ran away. Without the knowledge of either set of parents, we ran over with our twins to his grandma's home in Minnesota." She paused.

Sharon noticed her account of the events was like Luke's. Cynthia continued until Sharon realised the difference in the two accounts. The boyfriend's grandma collaborated with the nurse to sell Luke the younger twin without Luke's parents realising what they had done. It was the inability to provide for the twins that was the reason given. The grandma further persuaded Cynthia to return to her parents, a bid to make sure she got back her inheritance. In her naivety, she agreed and lost both children, one to the grandma and the other to adoption.

Mr Finland continued, "As fate will have it, Cynthia and I met again in college. After Cynthia left my life, I decided to work hard and make something out of my life, for the sake of the twins and Cynthia, the love of my life. After graduation, we retrieved George from my grandma. We reconciled with Cynthia's family and because we were grown and already had babies together, they allowed us to get married."

"So, how did you locate my parents?" Luke asked to make sure their story correlated with the story his parents told him.

"We threatened the nurse with prison if she didn't disclose the details of your adoptive parents. Immediately the nurse provided the details, we stayed in touch with her until we eventually lost touch. I thought we had lost Luke forever. We weren't sure about the kind of life he was growing up in. We hoped one day he would return to our family. We are glad he did."

"That does not answer why my parents lied to me or why the inheritance plan is at my disadvantage," George shouted in pain.

"George, we are sorry. We wanted to raise you whole. Losing one child was enough, telling you the truth and then lose you was our greatest fear. We vowed to love you as our only child, and as you know, I struggled to have another. The pain caused us to start the foundation in honour of your brother, Luke."

Cynthia pleaded with George to calm down, reaching out to hold him, wet tears falling on his hands.

His father continued, "The Will you discovered, George, is the old one. The revised version held by our lawyer divides the inheritance into three. One part for the foundation which will be divided equally among any grandchildren and held under your trusts until your children are 25 years old, and one part each for you two brothers. Things need to be right for the future. We made mistakes with no plans for you, Luke, and George. We couldn't do the same for our grandkids."

The twins' parents' words came out amidst eyes filled with tears. Sharon could not help but shed tears, too. The reasons all along, but assumptions and lack of communication had driven a wedge of pain into the hearts of the family.

The elder Finlands begged for forgiveness, while George struggled to come to terms with their revelations. Closing his eyes, George's life as he knew it ran images like a video recording through his mind.

"It was only 'make believe'," he muttered within the hearing of everyone.

Sharon led the whole family in prayer to the Saviour, thanking Him.

For the rest of the day, the brothers exchanged stories of childhood memories. Sharon watched as joy filled the room in place of the gloom a few hours ago.

Her husband chatted away, relaxed with his family. Luke repeated his desire to maintain his previous decision. He was standing his ground. She knew too well his reasons for leaving had something to do with her.

Luke would have to return to the UK. They agreed he would head the UK Finlands, replacing George. George would run the Houston head office to build new businesses and his marriage. Luke and Sharon parted with many unspoken words. He left for the UK permanently, taking a part of her with him.

Over the next few days, Luke transferred to the new office in London to avoid any encounters with Sharon, only to come home during the holidays.

Luke's life in London remained lonely and committed to the Saviour. Even though he prayed and prayed, he could not get Sharon out of his mind.

THIRTY - FOUR

Four years had passed for Sharon. It seemed only yesterday she had walked down the aisle with her Handsome Heart. Though her marriage had not always been a bed of roses, she had learned to adjust to living with her hot-headed George.

Their relationship was built around the Saviour at the centre of their lives, mitigating their differences. She often remembers the way her parents managed their relationship, their voices echoing in her ears.

"Loving your father is hard work, Princess. Don't think it is easy. You will soon discover," counsels Mrs O'Loan.

Her father will reply, "Yeah, I agree, but the day I said yes to you, I meant it with all my heart. I took up the challenge of keeping to that commitment. You were so hard to love. I am glad I won your heart at last."

Mr O'Loan would often finish his statement by placing a kiss on Mrs O'Loan's lips.

"Get a room, you two!" Sharon would exclaim in embarrassment and hilarity.

Their love life was fun to watch as a growing child, although she wondered why she never saw them disagree before her. Now, it is Sharon's turn to love and respect her commitment, no matter what.

It's hard work, her mind acknowledged. I am glad I have a man that makes it all worthwhile!

She was looking forward to her fifth anniversary, although George was on his usual business trip. Sharon and Luke had grown to be friends, and she enjoyed every of his visits. He often hosted their visits to the UK.

She remained careful about letting sleeping dogs lie regarding her overriding thoughts about Luke. Each time she went into the doldrums, she reminded herself of how vulnerable she was in her relationship with George.

But how can she explain that after almost five years, she had not gotten over Luke? George seemed to be aware of the struggle she was going through. He jealously guarded that which belonged to him.

She cast her mind to the first Christmas they spent together as a family. George had picked up Luke from the airport and dropped him off at the mansion.

She was aware of his growing insecurity that Luke still had a hold on his wife's heart. Once he returned home, they had their first argument because of the unspoken pressure.

Sharon was not pleased.

"How long are you going to keep up with this attitude toward Luke and myself? If I did not want you, I wouldn't have said my vows."

Sharon yelled at him, snapping the door behind her.

"I know we agreed he was spending the holidays with us, but..."

"But, what? You changed your mind?" she screamed back.

"Do you know you control everything about me lately? Do you ever think about what the Saviour thinks about how you think about Luke and me? Do you not trust me?"

"I am sorry! Beautiful Heart, I am hopeless in handling my feelings. You are my rock. You are better than I am." George apologised sincerely.

"I hate us quarrelling. I made a mistake, ignoring what we agreed. What I did was wrong. Please forgive me."

Listening to him sob, she pleaded with the Saviour.

I am struggling to understand why. Why do I have the two men in my heart? I am committed to loving my husband. Take every thought I have with Luke away. It is affecting my home life. This is emotional adultery. Help me!

She heard the muted voice of the Saviour speak to her.

"Sharon, your heart must love me first. When you do, you will learn to love the twins the way I created them to be loved by you. First as brothers, and then as a wife to George. If you lose your focus on loving Me, you will lack the love needed for your husband and sisterly love for his brother."

Sharon embraced her sobbing George. "I am sorry, I have only been concerned about the way I feel and not about you, dear Handsome Heart."

George responded by laying his head on her shoulder and whispered, "I will do anything to please you, Sharon. I was only protecting you the way I knew best."

"I know," she responded, thinking about the still small voice that had spoken to her.

They mutually agreed to follow George's lead and his protection of Sharon as his wife. She knew Luke was not the enemy, but the ever-occurring nightmares of her first encounter with him; was an ongoing problem.

Yet, she is learning to love and know him as a brother and family. She only imagines the amount of emotional struggle he was dealing with. That Luke had introduced no woman to them meant he was not ready to move on.

During one of his brief visits earlier that year, Luke offered to take her to lunch. Her heart went into overdrive like wild horses on a carter.

A meal with Luke alone was like a date, and she wondered how long she could do this. Remembering she was to love him as a brother, she willingly offered herself to his company with that in mind.

Sharon felt his eyes hovering over her as they ate their lunch. To distract him from her and towards business, she asked him,

"Luke, when will you be introducing her to me?"

"By her, you mean?"

"I know, George, and you have a closer bond than with me. I am only hoping you will let me into your confidence..."

"Hmm...!" He cleared his throat in discomfort, adjusting his tie.

His actions gave Sharon unease until he continued, "What version do you want to hear? The honest or the camouflaged version?" He smiled his tender, handsome grin.

Her heart melted, but she quickly remembered George.

"Okay, honestly, I don't have any lady at the moment." assured Luke to satisfy Sharon's curiosity.

"For real!?" she reacted, pinching her lips together. *O, dear!* She pondered in her heart.

I wish I had never started this conversation.

She brushed her wandering thought aside by sipping a drink before asking.

"Have you not met lady, from your community back home?"

"Not all men are lucky to meet and hang onto a beautiful lady like Sharon," Luke uttered before taking a sip of drink himself.

"I am sorry," she looked away in embarrassment upon the admission she was the centre of his inability to move on in his relationships.

"You don't have to apologise. By all means, I wouldn't mind you introducing me to one of your Nigerian ladies like your Aunt Bola suggested at your wedding," He laughed with ease.

Feeling relaxed by his joke, she took a deep breath and exclaimed.

"My only Aunt Bola is trouble no de finish."

"What do you mean by that?" he gazed at her.

"I mean the last few words you spoke."

"What words?" Sharon looking bewildered. Instantly, she realised, "Do you mean 'trouble no de finish'?"

"Yes, those words. I heard it a few times over the weekend at the wedding."

Laughing hysterically, she replied, "that's her family nickname. We know her to be the 'extra' aunt in the family. The 'never-ending trouble. We all love her yet avoid her 'extras' as much as possible."

"I see," Luke replied at the profound description of her aunt.

"Do you want a Nigerian lady, or you are joking?" Her eyes sparkled with excitement.

"I am joking, but you never know, the Saviour's ways are not our ways, remember! But getting married is not a priority, Sharon..."

"Luke, you are almost 40!" she exclaimed.

"I know. I have my baggage, too, Sharon."

"What do you mean by baggage?" her eyebrow boggled out, waiting for an explanation of his 'baggage.'

"Are you ready to hear my boring story? We have to head back to the office." Looking at her phone and dropping it.

Sharon replied, smiling, "You are the boss. I don't have any urgent appointment for the rest of the day."

"It's fine, let's get more drinks," Luke called the waiter and ordered more drinks.

He excused him to go the toilet and returning he said, "Where were we?"

"Your story, if I can remember?" she replied, getting ready to know another aspect of Luke.

"I have a daughter already!" he stated, gazing into her eyes to see how she would react to his revelation.

"How and where? Was she at the wedding? Who is her mother? Why have you not told any of us beforehand? Do you have more secrets?" Sharon threw all her questions at him at once without considering the implications of her raised voice.
Luke looked around and watched the eyes of other customers in the restaurant staring at him.

"Sharon," holding her hands, "Which of the question do you want me to answer first?"

"I am sorry. I bombarded you with questions." Turning her face from him to hide her rising emotions.

"Sharon, I have made mistakes too. In my mistakes, my Saviour, and my parents forgave me.

The process of reconciliation led to the strengthening of my family."

"I'm glad!" she whispered, placing her hand tenderly on his.

"When I was an undergraduate, I had a period of momentary wandering from my faith. I fell in love with a lady I met on campus through a friend. One date led to another, and we soon started having sex."

Watching her and getting no response, Luke continued. "She got pregnant and was ready to abort the pregnancy. After several pleas from my parents and with a promise to raise the baby; she agreed to give her baby over to my family. After that experience, I vowed not to start any relationship I was not ready to take on a long haul."

"What happened to the mother and the baby?" Taking a deep breath, tears filled Luke's eyelids. He took a sip of the drink before continuing narrating his sad story.

"She left the baby with my parents and continued in her lifestyle. About three years later, she had a terrible accident because of intoxication from drinking. We introduced my daughter to her mother, and every summer my mum allows her to visit her maternal grandparent the reason she was not present at the wedding. Besides, I didn't want to complicate things here, either."

"I am so sorry, Luke. That must have been a hard life for you."

"Hard is an understatement, but we have the Saviour's words as a rod and staff to lead us back to his will. I believe I am in his will and waiting on him to perfect his plans in my life. I am not in a hurry to rush things. Although, my mum often says she hopes to have more grandbabies."

Sharon smiled at the expression of grandbabies, remembering Mrs O'Loan often mentioned the same.

Luke continued, "I reminded her, the Saviour has a plan for grandbabies and will keep her alive to meet them."

"True, Luke. You are a wise man."

"I hope so. Wisdom, they say, comes with experience."

Turning his gaze back to her, Luke said, "What about you guys? When do you want to have babies? It's nearly been five years!"

Avoiding the question, she replied, "Did you not ask George?"

"You know your husband. He doesn't speak about his wife to anyone."

"I know, that's why I love my Handsome Heart!"

"You are so right, Beautiful Heart!" Luke teased her back, sounding just like George.

"I know we planned for kids as soon as possible. Just as you stated, His ways are rarely our ways."

"I understand more than you can imagine," he replied with a sense of disappointment at his own situation.

"But kindly give me the privilege to announce to you, Luke, I'm about eight weeks, you will soon be Uncle Luke."

"Excellent news!!" Luke exclaimed, standing up to hug Sharon. She responded warmly to his embrace. It was a kind of hug she had longed for over four years.

With that passionate hug, Sharon's senses suddenly returned. "I think we have to go, Uncle Luke."

Luke admitted, "I like the sound of that – Uncle Luke."

Picking up his phone from the table, Luke continued. "We need to head back. Cynthia will soon be searching for both of us."
Sharon picked up her bag, whilst Luke assisted her with her coat. He led her out of the restaurant.

"Luke, I hope you wouldn't mind if I discuss your past with George."

"If you feel comfortable, Sharon, but I would prefer to let the cat out of the bag myself."

"I will let you do that in your own time then. Thank you for sharing your heart with me, Luke."

Sharon had managed her relationship with her brother-in-law. However, the family was faced with their father's deteriorating health. Mr Finland Senior was in and out of the hospital yet remained in spirits.

He was glad he had his sons handling the affairs of the companies and estates.

On return from a business trip, Sharon received a piece of news after a relaxing dinner. Mr Finland was in an ambulance on the way to the hospital. Getting off the call she panicked and called out to George, Sharon squealed,

"George, Dad is on the way to the hospital!"

"Why didn't you tell me earlier, Sharon!?" yelled George impatiently.

"I could have headed to the hospital from the airport!"

"Why would you even say that when I just learned about your dad, myself? Also, I miss having you to myself," she added softly, using her hands to massage his shoulder.

Expressing outrage at her inappropriate actions, considering the circumstances, he busted out in anger.

"Not now, Beautiful!"

"We don't need to put aside our love, George! Dad is fine. I know he's been in and out of the hospital, but he is in excellent hands. I want you around! Our baby and I missed you."

She drew close to him for a cuddle, but he distractedly pushed her away, picking up his car keys.

"We have to go, Sharon."

"Tonight?" She exclaimed.

"It's 10.30 pm and way past hospital visiting hours. We can visit first thing in the morning."

Sharon had seen George in this state before. His agitation often led to something dangerous. She prayed silently that he calmed down, but he replied sharply,

"Are you coming or not?"

"George, you need to listen to me." She pleaded.

"I need you here by my side tonight. I missed you." She replied by pulling his hands.

"Sharon, we will be back before you know it. I need you by my side, visiting my dad."

Sharon thought they could continue with the argument or go to visit his dad. Besides, they would be back.

They had a lot to talk about, the baby, the office, Luke – how she couldn't keep the secret anymore.

"Okay, George, let's go." Responding with a kiss on her forehead, he replied.

"Beautiful Heart, thank you. Let me get your purse." George hurried into the bedroom.

George drove to the hospital as though he is in a police chase. Sharon pleaded with him to drive carefully. He ignored her plea and ran the first red light.

George ran the second red light when a huge Toyota truck suddenly rammed into the driver's side. His sports car rolled over several times, breaking glass, inflating the airbag, unceremoniously crashing into a tree.

The impact from the truck resulted in throwing George out of the window. His head contacted the cement ground. Dark crimson blood poured out of his head. Sharon remained under the rubble.

The night was cold and lonely, and the few bystanders rushed towards the accident. Others called the ambulance and the police. The smell of fuel leaking from the car didn't help the situation much. The bystanders had to cover their noses to breathe properly.

They rushed the unconscious Finlands to the nearby hospital. While they laid on the hospital beds in a coma, the police tried to locate their relatives.

From a search of the car rubble for their belongings, the police inspector found George's wallet. They immediately linked their identities to Graceoak Ltd. They contacted family members, one of whom was Luke.

THIRTY - FIVE

Mrs Finland was the first member of the family in the emergency room. She was out of her mind with worry, waiting for other family members.

In one hospital bed laid her husband, in ICU laid her son- and daughter-in-law. Cynthia was numb and had no memory of the past three hours. Her phone line rang continuously.

Luke booked a flight so Sharon's parents could be with their daughter. Friends and other family relatives started trickling in.

The Pastor was the first to arrive, next was the Peters'. The Pastor led prayers for the younger Finlands' recovery. Five hours later, the consultant walked into the relative room and asked,

"Can I speak to anyone related to Mr & Mrs Finland Junior?"

George's mum walked towards the doctor, she whispered.

"I am. Are my babies, okay? Is my grandchild safe?" tears rolling down her cheeks.

Looking down on his feet, the consultant paused before replying.

"I am Doctor Trump, the consultant on duty when the accident victims were brought in."

Everyone surrounded Cynthia, forming a ring of comfort around her.

"My babies, are they alright? Can I see them?" Her voice cracked in desperation for an answer.

The doctor adjusted his facial expression and replied.

"I am sorry, Mrs Finland, we lost George and the baby. But..."

"Noooo," she screamed, collapsed passing out as the Pastor caught her.

The doctor called for extra support. They rushed to resuscitate Cynthia. It was a nightmare she would not want to wake up from.

Eighteen hours later, Luke rushed into the hospital with the O'Loan, in search of his brother and Sharon. The receptionist who questioned him. halted his brisk movement.

"Day, Sir, can I help you?" she called out.

"Apologies. We are here to see family. Can you lead us to where the Finlands are admitted?" He questioned without waiting for an answer.

The receptionist replied, "I'm sorry, Mr ...?"

"Mr Luke Finland," he replied.

"Are you related to...?" Luke interrupted the receptionist.

"Yes! Yes, I am Luke. George Finland's twin brother." He replied in a much-expected panic.

"Oh!" she exclaimed in dismay.

"Let me get the physician in charge." Cut in the nurse standing beside the receptionist.

The nurse was not ready to say anything further. She picked up a file on the table. Luke stood helplessly in front of the reception desk, pale as a ghost. A few moments later, Peter and his pastor saw him from afar and rushed towards him.

"Luke, Luke! We are glad you are here." They exclaimed together, hugging him.

"Hey Peter, Tom. Thank you. Where is my family?"

They avoided his question until Peter asked,

"How was the flight?"

"It was bearable," he replied with a sigh.

"No one seems to have an answer for me."

"Let's get you some coffee. Everything will be fine." Tears filling his eyes, they led him to the relatives' room.

"I believe the physician will come in with some update soon." Peter handed a cup of coffee to Luke and added, "Luke, it will be alright, everything will be alright."

"For the nth time, is my Cynthia, Steve, George, Sharon, and the baby, okay?" he quizzed them faint-hearted.

"Everything will be fine; everything will be fine." There was a grave silent between them. Peter wanted to break the silence, so he repeated the question.

"How was your flight?"

"Peter, that's not important for now. How is my family?" Luke snapped back.

"Everything is going to be fine," the pastor said.

"Luke, we are very sorry, actually the doctors came about seven hours ago."

"What did he say?" Luke interrupted him.

"Hmm..." clearing his throat, "He informed us that George died in the accident. Despite their best efforts, they tried to resuscitate him but unfortunately were unable to revive him. But he's lost too much blood, and a irreversible trauma his brain."

"Oh no!" Luke bellowed.

"What about Sharon? What about the baby?" His body heaved, terrified to hear the next statement. Losing Sharon will be like losing my life. I would prefer to die, Luke reflected. The pastor stood up. Walked towards the window, looked out, and then back to Peter.

"We lost the baby, but Sharon is in intensive care."

"What? Oh, no!!" Luke held his head with both hands, gasping in pain. Peter drew close to support him.

"Sharon will head for her second operation in a couple of hours." he concluded.

"Oh God, this is too much to bear. What about Cynthia and Steve?" Peter took hold of Luke's hands.

"They admitted Steve to another hospital. That was the reason we were rushing out when we met you," Peter added.

"What happened?" Luke replied, confused.

"They rushed Steve to the hospital yesterday evening. The accident happened on the way to the hospital."

"What's happening to Cynthia? Is she okay?" Luke slid onto the floor, clutching his chest, weeping bitterly.

Screaming aloud and beating his chest, he cried, "Can't somebody tell me why all this is happening? It makes no sense!!"

For the nth time in his life, Luke felt he was losing it.

"Everybody, again!! When I came into their lives less than four years ago, I was hoping to rebuild my family bonds. What is all THIS!?" They waited until his sobbing quieted down.

"Cynthia will live. She fainted when the physician broke the news of George's death. The medical team had taken her in. We believe they are taking care of her. We all know she is as fit as a fiddle." Peter added.

His face still streaming with tears rolled down, Luke lamented, "What have I done? I should have stayed away, living my life in the UK!!"

"Why are you blaming yourself? You did nothing. Luke, you didn't cause the accident or your dad's sickness. You didn't cause anybody to faint. Let's not blame each other here. Let us keep in mind and not forget the words of the Saviour. All things work together for good..."

Luke cut in, saying, "Don't give me that now. I know, I know what the Saviour says."

"But yes, what is so important is for us to reflect on those words in tough times, lest we forget."

The pastor reassured him. He sat beside him on the floor and muttered, "Let's not forget what His words say. We keep praying."

They held his hands together and said a few words of prayer.

As they finished, the physician walked in with a grin on his face. "Everything is under control. We resuscitated Mrs Finland."

"Praise GOD!!" the Pastor exclaimed.

"This is Luke, George's twin brother, Doctor."

"Yes, she's OK. Our team is keeping a very close eye on her and monitoring her constantly. We have put her under with sedatives to rest. She should be fine. Mrs Finland just needs a few hours to rest."

"Thank you, doctor," Luke replied, relieved by the small positive sign that at least his mother was okay.

"Do you know the hospital where Mr Finland was admitted?" the doctor asked.

The Pastor informed him, "In the St. Peter's hospital down the road. He is doing fine."

"Is it possible to bring him over to this hospital so everyone can be under the same care facility?" Luke requested desperately.

"Yeah, we could arrange it, but we need to speak to the physician-in-charge of him. Also, we need to make sure we have an appropriate medical specialist in our hospital here."

They made all the arrangements to transfer Mr Finland from the hospital. Luke re-admitted his father into the same hospital with his wife and his daughter-in-law, Sharon.

The next six months after George's death, Sharon started coming to terms with her new reality. In the absence of Sharon, the family buried George and their baby.

The images of events before the night of the accident replayed in her mind as a constant torment. She couldn't understand how things turned from love to deaths in a split second.

Tossing and turning on many sleepless nights, she blamed herself completely for allowing George to drive her out that night. Sharon was released from the hospital after a few weeks. Though she would remain in a wheelchair for a long time, her doctor remained positive that she could work again. However, Sharon had lost faith that anything positive could happen to her after George.

"If you'll ever walk again," the doctor said in an encouraging tone. "You need to believe yourself are going to walk. Sharon, you will need to go through many months of rehabilitation."

"Doctor," Sharon replied, crying, "Everything is upside down! When George died and I lost my precious baby, it turned my world upside down." Hot tears flooded her pillows, rolling down her face on the sickbed.

Mr and Mrs O'Loan and Luke spoke words of comfort into her heart. Sharon's heart sunk deeper than their words could reach her.

"Beautiful Heart, remember the Saviour has not finished with you yet," Luke spoke to her, wheeling her out of the hospital.

"Don't say Beautiful Heart, Luke!!" Sharon burst out in anger. "Please, I rather you did not call me that!" shutting the door to expressions of affection.

"I'm so sorry, Sharon. I didn't mean to hurt you. I just felt it would be nice for you to hear these words..."

She interrupted and continued, "You sound so much like him!"

Luke stopped pushing the wheel as Sharon's mother bent before her wheelchair, staring into her princess's eyes.

Luke, confused, walked away to catch a breath of fresh air. Collapsing into her mum's arms, Sharon whispered,

"It's just that any time Luke calls me, Beautiful Heart, my heart tears apart. I hear George... I hear him. Why did he leave me alone when we agreed to leave this world together? He took my heart with him, Mum. How does he want me to survive?"

Mrs O'Loan pulled Sharon into a hug and muttered, "I'm so sorry. Sharon, I'm so sorry. Luke and George were born at the same time and are identical twins. They are bound to speak alike."
Her father joined his wife as they supported Sharon into the car and her new world.

After a month of nightmares, she finally agreed to fly back to the UK with her parents to recover. The same terrifying dreams kept coming back to haunt her night after night, causing me great distress.

Sharon now summed them up to be of George and not Luke, the stranger in the dream. In one of her recent dreams, she kept hearing George's voice whispering.

"My Beautiful Heart, please, don't go." In the nightmare, his voice would grow faint as the distance between them appeared to grow wider and wider. Sharon searched in tears, desperate to find the whisperer and always hearing her baby cry in the pitch-dark alleyway.

She always woke up in a cold sweat, trembling with fear as her mother rushed to her side to comfort her.

"Mum, I am losing my mind. Remind me again why God took my heart away!"

Holding her hands and pressing a peck on her forehead, her mum replied, "I apologise,

Princess, but I am unsure and cannot give you a definite answer. But we can only trust that in the pain and the suffering, a beautiful offering of praise will burst forth."

Sharon's sobbing each night opened Luke's heart towards her. Sharon had pushed him away several times now. He felt unworthy, defeated, and unable to comfort her until the night before they were to travel.

Mr O'Loan and Peter suggested an evening together, with Peter's wife and Mrs O'Loan giving womanly support to Sharon.

After the meal together, Peter spoke from the Saviour's words about not giving up on one another. Luke knew where the discussion was heading to. He listened to the older men as they advised him to play a role in Sharon's healing process.

He wondered how because Sharon hated him more since she lost his brother. To Luke, his pain was a multi-edged sword. First, losing his dream girl, then his brother and now hatred from Sharon, and all his losses, his daughter's mother, and his adoptive dad.

"What does the Saviour want from me?" Luke exclaimed with his troubled heart.

"You bet Joseph asked the same questions several times during his trials," Mr O'Loan replied.

"We could not answer all the questions on this side of things. We will have to wait like the rest of the saints for answers."

"Till then we will have to wait, trust and hope," Peter added.

"His promises, which we all know, never fail. All we know now is that Sharon needs all of us, especially you."

"But she will have her parents and all the medical care she needs. How do I come in? I need space to heal too. I only knew the second part of my heart for four years. Half of it, we lived in disagreement."

Luke broke down in deep sobs. "I am so sorry," He was swimming in tears.

The two men held him close as they sobbed with him. It was brotherhood of love producing much-needed healing. With a refreshed feeling, he understood why he needed to be by Sharon's side.

Mr O'Loan and Peter had handed comfort over to him, and they had become his brother and father. Their advice was more precious to him than gold.

THIRTY - SIX

After three years of hard work, of disagreement and pain, Luke and Sharon had settled into a new rhythm of life. The three years didn't come on a platter of gold.

Such had been Sharon's life experiences before George walked the shores of her world. A bitter-sweet Sharon was all too glad Luke had been a rock to her.

She couldn't remember what life would have thrown on her. The airport nightmares had struggled to leave her. To this day, the only constant comfort she had was the Saviour's words, like Mr O'Loan recited each day.

"All things work together for good for those that love the Saviour; and called according to His purpose."

Sharon had to remember each day that the words were not for only times, but it had to be a daily mix of the good and the bad.

Sharon finally took the first step to change her relationship with Luke on her wedding anniversary. The step forward was difficult. The pain of losing her dear heart, George, and her daughter – Mimi. On the other hand, what a joy she beheld in Luke's face as he grabbed her for a hug.

He held her to his chest as her feet gave way to her welcoming body, the fruit of their three years of hard work getting to know each other. For Sharon, all the horrible nightmares had faded away. Day by day, her friendship with Luke blossomed.

The night she took her first step towards Luke, she had a dream. This time she saw George and a 3-year-old girl dressed as saints, on one side of a chasm. Luke and herself were on the other side of the chasm, holding hands. This scenario was reminiscent of the Bible story of the Rich Man and Lazarus with a twist! In this scenario, a chilly breeze blew back and forth, with a horrible piercing sound rising from the chasm.

"Luke, you need to take care of my heart. She is now yours. Take my heart just like I did, and we'll see you soon on this other side." They turned around and walked away.

Sharon woke up from the dream with a smile on her face, waking up to Luke's soft voice.

"Hey, Beautiful, you're awake. I brought you breakfast. It good to see you woke up with a smile."

"Thanks, Luke. I had a pleasant dream; one I have longed for a long time."

"I can imagine. Would you mind sharing, Sharon?"

"Sure, I would love to share, Luke, not just with you, but with the rest of the family."

"Talking about family, I need to be in Houston tonight to meet with George Sr and Cynthia. I would have to be..."

They went on eating and talking for the next two hours until Mrs O'Loan interrupted them, coming into the room.

"Sharon, you still in bed? You need to stand up now. It's time for your exercises. Your physiotherapist is here."

"Mum, can't you see I'm having breakfast with Luke?"

"That is what you've been doing for the past two hours, having breakfast with him. Luke has to be in London for his meetings and then Houston tonight."

Sharon impatiently called out to her father. "Mr O'Loan, could you come over and get your heart? She needs to leave here immediately."

Mr O'Loan replied shouting back, "Mrs O'Loan my Heart, get out of there, and let Sharon find her own heart."

At his reply, they burst into laughter, whilst Mrs O'Loan tactfully left.

A smiling Luke spoke softly, "I'm so sorry Sharon, I need to leave now. My guess is that your mother is correct. I have to get down to Houston by tomorrow evening. I expect that is going to introduce me to the other aspects of Finland business. Also, I've not been to Asia, and I think Mr Williams needs a visit. I need to sort..."

Sharon spoke through gritted teeth, her disappointment evident.

"Okay, Luke, I was just having so much fun. So, you mean you will not be with me at the exercise today?"

"I'm sorry Sharon, I won't be at the exercise session today."

"Luke, I am counting on you, and I need you to come through for me. I make so much progress when you are here," she pleaded.

"Sharon, look at me, beautiful, look at me!" Turning her teary face at him. "Whether or not I am here, you can make progress. You can, because inside you is a strong, fierce woman who can climb every mountain. I know Mum and Dad will be here with you and I'll be back as soon as possible."

Sharon nodded with a "yeah!" Luke gave her a peck on the forehead, followed by a warm hug. He stamped out of the room, avoiding a further pull into her presence. Sharon fell back on the bed, with streams of tears rolling down her cheeks.

I was about to share the dream. I was just going to tell him all the nightmares since I met him. Luke, he's so distant, it appears he is still running. I hurt him so badly, he's completely closed to our having any intimate relationship.

Is there a chance both of us could ever be together? Saviour, you know, I never stopped loving him. Has he stopped loving me? Saviour, is there any future with him? Can you let me know? Please speak to Luke and me. Is there any chance? Am I meant to love him only as a brother alone? Could it be possible for us to come together in marriage?

Talking about chances, she took a chance on life when she married crazy George. The twins were so different in every sense of the word. George' proud and aggressive, and to an extent, hot-headed.

But he was passionate and loving and with his other qualities. He had swept her off her feet. Sharon found herself enamoured with him and could not stop thinking about him. There was no way she could let go of a life full of adventure with George.

I never knew myself until I met George. He brought out the best in me. He brought out the worst in me and I learned to be more like the Saviour with George on the side.

Sharon's mind continued travelling back and forth, comparing the brothers.

When it comes to Luke, it's fair to say that he's not anything like George. He is comely, gentle, and understanding. Although they speak with similar mannerisms, he is patient and a better listener. Luke is non-judgemental and avoids a disagreement at all costs. Even though sometimes I tried to push all his buttons as I did with George, he would never snap back.

If you snapped at him, he would turn it into a joke. He has a way of calming her. Why did I not get the chance of knowing him before George?

I guess, like Luke always says, "it's all about the Masterplan." He often repeated it was part of a masterplan that everything worked out the way it did. Sometimes I don't understand, I feel like I am caught in the middle of the Masterplan.

One week of Luke's absence went into two and then several months. He must have gone to see Mr Williams in Asia. Meanwhile, Sharon made excellent progress in her physical therapy.

After his return to Houston, things seemed weird between them. Luke rarely called or returned her calls. The last time they spoke was three weeks ago. He finally called to inform her of his decision to return to the UK in a few weeks.

It was time for Sharon to surprise him with a walk to the door in her clutches! It wasn't long before Mrs O'Loan's voice echoed repeatedly in her ears...

Sharon, please be careful not to overexert yourself during your exercise routine. I know you want to walk, but you can accomplish it at a slower pace."

"Please Mum, don't stop me! I'm trying my best to walk now. I'll try my very best to get on my feet. I am determined to get my life back." Losing control of her emotions, she snapped.

"I'm sorry, child, I don't mean to push you. Your father and I don't mean to stress you, but I was kindly trying to tell you that you need to take your time."

"Mrs O'Loan, I understand," a contrite Sharon replied. But deep in her heart, she promised to herself, *I'd go all the way to see if there's anything in me for Luke to love. Will he never stop blaming me for rejecting him and killing his brother?*

A few days later, Sharon, alone at home, hobbled into the kitchen to make dinner for herself when the doorbell sounded. She dragged her feet in front of the other, painfully willing her crutches to move along with her.

"I am on my way," she yelled out. Expecting a reply, but no one replied. Turning the doorknob, she opened to find Luke standing with a bunch of yellow roses, with his briefcase beside him.

"Hello, beautiful," Sharon stood with feet glued to the floor, burst into the pent-up tears she could not contain any longer.

"I am so sorry. I've been away too long." He rushed in, gathered her frail body against his broad chest. Sharon could not stop sobbing as she collapsed helplessly into his arms.

After a long pause, she regained her composure and whispered, "I missed your company, Luke."

"Same here, same here," he mumbled into the nape of her neck. Releasing her gently before picking up her crutches for her, he continued.

"Sharon, your achievement is truly remarkable, and you have done it! You are walking! This is beautiful, just as you are beautiful! I never doubted the strength in you. Thanks to the Saviour, you didn't prove me wrong."

He patiently placed each crutch under her shoulder to balance her while supporting her.

"I am sorry. It wasn't part of my plan to cry. I find myself in an embarrassing situation and it's causing me a great deal of discomfort. The only plan was to open the door for you myself."

Smiling to reveal his appreciation of that moment of humour, he replied, very much amused,

"Did you also plan when I would press the doorbell?"

"Seriously, Luke? When there is a will, there is always a way. It happened just as planned!"

"Talking about a plan, have you had dinner, beautiful? But first, where is your Mum and Dad, so I can say, 'hi'?"

"Don't ask. Nowadays, I see little of them and have no clue as to their whereabouts. But they are definitely not home. About dinner, I was about to make some for myself. Do you want some?"

"Yeah, but I think we should eat out. You have made so much progress, we should celebrate your success!"

"Not really. Not sure I have anything to celebrate. Not yet! When I can do without my crutches."

Holding her close, he gazed into her eyes with, "I agree. Could you celebrate my homecoming instead?"

Pursing her lips and contemplating, Sharon assented. "Okay. Can I get dressed into something more suitable?"

"For sure, take all your time, beautiful. I will drop my luggage in the guest room. I need to freshen up, too."

"I hope you are not leaving in the morning, Luke?" Turning around and dropping a peck on her forehead, he replied.

"No, Sharon, I need a break, too."

An hour later, Luke supported Sharon out into his car for an unknown destination.

Ten minutes of driving in silence, Luke stretched his hands to cover her. "Sharon, I am here."

In a hushed tone, she whispered her appreciation saying "Thank you". Instead of heading into a restaurant, Luke drove them into the local garden centre.

"What's happening Luke? It's evening. Why the garden centre?"

"Relax Sharon, follow my lead," he replied. Luke stepped out of the car to help her out. Learning to trust again, she held out her hands to receive the support she needed.

Stepping out of the car, Luke requested she rely upon him, leaving her crutches behind. He blindfolded Sharon, putting his hands around her waist to lead her to the unknown destination.

Luke led her through an unfamiliar path until he assisted her to sit down. He gently removed the blindfold to find herself seated at a well-planned dinner date.

The garden centre had a popular area used by romantic couples for romantic surprises.

"When did you find time to plan this? You just arrived, didn't you?"

"Hush...," Luke placed his finger on her lips to stop any further questioning. "Relax and enjoy, no questions tonight. Promise me."

"Yes, but," she replied once Luke lifted his finger.

"No, but Sharon, not now, you can ask later."

The garden was lit with the colours of the dress she wore on her first dinner with him. Lemon coloured lights.

"Where on earth did he find lemon bulbs?" Her mind ran in circles, flashing back to her first brotherly date with Luke. He decorated the table with red roses, but there was no food in sight.

After seating her, Luke seated himself and clapped his hands. Muted romantic music from her favourite artists started playing, 'A Love Like This' by Phil and Brenda Nicholas.

"Are you ready to fill your famished tummy?" he smiled indulgently, reaching out to fill her glass with the wine he had already popped open.

"Yes, I am ready, Luke. But I don't remember seeing any food here!"

Clearing his throat as though he was signalling to someone, Mr. and Mrs. O'Loan walked in with the first course of mild pepper soup.

"Mum, Dad, you are in on it!" Sharon exclaimed. "Now I understand why you guys never told me where you were going."

"No questions, remember?" Luke reminded her.

Mr O'Loan added, "Princess, you deserve much more. You have taken giant strides in your therapy lately. Sharon covered her teary eyes, while Mrs O'Loan pulled her husband away from the diners to give them privacy.

A few moments later, Luke walked over to the bend before her and asked gently,

"Sharon, does this bring too many memories? Do you want us to call it a night? I am sorry, it's too much for you to handle."

Sharon responded by throwing her hands around his neck.

"Luke, I am only overwhelmed. I want to spend every minute of tonight with you. As for my parents, they have some explaining to do."

They burst into laughter together.

Luke's discussion of his travels, Graceoak's businesses accompanied the meal. His daughter's teenage excesses, and his mum's new charity commitments.

He shared how his parents have missed her. Sharon was glad to listen to all the news. She observed Luke seemed more eager than normal.

After dinner, Mr & Mrs O'Loan bid them night and promised not to lock them out if they came in later than expected.

Luke assisted Sharon to another side of the garden, help her sit on a bench before bringing out a present.

"Sharon, I would like you to open this."

George was very good with surprises, didn't know Luke is equal in playing the game. I guess, that's why they were twins. Sharon deliberated for a few seconds, smiling at him before taking the gift to unwrap it. To Sharon's amazement, the box contained the very shirt she had accidentally poured coffee on nearly ten years ago. Unfolding the navy-blue shirt revealed a dirty patterned coffee stain.

"Oh my word!" Sharon was breathless. "Luke, you still kept this shirt!! Why? How? For what?" Her eyes were wide open. in amazement, and she demanded an explanation.

To answer her questions, Luke quietly drew her onto his lap, laid her head on his chest and whispered into her hair.

"That day, I saw you before you spilt the coffee on me. I loved you at the first sight. What I did not know was, it would take me ten years to let you know I never stopped loving you. Sharon, will you love me back?" Luke placed a kiss on her forehead.

Sharon remained speechless, as she heard the very words her heart has longed for from the first time, she set her eyes on him.

Yes, the Saviour does work all things together for our good, Sharon acknowledged. Praise the LORD!! Luke had changed from being her comfort into her only love! With a heart full of gratitude, she came to the realisation.

The End

ABOUT THE AUTHOR

Joan Hephzibah is a mum with two amazing girls and the director of Infohubme and the children's broadcast Reading with Joan RWJ. Joan had worked with various organisations for several years before picking up her pen to develop her creative skills. She has dealt with personal loss, fears of failures and insecurity in relating with people. These experiences have informed her depiction of a single intelligent lady under pressure to conform to the defined ideals of what a relationship means. She enjoys making music and writing poetry.

Other books from Quartjc Publishers and Infohubme CIC

She Smiled Series

- From the Ashes: She Smiled
- Broken Yet: She Smiled

New Me Series {Kids}

- Timi's Creativity
- The Race
- The Debate

Happy Mind Monthly Reflections Booklets {Kids}

- Change Perception
- Confidence
- Improve your Mental Health
- Emotions
- My sense of Identity
- My Physical Appearance
- Self Esteem
- Do I accept you?
- Peer Pressure
- Coping with School Challenges
- Social-cultural Awareness
- Express Yourself

Cultural Awareness Journal {Kids}

African Christmas Traditions {Kids}

Visit us on our website: www.readgroofy.com;
https://tinyurl.com/JoanHep

Printed in Great Britain
by Amazon